THE ACCIDENTAL TIME TRAVELLER

Rosie Harford is having a very odd day...

After a blazing row with boyfriend Will, she sets off for her latest reporting assignment – an interview at The Meadows, the location for a new reality TV show, *The 1950s House*. Stepping through the door, Rosie finds herself transported back in time, and as the days go by in this new world without mobile phones and Topshop, she realises that this is reality, not reality TV. She discovers that Will is also trapped in the past – but here Will is a devoted family man called Billy. Rosie falls in love with him all over again, but now he's out of bounds.

THE ACCIDENTAL
TIME TRAVELLER

The Accidental Time Traveller

by

Sharon Griffiths

Magna Large Print Books
Long Preston, North Yorkshire,
BD23 4ND, England.

LP

British Library Cataloguing in Publication Data.

Griffiths, Sharon
  The accidental time traveller.

  A catalogue record of this book is
  available from the British Library

  ISBN   978-0-7505-3224-2

First published in Great Britain by HarperCollins Publishers 2008

Copyright © Sharon Griffiths 2008

Cover illustration © Head Design

Sharon Griffiths asserts the moral right to be identified as the author
of this work

Published in Large Print 2010 by arrangement with
HarperCollins Publishers

Magna Large Print is an imprint of Library Magna Books Ltd.

Printed and bound in Great Britain by
T.J. (International) Ltd., Cornwall, PL28 8RW

For the Amos men – Mike, Adam and Owen –
with love.

Chapter One

'You all right, love?'

The taxi driver was looking at me oddly as I scrabbled in my bag. Mobile ... iPod ... notebook ... Dictaphone ... everything but my purse. Ah. There it was, right at the bottom, of course. I pulled a tenner out – I think it was a tenner – and pushed it through the window. Just peering in at the driver really hurt my neck.

'Here, thanks. Keep the change.'

'Are you *sure* you're all right?' he asked, swiftly folding the note into his wallet. Maybe it had been a twenty.

'Yes. Fine. Fine.'

But I wasn't. Not really. And it got worse.

As the taxi roared off – no one likes to hang around The Meadows longer than they have to – I stood swaying slightly on the pavement. My head was thumping, my eyes were hurting and I couldn't stop shivering. It was one of those Mondays when I swore I would never drink again. Or have a row with Will...

Right. No time to think about that at the moment. I tried to get myself together. I was here to do an interview for *The News*. Mrs Margaret Turnbull had been one of the first people to move in to The Meadows when it was built fifty years ago in the days when it was the Promised Land. Bit different now. You're lucky to come back and find your car still there. Even luckier if it's still got its wheels.

But *The News* was doing a special supplement to mark its fiftieth birthday. One of the big TV stations was apparently planning a reality programme where people have to pretend to live in the past – the 1950s house – and rumour had it that was going to be in The Meadows too. So I had spent the morning in the dusty little library at the top of *The News* building, reading through the bound files of yellowing newspapers from the 1950s – stories of new roads, new houses, flower festivals, pageants, mysterious deaths, and adverts for cigarettes and washing machines, and lots of housewives prancing around in pinnies. A different world.

Meanwhile, back in the present I leant for a moment on the gatepost as my head swam. Tidy gatepost. Neat path and pretty garden with tulips, primroses and violets. This was one of the nicer bits of the estate and a very posh front door showed quite clearly that Mrs Turnbull had bought her council house. Through the window, I could see a grey-haired lady in trousers and sweatshirt, looking up from some knitting, watching out for me.

But as I walked up that path I realised something was wrong, very wrong. My eyesight had gone haywire. The flagstones seemed somehow a long way away. It was hard to find them with my feet. Everything was at odd angles. My head was swirling. I wanted to shake it to clear it, but my neck wouldn't work properly. There was a pain in my eyes. This wasn't a hangover, this was something else. I was ill, really ill. I began to panic. I felt as if I was going to fall over. I got to the front door and pushed my hands out in front of me. Somehow, I rang the bell.

I suddenly wished – oh so strongly – that Will and I hadn't argued, that we'd said goodbye that morning with silence. I wished...

Then everything went black...

Things had started to go wrong on Sunday. As well as living together, Will and I work together too – he's the paper's Deputy News Editor – and so a weekend when neither of us is working is a bit of a treat. After a good Saturday night out with Caz and Jamie we had a nice – very nice thank you – lie-in, and then Will had gone to play football and I'd pottered around the flat having a bit of a pamper session and sorting out the washing. Just my washing – Will does his own. And his own ironing. You won't catch me starting down that route. Bad enough doing my own, so hooray for the tumble dryer.

Caz and I got to the pub at the same time. She was wearing a jacket I hadn't seen before, black and fitted, with fancy frogged buttons. Very romantic. 'Love it!' I said, as we made our way to the bar. 'New?'

'Don't be daft,' she laughed, doing a twirl so I could admire it. 'This was a coat from the charity shop reject box, because it had a stain on the bottom. So I chopped that off and found the buttons on eBay.' Clever girl, Caz. A real eye for what looks good.

With that, Jamie's car pulled up outside. Just

that glimpse of Will through the pub's small window made me smile. After all this time together, I got so excited to see him. He and Jamie breezed in, smelling of fresh air and full of the joy of victory. We managed to persuade them that no, they didn't really want to play table football, got our drinks, ordered some food and bagged the last table.

So, everything was fine until Leo and Jake came over.

But it wasn't their fault. Not their fault at all.

'It's OK. We're not stopping. We've just called in for some Dutch courage,' said Jake. 'We're off to lunch with Leo's parents. We have some news for them.'

'News?' Caz and I immediately sat up straight and took notice.

'We're getting married!' said Jake. 'Or civil partnershipped anyway. Midsummer's Day. Old Shire Hall. Marquee in the rose garden. Lots and lots of champagne. Lovely music. Lovely people too, if you'll come.'

Caz and I jumped up and hugged and kissed them both. Will and Jamie stood up and shook their hands in a manly sort of way, clapped them around the shoulders and said, 'Well done', 'Great news', and that sort of thing.

'Can I get you a drink to celebrate?' asked Will.

But no, Leo's parents were waiting. They didn't want to be late, and didn't want to be too drunk when they told them. It was an important day.

'Good luck!' we yelled as they went out, all pleased and excited.

'Well,' said Jamie, after they'd gone, 'what's the

14

form for a woofter wedding then? Do we have to wear pink?'

'Don't be so silly,' said Caz. 'And patronising. It will be good fun. And it's good they can do it. Makes sense with tax and money and all that sort of thing.'

'But that's not just why they're doing it,' I said. 'I think it's lovely. Public declaration and all that.'

'Do you really?' asked Will, and the sharpness of his tone surprised me.

'Well, yes,' I said, 'I mean they're obviously devoted to each other and it's great that now they can tell the world.'

'Yeah, guess so,' said Will, but he looked as though he wanted to carry on grumbling. Then our food arrived and we got stuck into eating. Drinking too. Afterwards we walked around to Caz and Jamie's place.

'Yes!' went Will as soon as we walked in. 'Oh that is just beautiful!'

Jamie laughed, 'Pretty neat, isn't it?'

I was behind them, pulling my boots off so couldn't see at first what all the fuss was about. Then I padded into the sitting room and saw it was a TV set, one of those huge plasma jobs. It was hanging on the wall like a picture. Caz raised her eyebrows in a 'Don't blame me, it's one of his toys', sort of expression.

'That is just mint!' said Will, standing in front of the set with his tongue practically hanging out. Jamie switched on some motor racing. It looked as though the cars were racing from one end of the room to the other. Impressive, but too much. Much too much. I went through to the kitchen to

15

help Caz dig out some ice cream she'd got from the farmers' market. More wine too.

'It's his latest toy,' she said.

'Don't you mind?'

Caz shrugged. 'It's his money.'

'Gerrrin there!' Will was yelling at the TV like a kid, he was so excited.

We took the wine and the ice cream back into the sitting room and I curled up on the sofa. My throat was a bit scratchy so I could kid myself the soothing ice cream was medicinal. Then Will said, 'I think we should get one of these TVs, Rosie.'

'In your dreams. We haven't got that sort of money. If we had, we'd be living in a bigger flat.'

This was a sore point. Our flat was actually mine, and it was tiny, which is why I had been able to buy it. When Will – and all his stuff – moved in a few months ago the plan had been we'd try and save to buy a bigger flat together. But you know what it's like, prices just keep going up and up... Money comes in. Money goes out. I'm not quite sure on what. But we needed more space. We didn't need a couple of thousand pounds' worth of television.

'Don't even think about it,' I said crossly.

Suddenly a row was in the air. Will had that slightly sulky expression that he has when he doesn't get his own way. But then Caz came downstairs, holding a photo and giggling.

'I was sorting out some stuff at my mum's, Will,' she said, 'and I found this.'

'Oh my God!' said Will. 'The outdoor activities week in Year Eleven!'

Oh yes. Will and Caz were in school together. They even had a bit of a fling at one time. About the time that picture was taken, long before I knew either of them.

Actually it was quite a funny photo. They must have been sixteen years old and on an outdoor week in the Yorkshire Dales – all climbing, canoeing and gorge walking. Caz was wearing one of those enormous geek-like cagoules. But she had the full make-up on – three different shades of eye shadow, blusher and lip gloss. Never a girl to let her standards slip is Caz.

In the picture she was gazing adoringly up at Will. Jamie snatched the photo from him. 'I bet you were hell for the teachers,' he said – and he should know, he teaches in the local comp – 'sneaking off to the canoe store for a quick snog. They all do.'

Caz and Will looked at each other very quickly and almost blushed.

Caz grinned. 'Thank goodness you don't choose your life partners at sixteen,' she said. 'Bad enough working with you, Will, let alone having to live with you. Don't know how Rosie manages it.'

'With difficulty sometimes,' I said, laughing. But I felt a small pang. I had fallen for Will the moment I'd arrived at *The News*, where he was already a senior reporter. He had to show me around on the first day and I knew, just knew, that he was the one for me. We were both slightly involved with other people at the time and as soon as we untangled ourselves, that was it. We were an item. It was as if we had always been together.

But we hadn't. And Caz had known him since they were eleven years old. They had a past, experiences, memories, daft jokes I couldn't share. And sometimes, just sometimes, I felt a twinge ... of jealousy, I suppose. Silly. He was with me now.

Jamie and Will started playing on the Play-Station.

'What about Leo and Jake then?' asked Caz, passing me some wine. 'I bet that will be a brilliant day.'

I laughed and started to say something to Will, but he was still gazing at that bloody television.

'Look, Will, you've only just got your new car,' I said. 'That's a nice new toy for now.'

'Well, you're the one who wanted to go to New York.'

'And you're the one who spent a fortune in Nieman Marcus,' I snapped back. 'How many cashmere sweaters does one man need?' A bit of a cheek coming from me, I know, being no slouch in the cashmere sweater department myself.

Things were getting snippy.

'Children, children,' said Jamie. You can just hear him with Year Seven, though at school he probably wouldn't have the lager can in his hand.

'Have you not thought,' Jamie went on, 'that perhaps if you didn't buy new cars and fly halfway across the world for a long weekend and a shopping habit, you might just be able to buy a bigger flat, or even a nice little house? Unless, of course, you don't really want to. And your subconscious is telling you to spend your money on fun and toys instead of being grown-up and sensible and salting it away for your future.

18

'Strange, isn't it,' he went on, 'that the only people in our group who are getting married are Leo and Jake? Takes a pair of gays to set the rest of us loose-living reprobates a good example.'

'Me, I don't see the point of being married,' said Caz. 'We're fine as we are, aren't we sweetie?' she said, patting Jamie's knee. 'We don't need a posh frock and a piece of paper. It might be different if we wanted kids, I suppose. But Jamie sees enough of kids in work. He doesn't want to come home to them as well.'

'But what about you?' I asked.

'Not a maternal bone in my body,' she laughed. 'Anyway I'd be an absolute disaster as a mum. I'd probably leave the poor little bugger's pram outside the pub. No, my unborn baby should be very grateful to me for keeping it that way.'

Jamie looked baffled. 'I always thought girls wanted to get married. You know, waiting for their knight in shining armour to come along and sweep them off their feet, rescue them from dragons.'

'We can fight our own dragons, thank you,' I said.

'See?' said Jamie laughing to Will. 'This lot have made us redundant. Out of work dragon-slayers, park your charger and hang up your plumed helmet.'

'Yeah, well,' said Will, now quite drunk and getting stroppy, 'maybe Leo and Jake have got something to prove. They want to settle down and play houses.'

Then, just like that, as if it wasn't really that important at all, he dropped the bombshell that nearly destroyed my world.

19

'As for me,' said Will, 'there's not much point in tying myself to a house if I'm not going to be around long.'

I was so shocked I gasped, as if he'd hit me. 'What do you mean? Where are you going?'

'Well, nowhere at the moment. But I might do,' he said, looking sideways at me. 'I might go out to work in Dubai, or somewhere. Mate of mine out there says they always want English journos. Plenty of money, easy lifestyle.'

Dubai? This was the first I'd heard of it. 'And is that what you want? Plenty of money and an easy lifestyle?' I snapped.

'Well, it's what we all want really, isn't it?' he said, taking a gulp from his can and sprawling back into the armchair.

I was furious. I was also drunk, which didn't help. And stunned. I had thought Will and I were pretty solid. Maybe even permanent. Wrong!

'Look, Rosie,' he put down his can, 'I just mean...'

He was probably trying to be conciliatory. I wasn't.

'Forget it,' I snapped.

'Coffee?' said Caz, very brightly. Just like the perfect hostess, only she staggered a bit and fell onto Jamie's lap, which spoiled the effect.

'No, no, I don't want coffee,' I said, angry and flustered and utterly wrong-bloody-footed, 'I think I want to go home.' I marched out into the hall, wriggled my feet into my boots and left.

Will came after me, and I didn't know if I was pleased or not. I could hear his footsteps but he said nothing. His long legs meant he soon caught

20

me up. He walked alongside me, matching his steps to mine, looking straight ahead. And we walked like that, side by side in silence all the way to the flat. My flat.

As soon as we got in, I turned to him. 'Are you really going to Dubai?'

'Who knows?' he shrugged. 'It's just a thought, an option, a possibility.'

'But what about me?'

'Well you can come too, if you like.' He hunched his hands into his pockets.

'If I like? If I like? You make me sound like an optional extra! I thought we had a future together.'

'Did you? Did you really?' Those big brown eyes flashed and I didn't like it.

'And if you think we have a future together,' he said, 'why is it that all I ever hear is what *you* want? *You* want to work in London. *You* want the bigger flat. *You* bought the bigger sofa, without even mentioning it to me. *You* pay the bills and just tell me how much to cough up. Fine, fine it's *your* flat after all, as you keep reminding me.'

I was stunned. 'I don't feel like that. I thought...'

'What did you think? Come on, tell me, I really want to know.'

'I was frightened,' I said. 'I didn't want to be dependent on you.'

'Why not? Don't you trust me?'

'It's not like that. No. It's nothing to do with trust. It's just that... Well, I don't know. We've never talked about the future, not really.'

And we hadn't. We've planned holidays and weekends away but no more than that, not what you would call a proper, grown-up, till death us do part future. Maybe it was too frightening to contemplate.

'Well let's talk about it now. Come on, Rosie, what do you want? What do you want from me? From us?'

'I don't know.' And that was honest. I had sometimes daydreamed of marrying Will. Not the big white wedding, but just being married to him, having him there all the time. He was the only person I've ever daydreamed like that about. The only one.

But I had never told him. Because there were times that the same dream could terrify me. The thought of being with just one person for ever. Well, it's seriously scary, isn't it?

And Will ... well, he wasn't exactly husband material. I mean, he was nearly thirty and he still acted like a big kid. Away from work all he and Jamie cared about was football and drinking and playing computer games and the bloody grand prix and flash tellies.

'You don't know?' he repeated, still waiting for my answer.

I looked up at him. 'Will, I love my job and I'm just beginning to get somewhere. I want to see how far I can go.'

'Fair enough. You'll go far, Rosie. We both know that.' Full of angry energy, he was pacing up and down the tiny sitting room. 'But I don't know if I'm part of your plan. Frankly, Rosie, I haven't a clue where I am with you. You want everything your own way.'

'But it's not like that...' I was stunned, struggling to find ways of saying what I thought.

And then he nearly floored me with his next question.

'Tell me, do you see yourself having children?'

'Hey!' I tried to joke. 'You can't ask questions like that at interviews. Not allowed.'

Will wasn't laughing. 'I want to know.'

'Well yes, since you ask, one day, probably,' I said. I'd daydreamed about that too. A boy and a girl, with Will's blond hair and big brown eyes. But not yet. Maybe I'd have them at some vague point in the future.

It was time for me to go on the attack. 'And what about you? Do you want children?'

'Maybe, one day. Depends.'

'Depends on what?' I asked. And the Devil got into me, because I snapped, 'On whether you can fit it in between the PlayStation and the plasma TV? Or another new car? You've got to be a grown-up to be a parent, Will, not an overgrown bloody kid yourself.'

Of course it all went downhill from there. We'd both had too much to drink and said too many things that shouldn't have been said and that I'm not even sure we meant.

I called him spoilt, immature and childish, among other things. He called me a selfish, un-thinking control freak, among other things. It didn't get us anywhere. In the end I went off to bed and I could hear Will still crashing around the sitting room, impatiently flicking through the TV channels, until he finally went to sleep on the sofa. My new sofa.

And me? I lay in bed and tried to re-run the row. Did I really want to be married? Yes of course. Maybe. But now? Frankly, the thought frightened me. What if Will went to Dubai? What if I went to London?

What if?

My head was thumping. I hardly slept, and in the morning my head was worse ... which is why when we got to *The News* on Monday morning – in Will's car, in silence – I'd been hoping to crawl quietly to my desk and just plod through the day – but the editor, Jan Fox, known to all as the Vixen, spotted me.

'Rosie! A word please!'

The Vixen was standing at her office door, eyes glinting, coppery highlights shining. In one hand she held a large sheet of paper, on which the perfect scarlet nails of the other hand were lightly drumming. It was not a happy drumming.

I realised that the piece of paper she was so obviously hacked off about was a proof copy of the next day's feature page. A feature on child-care, one I'd written. My heart sank even further. Happy Monday.

'Do you realise,' she said, shooting me one of her fierce looks, 'how incredibly young and silly this makes you sound? It's written as though everybody in the world has a responsibility to look after children with the sole exception of their bloody parents.'

'But I was just quoting from the reports and the government spokesman...'

'Yes, I know you were,' she sighed. 'I just won-der about your generation sometimes. You must have had it easier than any other in the history of the world, and it's still not enough, you're still asking for more.'

I just stood there, waiting, longing to get to the Ibuprofen in my desk drawer.

'OK, I've marked up some ideas. Get that done. And then there's something else I want you to have a go at.'

Just what, I found out at the morning conference.

The News Editor, Picture Editor, Chief Photographer, and others all crowded into the Vixen's office, with mugs of coffee and piles of notes balanced on their knees. Will was there too, not looking quite as polished as usual. I don't know if he was trying to catch my eye. I didn't give him the chance. I just kept staring at the photos of all the old editors on the wall above him. George Henfield, fat and bald, Richard Henfield with his pipe.

We'd whizzed through the plans for the following day's paper and much of the week's ideas, but the Vixen was still talking. 'Right,' she said. 'Now what about The Meadows? It's fifty years since the first families moved in and I think we should have a good look at it. At the time it was revolutionary, homes of the future, the perfect place to live.'

'Bloody hell, they must have been desperate,' muttered Will.

The Vixen, of course, heard him.

'Will, you haven't a bloody clue, have you?' she said in withering tones, which cheered me up.

Will tried to score some Brownie points. 'We've done quite a lot on the way the school's improved,' he said. 'We've had a few interviews with the new headmistress who's working miracles, Rosemary Picton, and we're always doing picture stories there.'

'Yes,' said the Vixen briskly, 'and I'm sure we'll be back to her. An amazing woman. But, as you know, they are using one of the houses on The Meadows for a new reality TV series, *The 1950s House*, so we need a good look at why people were so pleased to move there. What it was like at the beginning. Why it went wrong in parts. Why other parts are flourishing.

'We'll want to take a good look at life in the 1950s. It could make a series of features, but I want some meat on it, not just nostalgia. The Meadows seems a good place to start.'

By now I'd finished gazing at the old editors and was working my way around the myriad awards that *The News* had won under the Vixen. Suddenly I heard her mention my name. I sat up and tried to take notice.

'Rosie? Are you with us? I said I think this is something for you. If you wait afterwards, I'll give you some contacts.'

She always had contacts. I swear she knew everyone in town, not to mention the country. As the others picked up their notes and went back to their desks, she scribbled a name for me.

'Margaret Turnbull was one of the first people to move in to The Meadows, and she's lived there ever since. Nice woman, good talker. And she's actually Rosemary Picton's mother. When you've met Margaret you might get an idea of why her daughter's so determined to help the children of the Meadows. Anyway, here's her number. She'll get you off to a good start.'

With that she gave me an odd look. But her

eyes, in that immaculate make-up, were unreadable. 'I think you might find it very interesting,' she said.

Dutifully, I rang Mrs Turnbull and arranged to see her later that afternoon. Then I took a notebook up to the bound file room, where all the back copies of *The News* are stored in huge book-style files, and made a mug of camomile tea – all I could cope with – and settled down in the dusty little room. I didn't want to talk to anyone. Not even Caz and certainly not Will.

Was he going to go off to Dubai? Did I care? Well yes, actually, a lot. Could I cope without him? Yeah, course I could. Couldn't I?

It was probably easier to get on with some work. I felt rough though. My shoulder and neck hurt from lugging those old volumes around and poring over them. And my hands and feet were so cold. Bugger! My car was still in the car park at the Lion. So that's when I ordered a cab and went off to see Mrs Turnbull. Well, I thought she was Mrs Turnbull...

Chapter Two

Despite the pain in my head, I managed to open my eyes. The woman who opened the door wasn't the same as the one I'd seen through the window. Come to that, the window wasn't the same. Nor was the door. Oh God, what was happening?

I slumped against the door frame, my head

swirling, trying to make it out. What I really wanted to do was just slide down the wall and lie down ... but the woman was asking me something. Her voice seemed to come from a long way away.

'Are you the girl from *The News?*'

'Er yes, yes I am,' I said. It was about the only thing of which I was sure.

'Well you'd better come in.'

I wasn't sure if I could even walk, but I dragged my body together and followed her into a dark hallway. Something very odd here. I was sure that this sort of house didn't have that sort of long dark hall, or the sort of kitchen it led to. It had one of those cast-iron stoves, a bit like an Aga, only smaller. I could feel the warmth, which was wonderful. I was so cold. There was a strange smell. It took a while for me to realise it was coal and soot.

'Here,' said the woman, 'sit down before you fall down.'

There was a cat curled up on the chair by the stove. 'Shoo Sambo,' she said, pushing him off.

'You sit there for a minute,' she said to me, 'and I'll make you a cup of tea. You're as white as a sheet.'

I felt as if everything in my head had slid down to the back of my scalp and was made of lead. Never mind trying to make sense of what was going on. But at least I was starting to warm up. The cat, Sambo – Sambo! – jumped delicately back onto my lap and curled around. I rocked gently, feeling the warmth of the fire and of the cat. The room steadied. I wasn't feeling quite so

28

sick. I could even begin the attempt to make sense of my surroundings.

The woman perhaps wasn't as old as I first thought. Difficult to tell, probably only in her fifties, but definitely not from the Joanna Lumley school of fifty-somethings. She was wearing a heavy wool skirt and cardigan, a check apron and the sort of slippers that not even my gran wears any more. The room seemed incredibly old-fashioned. In the middle was a big table covered with a dark green cloth made out of that velvety stuff. Against one wall was a dresser covered with plates and jugs. Above the range was one of those wooden clothes racks that you see in trendy country magazines, but instead of drying bunches of herbs, this had sheets and pillowcases and what looked like old-fashioned vests and thick white underpants.

As the woman moved around the room between the dresser, the table and the range, it was like watching a film. She set out a tray with proper cups and saucers and plates, wrapped a cloth around her hand and lifted a huge black kettle off the top of the stove. She poured some water into a little brown teapot, went out of the room for a second into a scullery beyond and came back again, spooned loose tea into the pot and poured the boiling water onto it. From a hook by the range she lifted a tea cosy like a little chequered bobble hat and popped it on the teapot. She went into the scullery again and came back with a fruit loaf, cut a chunk off and put it on a plate in front of me. Then she passed me a cup of tea. It was strong and sweet – both of which I hate normally – but I drank it and could feel the warmth going through me. It was quite nice really, very comforting.

'I'm sorry about this, Mrs Turnbull,' I said.

'Oh, I'm not Mrs Turnbull,' she said.

'Oh my God,' I said and tried to stand up. 'Then I'm in the wrong house. I *thought* something was wrong. Look I'm really sorry. I'd better be on my way and find Mrs Turnbull. Is it the house next door? I must have come up the wrong path. I thought…'

'Sit down, girl,' she said, not unkindly. 'I'm Doreen Brown. If you're Rosie Harford from *The News* then you're in the right place. I've been expecting you.'

'You have?'

'Yes. And anyway, your trunk's upstairs.'

'Trunk? What trunk?'

'The things you'll need for your stay, of course.'

Stay? What stay? What on earth was going on? This was so confusing. I couldn't get my head around it. What was happening to my head? Maybe she'd slipped something in my tea. That was it. I had to get out. My mum always told me never to go into strange houses. And I reckon they didn't get much stranger than this.

'They sent it round from your office this morning. All the things you'll be needing in the next few weeks.'

I gazed at Mrs Turnbull who was now Mrs Brown and tried to understand what she was saying. My mind was so confused I expected one of those warning notices to flash up, 'You have performed an illegal operation. This program will

30

terminate.' And for a screen to go blank.

I felt sick. I promised myself I would never ever drink again. Too much wine, a blazing row and no sleep made a dreadful combination. Never ever again.

'You just sit there for a moment,' Mrs Brown said, letting me soak up the warmth of the fire and the cat. It would have been quite pleasant if my head hadn't been in overdrive.

Where was I? Why was I apparently staying here? What on earth was going on? I took deep breaths and tried my best not to panic.

By now I'd had two cups of tea and I suddenly realised that I really needed the loo. I couldn't deal with this on a full bladder.

'Upstairs, along the corridor, down a few steps and on your right.'

I tottered off. It was a bit like walking when drunk, I was almost hanging on to the walls of the passage. But I made it.

The bathroom was freezing. There was lino on the floor in a pattern of big black and white checks. Quite nice really. But the bath was hideous, huge with claw feet, a small brass tap and a big chrome one. It was all a bit Spartan. It smelt cold and clean and of old-fashioned rose-scented soap like one of Mum's aunties always used.

I got my phone out of my bag and tried to ring Will. I know we'd had a row, but this was really weird stuff. There was no signal. More than that, the phone was dead, as if the battery had gone. I sat on the loo and felt wretched. To be honest, I was frightened. Everything seemed strange. Even the loo paper was horrid. Nasty scratchy stuff.

And the loo had one of those big iron cisterns and a chain. Everything was somehow wrong, unfamiliar, just not quite right.

This house seemed to belong to another age. So old-fashioned. Can't have been touched for fifty years at least. What was I doing here? There must be some mistake. I had to get out. I stood up quickly. Too quickly. My head swam again and I leant against the door. I mustn't panic, I told myself. I must stay calm. Stay calm.

After a few moments I washed my hands, splashed some cold water on my face and gingerly made my way back downstairs, holding carefully on to the banisters. I would go downstairs, explain to the woman in the kitchen that, sorry, I had to go, and get out as soon as I could. Yes, that's what I would do. And as soon as I was outside, I would phone Will and ask him to come and get me. And if my phone still didn't work?

Stay calm. Stay calm. If my phone didn't work, I would just walk towards town. It wasn't that far. Even The Meadows must be safe enough in daylight. There might even be a phone box. And I would be all right once I was out in the fresh air.

I made my way back along the hallway, leaning against the wall for support. I made it into the kitchen but collapsed back into the rocking chair. I would just sit here for a while and get my strength back so I would be able to walk back into town if needs be.

My eyes lit on a calendar on the wall. There was a picture of the Queen looking very young. The calendar didn't look old or as though it had been sitting in a junk shop for fifty years. No, it looked new and shiny. In a 1950s sort of way.

I stood up. My head didn't swim. Good. I went through into the scullery to find Mrs Turnbull or Brown or whatever her name was. She was standing by a big stone sink with a wooden draining board, deftly chopping potatoes into a pan.

'Look, Mrs ... er Brown. I think I'd better be on my way,' I said. 'There seems to be a bit of a mix-up. I was meant to be meeting a Mrs Turnbull so I think I'd better get back and check with the office. Thank you so much for the tea and cake. I really appreciated it, but...'

'Oh you can't go yet, pet,' said Mrs Brown. 'You're meant to be staying. Anyway, Frank and Peggy will be back soon and supper won't be long.'

Meant to be staying? What was going on? And who were Frank and Peggy?

'I'll just get some fresh air, if you don't mind.'

'Carry on, dear.'

I picked up my bag and walked back along the hall. My head felt a bit better now. I'd tried to be polite about it, but that hadn't got me anywhere. I would just have to walk out. I hoped the front door wasn't locked. Strange. I was sure that when I'd walked up the path there'd been a modern white door, but here was this heavy wooden thing with stained glass at the top. I turned the handle, and opened it.

It was different. Everything was different.

Instead of the wide road of The Meadows with its rows of semi-detached houses and front gardens, parked cars and abandoned vans, the door opened directly onto a narrow cobbled street. Opposite was the high wall of what seemed to be

33

a factory or warehouse. No cars. No people. I stepped back into the house and shut the door quickly again.

Deep breaths. Stay calm.

Slowly, very slowly, I opened the door again. Still a cobbled street. Still an old factory. A light glinted as something caught the late afternoon sun.

I walked slowly back to the kitchen. That calendar. The Queen looked awfully young...

'Mrs Brown?'

'Yes dear?' she was manoeuvring some pans on the top of the range.

'Did you say my office arranged this visit?'

'That's right. And a young man brought your trunk around this morning. That's why I knew you were coming. All arranged with the editor.'

The editor. I thought back to the morning conference, which seemed a lifetime away. What exactly had the Vixen said? I couldn't remember. I'd been feeling so lousy and thinking so much about Will, that I hadn't really been listening. Think, girl, think. Something about The Meadows, of course, that's why I was here. And a TV programme. A reality TV programme. *The 1950s House...*

The 1950s House... It couldn't be, could it? When she'd talked about people living in a 1950s house for a television programme, she hadn't meant me, had she? She'd mentioned research. That's why I'd spent the morning in the bound file room. But she hadn't said anything about being here.

But she could have. I hadn't been listening. Hadn't heard. Wouldn't remember if she had. I had been away with the fairies all through conference.

But she *had* said in that meaningful way that I would find my visit to Mrs Turnbull 'interesting'. This is what it was all about. Was I taking part in one of those reality TV shows? I looked around for the cameras. I remembered that glint of light in the factory. I thought it had been sunlight on a window, but it could have been a camera.

A camera! I looked around. Was I being filmed now? Without thinking about it, I realised I had put my hand up to smooth my hair.

But how had they got me there? And how was outside completely different? It must have been something to do with that taxi driver I supposed. He had seemed odd and my head had been so rough I hadn't really taken much notice of where I was. And he'd followed me up the path. Maybe somehow he'd made me go somewhere else.

Maybe the path had been a stage set and that's why it had sent my eyesight funny. A trick, just projected on a wall or something. Maybe it had just been a façade, a front in front of this old house. It seemed a bit over the top, but there – for *I'm a Celebrity* they parachuted people into the jungle, didn't they? Walking up the wrong garden path was nothing compared to that.

And that factory. It could be the old rope works on the other side of town. There were a couple of indie TV production companies in there. The *Big Brother* house was in the middle of an industrial estate. This could just be in a car park. Maybe.

'All right, dear?' said Mrs Brown. 'You've got a bit of colour back. You just sit there for a bit while I get supper ready.'

Feeling a bit calmer now I thought I'd worked

this out, I sat on the rocking chair stroking Sambo, who purred quietly while I listened to Mrs Brown clattering away in the next room. So this must be the 1950s house and the Vixen must have volunteered me for it. And I was clearly staying for a while. I wondered what the rules were, who else would be there. I was just wishing I knew more, a lot more, when Mrs Brown called out, 'There we are, here's Frank and Peggy. Right on time.'

Frank was clearly Mr Brown, middle-aged in a thick suit, specs and moustache. He smiled at me and said, 'Well, you must be Rosie.' He shook my hand. A nice handshake.

'And this is Peggy,' said Mrs Brown.

Peggy was about my age, maybe a year or so younger. She had curly blonde hair and a pleasant open face that darkened when she saw me.

'Hello,' she said. That's all, and went to hang up her coat.

'So,' I said brightly, 'are we all in this together then? All play-acting in the 1950s? Did you enter a competition to get here? Or were you just volunteered by your boss, like I was?'

There was a silence. Peggy came and stood and looked at me as if I'd totally lost it. Mrs Brown came wandering out of the kitchen with her hands in oven mitts and a baffled expression. And Mr Brown took off his jacket and his tie, rolling it up carefully and putting it on the dresser, took a cardigan off the peg, put that on and swapped his shoes for slippers.

I realised I must have said something wrong.

'Oh sorry,' I said. 'Aren't we allowed to mention it's a programme? Do we have to pretend all the time that we're in the 1950s? I mean, I don't even know if it's like the *Big Brother* house and we're all competing against each other, or if it's just to see how we get on. Do you know? I mean, how did you get here?'

The silence continued. They were all still staring at me.

Finally Mr Brown said, 'We've rented this house since before the war. That's why we're here. You're here because our Peggy asked us to have you to stay, on account of you were working on *The News*. No more than that can I tell you.'

Right, I thought, that explains it. We clearly have to pretend at all times that we are in the 1950s. These three were obviously taking it desperately seriously. Like those people who dress up and guide you around museums and keep calling you 'thee' and 'thou' and pretend not to understand when you ask if there's a cash machine. These three were clearly In Character in a big way. No sneaking back to the twenty-first century, not even for a bit of light relief.

'I see,' I said and tried to enter into the spirit of the thing. 'Since before the war?'

'Yes. Our Stephen wasn't born and Peggy was just a toddler and now look at her.'

I did. She glared at me.

'Now then, young Rosie,' said Mr Brown. 'Tell me all about America.'

'America?' I said, not knowing what he was talking about. 'Well I've only been there twice, once to New York and once to Flor–'

'Now girl, don't be silly, I know you must be American, wearing trousers like that.'

I was dressed perfectly normally for work. Black trousers and a stretchy silky top. Though my jacket was a nifty little Jilly G. number that I had bought on eBay. Maybe Mr Brown recognised a style snip when he saw one. OK, maybe not.

'Never mind about that now,' said Mrs Brown. 'She's got plenty of other clothes in her trunk I expect.'

'Well she can't wear those to work,' said Peggy with sarcastic satisfaction. 'It might be all right in America but it won't do here. No. Mr Henfield won't stand for that. No women in trousers in the office.'

'Mr Henfield?'

'Richard Henfield, the editor of *The News*,' said Mrs Brown. 'Peggy's his secretary,' she added proudly.

Henfield ... Henfield...

I remembered the Vixen's office, the wall with the photographs of all the editors of *The News* that I'd gazed at in conference. Somewhere in the middle of them all I'm sure there was a Richard Henfield.

'Does he have a moustache and smoke a pipe?' I asked. 'I think I've seen his picture somewhere.'

'Well you would,' said Peggy, 'he's very well known.'

'Never mind that now,' said Mrs Brown. 'Peggy, come and mash the potatoes for me.' Mrs Brown was bustling around dishing up supper. She took a big casserole dish out of the stove and put it on the table.

'Well this looks special for a Monday,' said Mr Brown, rubbing his hands.

'Well, seeing as we have a visitor,' said Mrs Brown, through a cloud of steam.

So I didn't dare say that I don't really eat red meat. I'm not vegetarian, but I'm not really a red meat sort of person. And I didn't want to seem like one of those whingeing, whining contestants making a fuss about nothing, so I ate it up, and it was really quite good. Chunks of meat and thick gravy. Afterwards, from another compartment in the stove, Mrs Brown produced a rice pudding. I couldn't remember when I'd last had rice pudding, certainly not one that hadn't come out of a tin. Mrs Brown was definitely in character. Unless they had another kitchen out the back where they had a cook lined up to make everything, so Mrs Brown could just do the 'Here's one I made earlier' routine.

'So does your mother like cooking?' asked Mrs Brown.

'Well yes, I think so. She's worked her way through Delia and Nigella. I'm not sure she bothers much when it's just her and Dad, but when my brother or I go home...'

'Oh, don't you live at home? In digs, are you?'

'Digs?' I groped for a moment, trying to work out what she meant and thinking of *Time Team* and hairy archaeologists.

'Digs,' she said again, 'lodgings.'

'Oh, no. I have my own flat.'

'Oh you *are* a career woman, aren't you?' said Mrs Brown, looking a bit surprised. Peggy simply looked murderous.

'It's quite small, but it's in nice grounds and there's secure car parking.'

'You've got a car?'

'Well yes, just a little one. Nothing flash.'

'Your own flat and a car? Very nice I'm sure,' said Peggy, accepting another helping of rice pudding. 'All I can say is it must be very nice to be American. I hope you can manage to slum it with us.'

She really didn't like me...

'Look really, I'm not American.'

'Well you talk like one.'

'Do I?'

The Browns all had quite strong local accents. I didn't think I had much of any sort of accent really. I wished they didn't keep thinking I was American.

I offered to help with the washing up, but Mrs Brown was adamant.

'No, Frank will help me tonight, for a change. You two girls go and watch the television.' That sounded like a good idea. A bit of goofing out in front of the box was just what I needed. Some chance. The TV was a huge box affair with a tiny little screen showing a programme about ball-room dancing. It was nothing like *Strictly Come Dancing*. Somewhere there were a lot of tiny grey figures in grey dresses and grey suits waltzing across a grey ballroom.

Of course, they didn't have colour TV in the 1950s.

'Anything on any of the other channels?'

'What do you mean?' asked Peggy.

Of course, they wouldn't have Sky. But ITV, Channel 4?

'This is television. There's only this one.'

'Haven't you got ITV yet?'

'The one with adverts?'

'Yes, the one with adverts.'

'They've got it in London, but we haven't.'

Right.

I looked around the room, trying to spot where the cameras were. There were a couple of pictures on the wall, and they looked innocent enough, but the mirror above the fireplace – that could definitely be a two-way job with a camera on the other side. I looked straight at it and smiled – winningly, I hoped. Mrs Brown came in and picked up a big bag from behind the armchair and took out some knitting. This was clearly going to be a riveting evening.

'If you don't mind, I think I'd like to sort myself out,' I said.

'Of course, dear. What was I thinking of?' said Mrs Brown. 'Peggy, take Rosie up to her room, will you please, pet?'

Peggy clearly didn't want to be dragged away from the grey delights of television, but, sighing heavily, she led me up the narrow dark stairs, along a narrow dark landing, up a few more steps, to a small, icy cold room. It had been quite nice in front of the fire in the sitting room, toasting my toes, but once you went out of that room, the temperature plummeted.

'Here you are,' she said. 'It's really my brother Stephen's room, but he's in Cyprus at the moment.'

'Oh, lucky him,' I said, thinking of bars and beaches and all that clubbing.

She stared at me as if I were mad. 'Two soldiers

were killed there last week.'

'Is he a soldier then?'

'Doing his national service, isn't he?' she said and left me to it.

It was a bleak little room. Lino on the floor and a rug at the side of a narrow bed with a shiny green quilt, a chair, wardrobe, a bookcase with lots of Biggles books and football annuals, and a pile of football programmes. There was a trophy of a cricketer and some model planes, and that was about it. The only clothes in the wardrobe were a school blazer and a few old jumpers. Our Stephen was hardly a style icon, unless he'd taken all his possessions with him.

I looked around for cameras. Nothing obvious. Would they give us privacy in our bedrooms? Surely they would. But they didn't in the *Big Brother* house, did they? I looked around again. If there was a camera here, it had to be in the cricket trophy, I decided. Too obvious. Or maybe the model planes... I picked them up and put them in the wardrobe and shut the door. Then I picked up the Biggles books and put those in there too. That felt a bit safer. Now I could look in that trunk beneath the window.

A proper old-fashioned trunk, and on it were my initials RJH – Rose Jane Harford. I lifted up the lid. Clothes! So this is what I was to wear. I rummaged through them excitedly. Oh I do love clothes.

I tried to remember what sort of clothes they wore in the 1950s. I thought of Grace Kelly in *High Society* ... Audrey Hepburn in *Funny Face*. Or even Olivia Newton John in *Grease*. Oh yes. In my mind's eye I was already jiving with John Travolta, his hand on my nipped-in waist while my skirt swished and swayed beguilingly...

To my deep disappointment, these clothes were not at all beguiling. In fact, they all reminded me of my old geography teacher. And I mean *old* geography teacher. There were a couple of heavy wool skirts, one of which had a matching jacket. Some cotton blouses, and cardigans, hand-knitted by the look of them. And a pair of trousers, Capri pants in heavy navy cotton.

There was a dressing gown that looked like my grandad's. Oh and the underwear! The bras were made of white cotton and looked as though they were designed for nuns. I bet Grace Kelly never wore anything like those. Knickers too – white cotton. I don't think I'd worn pants like those since I was about three years old. In fact, even at that age my underwear had more style. These were dreadful.

There was a serviceable, very serviceable, raincoat and a bright red jacket like a duffel coat. I quite liked that. It had a matching beret too. I tried them on and did a twirl in front of the rather blotchy wardrobe mirror. Then I hung the dressing gown in front of it. Just in case of cameras.

A very functional wash bag contained a toothbrush, a round tin of bright pink toothpaste, a face cloth, a bottle of White Rain shampoo for 'normal' hair, and some cold cream. And at the bottom was a handbag, nice leather but brown and boring. I opened it to find a funny little purse containing money. But not money I knew. There were some notes, orange ones that said ten shillings and green ones that said one pound. One pound notes – I thought they only had those in Scotland – also lots of coins, not like Euros, but big and heavy.

I kept the jacket on. It was so cold in there. Out of the window I could hear the sound of rushing water. There must be a river. I looked out, but the streetlights were so dim I could only see the faint outline of some trees and a bridge. The view could wait till morning. I presumed I would still be here in the morning. I wished I knew exactly what was going on. I felt very unsettled and a bit, quite a bit actually, lost.

I missed Will. I tried my phone again. I have a video on it of Will just walking down the street towards me. It's wonderful because you can see he's thinking of something else and then suddenly he sees me and then he has a great big grin. I play it a lot, especially when I miss him. And never missed him as much as in this strange place where I didn't know what's happening. But the phone was absolutely dead. Nothing.

There was a knock on the door. Mrs Brown. 'Rosie, I've made a cup of tea. Or you can have cocoa if you like. Come downstairs and get warmed up.'

Cocoa! Such excitement, I thought as I went down into the kitchen. In the dim light, Mr Brown was sitting in the rocking chair, reading a copy of *The News* – the old broadsheet version, of course, very authentic. But there was someone else in there.

A small girl was sitting at the table. She was surrounded by exercise books. Judging by the dirty dishes near her, she'd also polished off the remains of the casserole and the rice pudding. She was wearing one of those old-fashioned pinafore dress things they had in the St Trinian's films – a gymslip? – a very grubby school blouse and a stringy tie. Her mousy, greasy hair looked as though it had been hacked rather than cut. And she had specs, the ugliest specs I've ever seen and so cruel to give to a child.

But as she looked up at me, I realised she was older than I had first thought – probably about eleven or twelve, and that behind those horrid specs she had a measuring, challenging expression that was a bit disconcerting.

'Are you the American?' she asked.

'I'm not American,' I said, already weary with that assumption.

'This is Janice,' said Mr Brown. 'She's very clever, doing well at the grammar school and she comes here to do her homework.'

I must have looked a bit puzzled by this because Janice said simply, 'I've got seven brothers. Two of them howl all the time.'

'Her mum cleans the post office where Doreen works,' said Mr Brown, 'so she always comes here when she's got homework to do. I used to be able to help her but I think she's cleverer than me now, aren't you, girl?'

With that Peggy came into the kitchen and to my surprise, gave the grubby little girl a big smile. Peggy looked really pretty when she smiled.

'Hiya kid!' she said. 'How's the French? Mrs Stace still giving you hell?'

'Of course. We've got a test tomorrow.' Janice

45

looked worried. 'Will you test me, Peggy, please? Perfect tense?'

'I have given.'

'*J'ai donné.*'

'He has finished.'

'*Il a fini.*'

'They have gone.'

'Aha, that takes *être! Ils sont allés.*'

'Well done,' said Peggy.

'Do you speak French, Rosie?' asked Janice.

'A bit,' I said. 'I did it for GCSE, but not like that.'

'Janice is smashing at it,' said Peggy amiably, almost proudly. 'One day she's going to go to France and she'll need to know how to talk to them all, order her snails and frogs' legs and wine.'

'It would be wonderful to go to France,' said Janice wistfully, 'wonderful to hear people talking differently.'

'Tell you what,' said Peggy – she really seemed quite nice when she wasn't talking to me – 'you don't need to do any more French, you know enough for today. Shall I wash your hair for you? You can use some of my new shampoo.'

'Oh yes please, Peggy!' said the little scruff, bundling her books into her satchel.

Soon she was on a stool, kneeling over the big white stone sink in the scullery, while Peggy shampooed her hair and rinsed it using a big enamel jug. She wrapped it in a rough kitchen towel and then combed it out for her quite gently and carefully, easing the comb through the tangles.

'If you like, I'll trim the fringe a bit for you,' said Peggy and went to get her mother's sewing scissors. She snipped away, looked at her handi-work a bit, turned Janice's head this way and that and snipped a bit more. 'There, see what that's like when it dries.'

It was already starting to fluff up in the warmth of the range. It looked so much better, shinier. There was even a hint of red in the mousy strands.

'Now now, Janice, Peggy, time to pack up.' Mrs Brown had come into the kitchen and was getting a cloth out of the dresser drawer. 'This is a kitchen not a hairdressers. I need that table for the breakfast things and it's time you were at home and in bed. Here,' she took a scarf out of a drawer and gave it to the girl, 'put that over you. You don't want to be walking the streets with wet hair, you'll catch your death.'

'Right-o, Mrs Brown,' said Janice, taking one last look in the mirror before gathering up her satchel. She smiled hugely at Peggy. 'It's lovely, Peggy, really lovely. Thank you. See you tomorrow.' She slid out of the back door, small and scruffy and still smelly too.

'She can't help it,' said Mrs Brown, noticing my expression. 'Terrible family. Father's out of work half the time. Mother's a willing little woman but has no idea really. All they seem able to do is make babies. There are seven boys and Janice, and two of the boys are simple. Still, Janice is bright and got into the grammar school, so let's hope it helps get her somewhere. She deserves a chance, poor scrap. Right. Tea or cocoa?'

I had cocoa – for the first time since a Brownie sleep-over when I was about seven – said my goodnights and took it up to bed with me. There were too many things I wanted to think about. I undressed, put on the great big dressing gown, scuttled to the bathroom, scuttled back, popped the dressing gown back over the wardrobe mirror and got into bed. Icy sheets. I reached for my notebook.

DAY ONE IN THE 1950s HOUSE
Very cold but headache better and at least I realise what's going on. Clearly, our reactions to a new situation must be part of The Test. Initial disorientation all part of this.

Must find out how long I'm going to be here for. What about work? My life? Maybe all will be explained soon.

Find video diary room.

What's the prize?

Find cameras. Smile at them. A lot.

Be nice to everyone.

Peggy – a test?

Have noticed that all Big Brother, It's a Celebrity, *etc TV shows are never won by the loudmouths, but by the quiet pleasant ones who win admiration and respect from all concerned, doing hard work, solving quarrels, being calm voice of reason all round. This is what I shall do. Practise being calm voice of reason.*

I tried to ring Will again, but the phone was still dead. That made me feel really alone and a bit down. But then there was a knock on the door.

'I thought you might like a hot-water bottle,' said Mrs Brown, handing one over and giving a strange glance at the dressing gown spread out over the front of the wardrobe. 'Are you sure

48

you're all right?'

'Yes fine thank you!' I said brightly.

The hot-water bottle was wonderful, warm and squidgy. I shoved it down between the sheets, which smelled of soap powder and sunshine and, as I wriggled down between them, with my feet nice and warm, I clutched my phone, the way I used to clutch my woolly cuddly cat when I was little. Even though my head was spinning, I was asleep in minutes.

I wished I'd been able to talk to Will, but if this was a challenge, then bring it on!

Chapter Three

Challenge? I'll tell them what to do with their nasty, manipulative, heartbreaking challenges. Today has been a nightmare. A glimpse into an alternative universe. I hated it. If I didn't think it was all a TV show I don't know what I'd do.

I never even asked to be in this. They can't just dump me here without asking, without any preparation or briefing. Shouldn't they have had my written permission? Contracts with lawyers? Big fat fees? Get-out clauses? Insurance? Maybe I could sue them for stress and anxiety. What happens if I break my neck on the stairs at The News? *Or die of pneumonia from the damp and cold?*

Or from a broken heart?

Today was my first day on *The News* 1950s style.

It had started badly. My clothes, my proper clothes, had vanished. Someone must have taken them while I was in the bathroom. Even my own handbag. All I had left was the handbag from the trunk, a dead phone and the notebook and pen from my bedside table. I thought of going down to demand my things from Mrs Brown, but then I remembered the Golden Rule of Reality TV which is Be Nice, Smile, Don't Make A Fuss. So after a wash – no shower, and I couldn't even have a bath because there's only one loo and that's in the bathroom and people kept banging on the door – I got dressed in my 1950s clothes.

Everything itched, scratched and dug in. There was no Lycra, of course. Dressed in the skirt suit I felt trussed up like a turkey. My suspender belt (when did I ever think they were sexy?) threatened to ping at any minute and my capacious cotton knickers kept disappearing up the crack of my bum. No wonder people in old photos look miserable.

And I still couldn't get anything on my phone... When I woke up it was on the pillow beside me, and I just grabbed it automatically. Nothing. Just a blank screen. The blankness of it just hit me and made me feel so dreadfully alone. Even if they were blocking the signal, you'd think they'd let me look at the stored pictures and messages on it, wouldn't you? It was a link to my world, my proper world, and Will.

And my hair! No shower, no dryer, no mousse, no straighteners. All I could do was comb it. Great.

After that grim start, the day got no better.

My usual breakfast was yoghurt and banana. Here it was porridge and boiled eggs. Compulsory. By the time I'd eaten it I felt so weighed down I thought I'd never lift myself off the chair. And the coffee ... the coffee came from a bottle that looked like gravy browning and tasted like it too.

To make it worse, because Mrs Brown worked mornings in a post office, Peggy and I, who apparently didn't have to be in work until half an hour later, had to do the washing up.

'You can wash,' said Peggy, handing me the porridge pan, with its burnt-on bits. 'It makes sense for me to wipe up and put away because you don't know where anything lives.'

'You could show me,' I said, but knew as I said it, there wasn't much point.

Do you want to know what I think of the 1950s so far? Well porridge pans really piss me off. Non-stick hasn't been invented yet. Neither has washing-up liquid, just disgusting green soap. You have to scrape the congealed porridge off with a knife and then, the real horror is when you have to scoop great blobs of it out of the plug-hole. That is so disgusting.

And Peggy. Peggy is a pain. Pisses me off even more than porridge pans. I am trying really hard to be nice to her and smile a lot (for the cameras, which I haven't found yet) but it's really tricky.

'Are these clothes all right for work, Peggy?' I asked.

'Very suitable,' she said.

'Do your clothes make you itch?'

51

'Of course not,' she said, but with such a filthy expression that I'm sure *her* knicks were stuck up the crack of her bum too. 'Come on. Time to get a move on.'

She handed me an Oxo tin. An Oxo tin? What was I meant to do with that? I must have looked blank because she said, 'It's your sandwiches, for your dinner.'

Off we went. I don't know how they're doing it, but it's very clever. Of course, Peggy led the way. (The more I think about it, the more she must be part of the team setting the challenge.) We went through some narrow streets and across a market square. (It's clearly a film set.) There was very little traffic, just a few old cars. (The sort they always have in period films.) And a delivery boy on a bike. (They always have that as well.) And there was a milkman with a horse and cart. (Which I thought was taking it a bit far really, but that might have been the one with the camera in it, so I gave the horse an extra nice smile.) The shops were small with crowded little windows, a bit drab, but the streets were very clean. No pizza boxes or burger trays. (Shows that it must have been all pretend.)

'Is it far to *The News?*' I asked, wondering how we'd get to the industrial estate.

'No,' she said. And that was it. No chatty girly conversation. In fact, nothing. Right, thank you, Peggy. But I remembered my winning ways and smiled and tried again. Tricky, because she was walking quite fast and I was struggling to keep up, and not just because of the shoes.

'Have you worked there long?'

'Five years.'

'So what's the editor like then?'

At this she went a bit pink and turned around to face me. 'He's a wonderful man,' she said vehemently. 'Wonderful!'

Bit of a giveaway wouldn't you say?

But now we were at *The News*. Not just off the ring road. It was right in the centre of town. And the funny thing was that it looked just like the old pictures we have hanging at reception in the industrial estate. A really old timbered building, with leaded windows. There were some big gates at the side, leading into a yard where I could see old-fashioned delivery vans. I don't know how they did it, but it was very clever.

As soon as we walked in through the door, Peggy changed character and was as nice as you like. Smiles and 'Good mornings'. She led the way upstairs.

Well, it was a newspaper office, but not as I knew it.

The place was chaos. A warren of small rooms, each one crowded with heavy wooden desks piled high with papers. The windows were small and grubby, and almost obscured by heaps of papers and files. There were papers everywhere. Piles of yellowing newspapers, on the floor, in corners, on windowsills, blocking doorways. Health and safety would have had hysterics. Especially as there was also a thick cloud of smoke. Everyone seemed to be smoking.

One stray fag end in that lot...

Peggy was leading the way along a narrow corridor of bare and battered floorboards. Then she led me into an outer office, hung up her coat and knocked reverentially on an inner door. 'Good morning Mr Henfield.' She was almost simpering. 'I've brought Rosie Harford.'

Richard Henfield looked exactly like his photograph. That was a nice touch, I thought, well researched. Middle-aged, specs, moustache and pipe. Nice eyes, weak chin. 'Ah yes, you're with us for a few weeks.'

'Apparently,' I said with a winning smile. There *must* be a camera in here.

'So tell me what you've done.' He leant back in his chair and stared at me. It wasn't a particularly nice stare.

'Well, after my degree, I did a post-graduate diploma in journalism and worked on a weekly paper for a while. For the last few years I've been a general reporter, then on the business desk, and now I'm a features writer, specialising in social and consumer issues.' Smile again.

'Well, aren't you a clever little girl,' he said, gazing at my boobs.

Really! My fingers itched to slap his pompous, patronising, sexist face. But smile, Rosie, smile. I smiled.

'Better see what you can do then,' he said, standing up to put his arm around my shoulders – not nice, he smelt of stale tobacco and sweat and half-digested meat. Didn't the man shower? – and led me back along the corridor and into one of the crowded smoky rooms, where an oldish man in a trailing overcoat was sitting with his feet on the desk reading a paper, while a woman talked on the telephone. Two other men were picking up their coats as if on their way out.

I ostentatiously removed myself from Henfield's arm. That smell was taking reality TV a bit too far.

'Is Billy about?' asked Henfield.

'Assizes,' said the man, hardly lifting his eyes from the paper. Seeing me, his beady eyes lit up too and he gave me and Henfield his attention.

'OK Gordon,' Henfield said. 'This is Rosie. She has a degree and a diploma and knows all about business and social issues.' He said it in a sarcastic, mocking tone.

'Very fancy,' muttered the woman behind him, putting the phone down and lighting a cigarette.

'She'll be here for a few weeks and no doubt she has many talents to reveal,' he leered. 'And a lot to show us.' He and Gordon gave each other knowing glances and then both looked me up and down, when, thank God, Peggy came along simpering, 'There's a phone call for you Mr Henfield,' and off he went.

'Smarmy bugger,' muttered the woman. Promising. Then looking at me, she added, 'I'm Marje, by the way. Well, let's see what you can do then.'

'Anything,' I said, all keen and eager and desperate to get stuck into a decent story.

'Kettle's over there,' said Marje. 'No sugar for me, two for him' – pointing at Gordon who'd gone back to reading the newspaper – 'and the cups need washing. Down the corridor at the very end and don't wait for the hot water, because there isn't any.'

Did I have a sign saying 'skivvy' stuck to my forehead?

Gordon was the News Editor. When he'd

stopped eyeing me up and down he had decided I was barely worth considering. 'You'd better follow Marje around for now,' he said as he took his tea without a thank-you. 'She can show you the ropes. There's a couple of golden weddings in the book. You should be able to manage those between you.'

Golden weddings! I hadn't done those since my early days on the weekly. But off I went dutifully with Marje. We had to walk to the old people's houses. There seemed to be only one van for the staff, and the photographers used it all the time. Reporters had to walk.

Marje strode briskly along.

'Have you been on *The News* long?' I asked, with the little breath I had left. She was setting a cracking pace and I was struggling to keep up.

'Since the war,' she said. 'I was on the switchboard and when all the men got called up there was only me and old Mr Henfield left, so I started doing everything.'

The war again.

'Young Mr Henfield, the one who's editor now, was in the army. And Gordon and most of the others. John, the Chief Sub Editor, was in the RAF – got the DFC but he never talks about it. The younger ones weren't, of course. Billy and Phil were just a bit too young, lucky for them. But they've done their call-up and their fifteen days since.'

'Fifteen days?'

'Yes, you know. Two years' national service and then fifteen days every year for three years. Don't they do that in America?'

'Oh yes,' I said vaguely, too fed up to argue about this American business. 'Something very like.'

I was really getting into this 1950s thing. It was almost as if I were really there. But it was a bit worrying that everyone else seemed to have done so much research. Maybe they'd had more notice than I had. That wouldn't be hard. Ah well, I would just have to wing it. Tricky though. I was trying to get my head around the fact that the war had only finished ten or eleven years ago, because that was as if, well that was as if it had been finishing just when I was doing A levels. Weird.

Walking along, I could see bits of the present town but not many. I had to say that the TV company had been very thorough. You could almost believe you really were back in the 1950s. There were so many more shops, for a start, lots of little ones. Lots of butchers, a couple of bakers. No candlestick-makers, but a fishmonger, two bookshops, lots of tobacconists, a wool shop, toy shop, baby clothes, another couple of chemists, a china shop, a couple of ironmongers. No supermarkets, but grocers' shops like Home and Colonial, and Liptons... To be honest, it all looked a bit run-down.

Then I could smell it ... coffee. Proper coffee...

'Oh Marje, can I really smell coffee?'

'Probably. Silvino's is just around the corner.'

'Silvino's?'

'Italian coffee bar.'

'Oh glory be. We haven't got time, have we? Just for a quick coffee. I'm longing for coffee...'

'No time, sorry,' said Marje and I had to ignore the tantalising smell as we hurried off to the first golden wedding. Nice couple. (Recipe for happy marriage – he always tipped up his pay packet on a Friday night and she always had a hot meal ready for him.)

Luckily, George the photographer turned up to take their picture when we were there. He was only a young lad, in a baggy suit that looked far too big on him, but he seemed to know what he was doing. And he had the van, which meant that Marje and I could squash into the rickety front seat and get a lift to the next golden wedding couple. Eric and Bessie had met in the church choir, still sang in it. They said the secret of a happy marriage was never to let the sun go down on a quarrel. Bessie looked smug and Eric tried to pinch my bum. Randy old goat.

I suppose they were all extras. There seemed to be an awful lot of them. I didn't realise that the TV company had such a huge budget. Still, I suppose when they did the *Castaway* series they took over a whole island for a year, so a big film set for a few weeks would be comparatively cheap. Looked very real though, fair play.

Afterwards, while George went off on another job, Marje and I walked back to the office and I remembered about my Oxo tin. I opened it carefully. Inside was a brown paper bag. It smelt of candles and polish and a musty under-the-stairs sort of smell. Inside that was a sandwich made with doorsteps of good white bread, filled with something that smelled a bit odd. I took a tentative bite and tried to work out what it was. It had a sort of fishy taste. Sort of. A bit like cat food.

Then I remembered my gran's kitchen cupboard, those funny little jars. Fish paste. I was eating a fish paste sandwich. I suppose it made a change from M & S's poached Scottish salmon with dill mayonnaise and watercress on oatmeal bread. And the bread was nice.

Then Marje had to show me how to type up a story.

What a chew! There was this mucky black paper, carbon paper, that made a smudgy sort of copy. You had to put three pieces of paper together, with two bits of carbon between them, and roll them into a typewriter. The typewriter took for ever. It was so heavy. You really had to bash the keys. And I kept forgetting to push the thing that made it go to the next line, so I kept typing on the roller instead of the paper. And you couldn't delete mistakes!

'Bet you wish computers were invented,' I said to Marje.

'Computers? Why?' She looked at me blankly. She was very good at pretending to belong to the 1950s. I think she must have been one of the testers rather than a competitor.

'Well, you know, quick and easy to type, correct your mistakes, spell check.'

'Spell check?'

'Yes, it corrects your spelling for you.'

'That's handy if you can't spell. How does it do it?'

'Um, I don't know really. But that's before you start on the internet.'

'The which?'

'Internet. You can find anything you want to know in seconds. About anything. Facts, figures, famous people, shopping. You can go on the internet, find things and buy them.'

'How does it do it?'

'I don't know, but it's wonderful. And–'

'You don't know much, really, do you?' said Marje, lighting another cigarette. 'Especially about spelling.' She turned back to my chaotic-looking copy and carried on swiftly marking up my mistakes. Most of them weren't actually spelling mistakes you understand, just typing mistakes from using the heavy typewriter.

'That computer thing must have rotted your brain. Here,' she handed my piece back to me, 'you'd better type it again or the subs will go mad. See you in the morning.' She picked up her string bag of shopping and went home to cook supper for her husband.

I typed up the golden weddings again and, because there were no messengers around, and because I was curious, took it along myself to the subs' room. The subs, all men, were smoking pipes or cigarettes and sitting around a long table, marking up the copy ready for the printers. As soon as I walked into the room I had that feeling you get in some offices – as though you'd walked into a private club and you're an outsider. Horrid.

One of the men looked up from the piece of paper he was writing on and whistled at me. Another sat back in his chair. Soon all the men, six of them, were sitting staring at me. The first said, 'Well, well, what have we got here? Hello girlie, who are you?'

'Rosie Harford. I'm here for a while as a reporter and features writer.'

'Features writer eh? We used to have one of those, but the legs fell off,' said one young man. They all laughed uproariously as if he had made the wittiest remark ever.

Another older man leant across the desk. 'Well Rosie, you've certainly got rosie cheeks. Rosie by name, rosie by nature. If I said you had a beautiful body, would you hold it against me?'

More sniggers.

'Watch yourself,' I said. 'That's sexist language.'

They looked shocked for a moment and then the laughter started again. Slowly at first and building up as each man joined in more noisily than the one before.

'Sex, is it?' said one, looking around with a broad grin at the others. 'Well, if you're offering.'

'No I am *not*,' I said and banged the copy down on their desk, 'and certainly not with you.' I turned to walk out.

'Will you just look at that,' one of the men said to my retreating view. 'A backside like two eggs in a hanky.'

I slammed the door but could still hear their laughter through it. My face was bright red. Pigs. Idiots. Stupid ignorant men. Bugger! I realised it was probably a test, to see how I'd cope. Well, I'd really blown that, hadn't I?

Flustered and feeling stupid, I went back into the newsroom. At least it was nearly going home time. Gordon was there, talking to another man. A tall man with sleek blond hair, standing with his back to me under the yellowing light at the far end of the newsroom.

I recognised him instantly even in the shabby

unfamiliar clothes. I would have recognised him anytime, anywhere. The set of his shoulders, the angle of his head, the gesture with his hands as he explained something to Gordon. Oh, I knew them all. I didn't need a second glance. I knew that body almost as well as I knew my own.

Will!

I was so happy I nearly let out a yelp of excitement and only just stopped myself running up and flinging my arms around him. I thought my heart would leap right out of my body with joy and relief. Here, in the middle of whatever strangeness was going on, and those stupid sniggering subs, I knew how much I needed him. With Will here, everything would be all right. He would turn the nightmare into an adventure. It would be a game, a laugh, a great story. Us two against the world. Suddenly it stopped being something strange and slightly sinister. Already, in that split second, it had started being fun.

It was all so wonderfully familiar, so reassuring. If Will was here, then I could cope with anything, from sexist subs to fish paste sandwiches, scratchy underwear and no showers.

'Will!' I said, going towards him. 'Will! Thank God you're here!'

Will looked around. He looked surprised. He looked straight at me. And he absolutely blanked me.

Will looked at me as though he'd never seen me before in his life.

Chapter Four

The silence seemed to go on for ever, to hang heavy in the air above the heaps of newspapers, the jumbled files and scuffed desks. It swirled with the dust from the overflowing ashtrays, and time slowed down as I gazed desperately at Will. I had stopped breathing, was just waiting for him to respond, to laugh, to step forward and hug me. But he didn't.

Sure, for a moment there was a flicker in his eyes – but it was that flicker you get in the eyes of any strange man when he sees you for the first time, the quick measuring, appraising look. And then – nothing. Not a hint, not a glint of recognition.

This was worse, much worse than any row. This was nothing to do with anger. Will was looking at me as though he had never seen me before. As though I were a stranger, as if we had no life, no past together. Nothing. And when I saw that blankness in his eyes my whole world shifted, as though the very earth I was standing on had been hollowed out from under my feet and I was in free fall. Without him, there was nothing to cling to. Nothing.

I wanted to run up to him, fling my arms around him. OK, we'd had a row. That was in another world, another lifetime. It didn't matter. All that mattered was that he was here. But not when he looked at me like that.

'Will?' I asked, tentatively, hesitating, terrified that he wouldn't even acknowledge me. I stood beside the desk, too frightened to move any closer.

Gordon was looking at me oddly. 'Billy,' he said to Will, 'you haven't met our temporary girl, have you? Rosie's here for a few weeks. From America or somewhere.'

There was a little spark in Will's eyes and then he smiled – oh that smile! – and held out his hand. 'How do you do Rosie,' he said. 'Welcome to *The News*.'

I looked at him, expecting an acknowledgement, a little secret smile perhaps. Anything. But no. I shook his hand. And that's when I had another shock. His hand was rough, callused. Not at all like Will's. I looked up at him, puzzled.

There were other differences too. His haircut, of course. Very 1950s, short back and sides. But his face looked different, more hollowed, angular, and he looked somehow older, different in a way I can't explain. I wanted to touch his cheek, follow those bones and hollows with my fingers, but he was looking at me as if I were a stranger.

I could still feel the impression of his hand in mine. But he had already turned away and was talking to Gordon about the court case he'd covered. It was as if I didn't exist. I studied him from the back, the way his short haircut went into a little curl at the nape of his neck, how his shoulders looked so broad, yet he seemed slimmer. Must be the 1950s clothes.

But why did he blank me like that? How could he be so cruel? I sat at my desk, a copy of *The News* propped up in front of me, though I couldn't have told you a single thing that was in it, while I tried to work it out. Yes. That must be it. We were in this 1950s house, but no one must know how close we were. We must pretend to be strangers. Then we can secretly work together, be a team. Together we could soon sort out what we should be doing and do it. But we mustn't let on.

It was the only explanation I could think of, and I clung to it.

I knew I had to speak to Will alone – ideally somewhere out of reach of any possible cameras, and the office was surely full of them. But I needed to stay in the office so I could watch him, catch him when he left. Looking at him bent over the typewriter instead of a computer, yet the same pose, the same frown, the same fierce expression as he thought of the next sentence, and then the half-smile as he bashed it out. That was the Will I knew. Even if here he was wearing baggy grey trousers and a rather shabby shirt, instead of the stylish suits he normally wears.

I sat and watched and waited. Brian, the Night News Editor, came in and was introduced to me. At last he and Gordon went out to see Henfield. Will and I were alone in the newsroom and I had to seize my chance.

'Will,' I said, standing opposite him in the dusty yellow light.

He didn't react immediately, just sort of looked up vaguely as if puzzled about who I was talking to.

'Will!' I hissed. 'What are we going to do? What's this all about? Do you know what's going on?'

He looked at me, baffled. 'Sorry, er Rosie, I'm

not sure I know what you're talking about. I'm nearly finished here. Have you done all your stuff? It's time to go home. You're not doing the late shift are you? No, you were here this morning.'

He looked back to his typewriter, typed a few more words, looked over what he'd written, pulled the papers and carbon out of the machine and folded them over. 'Have you sent your stuff along? If you give it to me, I'll drop it off with the subs for you on my way out.'

This was hopeless.

'Will! We've got to have a plan, work out how we're going to deal with this. Do you know who the other competitors are? Where are the cameras? And is there a video room? We've got to find out.'

Now he was lifting his jacket – a heavy, shapeless tweedy sort of jacket with pens in the front pocket and leather patches on the elbows – off the back of the chair and easing into it. 'Sorry Rosie,' he said, politely, 'I don't think I know what you want. Have a word with Gordon. Or if it's cameras you're interested in, talk to Charlie, the Chief Photographer, or young George. Anyway,' he said, picking up the papers off his desk – and that was another difference, his desk was absolutely immaculate and tidy, very un-Will – 'I must be getting a move on. I promised my wife I'd be home early. Goodnight. I hope you've enjoyed your first day with us. See you tomorrow.'

I didn't reply. I stood there, leaning against the scarred wooden desk, looking at his desk, and the seat that he had left. He'd promised his wife he'd be home early. His *wife?* He'd promised his wife? No. I couldn't believe it. Will didn't have a wife.

I was still sitting in the office when Brian came back in. 'Still here, Rosie?' he asked. 'I always knew Americans were keen.'

'Tell me,' I asked, 'Will, Billy. Is he married do you know?'

'Billy? Oh yes, love, a real family man. Got a couple of kiddies too. Three of them I think.' He smiled nicely. 'You're wasting your time there, love. Billy's definitely spoken for.'

Billy. Will. A real family man. Married. Three kids.

No. *No!*

I gathered up my stuff and headed out of the building and back 'home' through town. My mind was going crazy. Will couldn't be married. Not my Will. Certainly not so *very* married. Three kids? My skin went clammy with panic. Calm down, I had to calm down. Think. I tried to think of all the possibilities. This was all pretend. It was a challenge. Like the bush tucker trial in the Celebrity Jungle thingy, only much much worse.

Yes, that's what it was. It was just another challenge. I had my breathing almost under control. A challenge on a reality TV show. That's what it was. All pretend. Somewhere in a viewing gallery there were people watching me and laughing themselves silly at my reaction, overreaction. It was only pretend.

Of course Will couldn't say anything in the office. There were cameras in the office. That's it. I'd have to get him outside. Somewhere there weren't cameras. Somewhere where we could talk properly.

67

I was calmer now. It began to make a sort of sense.

But I couldn't forget that blank look. That blank look had seemed too genuine. Could Will be that good an actor? I tried to shrug the memory from my mind.

It was a test, that's all, just a test. But what a test...

Right now, what I needed was a drink, a very large drink. A large vodka would hit the spot. Or a nice rich red Merlot. Just the thought of it cheered me up and made life seem almost normal. I went out into the street and up into the Market Place, looking for a supermarket or an off licence, but there didn't seem to be one, just lots of little shops, already shut up for the night. It all seemed very dark. No wine bars. No restaurants. No burger joints. Didn't anybody ever eat out? Plenty of pubs though. Some of them looked a bit rough.

I carried on walking through the town centre. Then I saw The Fleece. Of course! The Fleece must have been a coaching inn centuries ago. It was terribly respectable, the sort of place that the Rotary meets. I bowled into one of the side bars. It was full of smoke and smelt really strongly of beer.

'Hey you! Get out!'

I made my way past the tables and headed for the bar. The bar was already quite full and I needed some big fat chap to move his chair a bit so I could get past.

'Excuse me,' I said.

'What?'

'I'd like to get past please.'

'You can just bugger off,' he said and turned back to his drink, with a grin at his companion.

'There's no need for that!' I said crossly.

'There's every bloody need. You shouldn't be in here,' he said, still not moving. The man with him laughed – not a nice laugh – and some of the other men joined in.

I wished to God I hadn't gone in that bar, but I wasn't going to be bullied. I squared my shoulders and said firmly, 'I have every right to be in here.'

'No you haven't. Now get out.'

I looked over at the barman. Surely he would do something.

'Sorry, miss,' he said, 'but you're not allowed in here. Men only.'

'Men only? That's illegal!'

'No it isn't, miss. This has always been a men-only bar. You'll have to go.'

'You can't have bars that are just for men!'

'Yes you can, miss. And this is one of them. Will you go now, please.' He made a move as though he were going to lift the counter flap and come around and chase me off.

What else could I do? With my face bright red I left, making my way past all the little tables, while some of the men still laughed. Horrid. Horrid. Hateful. Another test. I tried not to let it worry me. I pushed my way out and in the corridor opposite I saw a door marked Lounge Bar. That would be all right. I walked in, trying to calm myself down.

This room looked much nicer. Comfortable chairs, horse brasses, a log fire and an air of quiet calm. And there was a woman here – a middle-aged couple were sitting in one of the corners beneath a picture of a hunting scene. I'd be all right here. I walked up to the bar and perched on one of the stools. There was a different barman, older. He was wiping glasses.

'A large vodka and cranberry juice please.'

He carried on wiping glasses.

I waited for a moment. I was still getting myself calmed down from the other bar. But then the barman stopped wiping glasses and started stacking bottles on the shelf.

'Excuse me,' I said in my Like-I'm-here-can't-you-see-me? sort of voice. 'Could I have a vodka and cranberry juice please?'

This time he did at least bother to look up. He put his hands on the counter and looked around the room, towards the door.

'You on your own, madam?'

'Yes and I'd like a large vodka and cranberry juice please.'

He looked at me, not particularly pleasantly.

'Two things, madam,' he said. 'First, we haven't got any Russian drinks. And second, we don't serve unaccompanied ladies, madam. I'm sure you understand why.'

I was gobsmacked.

'No I don't actually. I haven't a bloody clue.'

'Language, madam, please. I can't serve you and I must ask you to leave.'

I looked towards the middle-aged couple, thinking they'd be sympathetic and help me out here. But they were suddenly intent on the pattern on the table.

'This is ridiculous,' I said, getting really angry now. 'If you haven't got vodka, then give me a large glass of Merlot.'

He leant forward menacingly and said, 'I'm not giving you anything, madam.' Then, in a fierce undertone, 'Now just sling your hook before I call the manager and get you put out. This is a respectable establishment. We don't want your sort in here.'

My sort? What did he think I was? A tart touting for custom?

And then it dawned on me. That's precisely what he *did* think. The idea was so ridiculous I started to laugh, despite myself. I slipped off the stool and made quite a good exit. But outside I was shaking. It was ridiculous but it was also insulting. I still hadn't got a drink. And Will had got a wife. Not a good day.

I headed back to the Browns'. I desperately needed to talk properly to Will. This was a challenge too far, no joke. I remembered his blank look and started to panic again, wanted to cry. But no, it was a game, a TV show. It wasn't real, I reminded myself firmly. It's not real. We'd sort it all out tomorrow.

I blew my nose on the silly little lace-edged hanky I'd found in my jacket pocket and headed for home. I wasn't sure of the way but I strode out purposefully and kept my head held high and my expression determined. I even tried to smile – just in case those cameras were watching.

Chapter Five

Oh they're clever, whoever's doing this. Clever and cruel too. But I must not let them get to me. I'm not going to let them. Whatever nasty sneaky tricks they pull.

I thought the 1950s house was going to be about practical things – like doing without decent wine and hot showers, wearing scratchy underwear and not being able to do my hair. Not psychological warfare. But then I remembered a piece Caz wrote last year about how cruel reality TV was getting. Every new series pushes the barriers a bit further. The last one locked people alone in the dark for days on end. They were so disorientated they lost all sense of reality and of who they were. Public executions are the next step, Caz reckoned. But I think she's wrong. I think it's mind games to see who can cope best. That's why there was no warning, no preparation. Well, no one's going to make a victim of me. Certainly not for a TV programme. Certainly not for a TV programme I didn't ask to be in. Not even after their latest trick.

We marched into work, Peggy and I, walking together, umbrellas up against the suddenly fierce spring rain, neither of us in the best of moods, neither of us saying a word. Not only had I not been able to get a drink last night, but when I got back to the house, supper was liver and onions and congealing cabbage, left in the oven for me, stuck to the plate with skin on the gravy. And that Janice was there again, doing sums about compound interest that stretched for pages and pages.

'Always get an interest-free credit card,' I'd offered as an attempt at a bit of cheerful advice, but then had to explain to her what a credit card was. It sounds so stupid when you try to explain it. And all the time my mind was full of thoughts of Will and his wife. And three children. It had to be a trick or a challenge, didn't it?

It was like that bit in *1984* where Room 101 is full of all the things that people dread most. Well, I realised that what I dreaded most was losing Will. Only I hadn't realised it until now. Obviously the TV people knew more about me than I knew about myself. Clever and cruel. No wonder I hadn't slept. My eyes felt raw.

At breakfast Peggy was being a real pain, obviously more than normal as even her dad kept asking her if she was all right, but she only snapped back at him. Anyway, his mind was on other things and Mrs Brown was worried about a friend who was having some problems with her husband. So everyone was a bit distracted really.

Mrs Brown had dashed out even earlier than usual. 'I want to go around to Joan's and sort out a few things for her there. Dennis has had one of his turns again. Smashed the kitchen up this time.'

'Good grief,' I said. 'Has she called the police? Is she safe? You don't have to put up with domestic violence.'

'He can't help it,' she said, gathering up her bag and scarf. 'It's them bloody Japs. They worked him almost to death in that prison camp. Before the war he was the loveliest, kindest man you could imagine. Now he gets these rages.'

'Isn't there some treatment he could have? Therapy? Counselling? Compensation? How on earth does his wife cope?'

I'd read all the articles on domestic violence, and written a fair few too. I knew the score and the helpline numbers.

Mrs Brown looked at me pityingly. 'She's just glad she's got him back at all. And it's not as bad as it was. It was fearful at first, like looking after a wounded animal. Now he's much better, most of the time. But then something will start him off, something will remind him, and she has to sit with him and hold him and talk to him and keep him out of the children's way. So I'll just pop round to give her a hand and at least I'll make sure the kids get a decent meal. You two can fend for yourselves. There's some ham in the pantry and some cheese and I'll pop a couple of potatoes in the oven for you so they should be baked when you get home. And there's some of that treacle tart left.'

'Right-o, Mum,' said Peggy, 'but I might be going out anyway.'

'That's nice, dear. In by ten o'clock, mind. You've got work tomorrow,' said Mrs Brown, but she was already halfway out of the door before Peggy could say anything in reply.

I expected her to sound off. In by ten o'clock! Peggy was twenty-six, not sixteen for heaven's sake. But she didn't say anything. Staggering. On the other hand, if Peggy's another competitor then maybe it was a test for her and she's better at not overreacting than I am.

We arrived at *The News* offices still in silence, and as we got to the front door, both of us sort of stopped and took a deep breath before we went into the building. I glanced across at Peggy. There was a hint of a smile, a glimmer of recognition and fellow feeling, but not enough for me to ask.

I wasn't sure about all this at all. If this was a reality TV programme then I should have had some rules, some instructions, some guidelines, some clue about what was going on. And if it was Narnia, then where was a helpful faun or a Mrs Beaver with buttered toast? Or an Aslan to make everything right?

I took a deep breath and went into the reporters' room, bracing myself for seeing Will. I could cope. Of course I could cope. This was only a TV programme, for goodness' sake. It wasn't real life. As I hung my coat up, I took a quick look around, oh so casually, and when I came to his desk, I prepared myself, controlled my expression ... but he wasn't there. I let out a huge sigh. I didn't know whether from relief or disappointment, but I'd been holding my breath so hard that my chest hurt.

Gordon was talking to the other reporters, Alan, Tony and Derek, allocating jobs.

'Billy's over in the district office today, chasing something up, so you can do his jobs,' he was saying to Alan.

'Anything for me?' I asked, keeping a desk between me and Gordon. I was careful not to stand too near to him. Already he had a habit of getting even closer and 'accidentally' brushing against my bum or breasts. He didn't smell too sweet either. Personal hygiene doesn't seem to have been a big thing in the 1950s. I felt like hitting him, hard, but remembering I had to be all teeth and smiles, I had, so far, restrained myself.

He looked up at me as if wondering who the hell I was.

'If she does all the shorts today, why doesn't she do the Prettiest Village feature tomorrow?' asked Marje quickly, lighting a cigarette. You only ever saw this woman through a cloud of cigarette smoke. 'I've booked a photographer but I've got a lot on.'

Gordon looked at me again. 'I suppose so,' he said grudgingly. 'If you've got other things to do, Marje. I suppose if she makes a mess of it, you can do it on Friday.'

The condescension of the man!

'Right,' I said, all brisk and businesslike. 'What does this involve?'

'You tell her, Marje,' said Gordon and went back to his desk.

'Well, now it's spring,' said Marje with a wry glance through the tiny grubby window to the rain outside, 'it's time to start our village feature. Simple idea, you know the sort of thing. Go along to one of the prettier villages, lots of lovely pictures and then maybe a few words with the oldest resident, squire, lady of the manor, vicar, that sort of thing. Anything newsworthy or interesting. Gets people buying *The News* and we might dig up a few stories for the rest of the paper while we're at it. We'll make a few contacts at least. You should be all right. The postman reckons it's going to fair up tomorrow. I was going to start with Middleton Parva. You all right with that?'

'Fine,' I said. It wasn't exactly cutting edge, but it was a lot more fun than Princess Margaret's planned visit to the local regiment. There are worse assignments. 'But how do I get there?'

'You can team up with George and take the van. But Charlie's out with it for most of today. So if you can just sort out some of those short pieces while you're waiting. Or check in the files on Middleton Parva.'

'No problem,' I said, quite looking forward to a day out of the office. With that the door opened and an oldish woman came in carrying a long narrow wooden box full of brown envelopes. Everyone stood around her as she gave them out.

'Rose Harford?' she said, looking at me.

'That's me.' And I went up to her, like a child going to Santa.

My present was a brown envelope full of money. I was getting paid for this, what a bonus. £8. 12s. 6d. to be precise. In my normal life that would buy a couple of coffees and a sandwich. Here it was meant to provide for a whole week. But judging by what I'd seen of prices, it would buy quite a lot. I put the money carefully away in my purse.

I'd just started my list of NIBs (News In Brief – mainly jumble sales, meetings and talks in the Literary and Philosophical societies), when one of the young messengers poked his head around the door.

'Billy in?' he asked.

'No. He's over in the district office. Why?'

'Oh his missus is downstairs wanting him. Probably wanting his money more like. I'll go and tell her she'll have to get the shopping on tick.'

Will's wife downstairs? An opportunity too good to miss. 'No, it's all right,' I replied, before I realised what I was saying, getting up quickly and abandoning the Gilbert and Sullivan Society's performance of *Yeoman of the Guard* in mid sentence, 'I'll pop down and tell her.'

'Suit yourself,' said the lad and walked off whistling.

My heart was banging as I clattered down the narrow crowded stairs. I stopped on the turn and hung on to the rickety banister to try and get my breathing under control. IN twothreefourfivesix OUT twothreefourfivesix. Will's wife. Will's wife. What would she be like? What sort of girl would make Will give up his freedom? What would she look like, sound like? IN twothreefourfivesix OUT twothreefourfivesix. It was no good. I hadn't got time to breathe properly. I strode on down.

But, closer to the front office, I slowed down, my steps heavier. Did I really want to meet Will's wife? Did I want to see who he'd chosen, who he had children – three children! – with? What would I say to her? How painful would it be? What sort of trick was this? How was I expected to play it? Too late, despite myself, I was pushing through the battered door. Whatever she was like, I had to know.

There were only two people in the scruffy reception area, with its old-fashioned heavy wooden counters and scuffed tiled floor – a woman and a small child. The woman was wearing a workaday brown coat. She had her back to me, leaning

78

down to talk to the child, yet there was something very familiar about her. Something I recognised, something I knew almost as well as I knew myself. The hair was the wrong colour, the wrong style but... She turned around.

'Caz!'

This time, I didn't get the blank look I had had from Will. Instead there was a moment's puzzlement and then Caz's face lit up. 'Hello!' she said. 'Are you the American? I've heard about you. I'm Carol, Billy's wife.'

Caz? Married to Will? Somewhere in the universe, someone was playing a very sick joke on me. And it couldn't be Caz and Will, could it? The two people closest to me in the world wouldn't do this to me, would they, not even as a joke, not even for a reality TV programme?

'You? You're really married to Will?' As I asked it, I heard the catch in my voice. Were Will and Caz really in league against me?

'Married to Billy. Yes 'fraid so. For eleven years and counting. Is he in?'

'No, sorry. He's had to go out to one of the other offices.' How did I manage to answer so calmly and politely?

Eleven years? Eleven years? Will was still in school eleven years ago. Why was he married to Caz? Caz of all people. This had to be a wind-up. And if it was, it was a pretty sick one.

'Oh well, never mind. It's not important.' She smiled and turned to leave.

'Can I give him a message?'

I didn't want her to go. I needed to keep her there, to talk to her. I needed to know more.

'No, it's all right.' She hesitated. 'Well yes, go on then. Tell him I've got a job. Next term, when this one,' she indicated the little girl who was staring up at me with a shy smile and Caz's bright inquisitive eyes, 'starts school, I do too. I'm going to be a school cook. They told me today. Isn't that grand?'

Her face was alight with happiness. This was Caz pretending to be delighted about being a school cook? Caz whose idea of sophisticated cooking was putting a bit of parsley on a ready meal? We needed to talk, away from the office, away from any cameras.

'That's brilliant!' I said, entering into the game, for it had to be a game. 'Why don't we celebrate? Look, I've got half an hour to spare. Why don't we go to Silvino's? My treat? I've just been paid.'

This world might be pretend, but at least the coffee would be real. And I guessed Gordon wouldn't miss me from the office for half an hour. Caz – in true Caz fashion – hesitated for less than a split second.

'Oh yes, if you've got time,' she said and turned to the little girl. 'Well Libby, isn't this turning out to be a good day?'

She sounded so like Caz, my Caz, that my heart sang. With Libby holding firmly on to Caz's hand, we went across the Market Place to Silvino's, squeezing past the women in their damp macs with bags of shopping and dripping umbrellas. The menu was strong on teacakes and buns and buttered toast, but the smell and the steam was of coffee, proper Italian coffee. And in among the noise of the steam, and the black-and-white-clad waitresses bustling back and forth between the crowded tables, was Silvino himself, I guessed, a tiny round beaming Italian in a long apron and a wide smile. Part of me just wanted to sit back and savour the normality of it, but there was something far more important to deal with...

'Right,' I said, once we'd ordered, and Caz was undoing Libby's coat buttons for her. 'Come on Caz, tell me what this is all about.'

'What? The job? Well, it–'

'No, not the job, you daft bat, this reality TV thing. Where are the cameras? What are the rules? Who else is in it? Who's running it? Were you just dropped in it too? How do we get out when we want to?'

The smile faltered on Caz's face for a moment. She sat back from the table, put a hand on Libby's arm as if to protect her and looked at me, baffled and wary.

Then I noticed that just as Will didn't look exactly the same as Will in this place, that Caz, or Carol, didn't look quite like Caz either. Her hair was a different colour. Well that's no surprise. Caz has been colouring hers for so long that not even she can remember what colour it was originally. But Caz's hair is always glossy and shiny, this Carol's hair looked a bit dull. To be honest, it looked as though it needed washing. Caz's never looked like that. Even when she was ill, the first thing she did was wash her hair because she said it made her feel better.

Then her teeth. Caz has neat, straight, white teeth. This Carol had slightly crooked teeth. And this Carol had lines ... the beginning of wrinkles

81

around her eyes and on her forehead. And now she too was looking at me as if I were a stranger – and a slightly mad stranger at that.

Suddenly, I wasn't so sure...

I put my head down. I felt utterly defeated.

'I'm sorry. It's just that you and Will, Billy, look exactly like my closest friends back home. And it's such a shock to discover that maybe you're not them after all.'

'Oh you poor thing!' said Carol, in such a Caz-like way that I was sure it *must* be her. 'How awful, especially if you're feeling homesick. It's such a long way from America. Are they nice, these friends?'

'The best, the absolute best.'

'Well, let's just hope Billy and I will do instead,' she said in a wonderfully cheering, normal sort of a way. 'Now come on, drink your coffee and have a bit of this teacake.'

She was treating me as though I were the same age as Libby, and for some reason, I suddenly began to feel better, especially when I noticed her eyeing my jacket. Very Caz that. Always keen on clothes. Whether she was Caz or Carol, I needed her company, a friend. I began to relax a little, though I wanted to ply her with a hundred questions – like Why are you married to Will? What's he like as a husband? Do you really love him? Weren't you young to have children? And please move along now, because I'm here and he's mine.

The thought of Caz being married to Will was too huge and horrible to consider. They were good friends, of course they were, had been since they were in school. But married! If the two people closest to me in the whole world were married to each other, then where did that leave me? Squeezed out in the cold and very much alone.

Even if this were pretend, I didn't like it. I didn't like it one bit. At the very least the pair of them must have ganged up to play this trick on me. Thinking that about your two best friends is not a cheering thought.

Yet here was Caz, sipping her coffee, her eyes huge over the rim of the cup, looking just like she had so many times I'd sat with her before. No longer looking worried, she now seemed only concerned for me. Just as if it were me and Caz as we had always been. Maybe there were cameras in here too, and she knew. Maybe this time it was she who was waiting for a quiet opportunity to talk to me and hatch a plot. In the meantime, we would just enjoy the coffee.

It was so what I wanted – to pretend it was just me and Caz having a coffee, like normal. I wanted to forget all this strange stuff that was happening, if only for a moment. So I relaxed and pretended. It was surprisingly easy.

'Oh look,' I said, with a mouthful of teacake, 'they've got music here tomorrow night.'

'Music?'

On the wall was a handwritten notice. 'Saturday night at Silvino's. The Skiffle Cats!'

'I'd heard he was opening up in the evenings to give it a go.'

'Give what a go?'

'The skiffle groups. Have you been in the back room?'

'No, what back room?'

'There's another room that you get to from the side alley. Silvino's got a juke box in there. All the kids go in there to listen to records in the evenings at weekends.'

'Will you go and see The Skiffle Cats?'

Carol laughed.

'No, that's for kids, not people like me. They haven't even got proper instruments. Just a washboard and a bit of string on a broom handle. No, I tell a lie, I think one of them might have a guitar. I spend enough time with my washboard as it is, without going out at night to watch someone else scrubbing away. But I like to hear a bit of decent music sometimes.' She looked wistful. 'I like the juke box. Tell you what' – and again she sounded just like Caz – 'I'll be in town for the market on Saturday. Will you be in town too? I could meet you, say at the cross at eleven-ish and we could get what we want and then go in the back with the kids for a coffee and some music. What do you say?'

'Yes, great. Why not?'

'Well that's settled!' said Caz/Carol, then she turned to Libby and said, 'Now we'd better go and do some shopping, otherwise none of us will eat tonight. See you Saturday, Rosie.'

She did up Libby's coat buttons again, took her hand and manoeuvred through the crowded tables. As they went, Libby turned around and gave a quick smile. She was the image of her mother.

I paid the bill (leaving 3d. tip, how confident is that?) and dashed back to the office, teetering between utter gloom and a strange almost-happiness. The thought of shopping with Caz/Carol made me feel more cheerful than I'd done ever since I'd got here. The thought that she was married to Will just seemed so bizarre that I could hardly accept it. It had to be a joke or a trick. Hadn't it? Maybe I'd find out more on Saturday. That was obviously what she was thinking. And even though she was making out that she didn't know me, she was still like my friend Caz. At least she was friendly and chatty, not like Will. But I wasn't sure if that was better or worse. Maybe she was trying to lull me into a false sense of security. Maybe this was even more devious...

Will/Billy didn't come back to the office at the end of the day. Every time the door opened and anyone came into the office, I geared myself up to see him, preparing my calm face while the blood raced around my system and pounded behind my eyes. Then every time it wasn't him, I slumped again. God knows what all this was doing to my stress levels.

In the end, when it was clear he wasn't going to be coming back, I went home early for my ham and baked potato. Janice was there again later. I couldn't help her with her homework – physics – but she asked lots of questions about newspapers.

I still couldn't believe that Caz was married to Will. That was such a sadistic trick by the organisers. I couldn't believe that they would have agreed to that. I remembered the silly feeling I had occasionally when I was a bit jealous of their shared past, but they wouldn't do this. Surely not.

But if I took it at face value, at least Caz was

here too and prepared to be friendly. That was something. Not much, admittedly. But right now it was all I had.

Chapter Six

Middleton Parva was a separate village. Amazing. I just thought of it as the bit by the ring road where the new B&Q and Tesco were. But we went out of town, past fields and off the main road and down a country lane to get to it. George's driving was erratic to say the least.

'Hey hang on. You nearly had us in the ditch there! You're on the wrong side of the road!'

'Sorry!' yelled George. 'Habit. Think I'm in Germany still.'

'Germany?'

'Yes. That's where I learnt to drive, when I was doing my national service in the army. On tanks, so the van took some getting used to.'

'You were in the army?'

Honestly, he didn't look old enough.

'How old are you, George?'

'Twenty.'

'Did you break any of the Fräuleins' hearts?'

'No,' grinned George – and bless him, he blushed – 'we didn't do much of that sort of fraternising. Plenty of drinking though! Those Germans know how to drink.'

Somehow, we got to Middleton Parva. And as we did, so the sun came out, just as Marje's

86

postman had said it would. It was really pretty. There was a proper village green with trees, a couple of little shops, a very attractive church, which I'd never noticed before, probably because it's hidden behind B&Q. This couldn't be a film set, could it? This was something else. Something much bigger. But quite what, I didn't want to think about just yet. Too scary. Much too scary. My skin went cold and clammy as I tried to think about it. No. Easier to get on with work.

While George went off to scout for pictures, I went to the post office and struck gold straight-away. The postmistress's family had been running the place since the days when mail came with the stagecoach, so that was a nice easy story to write up. Then I found the vicar, and we did pretty pictures of the church and talked about its history and looked at a few interesting graves.

'What now?' asked George.

'The lady from the post office said the pub was run by a cockney, a chap who came here as an evacuee during the war. He must have liked it to stay. No doubt he'll have a tale to tell. Shall we?'

'A pub will do me fine. We'll get a drink while we're there. But which one?'

There were two pubs on either side of the green. One, the Royal Oak, was low and squat and old-fashioned. It had small windows, and beams that made it look as though it had grown up out of the ground and would return to it given half a chance. The other, the Rising Sun, was a big flash newer sort of place with a car park. It had beams too, but you could tell they weren't very old. There was a sign in the window. I went closer to read it.

'No Gypsies! No Irish!' it said.

I stepped back, shocked.

'Can they really say that?'

'Yes, of course. The fair's been here recently, that's what that's all about. They don't want gyppos upsetting their posh customers. Is this the pub we want?'

'No, thank heavens. We want the Royal Oak.'

We went across the green and in through the tiny low door of the pub. It had no signs in its window. Inside there were flagged floors and a small log fire. Two old men, smoking pipes, were playing dominoes. They looked up when we went in, 'Afternoon,' they said, and went back to their game.

Since we'd walked in through the door, I'd been holding my breath. I was waiting for someone to shout at me, or say they couldn't serve me, accuse me of being a tart. Instead, the cheerful young landlord was saying, 'Right sir, and what can I get you?'

'Pint of bitter for me please,' said George.

'And for the lady?'

I hesitated. I could hardly believe I was actually going to get a drink at last. But I didn't know what to ask for, what to choose. Apart from the beer pumps, the stock on the shelves looked pretty limited. I could see gin and whisky and lots of bottles of Mackeson and Guinness. An advert on the wall showed flying toucans, watched by some RAF types. 'Lovely day for a Guinness' said the slogan. But perhaps not.

'No vodka, I suppose?' I laughed, as if I were

making a joke.

'No, this is Middleton not Moscow, miss.'

'Sorry, I don't know what to have.'

'She's American,' said George in explanation.

'Right darling. Why not have a shandy, a lot of ladies like that. Or a drop of local cider?'

'Cider. That sounds fine. Yes please.'

He disappeared for a moment and came back with a large enamel jug. He placed a half-pint glass on the counter about a yard away and lifted the jug. Cider poured from it in a long arc and fell, perfectly on target, into the glass. It was neatly done.

I took a sip. 'Cheers!' I said and nearly choked. 'God this is strong! What's in it?'

'Apples, mostly,' said the landlord, 'and a few dead rats of course.'

I trusted he was joking, but boy was that cider good. It hit the spot wonderfully. I remembered I'd left my Oxo tin at the office.

'Any food on? Sandwiches?'

'The missus can make you a sandwich if you like. Ham or cheese?'

We both chose ham and while the missus was making them, I told the landlord why we'd come. He was happy to talk, a good utterer, and he spoke in quotes. Easy peasy. George did a nice picture of him leaning on the bar, and by the time the sandwiches came, we'd just about finished, leaving Ray, the landlord, to serve his other customers.

George and I took our sandwiches – and a second drink – over to a table by the tiny window. The sandwiches were brilliant. Proper thick bread with black crusts, masses of butter (Diet? What diet?) and chunks of delicious home-cooked ham. Real food. But now we were just sitting down and not actually working or talking about work, I noticed George looked a bit uneasy. It took a while to dawn on me that sitting in a bar alone with an older woman was clearly something he wasn't used to.

'It's all right George, I won't eat you.'

He smiled uneasily and moved a little further away from me.

'Did you like the army, George?'

'It was all right. Once you'd got basic training over. All that bloody, sorry Rose, all that drill and bullsh– all that stuff you had to do.'

'Did you go straight from school?'

'No. I was a messenger on *The News*. Then I used to help Charlie with the developing and printing and things. I told them that when I got called up and I got to work for the information unit. Which was spot on. I worked with the army photographers, so when I came back Mr Henfield took me on as a proper assistant for Charlie, so I was pretty chuffed really. I think Peggy put in a good word for me.'

'Peggy?'

'Yes, Henfield's secretary. Oh you know, you're lodging at her house, aren't you? She's nice, isn't she? She was always nice to me when I was a messenger. Most people just take the mick all the time, but Peggy never did. She was always kind. She always said that there was no reason that I shouldn't be a photographer. She always makes you think you can do things if you really want to. And she's got a lovely smile.'

I have to say this was a completely different view of Peggy from the one I saw. But then I remembered how nice she was with smelly little Janice, and I didn't say anything. Young George clearly had a bit of a crush on Peggy, and who was I to disillusion him? Anyway, maybe it was just me she didn't like.

'Do you like it on *The News*?'

'It's good, yes. And I like driving the van. I'm going to get a car of my own one day. I'll have a proper wage soon when I'm twenty-one. Then I can take my mum on outings.'

'Do you still live with your mum then?'

'Yes. Just me and her. Dad copped it at Dunkirk, so it's been just me and Mum ever since.'

'That must have been hard.'

'No harder than for lots of folk.' He paused, took a long drink and glanced up and out of the window across at the Rising Sun.

'Looks like Henfield's popped out for his lunchtime drink. That must be his car. There aren't that many two-tone Hillman Minxes around here. Maybe he's meeting one of his floozies.'

Floozy, what a wonderful word. I thought my grandad was the only one to use it.

'Goes in for floozies, does he?'

'One or two. Another drink?'

'George, you've had two. You'll be over the limit.'

'What limit?'

'You're not meant to have more than two pints. You won't be able to concentrate properly.'

'Rubbish. I drive better after a drink or two. One for the road.'

As he was getting the drinks – and that cider

was good – I was still gazing out of the window. A bus pulled up on the other side of the green, a real old-fashioned country bus. A young woman got out and hurried across the green to the Rising Sun. There was something familiar about her...

I sat up straight and had a proper look. Yes, no doubt about it. It was Peggy – who should have been in work – rushing into the pub, the pub outside which Richard Henfield's car was parked. She vanished through the door just as George came back with the drinks.

So Henfield liked his floozies, did he? And he and his secretary just happened to be in an out-of-the-way country pub at the same time. Interesting. Very interesting.

Chapter Seven

DAY SIX IN THE 1950s HOUSE

If that's where I am. I'm not sure any more. I'm not sure of anything.

If this is the 1950s house, why wasn't I briefed about it? Interviewed, insured, had explanations, and introduced to it?

It's more than just a house and a newspaper office. It's a whole town, not to mention the countryside around it, and villages like Middleton Parva. That was no film set. And so many people! No TV company would pay for so many extras. It's all so real. It doesn't feel like a film set. I haven't seen any cameras. No one's mentioned a video room.

None of the other people seem to be competitors. Mrs Brown was expecting me. My trunk was here. Everyone seems to think I'm here for a few weeks. But where's 'here'?

Will and Caz. Ah. This is the really tricky one. Are they Will and Caz? If so, they wouldn't play such a trick on me, not for so long. Not pretending to be married, with children. They're my two best friends in the world. They wouldn't play a trick like that, not even for a minute. They certainly wouldn't do it for a poxy reality TV show. They just wouldn't. No. Not even for a 'psychological test'. They wouldn't play those sort of sick games.

Because if they would, then how could I trust anyone ever again? And who? Billy and Carol are identical to Will and Caz. But they're different too. They both look older for a start. What about Caz's teeth? The wrinkles? Will's hands? That's not make-up. But if they're not Will and Caz, who are they? Why is it all different? What the hell is going on?

When Lucy went through that bloody wardrobe into Narnia she knew straightaway where she was. I don't. I don't know where I am or why I'm here.

It's not really the 1950s is it? That's impossible. Isn't it?

But what else is it?

After I'd written that, I seized up. My whole body froze and I couldn't get air in and out of my lungs. There was just a pain, the pain of panic. I didn't know where I was. In time or space. I couldn't trust any of my senses. Nothing was what it seemed.

As I tried to breathe, in great panicking gulps, I

93

tried to get my brain to work, tried to think logically, calmly. Ha!

I had thought this was a reality TV show, yet nothing, absolutely nothing backed that up. This wasn't a single house, or even a single film set. This was more. This was an entirely different world, a world locked in the past of fifty years ago. I ran to the window and beat my hands on it as if it were the bars of a cage, because it might just as well have been.

I couldn't have gone back in time, not really back in the 1950s. But where was I?

All I knew for certain, the one sure thing, was that I wanted Will. I wanted his arms around me and his mouth whispering in my ear the way he did when I had nightmares, because this was turning into a real nightmare. I wanted to be home. It was only eight o'clock – on a Saturday morning off, for goodness' sake, and I'd already been awake for hours. I was still leaning with my head against the cool of the window, taking deep breaths, trying to control my fear and panic, when Peggy came in.

'You alright?' she asked, not unkindly.

'Yes, no ... oh I don't know.' But then I had a thought.

'Peggy, you know you asked your mum if I could come and stay here?'

'Ye-es.'

'Well who arranged for me to come and work on *The News?* You're the editor's secretary. It must have been arranged through you.'

'Yes, it was.'

'Well how?'

This was it, I thought, I'm getting close to the truth now. If I knew who'd organised my trip, the clothes and everything, then I'd know just what was going on. There'd be correspondence, letters about it. If I could see those, I'd have cracked it.

'We had a phone call from Lord Uzmaston's office.'

'Lord Uzmaston?'

'Yes, you know – the proprietor. I've never met him, but Mr Henfield has. He's been to lunch at Uzmaston Hall.' She said this with a sort of pride. 'He owns *The News* and quite a lot of other papers.'

'What did he say?'

'Oh it wasn't *him*. He wouldn't ring himself, would he? It was a man, a young man, I think. Just said that they had a reporter who needed a temporary job and that we were to fit her in. I can tell you Mr Henfield wasn't happy, not with the idea of a woman reporter. But you've got to obey orders, haven't you? Especially when it's the owner, and Lord Uzmaston does have some funny ways.'

'Was there any correspondence? Any confirmation in writing? Anything like that?'

'No. Nothing at all. It was all very strange. Most irregular. That's why I was glad I'd asked about the rent.'

'Rent?'

'Oh yes. They asked if we could find her – you – accommodation. And I thought of our Stephen's room, it being empty. But before I said that, I asked how much they would pay. And the man said "Whatever is usual. It would be easier if you pay it direct from your office?"'

'Oh and do you?'

I realised, to my shame, I hadn't actually given a thought about whether I should be paying rent out of my £8. 12s. 6d.

'Yes, I take it out of the petty cash, and Mr Henfield signs a chitty.'

'And no one's come back to you? Asked anything about it?'

'No, which was a bit worrying really. But everything seems to be fine. Why? Who were you dealing with?'

'Tricky to explain,' I said, which was the understatement of the year really, or maybe even fifty years. One more thought occurred to me.

'Peggy, why did you suggest I should stay here? Was it to get your mum a bit of extra cash?'

'No, not really – though I suppose that was part of it.' Peggy looked embarrassed. 'No, I thought it would be fun.'

And that really surprised me. If Peggy thought it would be fun to have me here, why has she barely said a word to me ever since I arrived? That was probably the strangest thing of all. She was still standing in the doorway with an armful of laundry. For a moment she looked almost concerned. Not surprising really, she probably thought all my questions where completely off the wall.

'Are you all right?' she asked again.

'Yes, yes, fine really. Fine,' I said, too baffled to say otherwise. But at least I had an idea now, something to do. Once I was back in the office on Monday, I could talk to the person Peggy had spoken to, and see who had arranged it. That was somewhere to start. I had a plan. I already felt I was doing something.

'Here,' said Peggy, 'I've brought you a clean sheet and some pillow cases. We change the beds on Saturdays.'

'Only one sheet?'

'Put the top one on the bottom and the clean one on the top,' she said with exaggerated patience. 'This isn't America you know. And if you bring the dirty sheet down and any white cotton things – knicks, hankies, I'll put them in the washing machine.'

After she'd gone, I made the bed. Tricky job with sheets and blankets. Hard to get it nice and smooth and neat. But it calmed me down. I straightened those sheets so there wasn't a crease or a wrinkle to be seen. If only my life could be as neat and tidy.

I gathered up the laundry and took it down to the scullery and put it into the funny little washing machine. Peggy looked scornful, at the thought of my stockings and suspender belt going in there too, so I stood at the sink and washed them by hand with something called Oxydol. Like being on holidays. Funny sort of holiday.

In the background, the radio – a huge thing the size of a fridge – played children's songs, 'The Teddy Bears' Picnic', 'There once was an ugly duckling' ... and something about pink and blue toothbrushes. It made *Top of the Pops* seem edgy.

The washing machine didn't rinse. Well, it did, but first you had to empty the sudsy water out and put clean in. Peggy took the dirty hot water and threw it across the back yard and then scrubbed the yard with a big brush. This was meant to be a lazy Saturday morning...

All the time we were doing this, I wanted to ask her about her visit to the Rising Sun, but she was looking pretty grim-faced so I thought I'd better leave it for now. Anyway, I had too many other things on my mind.

Then we had to get the clothes out of the washing machine (at which point the radio was playing something of demented jollity and good cheer called 'I love to go a wandering', which somehow made me think of the Hitler Youth), and put them through the mangle thing at the top. I remembered books I'd had when I was little, *Mrs Lather's Laundry* or *Mrs Tiggywinkle*. I was a real washerwoman. I thought fondly of my 1400 spin automatic washer-dryer. It was hard work turning that handle as it squeezed the water out.

'Careful,' said Peggy, 'a girl from school went to work in the laundry and she put her hand in the mangle. Got all broken and crushed.'

'Horrid!' I said. 'I hope she got some compensation.'

Peggy looked at me blankly.

'You know, a pay-out for her injury,' I explained.

'Course not. She should have been more careful, shouldn't she?'

Peggy took the washing down the small steep back garden to hang on the line, while I used the last of the water to mop the scullery and kitchen floor.

Then I had to dash as I was meeting Caz...

Town was busy. I looked around at the crowds

and thought uneasily that they couldn't all be extras. So many women, mostly dressed in coats, clutching baskets and shopping bags. Men seemed to be conspicuous by their absence. There were a few young men and one or two very bent old men on sticks, slowly making their way between the stalls, but otherwise it was a world of women. And children! There were children everywhere, many as young as seven, on their own and equally laden down with shopping bags. Little girls of not much more than ten years old were expertly managing not just the bags, but sometimes also a battered pram with a well wrapped-up baby inside, with a toddler trailing alongside as well. They stood in the queues at the market stalls and seemed to cast a keen eye over the limited number of vegetables available, confidently pocketing the change.

Was it safe for these children to be out on their own? Shouldn't someone be looking after them? I was still wondering about it when I spotted Carol standing on the steps of the market cross.

Carol or Caz? Which was she? My steps slowed. I stopped, needing to think about this. Was she my friend from my real twenty-first-century life, playing a very nasty trick, a conspiracy against me? Or was she Carol, a young mother of three, whose life and background was half a century different from mine?

She was talking to a young boy and handing over a couple of bags of shopping to him. He was about ten or eleven years old, and the image of Will, the same blond hair and big brown eyes. He was wearing short trousers, long socks and a big hand-knitted jumper, and he glowed with health and energy. Will's son. So that's what Will's son would look like, just like the boy I'd imagined in my daydreams. He looked exactly like a picture of Will his mum has on her mantelpiece. I felt I already knew him. He gave me a quick grin as Caz greeted me.

'Perfect timing. I've just finished the shopping. Right, Pete, go straight home, mind. Your dad wants you to help him this morning. And if you're good, I'll bring some fish and chips home for your dinner. Now scoot!'

The boy grinned and duly scooted, even though he was weighed down with all the shopping bags.

'Right,' said Caz. 'Let's go and look for some material. Will and I have got a posh do to go to next month and I must have something to wear.'

Will and Caz, posh do? I knew it couldn't be the real Caz saying this. She couldn't be so casually hurtful. I must stop thinking of her as Caz and think of her as Carol instead. Carol. Not Caz. It had to be.

Carol was already leading the way to the far end of the market where there was a clutch of fabric stalls. Great bolts of cloth lay out on the trestle tables, and men and women bundled up in layers of clothing casually lifted them here and there, expertly measuring out yards of material in stalls that looked almost like mini theatres. Most of the stalls seemed to have everyday-ish sort of materials, lots of wool and tweedy mixtures, ginghams and flowery cottons.

Carol darted between them and had stopped at a stall where the bales of cloth glinted with the richness of velvet and taffeta.

'Now then, Mrs West,' said the cheerful stall-holder, 'looking for something special today are we?'

'Yes please,' said Carol, putting down her shabby handbag and reaching into the mountain of material. She pulled out rolls of cloth, held them briefly against her, then put them down again.

'Have you got something in mind then?' asked the stallholder.

'Yes,' said Carol, 'but I won't know until I've seen it.'

'Well you're turning my stall nicely upside down,' said the man, with only the tiniest hint of resentment.

Then I saw it. Right at the bottom of the pile was a narrow roll of taffeta in a wonderful rich colour that hovered between a deep dark red, and black. It was exactly the same shade as a dress Caz had bought in the sale at Droopy and Browns, and made her look absolutely stunning. It would be just the thing for Carol.

'That's the one!' I yelled and tried to grab it.

All the rolls of material shifted slightly and I thought the whole lot would come down, when the man held them all back with one hand, while shuffling the dark red taffeta out with the other. He pushed it across at Carol, who unrolled a bit and held it up against her. Immediately it seemed to reflect hints of deep auburn into her mousy hair – the exact shade of auburn that Caz paid so much for, so often to achieve.

'Perfect!' I said. 'That's definitely the colour for you.'

Carol grinned, then unwound the fabric from

its roll.

'Not much left there,' she said, pursing her lips. 'Don't know if I'll be able to make anything of that. I'll be struggling and anyone any bigger than me would be left showing their underpinnings. No,' she said, making a show of putting it back and walking away, 'I'll have to look for something else...'

'Go on,' said the man, 'you can have it for eighteen bob.'

'Hang on!' Carol had grabbed another roll end from under a heap. It was a creamy cotton with a design – a picture really – on it in a deep pink. I couldn't quite see what it was, but Carol's eyes had lit up.

'Look, here's another roll end, neither use nor ornament to anyone.' She looked at him challengingly, with such a Caz-like glint that I had to laugh. 'You can throw that in buckshee, can't you?'

'Not on your nelly,' said the man, 'but go on, give us a quid for the lot and I'm a fool to myself.'

Carol had a pound note out of her purse like lightning.

'You're a gentleman!' she said. 'I shall tell all my friends and acquaintances to patronise no other stall.'

The man laughed and wrapped the material in a sheet of thin brown paper, and soon we were heading for Silvino's, with Carol clutching her purchases.

'Will you really be able to make that into a dress?' I asked as we made our way through the market crowds.

'Don't see why not, I've got a pattern I've used before, so it should work OK.'

'What's the big occasion anyway?'

'The Mayor's Ball. Very posh. At The Fleece.'

I shivered as I remembered my ghastly experience at The Fleece.

'But it will be lovely. A chance to dance. This is the first time we've been. The mayor's president of the football club, so he gave Billy some tickets, which was nice of him. Right, here we are.'

We were in an alley and going in through a small door into a room that looked as though it had only just stopped being a store room. The walls were roughly whitewashed, but I could smell coffee, and could hear the sounds of music beating out from a juke box. A wonderful machine! Just like in those old American films.

It was smoky and crowded, with people mostly in their mid to late teens or early twenties – Carol and I must have been the oldest people there. Their faces were bright and lively, but otherwise they were a drab-looking crowd. Boys in stiff, ill-fitting jeans, or baggy grey trousers, some even with jackets and ties. A few of the girls, like me, wore trousers. Most were in knitted cardigans and tops, tweedy skirts, apart from two girls, who stood in front of the juke box. Both had black polo neck sweaters and full skirts, one with a pattern of hearts sewn on, the other with stars.

They watched as each record was lifted up and spun into place to play. Then they danced by themselves in the small space, just deigning to move slightly out of the way if anyone came to put money in the juke box.

There seemed to be no waiters in this side. Instead the kids went up to a hatch that presumably opened into the main café and placed their orders, mainly for Coke or milk shakes it seemed, which they drank almost in parody of those black-and-white films about American teenagers. It was all warm and steamy and lively and smelt a bit of wet dog.

As we ordered our coffee, the juke box started playing 'Sixteen Tons'. That was really weird because my dad always used to sing a bit of it:

Sixteen tons and what do you get?
Another day older and deeper in debt.

And I'd never heard the rest. I listened carefully to get the words. Next time I saw Dad I'd sing it to him. Next time... But now the juke box was playing 'See you later, alligator', and more of the kids were up dancing in the little space near the front,

See you later, alligator.

And they'd all yell back

In a while, crocodile!

The two girls in the black polo necks danced with each other, taking no notice of anyone else at all, just totally absorbed in their dancing. They certainly had style. But this was another favourite of my dad's – and everyone was singing along. I knew the words and joined in happily. I felt part

104

of it, I belonged. It was good. I grinned at Caz.

'I don't see why just the kids should have the fun,' she said.

Then she took the package of material out and looked at it again.

'I've never had anything this colour before. Do you think it will suit me?'

'Nothing better,' I said. 'Trust me. Do you make a lot of your clothes?'

'Most of them. My gran gave me her sewing machine when Billy and I moved into our own place. I make most of the kids' clothes, most of mine. Much cheaper and I can get what I like.'

Again, she sounded just like Caz, when Caz talked about stuff she got from the charity shops or bought from eBay and added a twist that made things look stunning. Very talented. She loved old clothes. We're talking retro or vintage here, not your average charity shop stuff. She had a magic touch with them, seeing possibilities that the rest of us never could.

She did a lot of clever things with cushions and curtains too. And she'd helped with the costumes when Jamie had produced the school play. I guess she could make her own clothes if she had to, but then she'd never had to.

Carol was drinking her frothy coffee from the shallow Pyrex cup and swaying to the music. 'Rock, rock till broad daylight...'

'Do you listen to much music?' I asked.

'Whenever I can. But you know, when we get our new house, I'm going to get a wireless.'

'A wireless? You mean a radio? You haven't got one?'

105

'No electricity.'

'No electricity? How on earth do you manage?'

'OK,' she said defensively. 'We didn't have electricity at home till after the war. I'm not the only one. There's lots of people still haven't got electric.'

'No, I didn't think you were, sorry.' I was still thinking about what it would be like to live without electricity. I mean, a two-hour power cut can cause chaos. 'Well you can still get a radio. One that runs on batteries.'

'Do you know the price of batteries? And they don't last more than a few hours. No, we'll get a wireless. Maybe even a television. Billy would like a television. He loves watching it at his mum's.'

The rock and roll had finished. Another record was lifting out of the rack and being placed on the turntable. It had a gentle jazzy intro. Not Bill Haley or Lonnie Donegan. I recognised this. It was Frank Sinatra.

The way you wear your hat, the way you sip your tea
The memory of all that. They can't take that away
from me...

I thought of watching Will across the newsroom, the same pose, attitude, and mannerisms I knew so well. I thought of him at home in bed, the way he slept with one arm flung out over the duvet. I could hardly ask Carol if that's how Billy slept. But I knew it. It was strangely comforting. They couldn't take that away from me. Not how I knew Will, and my memories of him...

The kids were crowding back around the juke

box. 'Rock around the clock' came on again.

'It's no good,' said Carol. 'Time I was on my way. We have to have dinner early on Saturday. Billy goes to the match to do the football report for *The News*.'

'Oh, right,' I said. 'Well I guess I'd better be getting on home.'

'No need for that,' said Carol. 'Why don't you come and have fish and chips with us? Might as well, unless' – and she looked suddenly shy – 'unless you've got anything better to do.'

'No, fish and chips with you would be great,' I said.

We must have walked half a mile or so from the town centre, then down into a little side street, where I could see a long queue of people standing on the pavement. We joined the end of the queue until it was our turn to wait in the greasy steam and sizzling noise for our order. The woman behind the counter wrapped them all efficiently in old copies of *The News* and Carol produced a string bag from her pocket and shoved them all in.

We carried on walking. I didn't recognise this part of town. The streets were smaller and darker, many of them weren't tarmacked but were just potholed mud tracks. On the corner of one of the streets a group of boys, about half a dozen of them maybe twelve or thirteen years old, were gathered around a lamppost. On the other side of the street was an old advertising sign that had come loose. It swung back and forth on two screws – driven by the stones the boys were throwing at it. You could hear the whistle of the stones as they flew across the street. Then the heavy 'thunk' as they hit the soft and rotten board.

'Yeah! I win! I win!' yelled one of the boys, who had managed to hit the exact centre of the board, while the others muttered and grunted and shouted back at him.

Instinctively I'd drawn in on myself. Looked down, avoided eye contact. Gangs of thirteen-year-olds are never good news, especially when they're bored and they've got pockets full of stones. I was busy hurrying along, gazing at my feet, when I realised Carol had stopped. What's more, she was challenging the boys. Was she mad?

'Hey you lot!' she said. 'Haven't you got anything better to do on a Saturday afternoon? And you shouldn't be throwing stones – you could hit someone and hurt them. What would your mothers say if they could see you now? Or your dads? I bet they've got plenty of jobs you could be doing for them.'

To my utter astonishment – when I dared to look up – the boys looked abashed and embarrassed. 'We weren't doing any harm, Mrs West,' said one.

'No, not now, but you soon would be if I know you lot. Now go and find yourself something useful to do and stop making such a racket.' And she started walking again while the boys shuffled a bit then ran off yelling down the road.

'Little blighters,' said Carol. 'And they've all got mothers who could do with a bit of help. What makes them think they've got time to hang around street corners, I don't know.'

I was lost in admiration.

'You know, Carol, I wouldn't have dared speak to them like you did.'

'What? They're only a gang of kids.'

'Yes, I know, but where I come from, you just wouldn't. They'd beat you up, have your purse off you soon as look at you.'

She looked at me, astonished. 'But they're only kids, Rosie. Surely you can deal with a bunch of kids?'

'Well no, actually, we can't. Somehow we seem to have lost the trick.'

'Then you're off your heads if you ask me,' said Carol. 'Come on, here we are. Home sweet home.'

We had turned down a narrow steep lane and at the bottom at the side of a stream was a derelict mill and a tiny cottage.

'Oh isn't that pretty!' I exclaimed.

'You wouldn't think so if you had to live here,' said Carol, and even she almost had to stoop to go in through the front door.

The rooms were small and dark, so much so that I could hardly see anything. Carol went through to a kitchen and then out into a back garden that spread up the hill. It was huge. And in the middle of it was Will.

All the time I'd been walking home with Carol, I had tried to put out of my mind the fact that Will would be here. He was, after all, her husband.

And here he was. And what's more, gardening. Will gardening! This place got stranger and stranger. Will in baggy army trousers carrying an old window, with young Pete hanging on the other end. What if he dropped it? What if it smashed?

'Careful now, Pete,' Will was saying, 'just bring it around to the side of the house, next to the other one.' The two of them manoeuvred it carefully into place, looked at it admiringly and then Carol called out, 'Dinner's ready. Come and get your chips!'

Pete dragged his eyes away from the window frame and came running down the path. 'Can we have them in the paper, Mum? Not on plates?'

'Course you can,' said Carol, 'save on washing up. We'll eat them out there, pretend we're on holiday. Where's Davy?'

'Gone around Rob's on his bike. *My* bike.'

'I know dear, but it's too small for you now, isn't it!' said Carol. 'Come on, Libby.'

The small girl who'd been with her in the office was crouching intently over a small patch of earth. 'I'm planting lettuces,' she said.

'And we've been building a cold frame,' said Pete, jumping up onto the low wall and reaching for his chips. 'Dad and I have built one half and we've got the framework and bricks ready for the second half. We just have to make them secure now. And put the hinges on.'

'Good boy,' said Carol. 'Here you are, Billy.'

Will/Billy wiped his hands on his trousers and perched on the wall, looking out over his garden, as if he were still thinking about it, planning it.

I was suddenly shy with this Will, Billy, I hardly seemed to know him – a man who was competent and capable with practical things. 'Big garden you've got,' I said. The garden seemed to spread up the hillside. It was wonderfully neat

110

and tidy, lots of rows, with small green shoots springing out.

'I didn't have you down as a gardener. I don't know why,' I said, though I did know why – because I couldn't imagine Will gardening.

'My dad always had an allotment. I kept it going during the war. Then the scouts had a couple of allotments too, so I had plenty of practice.'

'You were in the scouts?'

'Oh yes, we were always busy for the war effort – digging for victory, firewatching, collecting scrap metal. Though whether anyone's garden railings ever did go to build Spitfires I have great doubts. But it kept us busy.'

Carol was giggling.

'He was a good scout,' she said, 'but if he'd remembered to Be Prepared, we wouldn't have had Pete, would we?'

So that's why... Caz had been pregnant and that's why Will had married her. That's why they were married so young. Even as I worked it out, it hurt. Caz's giggle and Will's answering grin, their shared complicity – not to mention their shared lives and shared children – cut me out. They were the couple. I was the outsider. It suddenly felt very lonely.

Billy ruffled Peter's hair affectionately. 'Wouldn't be without him. You've worked well this morning, son.'

I ate my fish and chips – growing cold and more batter than fish, to be honest – and tried to take in this new Billy. At the end of a long working week, he had spent a morning doing hard physical work and soon he was going off to work

111

again. Yet he looked really happy.

'Right,' he said, screwing up the fish and chip paper. 'We'll just have time to get those hinges fixed before I have to go to the office. Come on, Pete.'

Pete gobbled the last of his chips. And the two of them went back up the path. I could see Billy explaining the job to Pete as they fastened the old window frame to the framework on the wall beside the shed. Billy did one bit, then handed the tools to Pete who did the next while his father stood and watched approvingly, just making an occasional suggestion, or holding the boy's hand steady, while taking the weight of the window with his other hand. Then they tested the frame, lifting it up and down and laughing, pleased with their work.

'Tea's made,' called Carol.

Billy strode down the path with his arm around Pete's shoulders and then turned off down another path into what looked like a guardsman's sentry box. What a funny shed, I thought, and then realised, as he came out, adjusting his trousers, that it was the loo. And with no water plumbed to it. It didn't bear thinking about.

'I'll just get a wash before I have that tea,' said Billy, going into the house.

I could hear the sound of water running in the kitchen behind me. He was having a wash at the kitchen sink. And he came out, changed into his work trousers and tweedy jacket and tying his tie.

'Right, see you later,' he said, drinking his tea quickly. 'Pete – make sure you put all the tools back in the shed please – in their proper place.

And I'll go and earn my corn. Or maybe enough for a new bike for somebody,' and he grinned at Pete, whose face lit up.

'Really? A new bike?'

'Well, if there's anyone with a birthday coming up, whose bike is too small for them...'

'Yippee!' yelled Pete.

Billy put down his teacup and picked up Libby. 'And soon we'll have the most delicious lettuce in the world for our tea,' he said, kissing the top of her head. 'But now Daddy's got to go to work. See you later everybody.'

He nodded towards me, 'Nice to see you, Rosie.' He ducked back into the dark kitchen and in a few minutes I could see him striding easily up the hill. The very picture of a family man. Will as a family man... It took some getting used to.

'He seems very grown up,' I said, staring after him.

'Yes, he's a good help around the house and he loves helping his dad,' said Carol, looking fondly at Peter.

'Oh I didn't mean Pete. I meant Wi– Billy.'

'Billy? Well of course he's grown up, you daft ha'p'orth. He's twenty-nine years old and if that's not grown up I don't know what is.'

I thought of Will and Jamie playing table football, of them drooling over the motor racing. Twenty-nine? Grown up? Not always.

As instructed, Peter was carefully putting all the tools back in the shed. Libby had abandoned her lettuce planting and was busy with a battered dolls' pram, tucking her charges in under many layers of blankets.

'Tell you what, while they're busy, let's make a fresh pot of tea,' said Carol.

I followed her into the kitchen and, once my eyes had adjusted to the gloom, took a good look around. It was quite a big room but low ceilinged, very crowded and smelt of earth and damp despite the fire burning in the range. Above it was a clothes rack covered in folded ironing, just as at the Browns. There were two battered armchairs on either side of the fire, and an alcove full of books.

There was a table covered with a cloth, and a cheap metal cupboard with plates and cups and a few packets of food – I could see a tin of peas and a packet of Puffed Wheat, and on a drop-down shelf, a loaf of bread, and a dish of butter. Against one wall was a big stone sink with a wooden draining board, scrubbed white, with a mirror above it. And on a shelf alongside were a couple of mugs. One held a family of toothbrushes and another held a shaving brush. So this is where Billy shaved in the morning. I thought of Will and our power shower and his whole shelf full of gels and foams and aftershaves and skin care. The big tin bath I'd seen on the wall outside, I realised suddenly, that was their bath...

Beneath the sink was a gingham curtain, hiding pots and pans I presumed. And on top of the stove was a big covered pan.

'Something nice cooking for supper?' I asked.

'No! Billy's underpants boiling.'

Oh God, definitely too much information.

'When we move I'm going to have a proper electric wash boiler, maybe even a washing

114

machine. You can get one on the never never. It'll be grand. No more pans of towels. No more standing at the sink scrubbing.' She looked wistful. 'Tell me about America, Rosie. Tell me about the things you have.'

'I'll tell you about my friend Caz,' I said, 'the one who's just like you.'

'OK,' and she settled down happily, with her cup of tea, like a child having a story. Just like Caz in fact, when I have a juicy bit of gossip for her.

I told her about Caz.

'She lives with a teacher called Jamie.'

'What, just lives with? Over the brush? They're not married?'

'No.'

'And he's still allowed to be a teacher?'

'Well yes.'

'Didn't think the parents would like that. Not a good example.'

'Half the parents aren't married either.'

'Oh well. Funny place America. So what's their house like?'

'It's a Victorian terraced house.'

'What, an old-fashioned thing, not a nice new one?'

'With four bedrooms, two bathrooms.'

'*Two* bathrooms? Blimey, I'd be happy just to have one!'

'And it's all decorated in neutral colours.'

'Neutral?'

'Yes, you know, whites and creams and beiges.'

'Sounds boring.'

'Not really because Caz has made great

115

cushions and they have wonderful paintings on the walls.'

'Paintings? They must be rich these friends.'

'No, as I said, Jamie's a teacher and Caz works with me on the paper.'

'Have they got a telly?'

'Oh yes, Jamie's just bought a big one, about four-foot long. The colours are really sharp.'

'Colours? You've got TV in colour?'

'Yes, almost all our TVs are in colour. And we can have over a hundred different channels to watch.'

Carol just gawped at me. I told her about Caz and Jamie having a car each, how they went skiing at Christmas and were planning to go to Thailand in the summer, but I don't think Carol believed me. She certainly seemed unable to take it all in.

'Have they got any kiddies?'

'No. No. They don't want any, not yet anyway. And I'm not sure if they ever want any.'

'Well you get what you're given,' laughed Carol, 'even if the timing's not quite right. But I wouldn't be without them.'

Libby had come in, sucking her thumb and carrying a doll in her other hand. She snuggled into Carol, who put her arm around her. 'Wouldn't be without you, would I my precious? Nor your big brothers.'

'And what about Billy?' I asked, my heart thumping and my voice suddenly shaking.

'He's a good dad,' said Carol. 'Works hard, brings his pay home, does the garden. No complaints.'

116

'And you're happy?' I hesitated but had to ask. 'You still love him?'

'Love him?' Carol laughed. 'Don't know what love's got to do with it. But we've rubbed along for a long time now and he's a good man, a decent man. Never hesitated about getting wed and been a good provider ever since. Could do worse.

'He earns the money and looks after the garden. And I look after him and the kids and the house. And when we get our new house, we'll all be made up won't we?'

'Where is your new house going to be?'

'Up at The Meadows.'

'The Meadows?'

I thought of that vast estate, the few good areas and the stretches of bad parts, where joyriders terrorised the streets and then made bonfires of the cars they'd stolen. The wrecks sat in the streets for weeks, blending in with the other rubbish dumped in front gardens of houses with boarded-up windows sprayed with graffiti. Litter blew in the wind and aggressive young girls, all sulky expressions, bare midriffs, cheap thongs and tattoos, sat on walls, chain-smoking, throwing insults at passersby while their babies sat ignored in buggies.

'Yes, it's going to be great up there. The houses are lovely, really lovely. They've got big windows so they're all light and airy and we'll have a bathroom and three bedrooms and there's a kitchen, with a proper cooker and a sitting room with a back boiler and a little dining room as well. We'll be so posh, won't we Libby? And you can have a bedroom all on your own. Won't that be lovely?'

There was a crash outside the door. A small boy came bursting through. He too looked just like Carol but with Will's big brown eyes. 'Hi Mum. Is there anything to eat? I'm starving!'

'Then you should have been home for your dinner. We ate all your chips. But if you're good I'll get you some bread and jam – and will you look at the state of your clothes! What have you been doing?'

'Building a den, but then Rob had to go and see his gran.'

'Right, get out of those clothes and I think we'll get you in the sink and wash you down.'

Time for me to leave. 'I'd better be going and leave you to it. It's been great really. Thanks for the chips and the tea, and everything.'

'Will you come again?'

'Please, if you like. Or maybe we could have a coffee again in town if I can get out of the office.'

'Smashing,' but she had already turned to Davy and was peeling off his filthy jumper. She was caught up in domesticity. I let myself out and walked back through town, turning over what I'd seen. How strange to see Caz with kids, and kids she clearly adored, at that. And coping with them in that small, dark, damp house. Caz!

I wondered about what she'd said about her and Will. What's love got to do with it... It was almost like a business partnership. Yet they had three kids, so it certainly wasn't platonic. And that look and grin they'd shared... I didn't like to think of Caz and Will in bed together, so I hurried on, concentrating on finding my way home, thinking of this new Will I'd seen. Will as a family man.

When I got back to the Browns' house, I was desperate for the loo. Somehow, I hadn't fancied the sentry box at Carol's. Doreen and Frank seemed to be out, but Peggy was in the bathroom. I waited a while, then finally I had to bang on the door.

'Peggy, could you hurry please? I'm getting desperate!'

Eventually she flung open the door and came out surrounded by billowing clouds of steam.

'Good grief. It's like a sauna in here,' I said, getting past her. I'd never known that bathroom so warm. And that was another odd thing. I could have sworn she smelt of booze. I mean, I occasionally like to lie in the bath with a glass of wine but I didn't think that was Peggy's thing. As I sat on the loo, I could hear her crashing around in her bedroom. She sounded almost as if she were drunk. But that was just daft. Peggy wasn't the drinking type.

Chapter Eight

Sometimes I think about the third circle of hell ... Heathrow on a bank holiday ... Will and Jamie explaining the offside rule ... waiting for an hour to get through to a computer helpline, and finally talking to someone in a far-flung country who says his name is Kevin, just before the phone goes dead...

None of these compare to Sundays in the

Browns' house.

Saturday evening had been OK really. Just after the Browns got back, two lads had called round. They were friends of Stephen on leave from the forces. They'd come in and Doreen had made some sandwiches and Frank had nipped out for a few bottles of beer and it had been a bit of a laugh. So I wasn't prepared for Sunday.

It started with church. Now I've got nothing against church. I go regularly myself – oh, at least once every other Christmas to keep my mum happy. Not that she goes much more often. But I thought, in the Browns' house, it would be a nice thing to do. Right?

Wrong. It was grim. If that was what church was like, no wonder everyone stopped going. I couldn't find my place in the service book and when I got the words wrong, people glared at me. Surprisingly, I knew the first hymn, sort of. 'Praise my soul the King of heaven' – I've sung it at weddings. But then I dropped my hymn book and you'd think I'd farted by all the tut-tutting around me.

As for the sermon ... it was so riveting that I started counting pieces of stained glass, and I can tell you that in the window behind the altar there were thirty-three blue bits, five fewer than in the window to my right.

And yet, maybe something got through, some yearning for something, but I didn't quite know what. Not so much the service, but something about the building itself and the thought of all those people going back hundreds of years, who had come here to worship, to say the same prayers. In a way, I could almost feel them there around me.

And it gave me a chance to think about Will, or rather Will as Billy, a family man. I know Carol had laughed, but the only way I could describe him was 'grown up'. He was doing things for his family, literally providing for them by growing food, and teaching them, showing Pete how to make that cold frame.

Gosh, even Pete seemed more grown up than Will in some ways.

Would Will be like that if we had a family? Would he take responsibility?

Billy had taken responsibility since he was seventeen, when he became a dad. At eighteen, he was married, a father and a soldier. Is this what they mean by making a man of someone? I thought of the way Billy had shown Pete how to do that cold frame thing, a father passing on skills to his son. He wasn't making a big deal of it, he was just doing it. And it was brilliant.

Oh God, I wanted to cry. Thank goodness it was the last hymn and soon we were all shuffling out and putting our hymn books back on the table at the back and out into the fresh air away from the musty smell of moth balls and peppermints.

As soon as we got home, Mrs Brown changed out of her Sunday best, rolled up her sleeves and started on the lunch.

Now my mum makes a mean Sunday dinner. The best. She always does it for my brother when he goes home and it's good enough to make me forget I don't really like red meat – roast beef and all the trimmings. But Mum manages to do it

121

while knocking back the best part of a bottle of Merlot and in between sitting at the kitchen table reading the *Sunday Times*. It never seems a big deal.

This was. Peggy had emerged from her pit and was trying to read the *News of the World*. Not that I think she was reading it really, she seemed more to be hiding behind it. But not for long. Mrs Brown has us both peeling (more bloody potatoes) and chopping. She had the cloth off the kitchen table and was making pastry.

'Rosie, can you go down the garden and pick some rhubarb please?' she asked.

Rhubarb?

The back garden was steep, narrow and treacherous, a sort of series of terraces leading down to the river, which went rushing past below. It was easy to see from the debris on the steps that the river had been halfway up the garden recently. I looked around for rhubarb and tried to think what it looked like. Long pink sticks.

Anyway, I went up and down those slippy steps, along the little patches of garden and couldn't see anything looking like rhubarb. I was so long, that Peggy came to look for me, stamping down the steps in a mood.

'I can't find it, sorry,' I said.

She just gave me a withering look and marched over to a big upturned metal bucket. She picked it up and beneath it were some long thin pink sticks of rhubarb with large pale green leaves.

'Well how was I meant to know it was under a bucket?' I said.

'Where do you think rhubarb grows?' she said,

122

very sarcastically.

I wanted to say 'in a long polystyrene tray just on the left when you go into Sainsbury's', but thought I was probably wasting my breath...

I had to get some apples from a shelf in the pantry. They were from the twisted old tree in the garden and had been packed in the previous autumn. Talk about past their sell-by date. The apples were all individually wrapped in newspaper and were soft and waxy. I peeled them and chopped them and stood stirring them on the side of the range until they went mushy. All this just for some apple sauce.

The meal was a production. It was like something out of *A Christmas Carol*. Mrs Brown produced the meat, Mr Brown carved it. We were all meant to say ooh and ah... Gosh, it would have been so much easier for us all just to go to the pub. The only excitement came when we were working our way through the meat. And I said, ever so casually, to Peggy, 'Do they do good food at the Rising Sun?'

She gave me a filthy look and said, 'How should I know? I've never been there.'

'Oh,' I said, 'I thought you might have been there on official business, with the editor maybe.'

'Well you're wrong. I haven't,' she snapped, banging down a rhubarb pie on the table. She looked really upset and a bit pale, which made me feel guilty, so I left it at that. But I'd clearly touched a nerve.

Finally, when we were all too full to move, we had the washing up to do. It took hours. It was like the porridge pot only much more of it, all cleaned with a bit of wire wool and some grey powder.

And that was it. That was the excitement for the day.

Peggy said she was going to see a friend and tittled off. Mr Brown sat at the dining-room table and did some parish council work, and Mrs Brown did the ironing.

Oh yes and Stephen's girlfriend Cheryl came around. She was a mousy little thing, but only seventeen years old. She'd brought a letter from Stephen to show to the Browns. Mrs Brown stopped ironing and went and got her latest letter from Stephen from behind the clock in the kitchen. The two women compared notes while Mr Brown paused in his parish council work

As far as I could tell the lad had written the same thing to both mother and girlfriend. It was very hot, there had been a spot of bother and they hadn't been allowed any free time that week. They were still in the Nissen huts but hoped to move to proper barracks soon. Maybe his girl-friend had a few more kisses than his mother. And that seemed about it.

'Oh he won't like it in the heat,' said Mrs Brown. 'He always gets that itchy rash on his back.'

'And behind his knees,' said Cheryl.

Heat rash? As far as I could tell Cyprus was in a state of riot after they'd got rid of Archbishop whatnot. There was shooting in the streets. Goodness knows what the 'spot of bother' was that Stephen had mentioned. And all his mother and girlfriend could worry about was the rash on the back of his knees.

It baffled me. It really did. This couldn't be real.

I went up to my room, lay on my bed. Sambo followed me up and lay beside me purring happily. I listened to the river and tried to make sense of it all. And there was so much to make sense of.

I am no nearer at all in working out where I am or why I'm here but I'm beginning to think that it can't be a reality show. There are no cameras, no rules, no video room, no perky little Geordie comics commenting on it.

It's too big. You can recreate a house, a newspaper office, a street even, but not a whole town.

Then there are the people. Carol and Billy are not Caz and Will. Almost like them. Just like Caz and Will would be probably if they had grown up in a different time. If they had been transplanted to the 1950s for instance. I mean, Caz has always said she doesn't want children, and here she is with three of them on whom she absolutely dotes. But Caz hasn't missed them. Carol's dead excited about getting a job as a school cook. If she hadn't fallen pregnant at sixteen, then what could she have done?

It's ridiculous to think of Will and Caz as a couple. But Billy and Carol seem a real partnership, working together for the kids. If they'd had to, could Will and Caz have worked it out like Billy and Carol? Maybe. All very weird.

I thought of the hymn we'd sung in church that morning. There was a line in it, 'dwellers all in time and space'.

We were all dwellers in time and space. We think we're restricted to one little place, moving along a narrow path, always in the same direction, a bit like railway lines. But what if it's not like that at all? What if we can move around in it like astronauts in the weightlessness of space, bobbing here and there without much control over where we go? Could I really, perhaps actually be in the real 1950s?

It was a terrifying thought, so terrifying that I had been refusing to consider it. But now the thought would not be shoved to the back of my brain. I had to face it. I went hot and cold. My heartbeat raced and my skin went clammy. I took deep breaths to try to calm myself down.

The real 1950s? It couldn't be. Things like that don't happen. People don't go back in time, not really, not to a different world. It's not possible.

But what else could it be?

I had thought and thought about what was going on, had twisted ideas this way and that, but there was one idea I had dared not face up to.

That this was real. That I had somehow gone back in time. God knew how – or even why – it had happened. But it was beginning to be the only solution that made sense. I remembered a bit in *The Lion, The Witch and the Wardrobe*, where the older Pevensie children went to talk to the Professor about what Lucy had said about the land of Narnia. Basically, said the Professor, when you've eliminated everything else, then what is left must be the truth...

I was breathing more evenly now and suddenly felt strangely calm. Maybe I really was back in

126

the 1950s. In a way, mind-blowing as it seemed, it was the only thing that made sense. I had time travelled. No. I couldn't have. But how else to explain it? How or why, I didn't know or understand. Couldn't begin to get my head around it. But I was here. And if I needed reminding, the scratchy underwear and slippery eiderdown told me so.

I didn't fit here. I didn't belong. If I stayed here – God, I'd be older than my parents. Panic surged through me again.

But no. Deep breath. Everyone seemed to think I was here for only a few weeks. The Browns had said so. Richard Smarmy Henfield had said so. This wasn't a full-scale exchange, just a time trip, a holiday in another age. It wasn't for ever. I had to believe that.

But what about my life at home? Did Mum and Dad know I was here? What if they were ringing me and not getting an answer? What if they were worrying? My heart raced again. *It wasn't for ever.* That was the important bit. *It wasn't for ever.* At least, I didn't think so. And just in case, I'd keep smiling for those cameras...

At teatime we had tinned salmon sandwiches, which were clearly a treat, and a cake that Mrs Brown had made that morning. Listen, I was so desperate for entertainment that I learnt to knit. Seriously. When *What's My Line* came on, Mrs Brown dragged her knitting bag out.

'Do you knit much?' she asked.

'Not at all,' I said. 'Never learnt.'

Well! Do I eat babies for breakfast? Or push little old ladies under cars? You'd think I did, the reaction I had from Mrs Brown. Anyway, it all ended up with her digging out a pair of needles and some scraps of wool and teaching me how to knit. I was apparently knitting a scarf. I have done at least three inches of it. So far, it was black, and red, and yellow, and further colours will depend on the scraps in Mrs Brown's knitting bag.

Once I'd got the hang of it, it was quite soothing really, click, click, click, as I watched the little grey people on the television signing in and then going through their mimes of the jobs. A lot of Hollywood stars have taken up knitting, haven't they? Say it's very good for their stress levels on set. I can believe it too.

I thought of Carol's children and their hand-knitted jumpers. I suppose Carol had done that too – in between making most of their clothes, washing by hand and trying to keep that small dark little house clean. Very different from Caz. Don't get me wrong, Caz is a worker. I've known her do twelve-hour shifts at work and not moan at all. But on her days off she believes in as little effort as possible. I thought of their bathroom – power shower, deep tub, surrounded by bottles of bath oil and candles. Couldn't imagine Caz settling for a tin tub in front of the fire. But if there was no alternative...

I'd just come to the end of the red wool and was ready for a break from all this creativity and thinking – that's the trouble with 1950s Sundays, too much time to think – when I heard a strange noise from the kitchen. When I went out there, it was young Janice, in a grubby shapeless kilt and jumper, eating what looked like a beef sandwich while walking up and down, with her eyes closed reciting a poem.

"'Ish there any body there?" shaid the Traveller,
  knocking on the moonlit door.
And hish horse in the silence champed the grashes
Of the forest's ferny floor.
And a bird ... and a bird... [Oh blow.]
And a bird flew up out of the turret,'

'*Above the Traveller's head,*' I said, having picked up the book and looked.

Janice jumped and sprayed crumbs all over the kitchen.

'Sorry Janice, didn't mean to make you jump. Is this part of your homework?'

'Yes, I've got to learn it for first lesson tomorrow. And it's impossible to do it in our house with all the howling.'

'Well I'm sure if you explained that to your teacher, she'd let you off.'

'No she wouldn't. If things are difficult, she says you just have to try harder. Anyway I'd feel silly, wouldn't I? If all the others learnt it and I hadn't just because my brothers howl all the time.'

I had to admire her. Even with her new haircut – already looking pretty grubby and greasy again – the poor kid didn't have much going for her. But she was determined, I'll give her that. She wasn't making excuses even though it seemed she had a house full of them.

'Well, come on, I'll help you.'

So we walked around the kitchen, Sambo weaving between our legs, chanting it together.

'But only a host of phantom listeners
that dwelt in the lone house then
Stood listening in the quiet of the moonlight
To that voice from the world of men...'

Until Janice was word perfect and triumphant and I too had got it by heart. Knitting and learning poetry. Was this what Sundays had come to?

After Janice had gone home I went back into the sitting room and sat on the sofa in front of the fire. A draught chilled my shoulders and the back of my neck, while the fronts of my legs were almost burnt by the fire. I felt edgy and restless and could feel Mrs Brown beginning to get impatient with me, so I picked up my knitting again. It gave me something to do with my hands while I carried on with my thinking. I looked at the pictures in the flames and knitted my scarf. And did some thinking. So much thinking.

Click click *'Is there anyone there?'* said the Traveller.

Click click *Dwellers all in time and space.*

Click click *When you've eliminated everything else, then what's left must be the truth.*

Click click *They can't take that away from me.*

Click, click, click...

Chapter Nine

Maybe it was the knitting... OK, maybe not. Trust me, its therapeutic effects are overrated. But on Monday morning I felt a lot calmer. Maybe this was just an adventure. Part of me was still bewildered, trying to work it out and if I thought too hard about it, I guess I could feel the panic rising again. But I clung on to the fact that everyone said I would be here just for a few weeks. So the other part of me was curious, excited almost. This was an adventure and I wanted to see what happened. After all, I thought, it could be a great story...

After such a stodgy Sunday I practically ran into the office. I was actually looking forward to work. I went into the reporters' room expecting to be greeted by Gordon's demands for tea. But he wasn't there. Instead Billy was standing with the big diary in front of him, marking up the stories.

'Hello Rosie,' he said, pleasant and friendly but still like a stranger. 'Nice to see you on Saturday.'

I was completely wrong-footed. For some reason I hadn't expected him to be there, didn't know what to do with my hands, the expression on my face. 'Yes. I enjoyed meeting Peter. He's a great lad, isn't he?' Gosh, I was making conversation like an old granny with the vicar.

'Not bad,' said Billy, but he looked pleased.

'Right,' he went on, 'Gordon won't be in for a

week or two. He's broken his leg, fell downstairs apparently – while stone cold sober, before you start. He's in the Victoria Infirmary at the moment and they won't let him out until he's mastered the crutches. So it'll be a while before he's back at work.'

I thought of Gordon trying to negotiate those long steep narrow cluttered stairs on crutches and for a moment – a very brief moment – almost sympathised.

'So I'm taking over the desk for now and I've had to reorganise some of the jobs. Alan, you'll have to get to the council planning meeting today. It's the day they decide on the ring road. That's a must. Tony's down at the petty sessions. Derek's gone to an accident on the Netherton Road. Marje – I've got you down for the Duke and Duchess opening the new school. OK?'

'Fine by me,' said Marje.

'What about me?' I asked.

'Dan and Doris Archer are opening the spring flower show in the Shire Hall, but that's not till lunch time, so if you can get on with some shorts till then...'

'What, off the radio show? *The* Dan and Doris? Gosh my mum would be jealous. She loves *The Archers.*'

'Not a patch on *Dick Barton*,' muttered Marje. 'They're all yours.'

First I had a phone call to make...

Making phone calls was tricky because there were only three phones in the office, none of them on my desk. And everything had to go through the operators downstairs. You couldn't just dial a

132

number, you had to wait for them to put you through. The upside of this was that often you didn't even need to know the number you wanted – just left it up to them.

I waited until the office was quiet, then I went over to Gordon's desk, took a deep breath and picked up the phone. There was a quick click and a voice said, 'Switchboard!'

'Could you put me through to head office?' I said briskly, in my best businesslike tone.

'Who is that please?' asked the switchboard operator suspiciously.

'Rosie Harford.'

There was a pause and I could hear them dithering over whether to connect me or not. Obviously, humble reporters never dared ring head office.

'I have a few details I need to clarify with Lord Uzmaston's secretary.'

'Oooh, right you are love,' said the operator and, many clicks later, I was speaking to another operator who sounded as though she were on Mars, or underwater.

'This is Rosie Harford on *The News*. I have a few questions about my attachment here and I would like to speak to the person who arranged it.'

'Have you a name for that person, caller?'

'No I don't, sorry.'

'Right, I'd better put you through to Lord Uzmaston's office.'

Good. This was sounding promising. The phone was answered by an incredibly posh-sounding woman. I just knew – *knew* – that she was wearing pearls. She had that sort of voice. I went through my request again.

'And who was the person who made this arrangement?' Bugger. This would make me look a lot less businesslike. 'I'm sorry, I'm not sure. I believe it was a young man who is an assistant to Lord Uzmaston.'

'Ah. That would be our Mr Simpson.'

'Could I speak to him please?'

'No, unfortunately not. He is away from the office for the next two weeks.'

'Is there anyone else who would know about it?'

'Not if Mr Simpson was dealing with it. No.'

'Does Mr Simpson have a secretary? Do you have an HR department? Who deals with jobs and training? There must be somebody.'

'That would be myself. If I don't know about this ... arrangement ... then I'm afraid nobody will. You will have to speak to Mr Simpson. I can't help you any further.'

And she put the phone down. Great. Two more weeks before I could talk to our Mr bloody Simpson. Two more weeks before I could get any further with this mystery of where I was and why I was there. I felt frustrated and, to be honest, a bit lost.

Which gave me another thought. I started dialling my parents' number. Maybe they'd be there. Maybe they were here too. Maybe they could put things right. So often in the past I remember ringing them when I was stranded or ill or the cash machine had swallowed my card. And they would turn up, one or the other or both of them would come and put it right. Once, when I was ill at uni, they turned up at midnight, wrapped me in my duvet and took me home. I can still remember that glorious feeling when they arrived, that from that moment on I could just give up. They would take over. They would make things right. Maybe they could put this right too...

It was a moment before I could remember the string of numbers – I was so used just to clicking 'Home' on my mobile. But it didn't matter. I hadn't got past the area code when a voice interrupted briskly. It was the switchboard lady asking bossily, 'Can I help you? Which number do you require?'

'It doesn't matter,' I said, deflated. Then I remembered. Suddenly I was small again – about four or five years old and lying in my parents' bed when they still had the old dark red telephone, one with a dial, on their bedside table. Back then it still had a sticker with the original number from the small local exchange.

'Just a moment. Yes, hang on. Could you get me' – I closed my eyes and tried to picture that old telephone, trying to read the sticker – 'Could you get me Barton 463 please?'

'Just a moment, caller.'

There were clicks and rushing sounds. I held my breath, hoping that Mum or Dad would pick up the phone and all would be well again.

But no.

'Sorry, caller. I'm unable to connect you. That number is not in service.'

No. I didn't think it would be. But it had been worth a try. For a moment I felt bitterly, desperately disappointed. I had so wanted Mum and Dad to make things better, to take all this confusion away. But I guess I was a grown-up now. I blew my nose and got back to work, glad of the boring routine of News in Brief paragraphs until I realised that without Gordon barking orders, I hadn't made the tea. I just had time for a cup before I went to see Dan and Doris. I was just going out of the office to fill the kettle when the phone rang.

'Newsroom,' I said importantly – and felt as nervous doing it as on my first work experience week, years before.

'This is Ron Neasham, the newsagent in Friars' Mill,' said a voice. 'Do you know what's going on down here?'

'No I don't, Mr Neasham,' I said, 'should I?'

'Well there's all sorts of police here, with dogs and all. I think a kiddie's gone missing.'

'A missing child? Are you sure? They didn't say anything to us when we made the calls this morning.'

'I think it's just happened. You'd better check it out.'

'We certainly shall, Mr Neasham. Thank you.'

He'd already put the phone down just as Billy walked back into the office.

'Missing child in Friars' Mill apparently,' I said. 'Someone called Ron Neasham rang to tell us there's a lot of police activity there.'

'Good bloke Ron Neasham,' said Billy. 'Used to be one of our van drivers so he often passes us snippets. Odd though that the police didn't mention it on the calls.'

'That's what I said.'

Billy looked around the office desperately,

136

trying to find someone to send on the story. But he couldn't. There was only me.

'Look, you get down to Friars' Mill and find out what you can, and ring me as soon as you've got something.'

'Right.' I'd grabbed my bag and was out of the office before he could change his mind. I'd miss Dan and Doris, but what the hell – there'd be another fifty years to catch up with them.

Friars' Mill was about two miles out of town. Which would take me forty minutes to walk and by the time I'd done that the Chief Inspector would probably be back in his bloody office. Bugger!

Then I remembered Dan and Doris. Young George was out there waiting to take their picture. I dashed out and pushed through the crowds to find him.

'Are they here yet?'

'Just arriving,' said George.

'Then just take a picture as quick as you can and let's get out of here. Just do it George. Please.'

With that, Dan and Doris arrived looking a lot more like actors than a farmer and his wife. God must have been on my side, because as they went up the steps to the Shire Hall, they stopped half-way to wave at the crowd and a small child shoved a toy lamb at them. Brilliant. George got them perfectly. And soon we were bundled in the van and heading for Friars' Mill.

It must be part of the town now. I know there's a Friars' Mill Road, but that's about it. Though there was something about the name that kept niggling at my brain. I knew it for something but

I couldn't recall what. Anyway, the place I went to with George was in the country. There was a green, and a river with a weir, and a duck pond, and a row of small cottages. There were a couple of black cars parked on the green, and I could see two policemen in their old-fashioned uniforms, talking to someone on a cottage doorstep.

In the middle was what looked like an old army hut made out of corrugated iron but it had newspaper bills outside, as well as sacks of potatoes and gas cylinders. Tesco Express it wasn't. This must be Ron Neasham's shop. We headed there. Ron was busy marking up a ledger, but looked up eagerly when he saw George and his camera and realised who we were.

'It's the little girl from the big house, the housekeeper's daughter,' he said, so full of importance and keen to tell us all he knew.

'She set off to school this morning as usual, about half past eight. Then her mum went down the school about half past ten to take her to the dentist and she wasn't there. Never got there. Apparently, when Joyce Williams – that's little Susan's mother – was asking her friends at school if anyone had seen her, Charlie, one of the little 'uns, pipes up that he saw her being pulled into a van by an old man.'

'What! Well why didn't he say anything before?'

'Little lad's only five years old.'

I was scribbling quickly in my notebook as he spoke.

'Well, when she heard that, the headmistress got straight on to the police and the police came right out. They're up at the house now, and those two over there have been going from door to door asking people what they've seen. As far as I can tell, no one's seen anything, apart from that little lad.'

'And if he's only five, he could be making it all up.'

'Maybe, maybe. But if you want to talk to the man in charge, I think he must be up at the house. Look,' and he pointed out an impressive gateway at the far end of the green. 'That's the entrance, but the house is about half a mile further up the drive.'

'Right Ron,' I pushed the notebook into my bag. 'Thanks a lot. You're a real star.'

'Just like to help the old firm, you know,' he said, looking pleased with himself.

I got George to take a picture across the green with the policemen in the background. Then we went up the drive to The Grange. It was a big house, not quite a stately home, but pretty impressive all the same. The drive swept around in front of well-tended lawns. I could see a tennis court, and what looked like stables and a paddock.

'Better find the tradesman's entrance,' said George, and we turned up, past two small cottages and stopped in a back yard where there was a big black car and a young policeman guarding it.

'Press,' I said confidently, 'from *The News.*'

'Blimey, you were quick,' said the policeman, who was pink-cheeked and looked about sixteen.

'Is the Chief Inspector about?'

'He's in there. But I don't think...'

'Thank you,' I said and I went in, with George following.

We went into a room full of old coats and welly

139

boots and dog baskets, along a passage until we heard voices, which we followed to a huge high-ceilinged kitchen. As we stood in the doorway, a young woman almost ran towards me.

'Have you found her?' she asked. 'Have you found Susan?'

'No, I'm sorry. We're from *The News*. Someone rang to tell us what had happened,' I said quickly, before the Chief Inspector could throw us out. 'They thought we could help.'

'Help? How could you help?'

An older woman, grey-haired, very erect, was standing by an Aga. She was clearly the lady of the manor. I learnt later she was Caroline Cavendish.

'My apologies,' I said, as politely as I could, while trying to look friendly, concerned, un-threatening, and helpful all at the same time. Quickly (I could sense the Chief Inspector homing in on me), I spoke to the housekeeper.

'I'm sure Susan will be back home again by teatime,' I said. 'I'm sure the Chief Inspector has told you that nearly every child who goes missing wanders back fairly soon, safe and sound in a matter of hours.'

Joyce clutched her hanky, sniffed and said yes, he had said that, he had and she really hoped it was right.

'I'm sure she will be back. But, as I say, just in case, as a sort of safety net, just to be on the safe side, if we had something in tomorrow's paper, then by six o'clock in the morning you could have 100,000 people looking for her. If we had a picture, then people would see it and be on the lookout.'

'She's right,' said the Chief Inspector. 'The press can be very useful on such occasions.'

'If you're sure, Mrs Cavendish,' said Joyce, looking beseechingly towards her employer.

I turned to the Chief Inspector.

'Are you having a press conference or briefing soon?'

He looked blank.

'Press conference?'

No, of course, no press conferences. No reconstructions, handout pictures, interviews for TV and radio. I spotted a picture on the dresser. Clearly a school photo, a little girl with blonde plaits and a gappy grin, arms folded above an impressive-looking encyclopaedia. 'Is this Susan?'

'Yes,' said her mother, snatching the photo and holding it close to her.

'Maybe,' I said gently, 'you could just let George here borrow it for a moment and he could take a photograph of it, a copy of it. It's all right, we'll just take it out of the frame, but you can have it straight back. Can't she, George?

'And while you're doing that, perhaps the Chief Inspector and I can just go outside for a moment?'

Outside, the Chief Inspector recapped on the details of the case for me, then added, 'Little Charlie thought Susan was waiting for him, you see, when a van appeared, a grey one, he says, driving very fast. A "fat man" got out, shouting, and dragged Susan into the van and roared off.'

'Do you think he's telling the truth?'

'Probably, yes. We can't be sure, of course. He's only five, and they can get muddled at that age. But he seems quite sure, and quite consistent. He thinks the van came from the woods.'

'Could it?'

'There's no road there, but a good track, and in this dry weather it would be quite passable. Bumpy, but passable.'

'Any idea of the van?' I asked.

'No. Grey vans are ten-a-penny.'

'Who lives in The Grange?'

'The Cavendishes. Mrs Cavendish you've seen. Husband Colonel Cavendish is up in London during the week. There's a daughter at boarding school, and a son, Jeremy, up at Oxford, though he's home for the holidays at the moment. He went out to see friends over in Upper Middleton last night, presumably stayed the night and isn't home yet. They don't own a grey van.'

'So what happens now?'

'Well, I still think that Susan will turn up by teatime. Amazing the number of kids who remember to come home when they're hungry. She's probably gone off in a dream, or had an arithmetic test today or something.'

'And if she doesn't?'

'If she doesn't, then in view of the evidence of the little boy, we'll start a full-scale search. But I'm sure it won't come to that. OK?'

'Thanks, Chief Inspector.'

I went back into the house and had a chat with Susan's mother Joyce. Susan had never missed a day at school, not even been late, loved school, was doing well, wanted to be a teacher. She would be home soon, wouldn't she?'

Of course she would, of course she would.

'Right,' said George. 'What now? I've taken the

copy of the kiddie's picture. I've got the police and her mum. Any point in staying?'

'No, I guess not. Anyway, I need to tell Billy what's happening.' I reached instinctively for my mobile before realising how hopeless that was. Down the drive I could see a policewoman coming up, firmly holding on to the hand of a small boy, no doubt Charlie. By now it was a quarter to four. Nearly teatime. Let's hope Susan would get hungry.

George and I were just getting into his van (thank goodness it was black, not grey), when I saw a young policeman running up the drive like a champion sprinter, his helmet bobbing up and down and his great long coat flapping behind him. 'Sir, sir!' He was calling to the Chief Inspector, who was just going into the gardener's house behind the policewoman and little Charlie. The young policeman stopped, and dropped his head down onto his knees in his breathlessness, then looked up.

'Sir, we've ... we've found a body.'

'Oh no,' said the Chief Inspector, the colour draining from his face. 'Not Susan.'

'No sir, not Susan. It's a young man. We think it's Jeremy Cavendish. He's been shot.'

I was out of the van in a flash. But the Chief Inspector held up his hand, his former friendliness vanished under an air of grim authority.

'No, I have nothing to say until I know more myself. Will you please leave now. When I have something I can tell you, I will telephone the paper.'

'But–'

143

'Please. Leave. Now.'

I needed to talk to Billy anyway, and George had to get his pictures printed.

We raced down the drive, my teeth rattling in the little van. I thought of that erect grey-haired woman who had been standing at the Aga, dealing with officialdom on behalf of her house-keeper. Now her son was dead.

Back at *The News* I raced up the dusty wooden stairs. Billy was talking to someone on the phone, writing in his notebook as he listened. It was very Will-ish. But I had no time to think of that as I waved to get his attention. He brought the call to a quick, but very polite end, and turned to me. I told him what had happened, as quickly, clearly and as professionally as I could.

Billy took it all in, thought for a second, and then said, 'Write up the story of the missing girl, but don't mention the body until we get official confirmation.' He turned to the other reporter in the room, 'Derek – have you got your stuff written up?'

'Just about.'

'And have you got your bike here?'

'Of course.'

'Right, get yourself up to Friars' Mill. Don't annoy Watkins, but try and get the gen on this body. They're going to have to open an inquest, so there's bound to be an ID. We need to know exactly what's going on.'

'But it's my story!' I said.

'Yes Rosie I know, and I'm not taking it away from you. This is a team effort. You get your stuff written up as quick as you can.'

I typed as quickly as I could, with all that fiddly carbon paper. I had just finished when I suddenly remembered.

Back before all this strange Narnia type adventure had happened, when I'd been sitting in the bound file room, going through all the copies of *The News* from the 1950s, there was that small paragraph. A sixteen-year-old girl had died in the river below the millpond at Friars' Mill. I remembered it simply because it was such a small paragraph, such a sad memorial to a young life, and because the verdict had been Accidental Death, but something about the way it had been written had made me think it had really been suicide.

'Friars' Mill,' I said to Billy. 'Wasn't that where a young girl drowned recently?'

'Yes,' said Billy, 'I did the inquest. She was only sixteen. What we didn't say in the paper was that she was pregnant. It was pretty clear that she'd killed herself, but the jury decided to spare the family's feelings and say it was Accidental Death.'

'Pregnant and abandoned?'

'Yes.'

'Do we know who the father was?'

'No, it didn't come out in court. There was something from a friend of hers saying that she'd been worried, her boyfriend came from a good family apparently, something about him being a student but refusing to give up his studies and do the decent thing and marry her because his family wouldn't approve. Wouldn't even consider it.'

'A student? Good family?' I looked at Billy.

'Jeremy Cavendish?' he asked, looking back.

'That would explain why she did the deed in

Friars' Mill, wouldn't it? Right on his doorstep. Who was the girl? Can you remember her name?'

Billy frowned. 'Amy something. Amy... Amy... She was a farmer's daughter, lived the other side of town, I think. Oh,' he banged the desk in frustration, 'if only I could remember her name!'

Today at *The News* of course you'd just type 'Amy sixteen-year-old suicide' into a computer search engine, and the story would flash up in front of you in seconds.

Not in the 1950s.

Billy started rifling through the big bound back copies that lived on a shelf at the end of the newsroom. He was turning pages swiftly, searching. Meanwhile, I ran up to the library. This consisted of shelf after shelf of brown envelopes packed with curling cuttings. First go I grabbed a fat envelope marked 'Friars' Mill' and shook the cuttings out onto a desk. There were cuttings about garden parties at The Grange, about archaeological digs, about the leek show, the spring fair, an overturned milk lorry and the WI planting daffodil bulbs. But absolutely nothing about a sixteen-year-old girl 'accidentally' falling into the river.

'Rosie!' Billy was running up the library stairs. 'I've remembered. She was Amy Littlejohn, and her father has a small farm about two miles from Friars' Mill.'

'A farmer would have a gun, wouldn't he?'

'Yes. Of course we could be barking up completely the wrong tree here.'

'Of course we could,' I agreed. 'But it does seem to fit. So what shall we do?'

146

'Phil's the reporter on night shift. He's already in. We could send him up to have a look around. Or...' and he grinned. My heart lurched. It was a real Will grin, 'Or we could borrow his motorbike and go ourselves.'

'Just to have a little look around, of course,' I said.

'Of course.'

'What are we waiting for?'

Five minutes later, I was perched on the back of the borrowed motorbike, my hands gripping Billy's shoulders, and we were roaring out of *The News* yard in search of the story.

Chapter Ten

It was a long time since I'd been on the back of a motorbike – not since I briefly had a rocker boyfriend when I was about fifteen – and it's amazing how vulnerable you feel without a helmet. And uncomfortable, too, when you're wearing a skirt and stockings. The draught...

As we roared around bends and along the narrow country roads, I wanted to wrap my arms around Billy, hold him tightly, bury my head in his shoulder. Instead, I just hung on as lightly and as distantly as I could, sitting upright, rather primly I thought. Think Audrey Hepburn in *Roman Holiday*. OK, maybe not.

The roads were getting bumpier now and Billy was driving more slowly, searching through the gloom. 'Right, I think that's it.'

We got off. I was already feeling stiff and cold. Billy tucked the bike in a gateway and pointed across the road.

'I think that's Littlejohn's down there.'

A short, steep, muddy track twisted down into a hollow where there was a small farm. Even in the fading light it looked grim. The house had once – long ago – been whitewashed, but was now dirty and mottled, as if it had some nasty disease. The windows were dirty and the curtains drooped. A heap of logs lay scattered across the mud-covered yard along with bits of machinery that seemed abandoned rather than functional. The whole place reeked of neglect and despair.

As we stood silently gazing I suddenly heard a huge cough a few feet away from me. I leapt and gave a little yelp. 'What's that? Who's there?'

Billy was laughing. 'It's only a cow,' he whispered. 'Haven't you heard a cow cough before?'

'You know, I don't believe I have.'

But Billy was by now wriggling his way through the fence, which wasn't so much a fence as a few rusty old iron bedsteads roughly pushed into position. 'Come on. We'll have a better view from here.'

He took my hand – it was wonderful to feel his hand on mine – and guided me into the field. My feet squelched in something disgusting. 'Ugh!' I said, not liking to think what it could have been. Down below we could hear a dog giving a few muttered barks.

'Look!' said Billy suddenly.

Below us, tucked into the shelter of one of the

148

barns, was a van, a small grey van. 'Coincidence?' said Billy drily.

'The inspector said small grey vans are ten-a-penny.'

'Maybe, maybe.'

'So what do we do now? Should we tell the police?'

If only I had my mobile, I could have rung them. Easy peasy. Instead, I was stuck in a field in the dark, with possibly a murderer and a kidnapper down below me, and one foot covered in cow shit. Great.

Something was happening in the house. We saw a movement in front of a window and then a light went on, a soft, dim glow. From an oil lamp, I realised. Someone was carrying it across a room, and for a second I saw two shadows. A very big one and a very small one. The small one had pigtails...

'Oh God, Billy, that must be Susan. He's got her there. What shall we do?' I hissed.

Billy was calm, rational. 'It could be a perfectly normal farmer and his daughter or grand-daughter. We have no reason to think it's Susan. Only a string of coincidences. On the other hand, if that *is* Susan, we can't abandon her. God knows what Littlejohn will do. But we need to get help. There was another farm about half a mile back. They might have a phone. You go there and call the police. Tell them the story. Let them come and see.'

'Can I take the motorbike? Then if there's no phone I can get to town quickly.'

Down at the farm, the dog began his muttered barking again.

Billy gave me a quick look. Even in the dark I could see his grin. 'Can you ride a motorbike?'

'I think so.'

'Well be careful, girl. Here.' He handed me the key and I turned to go back up the slope to the rusty bedstead and the road. As I did, I slipped again and – stupid woman – gave a small yelp. The dog went mad. It was as if he were saying I *thought* there was someone up there and now I know. I could hear his chain rattling. He was barking so furiously and trying so hard to get to us he was practically choking himself. It was a dreadful sound. I prayed that chain would hold.

Then the door of the farmhouse was pulled open. In the doorway, the light of the oil lamp behind him, stood a man, a giant of a man. In his hands he had a shotgun. He was pointing it up the slope towards us.

'Who's there?' he yelled. 'Whoever you are, show yerself, before I set the dog on you.'

We stood stock still, not daring to move, not daring to breathe, though my heart was thumping so loudly I was sure the world could hear it.

'Run!' hissed Billy at me. 'Run!'

I turned to go, but with that the farmer came out into the yard and started striding up the slope. For a big man he moved quickly, confidently, easily. And now he could see us clearly.

'No you don't,' he said, his gun up at his shoulder, ready to fire. 'Don't you go anywhere. You just stay where you are.'

I turned back down the slope and stood next to Billy. I could smell the damp grass and the cows. And there was another smell I couldn't identify –

possibly my own terror. By now the farmer was just a few feet away from us. He was a huge man. More than six foot tall and nearly as wide, though his clothes hung on him. He wore a big tweed jacket that flapped around him. 'Get down,' he said, pointing at us with the gun, 'get down to the yard.'

Billy held a hand up, warning me to be quiet. We slithered down the slope. The farmer motioned us into the house and stood behind us with the gun. The dog ran towards us, growling deep down in his throat. It was a terrible noise.

We stumbled into the house. It stank. Absolutely stank. We were in the kitchen, but the big range across the far wall was dead and cold. In the dim light of the oil lamps I could see newspapers heaped on a chair, bits of sacking and rusty buckets littered the floor. A bit of machinery lay in pieces on the filthy table. Beside it was a heap of cartridge cases and an almost empty whisky bottle. And in the corner, just where the circle of light faded into black, huddled up on a wooden settle sat a small girl with blonde pigtails, shaking with sobs.

'Susan?' I asked. 'Susan?'

The little girl looked up at me, terrified, and then back again, clutching her knees.

'Will you shut that bloody row!' yelled the farmer.

'She's frightened,' said Billy, in a reasonable, noncommittal sort of voice, as if he were commenting on the weather.

'Well she's no need. I won't hurt her.'

'She's cold too.' Billy was taking off his jacket.

'Can we just put this around her? Just to warm her up a bit? It might stop her crying.'

The farmer grunted. Billy took this as assent and threw the jacket at me. Quickly and not daring to look at the farmer with his gun – I ran over to the settle and wrapped the jacket around Susan. She clung to me and I sat down on the settle next to her. I could feel her trembling. I wrapped my arms around her, partly to comfort her, partly to keep her warm, and partly to stay her sobs so she wouldn't annoy Littlejohn any more.

Whatever the reason, her sobs quietened. I could still feel her trembling as she huddled right up to me, but the crying had almost stopped. It somehow made it easier for all of us to breathe.

Billy was standing there in his shirtsleeves. He wore braces. He looked relaxed, in control. It was an impressive performance. 'There, that's better, isn't it?' he said to Littlejohn. 'She's only a little girl after all. Why did you bring her here? Why the gun?'

The farmer was still pointing his gun at us. I was scared to move, apart from to stroke Susan's back through the rough tweed of Billy's jacket. It was like trying to calm a horse or a frightened dog. I knew I was trying to calm myself as much as the little girl. Littlejohn seemed so angry, so unpredictable.

'She saw me.'

'Saw you?' asked Billy, still in this calm, it-doesn't-matter-if-you-answer-or-not sort of tone. 'Saw you? Did that matter?'

'She watched me coming down the track from

the woods. She saw the van. Anyway,' he suddenly jerked the gun back up again so it was pointing straight at Billy, 'who are you? What are you doing here?' He peered more closely at Billy.

'I know your face. I've seen you before. I know! You're the reporter from *The News*. You were in the court, weren't you?'

'That's right, Mr Littlejohn, I was. It was a very sad occasion. I was very sorry for your loss.'

'She was a good girl, you know. A good girl. Ever since her mother died...'

'Was that a long time ago?'

'Amy was only nine when Megan went. She tried to look after her, tried to look after me...'

He was still looking towards Billy, still pointing the gun at him, but his eyes and his mind were elsewhere.

Somehow, sometime, a long time ago, someone had tried to make the kitchen homely. The curtains, now drooping, were made of pretty flowered material. The cushion on the settle I was sitting on was filthy and ragged, but it had once been brightly coloured patchwork. Some woman had sat here, maybe by the range when it was polished and warm, sat here in the light of the oil lamp making a cheerful cushion for the family kitchen.

Most of the dresser was given over to bits of machinery and papers, but from the hooks on the top shelf there still hung some jugs and mugs. Among them was a Coronation mug for Queen Elizabeth. Amy must have put that there, years after her mother died, when she was trying to keep the home going.

'Megan had cancer,' the farmer said, as if trying

153

to make Billy understand. 'She was a long time dying, a terrible long time. If she'd been a beast I'd have shot her, put her out of her pain. But I just had to watch and do nothing.'

'It must have been a terrible time. For you as well as her.'

Littlejohn gave Billy a sharp look. But Billy seemed quite open, honest and straightforward.

'So then it was just you and Amy?' asked Billy, his eyes never leaving Littlejohn's face.

'Ay, and she did her best. I wasn't much good, I know that. The girl needed her mother. There was too much to do, and it was hard. She was a young woman, I didn't realise.'

'Of course you didn't,' said Billy soothingly. 'They grow up so quickly, don't they?'

Littlejohn nodded dumbly.

'And then I looked at her one day. She was bending over, putting coal on the range. And she looked just like my Megan did when she was carrying Amy. I knew then.'

'That she was expecting a baby?'

Littlejohn nodded.

'So you were angry with Amy?'

Littlejohn looked astonished.

'No, not with Amy. Ay, she'd been foolish right enough, but plenty more have been no wiser. No, I wasn't angry with her. Not with her. But with that stuck-up cowardly lad she'd got involved with, that namby pamby boy with his la-di-dah accent and his college scarf. I was angry with him. And when he said he wanted nothing to do with Amy, nothing to do with his baby. That he didn't want Mummy and Daddy to know because it would upset them – upset them! – then I was really bloody angry.'

He slammed the table with one hand, and bits of machinery clattered about. Susan whimpered and clung even closer to me.

Despite the current nightmare, I was beginning to feel sorry for Mr Littlejohn. But even more sorry for Amy. She must have been left pretty much to bring herself up. What a bloody tragedy she'd hit on Jeremy Cavendish.

Despite my fear, curiosity overtook me. How on earth did a grubby little girl from this neglected farm get to meet the likes of Jeremy Cavendish? How on earth did their worlds ever collide? I must have asked the question aloud because Littlejohn looked at me and said, 'The Hirings.'

The Hirings? For a minute I was lost, then I remembered what I'd read in those old newspapers in the bound file room. The Hirings was the old name for the annual fair in the town, famous throughout the country. Everyone went to The Hirings, all ages, all backgrounds, all rubbing shoulders in the dark and the music and the excitement. Easy to see how Amy and Jeremy could have bumped into each other there.

'So what happened?' Billy asked in a low, coaxing voice.

'I wanted that Cavendish to come here and face me like a man, wanted to know what he was going to do for Amy and his child she was carrying. But he wouldn't come. He laughed at Amy, told her that he would never want anything to do with the likes of her, and she should have known that all along. Told her she must be mad if she thought he'd marry her. He was at the university and he had to get on with his studies. Nothing must interrupt that. His books were more important than my little girl and the baby.

'I didn't want his money. But Amy loved him and if she wanted him I wanted her to have him. I'd done so little for her, you see, given her nothing. If I could give her him, then maybe that would make things better...'

He was lost for a moment in his thoughts, gazing blankly at the dismal room. Billy just stood there, pleasantly, sort of caring, not threatening at all. Mr Littlejohn went on.

'I was going over there after she told me, that night, even though it were nearly midnight, I wanted to go there and see him and his precious Mummy and Daddy and tell them that it was my little girl, my baby that he ruined. But Amy cried and sobbed and made me promise to wait till morning when I was calmer. So I said I would.

'But next morning she was gone. I looked all over and she was nowhere here. I knew something was wrong, something had happened. And then they came and told me they'd found her in the river...'

Tears were streaming down his unshaven face. Susan and I clung closer together on the settle. But Billy just stood there so calmly. As if it were the most natural thing in the world that this old man should be telling him all this. And the old man just carried on talking.

'He broke her heart. And I could never forgive him for that. You know he never turned up at court, did he? Didn't have the decency to do that

156

for the girl he wronged. Just wiped his hands of her like she was a bit of muck and got back to his precious studies.

'He was useless, a weak and useless excuse for a man. I despised him for what he'd done to Amy and her baby.

'Then, last night I saw him. I'd been in the Blue Bells at Barton, and as I came through Witton I saw him. Gone midnight it was and he was with some of his hoity-toity college friends, leaving the Lion in Witton, laughing, happy as you like, not a care nor a trouble in the world.

'Now that's not right, is it? You can't go ruining someone's life and then go laughing. Not when a girl and her baby are drowned in the river. And she looked so like her mother.'

He paused, and still with his hand on his gun, picked up the whisky bottle and took a huge gulp.

'So I followed him. I knew which way he'd go. I waited till he was alongside the woods, then I drove up and got him. Didn't even put up a fight. He whimpered like a dog. I shot him, like a dog. The world's well rid.

'I was there in the woods, thinking about Megan and Amy and what had happened. Then I realised it was well past dawn. I tried to cover him up, till I realised how late it was. I took the track through the woods. Nobody uses it, but then the little girl saw me. So I picked her up and brought her too. I shouldn't have done that, I know, but I wasn't thinking straight.

'I wasn't going to hurt her, you know,' he said, and I believed him. 'But I didn't want her telling

157

everyone that she'd seen me. I'm sorry I frightened her, but I was never going to hurt her. There's too many been hurt already.'

He looked at me. And despite it all, I felt sorry for him again. He was a desperate man driven by despair. He nodded his head at Susan, wrapped in my arms.

'Why don't you take the little lass out of here? Take her somewhere warm. It's too cold here and I've no food to give her. She'll be hungry, poor thing. Take her back to her mother. If she's got a mother, she'll be pining for her.'

Billy nodded at me. I took hold of Susan and practically carried her out of the house. I had difficulty opening the big old-fashioned latch on the kitchen door, but finally I was out into the darkness and foulness of the yard. The dog growled, but made no attempt to come near me.

I stood out in the filthy yard, hardly able to breathe. I couldn't believe I'd got out of there. And got Susan out as well. My legs had turned to jelly. They were shaking. I wasn't sure they could hold me up. I wanted to know about Billy. I wanted to see him safe out of there too. But Susan was still clinging to my arm. I had to think of her.

What now?

'Right, Susan,' I said as brightly and encouragingly as I could. 'We're going to walk up this track to the road and then see if we can find the motorbike. Are you all right?'

She sort of nodded, but by now, the tears were streaming down her face, and who could blame her? We trudged up the mucky track, Susan still wearing Billy's jacket and blowing her nose on

158

the handkerchief she'd found in his pocket. Then I heard the sound of cars coming slowly along the road. As the first one rounded the corner, I snatched the hanky off the bewildered Susan and waved it, so the driver could see us in the dark. The cars stopped. In the light from the head-lamps I could just make out the distinctive shapes of police uniforms. I have never in my life been so relieved to see the police.

'Chief Inspector! Am I pleased to see you.'

'Rose Harford! Is this Susan Williams? Thank goodness you're safe. Are you all right?'

Susan nodded, and we bundled her into the car. It smelt of leather and tobacco.

'Where's your colleague?'

'He's still in there, with Littlejohn. Littlejohn's confessed to killing Jeremy Cavendish. He's just let us go. He's got a gun, but I don't think he's dangerous.'

With that a gunshot rang out. The sound shattered the night. It echoed and bounced around the farmhouse in the little dip. The dog barked wildly and ran around the yard, the chain clanking. Susan clung to me, and I gasped, 'Will!'

Oh please God, not Will, not Billy. He'd got the little girl and me out safely. Please God don't let him be killed. I started to run back down the muddy slope, but the Chief Inspector grabbed me. 'Stay there!' he snapped. 'Look after the girl!' And he and the other policemen swarmed down the hill to the farmhouse.

Susan was curled up into herself in the back seat of the car. She was rocking herself back and forth and making small whimpering sounds. It was heartbreaking. But my heart was breaking for Billy too. He had been so calm, so clever, so utterly brilliant. He had to be alive. He had to be.

I leant into the car and stroked Susan's arm. 'There, there,' I crooned. 'It will be all right, don't worry. You're safe now. You'll soon be home, back with your mum. You're safe, don't worry.' All the time I was trying to look past her, to see down the hill to the farmhouse, trying to calm myself as much as the little girl.

The Chief Inspector was giving orders while his men waited in the shadows. They were facing a man with a gun – a very angry and disturbed man who had already killed someone – and they weren't armed.

Armed?! They didn't even have flak jackets or shields. They had nothing, no protection at all. Just their helmets and native wit. It was madness, but they hadn't seemed to hesitate. How brave they were, I thought. To do what they were doing took huge physical courage.

I carried on trying to soothe Susan, but by now I was so tense, so anxious about Billy that I could hardly breathe, let alone speak. What had happened in that kitchen? Please God let Billy be all right. Please God.

Then the farmhouse door opened. A small gleam of yellow light gradually fanned out in front of it. My hand froze on Susan's arm as I tried to make out what was happening. I could see a figure in the doorway, illuminated in the lamp-light. It was impossible to see who it was. Fear filled my throat. Then the figure moved forward. He was tall and slim, in shirtsleeves...

Billy. It was Billy. Thank you God. Thank you. Billy was walking out of the house. He was safe. Susan saw him too and gasped. I wanted to run back down the hill and fling my arms around Billy, but Susan was clinging to me. We hugged each other, shaking and sobbing from relief.

Down in the yard Billy was surrounded by policemen. I could see him talking to them, pointing back inside the house. They went in while he walked slowly, wearily up the hill and got in the Chief Inspector's car.

I still had one arm around Susan, but I stretched out with the other towards Billy. I just had to touch him, to know he was really alive. He returned the pressure gently, then over Susan's head, he put his finger to his lips. Then he bent his head down towards her and said, 'It's all right sweetheart. We're going home now.'

He leant back against the leather upholstery of the seat, closed his eyes, blew a sigh and shook his head as if to clear it of the things he had seen.

More police cars came, their lights bobbing along the narrow road. A policeman took us back, first to The Grange, where Joyce Williams hugged her daughter so hard that she must almost have broken her ribs. She took her into the house, but I don't think there was much wild rejoicing because, after all, Jeremy Cavendish, her employers' son, was dead.

Then Billy told me that Littlejohn had shot himself.

'Didn't you try to stop him?' I asked.

'What? Just so he could hang instead?' said Billy. 'It was a kindness to let him do it. It was the only decent thing he could have done. Saved the trouble of a trial and the hangman's noose.'

I thought of those flowery curtains, the patchwork cushion. Twenty years ago that must have been a happy home. And it had come to that. I started shivering and couldn't stop. Billy put his arm around me, kindly, companionably, concerned.

He smelt of sweat and mud, a very masculine smell, strange but very comforting. He squeezed my shoulder gently. The place where he had touched me flushed with heat. I grasped his hand. I longed to cling to him, hold him tightly, make sure he was really all right. I wanted to hold his face in my hands and kiss every little hollow of his cheekbones in gratitude that he was here, alive and well.

He smiled at me, and, as his eyes held mine, for a moment I thought I saw my emotions mirrored in his. But then gently, wearily, he eased his hand out of mine, putting a distance between us, and we just sat like that in the back of the police car as they drove us into town.

'G'night,' said the policeman as he stopped to let us out in front of *The News*. 'I'll read all about it in the morning.'

'We've got to write it first,' laughed Billy, taking my hand to help me out of the car. We went into the yard, past the vans and the newspaper hoist and in through the back door, to the shabby back staircase. Billy stopped in the shadows at the foot of the stairs, and put his hands on my shoulders.

'You were terrific tonight,' he said. 'The way you looked after the kid and calmed her down.'

'You were pretty fantastic yourself,' I said. 'My God, he could have shot you! One wrong word and, oh, I don't want to think about what could have happened.'

'We must be a great team, then, mustn't we?' He smiled down at me and for a moment, just a moment, I thought he was going to lean down, put his head close to mine and... But no.

'Come on! We've got a story to write and we'll make the last edition if we're quick.' And he was bounding up the stairs ahead of me. I trailed behind, my legs suddenly weary from fatigue and disappointment.

Phil was the only person left on the editorial floor. Billy told him what had happened, then swiftly and efficiently wrote up a brief account for the last edition, occasionally asking me about a word, a sentence, making it a joint effort. He took the copy down to the works, then went into the editor's office, returning to his desk with a bottle of whisky. He poured generous measures for the three of us into the quickly washed teacups. 'I think we've earned this,' he said.

As we filled in more of the details, Phil knocked back the last of his whisky and said, 'Two things. One, where's my motorbike? And two, what's that stink?'

I looked down. My left leg was still covered in cow shit.

Chapter Eleven

Next morning all I wanted was to see that Billy was all right. I ran across town and clattered upstairs to the newsroom.

He was there. He was sitting at his desk typing, and as I walked in he looked up and smiled at me.

'Good morning!' he said. 'Isn't it nice to be here?'

And I didn't care what anyone thought. I went over to him and put my hands on his. 'Are you OK?'

'Yes, of course.' He didn't move his hands away but instead curled up his fingers until they were wrapped around mine. I gazed at him. He looked pretty bleary too, but his hands were warm and rough on mine. I untangled one of my hands and put it on his shoulder, reaching up, gently to his head.

'Bad dreams?' he asked.

'Just a bit. I needed to know you were all right.' And I just stood there for a while, feeling the warmth of his hand.

'Takes more than a mad farmer with a rusty shotgun to get rid of me.'

'I thought ... I thought you were brilliant with him. Great negotiating skills.' I tried to laugh.

'You were good with the kid. Very calm. It helped.'

'Good.'

We were still and silent for a moment. Me standing, him sitting, still touching, just looking into each other's eyes, saying nothing, saying everything.

Then he gave my hand a final squeeze and moved his hand away.

'And now we'd better get down to some work,' he said briskly. 'And you'd better go around to the police station and make a statement. I've already done mine.'

The working world came back into focus. My heart slowed down to something more normal. Billy wound paper and carbons into his typewriter and started tapping away on a longer fuller version of the very brief report we'd done just a few hours earlier. Billy talked it through as he wrote it, and, although it was tricky, what with Jeremy Cavendish being dead and Littlejohn having shot himself, I added bits, suggested bits and together we made a decent fist of it. If I'd been writing it up in the twenty-first century, I would have been plastered all over the pages, with my picture. But then it was a much more sober affair, and the only byline was 'Our Reporters'.

But after that night and that story, everything seemed to get easier. I began to feel accepted as part of the team at *The News,* and the others started treating me like one of them, which was good. It helped, of course, that the old lech Gordon was still hopping around on his crutches and couldn't get in. I still kept clear of the subs' room, mind.

I began to feel less fraught about what was

165

going on. Where I was in time and space – Narnia or over the blessed rainbow – didn't seem to matter quite so much.

Working with Will got no easier. Seeing him every day and not being able to hold him, talk to him, be with him the way I once had was torture. And the friendlier we became, the more companionable and easier with each other, the worse it was.

But that morning, everyone wanted to know what had happened. Even Peggy was quite chatty and she made me a cup of tea – using the editor's kettle, how honoured – while I told her all about it. I'd just got to the bit where I was telling her how Billy had calmed Littlejohn down. 'Littlejohn was so angry and Billy just spoke to him quietly and it was like magic…' when Leo walked in.

Leo! I thought back to when I'd seen him the day before all this began, in the pub with Jake, arm in arm, laughing, and so excited about their civil partnership plans.

'Leo?' I asked. 'Is it you?'

He looked at me blankly, and it was Will and Caz all over again. But I think I was sort of expecting that. Peggy jumped up from her desk. 'Hello Lenny!' she cried. 'I've got a great pile of books here for you.'

She turned to me. 'This is Lenny. He does a lot of our book reviews. He reads an awful lot.' She giggled archly. 'That's why he's got no time for girls.'

'So that's why, is it?' I said and put my foot in it big time. Well I mean, when Peggy said that he had no time for girls I thought she *knew* Leo/ Lenny was gay. I mean, why else would she say something so stupid unless she meant it as a joke, however feeble?

'So how's Jake?' I asked. 'Are you still with Jake Andrews? Or is that different here too?'

Lenny looked as if I'd hit him. He really did. He went white, then red, and gazed at me as if I'd told him the worst news in the world.

Peggy was fussing about with a pile of books on the shelf behind her desk so, luckily, couldn't see Lenny's expression.

Lenny seemed terrified. 'I don't know what you mean,' he said. Then he picked up his briefcase, hurriedly, awkwardly. 'I have to go, Peggy. I'll see you later.'

'What about...?' But Lenny had gone, practically running from the room.

'Well, what's the matter with him?' said Peggy. 'He's normally so nice and chatty. Ah well, must have got out of bed the wrong side. Right, now tell me about the farmer. Did you actually see him shoot himself?'

Sighing, I finished the story.

Later, when Billy and I were checking the page proof of our story, I said, 'Billy, can I ask you something?'

'Mmm?' He was drinking a cup of tea while reading the proof. It was such a Will attitude and response. Ouch. I was getting better at separating Will and Billy, but it wasn't easy.

'Tell me, is it acceptable to be gay around here?'

He looked at me a bit blankly.

167

'Well, er, of course it is. You can be as gay as you like. Laugh, sing, you don't have to be gloomy. A bit of gaiety is always cheering.'

Now it was my turn to look blank. 'No, not gay like that, I mean *gay*.'

Blank look.

'Gay as in homosexual.'

A faint light began to dawn in Billy's eyes. 'You mean like er, like…' He was clearly a bit embarrassed, which was sweet.

'I mean one man loving another man.'

Was Billy blushing? Just a hint of pink on his gorgeous hollow cheekbones?

'Like, um, queers and nancy boys?'

'Exactly like that. Is it acceptable? I guess by your reaction it isn't.'

'Well it's against the law for a start.'

Oh God, of course, I'd forgotten. Homosexuality was illegal until, oh I don't know when, the 1960s I think. 'But even though it's illegal…' I mean, a lot of things are illegal but quite acceptable, aren't they? Like speeding or smoking dope, or dodging your tax. '…even though it's illegal, is it still, well, all right?'

Billy was definitely blushing now.

'Well, er yes, there are people you know, who are, well, who are … there were a few in the army. But, well, you don't make a song and dance about it, because well, you just don't. Right now, can we just get on with this please?'

He was *so* embarrassed, poor boy. I wondered whether it was because he was talking about gays, or just because he was talking about gays to a woman. Very funny really. But it told me what I

168

needed to know, and it looked as though I had dropped Leo/Lenny right into it. I wondered whether I should tell Billy about some of Elton John's parties. Maybe he wasn't quite ready to hear that from me...

I was just smiling to myself about that when Phil, the reporter on night shift, came in. 'Have you got your motorbike back?' I asked.

'Yes thanks. Only a young copper seemed to think there was something very suspicious about it all.'

'Is there much activity up there?'

'No, we sent a reporter up earlier, but I think the police have more or less finished there now. Up to the solicitors now, I suppose.'

'I wonder what will happen to the house, if there's anyone to inherit it. If so, they should have helped Littlejohn when he was alive.'

'It will probably be a tenancy. The estate will take it back and let it out again to someone.'

'Let's hope they have better luck there. Anyway, what are we going to do about a follow-up?'

'Follow-up?' Both Billy and Phil looked at me as if I were talking a foreign language.

'Yes. I mean this has been a terrific story, but shouldn't we be getting more background about the Littlejohns? What led up to this tragedy, etc, etc? And see how Susan's coping? And her mum? You know, "My Night of Anguish, by shotgun girl's mum"?' I was looking at them eagerly. They were looking at me blankly.

'I don't think so,' said Billy. 'Let's just let them get on with it in peace now,' he said. He took some papers and walked out of the office, leaving me feeling a bit of an idiot.

'Look, Rosie.' It was Phil's turn to look a bit embarrassed now. 'Tonight's my last day on nights. I've got tomorrow off, then I start on days again. Would you like to come to the flicks with me on Thursday?'

I looked at him. I was still thinking of follow-ups, and he was asking me out. A date! It was ages since anyone had asked me for a date. Because of course, I was with Will. But not here I wasn't. But my heart was... Oh why not? This was only a pretend world after all. I smiled. 'Right, yes. OK Phil, that would be really nice. I'd like that.'

'That's good,' said Phil. 'I'll see you Thursday then. We'll go straight from work.' And he gave me a sweet smile and got on with making the first calls of the evening.

When I got home everyone wanted to know about the kidnapping and the murder. So I had to tell the story all over again, over the sausage and grey-looking mash.

'Well I don't care what anyone says,' said Mrs Brown firmly, as she cleared the plates away, 'all this started when that silly girl got herself in the family way. If she'd had more sense...'

'But she didn't get herself pregnant on her own, Mrs Brown,' I said. 'She must have been desperate to kill herself.'

'She drowned herself in Friars' Mill, didn't she?' asked Peggy quietly.

'Yes,' I said. 'Jeremy Cavendish had presumably said he'd stand by her, and when he didn't she shamed him by killing herself almost on his doorstep.'

'Ha! There's a lot of girls have trusted a fellow and look where it's got them. Silly girl. Should have kept her hand on her ha'penny. No better than she should be and look where it's led to,' snapped Mrs Brown, coming back to the table with the pudding.

And that's when I opened my big mouth...

'If only they'd been sensible,' I said. 'If only she'd been on the pill or something.'

'Pill?' asked Peggy sharply.

'Yes, you know, the contraceptive pill. No, actually you probably don't, do you? There's a pill you take that stops you getting pregnant. And if you slip up then there's another, the Morning After pill, which you can take up to three days after unprotected sex and...'

'And that's quite enough of *that* thank you,' said Mrs Brown banging down a dish of stewed apples so hard that they slopped over the edge and onto the tablecloth. 'We won't have any of that sort of smutty talk in this household.'

Bang! A jug of custard was also slammed down and slopped over.

'I've never heard of such a thing. And you think you can come out with filth like that while we're having our supper. Oh no lady, I don't know what you do in America, but we don't have that sort of thing here. I will not have that sort of talk in my house, if you don't mind.'

She almost threw the spoonfuls of apple into the bowls and pushed them in front of us. I realised I had genuinely upset her.

'I'm very sorry, Mrs Brown,' I said contritely – she was a seriously scary woman – 'I didn't mean to upset you. It's just that where I come from we talk quite openly of...'

'Enough!'

I shut up and concentrated on my apple and custard. There was much spooning and slurping, but otherwise a deadly silence. Then Mr Brown, bless him, pointed out that they had more important matters to discuss.

'We'll soon be saying goodbye to this house, then,' he said.

Overshadowed by the dramatic events at Little-john's had been the council meeting that Alan had been to cover. The plans for the bypass and new inner ring road had been approved.

'Well, that's it then,' said Mr Brown. 'Just as well we never got you that fancy kitchen you wanted.'

'Why?' I asked. 'Will it affect you?'

'Whole street's coming down.'

'Oh gosh, really? Are you sure?'

'This one and all of Watergate and Fisher Quay.'

'Oh, but they're lovely old buildings!' I had passed and admired them on my way to work. They were an interesting collection of higgledy-piggledy timbered buildings, not a straight line to be seen. True, they were a bit dilapidated, but they were interesting and historic and beautiful, over-looking the river. They must have dated back cen-turies, and were a real part of the town's heritage.

'Get away with you!' said Mr Brown scornfully, as Mrs Brown passed him a cup of tea. 'The Quay's been a right warren of slums ever since I was a lad. Terrible place, only good for rats and

172

thieves. Best thing to pull it down. Pull the whole lot down as far as I'm concerned. Let's have something new and clean in the town. Something modern.'

'But this is your home! Where will you go?'

'They told us we'll get one of those new houses they're building up at The Meadows. Nice-looking houses they are. They're what I call proper houses. Nice and light with big windows. And they won't have the water and rats flooding into the cellars every time there's a bit of rain. They'll be all new and modern, with a proper garden on the flat and all.'

'What about you, Mrs Brown?' I was trying hard to get back into her good books. 'Won't you miss this house?'

'Not a bit. They can have it. I want a nice new house without damp in the walls, and cracked old cupboards and shelves that you can't keep clean however hard you try. And no more blooming mice. And a front garden! Oooh, it'll be lovely to have a front garden, not to walk straight in off the street with every Tom, Dick and Harry staring straight in your windows.

'Mind you, I've brought my kids up in this house, so it's got happy memories. But now I want some comfort and convenience in my old age. No, I won't be sorry to leave here.'

I looked at the proposed plan as shown in *The News*. It showed the inner ring-road sweeping over a new bridge and alongside the river. It looked familiar. Of course! That's how the town used to be until just before I'd started on *The News* when they'd closed the original inner ring-road, and pedestrianised it. The area alongside the river now had smart new bars and restaurants, and an arts centre. Funnily enough, they'd called it Fisher Quay. If only they'd kept some of the original buildings...

In my time we were desperate to hark back to the past, to hang on to anything old, however useless and dubious. But here the Browns were longing for the future. They seemed to think that everything could only get better, that the future was new and exciting, a great big present just waiting to be unwrapped.

And who was I to disillusion them?

Chapter Twelve

I was just on my way back to the office, dodging through the stalls of the midweek market, when I saw a familiar figure in her brown coat. Carol was struggling with a basket, a string bag full of vegetables and a brown paper carrier bag as well. 'Here, let me take one of those.'

'Oh hello, Rosie. Thanks. I got a bit carried away, all these carrots and potatoes.'

I took the string bag from her. A little shower of soil fell to the ground. You don't often see vegetables with soil on now, do you, unless you shop at the farmers' market.

'Libby not with you?'

'No, she's playing at a neighbour's house so I thought I'd take the chance to dash into town.

174

You been doing anything interesting?'

'An exhibition at the town hall. Very boring.'

'Can't always be murders and shootings then. Bit too exciting that, if you ask me.'

'Billy was brilliant, Carol, absolutely brilliant. So calm and brave. Littlejohn was so unpredictable, he could have done anything, but Billy really calmed him down. Weren't you worried about him?'

'No, because by the time I knew about it, it was over, wasn't it? And he was all right. No point worrying over something that didn't happen. Let's just be thankful that little girl was safe and didn't get hurt. Sad about the young lad though, but mind you, he sounded a bit of a rotter. Leading that girl on and walking out on her. Poor cow. I don't know what I'd have done if Billy'd walked out on me. Still, it didn't happen, so no point worrying about it. Look, I can manage from here, if you've got to get back to work.'

'No, it's all right. It's a pretty quiet morning and they're not expecting me back yet anyway.'

'Fancy a cuppa?'

'Why not?'

We walked companionably on, carrying the shopping between us, along the narrow street and down the hill into the low, dark, damp house. I glanced up at the garden.

'Billy spent all yesterday evening fussing on with that old shed,' said Carol, pushing open the door. 'I think he's wasting his time, it's had it. Still, he might treat himself to a new one when we move.'

I tried to imagine Will getting excited over a

shed. Tricky. Not quite as sexy as a widescreen plasma TV.

In the kitchen – the mouldering smell of damp hit me as I walked in – Carol moved the kettle from the hearth and put it on the fire on the actual coals. She gave them a quick poke and soon the coals were glowing and the kettle steaming.

'Ugh! What's that?'

A large bowl on the wooden draining board seemed to be full of swirling blood and raw flesh, with some very functional looking tubes. Carol looked surprised. 'Hearts, soaking for supper.'

'Hearts? You'll eat them?'

'Yes, haven't you ever had them? Got a bit of stuffing for them. Very tasty.'

She lifted the kettle off the coals, made the tea and put the pot down on the table. I sat down, with my back to the bowl with the hearts in. Despite the gloom, it was a cosy kitchen. There was a jug of daffodils on the windowsill, a brightly-coloured rug in front of the fire, and pretty patchwork cushions on the chairs.

On the arm of the chair next to the table, half hidden by a Sooty glove puppet, was a library book.

'Oh, who's reading *Lucky Jim*?'

'Billy. He's really enjoying it. Says I'll like it when he's finished.'

'It's one of Will's favourites.'

'Tell me about this Will then,' she said, pouring the tea.

'Well, he's very like Billy. Very like. Amazingly like.'

'Are you going to get married?'

176

'I don't know. I'm not sure he's ready for it yet. Not to settle down.'

'How old is he?'

'Same age as Billy.'

Carol laughed.

'Well that's old enough. Billy and me have been married for eleven years.'

'Yes, but it's sort of different.'

'Is he good to you?'

'Oh yes.'

'Does he make you laugh?'

'Often.'

'Is he kind, generous?'

'Very.'

'And is he, you know, do you like him, does he make you go tingly all over?'

'Oh yes, definitely!'

'Then what are you waiting for, girl, snap him up!'

'But what if he doesn't want to be snapped up?' I put my cup back in its saucer and looked at Carol. I really wanted to know the answer.

'Oh men do. There's not many men that's happy on their own. They pretend they want to be roaring lads off with their mates, but really, they just want a family to look after. They want someone they can trust beside them. You know what they say, "Behind every great man is a woman". Well, they need us. Useless without us.'

'Where I come from, a lot of men don't get married. Women neither. They might just live together for a while, sort of semi-detached.'

'Oho, try before you buy, is it?'

'No, not like that. It's sort of more short-term.

You can give each other lots of space.'

'Space?' Carol glanced around the crowded kitchen. 'Space?'

'Well, not thinking too far ahead. Lots of women choose not to have children. They have jobs, same jobs as the men.'

'Someone's got to look after the kids though, haven't they? That's why I'm going to work at the school. Fits in nicely. Don't want my lot to be latchkey kids.'

'Yes, but...'

'Anyway, you don't want to be left on the shelf. If this Will is anything like Billy, what are you waiting for?'

'I don't know any more. I really don't know. When I see him again...' I imagined Will in front of me. But it was hard, as he kept getting confused with Billy. I shook my head to clear the vision.

'Anyway, I'm going out with Phil tonight. Just to the pictures. Nothing, you know ... just as a friend really.'

'Ooh, what would your Will say about that? Still, what the eye don't see, the heart don't grieve over. You have a good time while you can. But he's a nice lad, Phil, so don't you go leading him on and breaking his heart.'

'That is the last thing I want to do. It's just a night out. But I'd better get back to work. Thanks for the tea.'

'Any time. Enjoy yourself tonight.' She was already wrapping her apron around her, ready to tackle that heap of vegetables and the bleeding hearts.

Phil had been looking at me knowingly all day and every now and then, despite myself, I'd feel quite excited. Well, excited is probably too strong a word, but anticipatory perhaps. And then I'd look at Billy and know that he was the only man I ever wanted, and that it was pointless to go out with anyone else. But it was better than sitting at home at the Browns, watching the tiny black-and-white TV screen. So, when Phil came along to my desk to collect all my ready copy, and grinned shyly saying, 'I'm ready to go now,' I went along to the tiny awkward cloakroom and had a wash and cleaned my teeth and did my best with the make-up.

Feeling a bit fresher, if not exactly glammed up for a night on the razz, I came back to the newsroom.

'Oh ho, so that's the way it is then, is it?' said Charlie the Chief Photographer as we walked out together. Billy looked up from his typewriter and gave me a strange look. Our eyes met, and for a moment, I thought he was going to ask what I was doing and try to stop me. He frowned, then forced a quick smile. 'Enjoy the film,' he said.

'We shall!' yelled Phil back at him and we manoeuvred our way down the chaotic narrow stairs.

Downstairs, outside on the pavement, he hesitated for a moment, a bit unsure. Not as unsure as I was. I mean I'd never been on a 1950s date. Come to that, not even my parents had been on a 1950s date. And I had never talked to my grandparents about dating...

'I thought we'd get something to eat at the Odeon,' said Phil.

179

'Oh, can you eat there?'

'Yes, they've got a café upstairs. It's about the only place you can get food at this time of night. The Copper Kettle's closed. Silvino has the back place open, but that's full of kids.'

'Right. The Odeon it is.'

The Odeon was a wonderful old cinema. All red plush and gold curly bits. Two huge staircases curved upon either side of the foyer. In the middle was a tiny little booth of a box office where Phil bought our tickets. The best in the house – 3/9 each, which isn't even twenty pence in modern money. We went up one of the staircases – it felt terribly grand – and found ourselves in a café. One wall had windows overlooking the street and the other had windows that looked out over the auditorium, so you could sit there and eat and watch the film if you liked.

I was longing to eat something spicy or garlicky. Everything I'd eaten lately seemed to have been so bland. Some garlic ciabatta or a Thai green curry would have gone down a treat.

The menu offered poached egg on toast, scrambled egg on toast, cheese on toast, beans on toast, sardines on toast, mushrooms on toast, tomato soup or ham sandwiches, cheese sandwiches, egg sandwiches. Right. No low carb diet here then.

'What are you having?' I asked Phil.

'Poached egg on toast for me.'

'I'll have the same please.'

'And a pot of tea for two,' said Phil to the middle-aged waitress in dusty black dress and white pinny.

I ate my poached egg, drank my tea and thought wistfully of our local curry house...

'So how did you get to be a reporter then?' asked Phil.

I told him about my A levels and the degree and the postgrad course.

'You did a degree? Just to be a reporter? And then spent another year learning all about it?' Phil was so astonished he had difficulty not spraying egg everywhere.

'Well yes. It's the usual way now.'

'But you must have been twenty-two when you got your first job.'

'Yes. Twenty-two and a half when I started on the *Swaledale Courant*.'

'Blimey, I'd been working seven years by then. Eight if you count all the stuff I did when I was still at school.'

'What, you were writing for *The News* when you were fifteen?'

'Fourteen actually. Did sports reports, not that there was much sport on during the war. And I wrote pieces about the concerts and the fundraising efforts until in the end old Mr Henfield was asking me to do things official like. There weren't many people around. He was glad of anything really. So I just did what I could. Taught myself to type and learnt shorthand at evening classes.'

'Have you been on *The News* ever since?'

'Apart from national service, yes. I keep thinking I might go to Fleet Street, but I'm not sure. What I'd really like to do is go to Australia. All that sunshine would be wonderful.'

And he hadn't even seen *Neighbours*.

181

Our eggs and toast finished, I realised Phil was waiting for me to be 'mother' and pour the tea.

'You could make your name in Fleet Street,' I said, passing him his tea.

'Well, there was a chap in the army. He's on the *Express* now. He says there's a job there for me if I want it.'

'Go for it!'

'Do you think I should?'

'Of course I do. A job in Fleet Street! No question. You're young, single. You're a good journalist. Have you anything to keep you here? Family?'

'Well, there's my parents, but I've got two sisters who live locally. They're both married with kids so Mum and Dad wouldn't be short of people to keep an eye on them.'

'Do you want to be on *The News* for ever?'

'No. I mean I like it well enough, but there are other places, aren't there? Other things to do? When I was in the army I met all sorts of different blokes, and here, well, here I just meet the people I've always known. Or who know the people I've always known. That's why it was so great when you came here. You're so different, from the other side of the world with different ideas, a different way of doing things. I really like that.'

Oh dear, he was beginning to look at me. Meaningfully. I wasn't sure I could cope.

'You'd love it in London,' I said quickly. 'All those new people, all those stories. And a real chance to make your name. You could be famous, get to cover all the big stories. And you could do it. You're as good as any of the national people.'

'Well, I could have a go. I know I'd be as good

as my mate on the *Express* and he's doing all right for himself.'

'Well there you are then. Go for it. It could be great.'

'It would, wouldn't it?' he grinned. 'Well maybe I shall.'

He paid the bill – refusing my offer to go halves – and we went into see the film. It was *Blackboard Jungle,* and had music with Bill Haley. 'Best be careful,' said Phil, 'when they showed this in some places the teddy boys started ripping the seats.'

'Oh, a riot. Be a good story though wouldn't it?'

He laughed as he led the way to the seats.

I was looking forward to seeing *Blackboard Jungle.* I remembered watching it at about two in the morning when I'd come in from a not very good party. That would have been tricky to explain to Phil... But when the film started it wasn't *Blackboard Jungle* at all, but some feeble cowboy film. I was about to tell Phil we were in the wrong studio when I realised that this was the supporting film, the B movie.

There was an interval and we had an ice cream and then settled down for the main feature. When the titles rolled and the Bill Haley music blasted out, a group of kids near the front yelled and whistled and tried to bop a bit, but everyone else told them to 'hush!' and the usherette came down the aisles with a big torch and said loudly, 'Any nonsense from you lot and you're OUT,' and they all settled down quietly again.

'No riots here then,' whispered Phil. 'Think we've missed our page one lead tomorrow.'

'Unless it's "Usherette curbs teenage gang violence with her torch",' I whispered back. I could just see Phil's grin in the dark.

'Good thing our schools aren't like that, eh?' he said later.

I thought of the story I'd done on The Meadows before the new headmistress had arrived there. Disaster. Kids on strike, drugs in school, stabbing in the playground. Mayhem. 'Oh yeah, good thing,' I whispered back.

When the lights went up, Phil grabbed my hand. 'Come on!' he urged and we scuttled out. Odd, I thought, then I heard a creaky rendition of the National Anthem and those people who weren't leaving, like us, were in their places, standing to attention. Sliding out just ahead of us were Leo/Lenny and Peggy. They must have been sitting a few rows behind us.

'Well, that's something I thought I'd never see,' said Phil. 'Still, nowt so queer as folk, as they say.' He looked at me in a sort of knowing way...

I smiled quickly, to show I understood, but after my very awkward conversation with Billy, I said nothing. It was dark now, and the town was quiet. There were just a few people coming from the cinema and leaving pubs, shouting their good-nights. The evening was over, people were clearly heading for home. I wished I was going home, proper home, wandering along the pavement with my arms wrapped around Will, after something as ordinary as a film. Home together. We could have a nightcap, curl up on the sofa together, go to bed...

I missed him so much I almost gasped with the pain of it. Instead, here I was with Phil, who was a perfectly nice, decent sort of bloke. But he wasn't Will.

I looked at my watch.

'What time do the pubs shut?' I asked Phil.

'Ten o'clock,' he said.

Too late even for a drink. Probably just as well.

After we left the town centre, we seemed to have the night and the streets to ourselves. Two buses pulled away from the Market Place, but there were only a handful of cars around. It was very peaceful. The noise of our footsteps echoed along the silent houses, until we got to the Browns'.

So what happens now? I wondered. 'I'm not sure if I can ask you in,' I said. 'It's not my house and...'

'It's all right, don't worry,' said Phil. He too looked hesitant.

'Well it's been a nice evening,' he said.

'Yes it has,' I said, and meant it. 'Thank you very much. And you should definitely have a crack at the Express. Really.'

'Yes I think I might, but don't mention it to the others, will you?'

'No, of course not.'

'No well, thank you.'

'Thank you.'

'See you tomorrow then.'

'Yes, see you tomorrow.'

He shifted his mac, which he had been carrying, from arm to arm and back again, then said again, 'Right. Well, see you tomorrow then.'

'Yes.'

'Goodnight Rosie.'

'Goodnight Phil.'

185

He turned and strode off up the road, leaving me with the key in the lock, wondering about not even getting a goodnight kiss...

Phil was a friendly face around the office, however. Someone to share a joke with, nip out for a coffee with. He was a lovely straightforward sort of chap and easy to talk to. Gordon had been a lech. Henfield still was. Alan more or less ignored me, and after that first disastrous evening, I avoided the sub editors as much as possible. Phil was the nearest to normal I had.

I was into the 1950s way of working now, adapted to a very different rhythm to the one I was used to. For a start, the phones didn't ring as often. People were more likely to turn up at the office, so I was constantly running up and down the stairs to see them. Or we would be out and about a lot more. Many of the people we interviewed didn't have a telephone, or wouldn't be comfortable interviewed that way. It was all face to face.

I didn't keep stopping to check texts on my phone – still dead and useless. And, above all, there was no internet, no emails, no constant bombardment of information and press releases and news flashes. It was surprisingly restful. You could get on with doing something in your own time without constantly checking your inbox. Getting information was tricky, but up on the top floor, the librarians waded through files and cuttings and found out most of what we wanted. It just wasn't instant. No one expected things to be instant. And after a while, neither did I. All our twenty-first-century toys were designed to save us time and energy, so why were the 1950s so much less stressful? Weird. I would love to have talked about it to someone, if not Will, then Phil, but I wouldn't have known where to begin.

'You know I'll be going back home soon,' I said to him one day as we'd sneaked out for a coffee. 'And you'll be off to Fleet Street.'

He looked crestfallen for barely a second as his thoughts of a future with me fought with a future in Fleet Street. To my relief, Fleet Street won hands down. 'I've gathered some cuttings together, to show what I can do,' he said. 'I'm going to send them to my mate so he can show them to his editor.'

'Good move,' I said.

Phil was straightforward enough. As for Billy ... it was tricky being alone with him. I found it hard remembering how to behave, hard to behave naturally. Sometimes I could feel him watching me, but when I looked he was always intent on his story on the typewriter. Until one day I must have been quicker and caught his glance. And what a glance.

We gazed at each other across the newsroom. It was no ordinary look. I could feel myself blushing. With that Phil came in with a bag of currant buns.

'Feeding time at the zoo,' he announced, offering the bag around, 'courtesy of Councillor Armstrong, baker of this parish. Hopeless councillor but, luckily, a very good baker.'

He bowled a bun to Billy who batted it away with a ruler. Instinctively I reached up and caught it, to cheers from them both.

'Owzat!' shouted Phil. Billy smiled. An ordinary friendly sort of smile, which was both a relief and a disappointment to me.

A sort of camaraderie developed. But the real breakthrough came a few days later.

Billy was in with Smarmy Henfield. Alan was at a council meeting, and Phil was on the phone. The office was quiet and peaceful. I was typing away at some odds and ends of stories, when a messenger came up from reception to say there were two ladies downstairs who wanted to talk to a reporter. Off I went.

'Theatricals,' said the young messenger knowingly. Certainly the girls had stage presence. They were about eighteen years old, very smartly dressed and very heavily made up, with vivid red-painted nails. In the dusty reception area of *The News* they looked positively exotic.

'Are you a reporter?' one of them asked me, eyeing me up and down and not looking terribly impressed. 'A *proper* reporter?'

I assured them I was.

'Well we've got a story to tell and we want it told. He shouldn't be allowed to get away with it.'

'No he shouldn't,' said the other.

'We're decent girls.'

'Never heard of such a thing.'

'Perhaps,' I said gently, 'if you were to start at the beginning...'

Their names, they told me, with perfectly straight faces, were Marcella and Loulou. They were actresses with a touring company that was appearing at the Civic. I'd seen the notices and the reviews. It wasn't going well. It was a sort of French farce, I think.

'We play the maids,' said Loulou, or it may have been Marcella. 'We wear very short skirts that show off our assets.'

I bet, I thought.

'But we have a lot of lines to say. We're actresses.'

'We can sing too. And dance.'

'We used to be Dinky Diamond Dancers, but that was when we were young. Now we are developing our careers.'

'Good for you. So what's the problem?'

'Mr Hennessey.'

'He runs the company.'

'It's not going well. Hardly anyone in the audience even though he's given tickets away.'

'Hardly a snigger when he drops his trousers.'

'Even though he's wearing huge spotty underpants.'

'So he said,' and here their brassy confidence faltered a little. 'He *told* us.'

'That it would be better if, instead of him taking his clothes off, *we* did it.'

'If *you* did it?' I looked up sharply from my notebook. 'He wants you to take your clothes off on stage?'

'Yes. He says we'll be behind a screen – sort of hiding – when one of the wives comes in.'

'Then the juvenile lead rushes in and "accidentally" knocks the screen over. And there we are.'

'With nothing on.'

'As nature intended.'

'My mum will kill me.'

'My dad'll disown me.'

'But he said it will get the audiences in. All the men will come.'

'Good clean family fun, he says.'

'But we don't want to do it.'

'We're not going to.'

'We've got principles.'

'So we're going home. Leaving the company.'

'Right,' I said, trying to sort this out. 'Your boss wants you to be naked on stage and you don't want to be, so you're walking out. That seems sensible. So what's the problem?'

'He hasn't paid us.'

'Not for four weeks.'

'Says there's no money and there won't be unless we take our clothes off.'

'No punters, no pay, he says.'

'And certainly not what's owed us.'

'We're actresses, not strippers.'

'Why should we?'

Exactly. The phrases 'constructive dismissal' and 'sexual harassment' floated around in my head, but I didn't even think about it. Not where we were.

Instead, I got Charlie down to take a picture of the girls who, serious actresses that they were, pulled their skirts up above the knee and puckered up provocatively. I went around to see their actor manager, who was a slimy little beast. It was hard to imagine him as a jovial cove in huge spotty underpants. He was also a calculating old rogue and knew the value of publicity. He said if the girls would come back until the end of the run –

another two weeks – even with their clothes on, he'd pay them all he owed them and they would be free to go.

'And what about some compensation?'

He looked at me angrily.

'What do you mean compensation?'

'I mean you've upset those girls, bullied them into walking out of their jobs. Not to mention the fact you haven't paid them for a month.'

'Upset? Those two? Hard as nails, the little trollops. They're lucky to have a job at all. Have you seen the way they move on stage? Like baby bloody elephants. No one's queuing up to give those two jobs, believe me. And don't tell me that they wouldn't show all they've got if they had the chance. They'd have gone to Fanshaw's Follies and worn nothing more than a few feathers and a smile if they could. But they haven't got the ankles.'

I thought ankles were probably the most irrelevant qualification, but no matter.

You could see the actor/manager was dreadfully torn between paying up and the chance to turn bad publicity into excellent publicity. His business brain finally won. Eventually, we agreed that the girls would get all the wages due to them today, and that if they stayed to the end of the run, they'd get an extra fiver each.

'How can I pay them if the punters don't come in?'

'But you can, because they will. And you know that. But you'd better not bully any more young girls.'

The deal was done – maybe I'd missed my vocation as a trade union leader or UN negotiator –

and I was quite pleased with myself. The girls were waiting for me in Silvino's, and they took about five seconds to agree to the deal, so I went back to the office, and shared the story with the others. We were all laughing about it as I typed it up.

'Good result. Good story,' said Billy. 'But you realise that they'd probably have been quite happy to strip off if the price had been right?'

'Maybe, maybe not.' I actually wasn't so sure. 'But if they're going to do it, let them do it on their own terms, not bullied by some weaselly little beast.'

The men, of course, were suddenly all volunteering to be theatre reviewers.

'Boys, boys, what sorry lives you lead,' I said. I was just typing the last sentence when Billy came over.

'Phil and I are going over to The Fleece,' he said. 'Fancy joining us?' His eyes were still smiling from our laughter. Phil came and stood alongside him, smiling too.

'Yes come on, Rosie. I think we've all deserved a drink today.'

This, believe it or not, was the first time I had been invited to the pub with the lads. A couple of them went over most days, sometimes after work too, but they had never asked me. I don't know if they ever asked Marje. She always seemed to be scuttling off with her string bag to do her shopping. And I'd missed it. Not the pub necessarily, but the companionship I suppose, being part of a team.

So yes, I jumped at the chance to go to the pub.

I ripped my story out of the typewriter, folded it ready to go to the subs, and grabbed my bag.

'Afternoon, Jack,' said Phil as we walked into the small bar. 'Two pints of the usual, and ... what would you like Rosie?'

'Cider please.'

'And a half of cider.'

Who said I wanted a half? But I wasn't going to argue. See, I already knew my place.

'So who's this then?' asked the landlord as he pulled the pints.

'This is Miss Rosie Harford, a visiting journalist from America.'

'I'm not...' and I gave up again.

Phil got some crisps and we all sat in the corner and laughed again at the story of Marcella and Loulou. We had a game of darts and shared the last two curling cheese sandwiches, from under a plastic dome on the counter. Billy bought another and then, when the glasses were empty again, I got up. 'My turn,' I said, getting my purse out.

The landlord looked surprised, and Billy and Phil both objected.

'No,' I said. 'I insist. Where I come from, if we work we pay our turn.'

'Can we accept that?' said Billy, turning to Phil in mock seriousness.

'Do you know,' said Phil, equally serious, equally mocking, 'I think we can.' And they took their pints.

'Cheers,' said Phil companionably. Billy raised his glass and said, 'Your very good health, Miss Harford.' And his eyes smiled into mine. I leant back, sipping my cider, and a ray of dusty sunshine fell across my face. I relaxed. I almost felt I belonged.

Until I went home alone and Billy went home to his wife.

Chapter Thirteen

Peggy had beaten me to the bathroom. While I was being helpful and taking out the dishes she'd nipped upstairs and was now ensconced behind a firmly bolted door. I could hear the hot water gurgling and could smell Yardley soap and bath salts.

'She's got to make herself beautiful for her young man,' said Mrs Brown equably. 'She seems to be seeing a lot of him these days.'

'That Lenny do you mean?' asked Mr Brown over his copy of *The News*.

'Yes. Such a nice young man.'

Mr Brown snorted. 'Too bloody nice if you ask me,' was all he said and went back to the paper.

'Well he's obviously making our Peg happy and that's what's important.'

'Doesn't seem very happy to me. Don't know what's got into the girl lately,' said Mr Brown. He looked prepared to put down his paper and discuss it.

'Oh, you know what girls are like, especially when they're in love,' said Mrs Brown, dismissing his concerns. She was busy putting her shopping away. Every time she took something out of her basket, she took the brown paper bag it was wrapped in, shook it out, folded it carefully and put it in the cupboard next to the range. The cupboard that smelt of polish, candles and mousetraps.

'We don't seem to see her smiling much any more. She's normally a real smiler,' Mr Brown persisted. But Mrs Brown had disappeared into the pantry.

'Now Rosie,' she said when she emerged. 'We're off early tomorrow morning. We're going to a christening. What a journey it's going to be. A train and two buses. So you two girls will have to fend for yourselves. There's plenty of that rabbit pie left, and you can do yourself some potatoes with it. And mind our Peggy doesn't leave you with all the pots to do.'

I just wished Peggy would hurry up. Phil had said he would probably call round and I wanted to be ready for him.

There was a click of the latch at the back door and Janice appeared to creep around it. Even by her normal small and scruffy standards she looked particularly woebegone.

'Hello pet,' said Mr Brown. 'Why, what's the matter with you? Lost a sixpence and found a ha'penny, have you?'

Janice came and stood next to the range, as if trying to absorb all its heat Her hair looked lanker, her face paler and bleaker than usual. Her socks had fallen down her bony grubby legs, and her shoes were so scuffed and battered it was impossible to tell what colour they had been. She looked like a little brown animal seeking shelter.

'They've taken our Kevin and Terry away.'

'Away?' Mrs Brown looked alarmed. 'Where to?'

'Parkfields.'

'Ah.'

There was a long silence. The room that had seemed so warm and cosy now suddenly seemed chill.

'Parkfields?' I asked hesitantly.

'The asylum,' said Mrs Brown

'The mad house,' said Janice.

I realised that they were talking about the huge Victorian mansion I'd passed while in the van with George one day. It had locked gates and a high wall. 'How old are Kevin and Terry?'

'Thirteen. They're twins. They're the ones that howl,' said Janice simply, in explanation.

'But that's dreadful! They can't take children to a place like that.'

'They say my mum can't cope any more.' Janice was rubbing her hand round and round the lid on the range's hot plate.

'Well it's been very hard for her,' said Mrs Brown kindly. 'I don't know how she's lasted that long with them. And with all the little ones as well.'

'But Kevin and Terry are getting better!' said Janice fiercely. 'They can do jobs around the house. They can feed themselves and dress themselves and they dig the garden. They can do all sorts now!'

'I know, pet. But they're not little boys any more. They're turning into young men, getting bigger all the time. It will be hard for your mother

196

to cope with them. And your dad ... well.'

'Dad works very hard!' said Janice defensively.

'Yes he does. He can turn his hand to anything in all weathers. But because he's out working so much, it's hard for him to do much for them, isn't it? And after the window...'

I looked enquiringly.

'When Janice's mother comes to clean at the post office, she has to leave the twins at home, so she locks them in their bedroom. A few weeks ago they got so angry that they smashed the window and tried to get out. They were terribly cut. Blood everywhere, ooh it was a real mess.'

'That's when the doctor said it had to end. That if we didn't do something, they would kill each other, or Mum, or someone else. But they wouldn't, I know they wouldn't.'

I expected her to be in tears, but she was fierce and dry-eyed.

'What exactly is the matter with them?' I asked.

'They're not right in the head,' said Mrs Brown, with great brevity but not a terrific amount of clinical accuracy. 'Never have been. There's a few like that in her father's family.' While she'd been talking she'd been making a pot of tea and now she poured a cup for Janice, who took it and scuttled back to the shelter of the range

'It's for the best. It really is,' said Mrs Brown kindly. 'They'll be looked after there by people who are used to dealing with them. They'll have those nice big grounds to be in. They can play cowboys there. They like that, don't they?'

Janice nodded.

'And your mother will be able to spend more

time on the rest of you, won't she? There'll be more time and space for them too. You'll still have four brothers at home and that's more than enough! They're all shooting up and wanting to be fed and clothed. Your mother will have her hands full enough. It's for the best.'

'Tell you what,' said Mr Brown, 'why don't we find some polish and clean those shoes for you? You're such a smart little thing, let's look smart on the outside too.'

Janice pushed her shabby shoes off and almost hid behind the cup of tea. I tried to imagine those thirteen-year-olds in that institution, and hoped that Janice was comforted by the Browns' kindness.

Into the gloomy silence came a cheery yell from upstairs. 'Bathroom's free!'

I went up and was almost knocked over by the smell of bath salts, talc, and the scented soap that Peggy had used in abundance. Lenny didn't know how lucky he was that night. I stayed upstairs until I heard him arrive to call for Peggy. I thought it best, really, that I didn't see him. I didn't want to upset him.

When I went downstairs, Janice had gone.

'Best thing that those boys are going to Parkfields,' said Mrs Brown again. 'How that woman's managed all these years I've no idea. That husband of hers – well, he's a worker I suppose, but he hasn't got much up top either. All he's good at is making babies. And look where that's got him. And the house! Well, she does her best. But there's no money, and what she does manage to do, those twins wreck.'

'What are the other children like?'

'Well, they're normal enough I suppose, as far as you can tell, because they're only young. But they're not going to set the world on fire. No, little Janice has got all the brains in that family. Pity really that the only girl should be the clever one. It would have been much better if one of the boys had had the brains. They could have done something with them then.'

'Little Janice might. She's very bright,' said Mr Brown peaceably.

'Yes, well, that's all very well, but then she'll only go and get married and have babies like her mother's done. A boy could really make something of himself.'

I was just drawing breath to leap in and slice this argument to pieces when the doorbell rang again. 'That'll be your young man, Rosie,' said Mr Brown. 'Aren't our girls popular tonight? You get your coat, I'll let him in.'

I swallowed hard and just contented myself by saying pleasantly to Mrs Brown, 'And I'm sure Janice will make something of herself too,' then I went to the hall where Phil was standing shyly.

'I've got the bike, I thought we'd go out into the country,' he said. 'A pub perhaps?'

'Great idea,' I said as we went outside. I clambered on the back of the bike. I didn't feel quite as nervous as before without a crash helmet, but I did still feel a bit vulnerable. I put my arms around Phil's waist, companionably. I didn't long to cling to him and get as close as I could, not the way I had with Billy. We went up into the hills that surrounded the town. The road was narrow, not much more than a track in places, as we got higher into the hills. Then we were going along a ridgeway, looking down at the valley below. We came to a row of houses – you couldn't really call it a village – and Phil stopped in front of a small pub with a bench outside.

'Cider?' he asked, taking off his big leather gauntlets.

'Yes please. Can we sit out here?'

'Of course. I thought you'd like the view.'

It was terrific. You could see for miles. I was trying to place the village we were in on the modern map that existed only in my mind and memory. It was on the edge of my consciousness somehow. I couldn't quite reach it.

'Here you are,' said Phil, coming back with the drinks, which he placed on the rickety table, a table that clearly lived outside all winter and in all weathers.

'Thanks.' I took a mouthful of cider, still gazing at the view – the ridgeway, the sharply sloping hill, the town in a sort of bowl at the bottom...

'It's the motorway!' I said suddenly. Phil was looking at me over his pint. 'Sorry. What did you say?' he asked, looking puzzled.

'Oh nothing, nothing at all,' I said quickly and confused. 'I was just admiring the view.'

What I wanted to say was that I recognised it because I always came back this way from seeing my parents. You come across the view suddenly, just past the Long Edge Services, so it sort of hits you – I always know that I'm nearly home, nearly back with Will. But here there was no motorway. Just a country road, and a cluster of cottages, and the baaing of sheep, sounding louder now the light was beginning to fade.

'What's this village called?'

'Long Edge,' said Phil.

I sipped my cider and looked at the view, relished the silence and peace of it. I thought of the narrow road overlaid by the six-lane motorway. This little pub is somewhere under the service station now, all flashing yellow and red neon signs and constant traffic and noise and people. It was a hard idea to get my head around.

'Penny for them,' said Phil, smiling.

'What do you think this place will look like in fifty years?' I asked him.

'Probably much the same as it does now,' said Phil. 'It hasn't changed much in the last thousand years, so can't see fifty making much difference.' He lit a cigarette as though that ended the matter.

'I liked your story about the dog that caught the train,' he said. I'd done a shaggy dog story about a dog that hopped on a train every day to meet his master coming from work. It was a bit daft.

'Billy reckons you've got a really nice touch with light stories – as well as the big stuff like the Littlejohn piece. He thinks highly of you.'

I wanted to punch the air with glee. I was glad the light was fading so Phil couldn't see me blush, or see the eagerness in my face. Trying to keep the conversation about Will going would be the next best thing to being with him. I wanted to talk about him, find out more of what he was like at work, what Phil knew about Carol and the family. I was trying to frame ways of asking questions without seeming unreasonably interested but Phil was telling stories about stories, the way newspaper people always do when they get together.

We had another drink or two and talked in easy, friendly fashion about work. All the time I was thinking about Will.

Finally it was dark. We still sat there on the bench outside the pub, with the sound of the sheep, and the muffled buzz of conversation and clatter of dominoes from the few old men inside. Phil put his arm around me and then he kissed me. Not passionately, but nicely. I was a bit shocked. Not because it was Phil but because it wasn't Will. Surprised really.

And I kissed him back, a bit absent-mindedly but quite nicely, politely. And we got on the bike and rode down the hill into the deep darkness, with just a few pinpoints of light from the occasional house. And I thought about all the lights and the gantries on the motorway and it was a bit odd really.

When we got back to the Browns' house, I hopped off the bike and gave Phil a swift kiss on the cheek before he could get the bike propped up and get me into a clinch.

'Thank you for a nice evening, Phil,' I said, and went quickly into the house and upstairs to bed where I could devote myself to thinking about Will without any distractions.

Just before I drifted off to sleep I wondered briefly about Peggy's big night with Lenny.

As I lay in bed on Sunday morning I could hear the Browns getting ready for their day out. The rattle as they cleared the fire. The back door banging and the stamping of feet as they took ashes out and brought coal and sticks in. Familiar morning sounds now. They were making an early start for their complicated journey. They seemed to be pottering on for ages until finally I heard the front door close and their footsteps receding along the quiet Sunday street.

Once they'd gone, I made a pot of tea and sat at the kitchen table reading Mr Brown's *Sunday Pictorial*, a real scandal sheet, but still with a surprising amount of news in it. What bliss. No thought of church, or of peeling vast amounts of vegetables for lunch, or anything. Nothing to do at all. I finished reading the *Sunday Pictorial*. Had a second cup of tea. Sambo, for lack of anyone else, leapt up gracefully and settled down on my lap. I stroked him absently.

Now what?

I was restless and didn't know what to do. I had no friends to meet, apart from Phil, and he'd be having a lazy day because he was back on night shift tonight. Anyway, I didn't want the poor chap to get the wrong idea by appearing too keen. I liked him too much for that. It was Will, of course, I wanted. But...

I decided I'd go for a walk, use up some energy. I put on my little red jacket, scribbled a note for Peggy and set out. I meandered through the town and found the path alongside the river. It was a pleasant walk, with that scent of spring in the air, still chilly but suddenly warm in the sun. I was enjoying walking. I noticed that I had much more energy than I had in my normal life. Getting more sleep helped, I suppose. And not drinking so much. There had to be some benefits.

I had no idea where I was going and I was trying to superimpose my route on the mental map of the modern town I knew, but I couldn't marry the two. I walked on, glad to have an outlet for my restlessness. And then I laughed. Instinct was an amazing thing.

Somehow I had walked around the town until I was on the opposite side of the river from Billy's house. There it was, at the bottom of that narrow lane, perched on the river bank, with the long garden stretching up behind it. I walked up some steps to a bench in the shelter of the old town wall where I could sit and look across. From here the neat rows of vegetables just beginning to come through had all the organisation and formality of a medieval garden. There was an intricate pattern of paths and squares. It reminded me of those Victorian samplers, neat, ordered.

Two small figures were running around the lower part of the garden. Peter and Davy, I guessed, chasing a ball. Then I saw Billy. He was coming down the path, carrying some sort of rake or hoe or something. He propped it up by the shed, then, wiping his hands on the seat of his trousers, he intercepted the ball. The two boys' delighted yells of mock indignation floated across the river. I wasn't the only one watching then. Another figure carrying a tray was coming up the steps. It was Carol who stood watching them all, while a tiny figure, Libby, clung to her skirts. One of the boys mis-kicked the ball and it headed straight for their mother. I waited, tensed for the tray to crash, but no, Carol had sidestepped neatly and then kicked the ball back towards the boys. She put the tray down somewhere just out of sight and they all gathered around her as she seemed to be dishing out drinks and biscuits.

It was a tiny snippet of family life. The sort of thing happening in hundreds of back gardens all over Britain. Nothing special at all. And it broke my heart.

They were a family, enclosed, happy together. And I was on the outside. I had no place with them. Watching them I was like a voyeur, watching people who had something I wanted so badly, something I couldn't manage on my own.

I stayed there, watching and immobile, while they finished their elevenses. I saw Billy put a cup back on the tray and walk back up the garden to carry on with his work. I watched him as he picked up a spade and dug a small patch. It must have been hard work, but he worked quickly and easily in a smooth steady rhythm. I just stared at the sheer physicality of him.

This was an aspect of Will I had never seen. I had never, I realised, seen him do any physical work. Sport, yes, but not work. Billy seemed to spend much of his time doing practical useful things for his family. Will just seemed to amuse himself.

Then the two boys were having a pretend fight. Billy called something to them. He must have sent them on an errand because they came back with a bundle of long sticks and a ball of string. Billy stopped what he was doing and came over. He divided the sticks into smaller bundles, cut up the string and tied the sticks together. He was doing it slowly, obviously explaining to the boys what he was doing. They stood and watched, then they too tried the trick and Billy guided them, helped them. Then with great triumph, they put the bundles of sticks upright and spread them out and I saw that they had made two perfect sort of tent frames, tepee-shaped, which they set up in the vegetable patch. Presumably they were a framework for some vegetable to grow up. The boys looked pleased with what they had done and Davy ran back down the path, dragging Carol back up to see.

As they admired the boys' handiwork Billy and Carol stood close together. He casually put an arm around her shoulder and she looked up at him. I couldn't see their expressions, but I knew they must be smiling at the newly found skills of their children. I couldn't watch any more.

My hands had gone numb while I'd been watching, trying to get as close as I could to that little family scene. My fingers were white and bloodless and scratched from the splintered wood of the bench. I liked the chilly numbness. It seemed right and fitting. It was how I wanted my mind to be, my emotions too.

How could I still want Will when he so clearly was happy with someone else? Will and I could never be together in this bloody awful place at this bloody awful time.

I hated myself and I hated what was happening to me. This challenge was too real, too painful. I remembered dimly the time when I had thought that it was meant to be a television programme. But that seemed like a dream now. All my other life did. I had to concentrate hard to remember it. Reality was here and now. Caz and Will, Carol and Billy. My two best friends, leaving me out and alone.

I jumped up from the bench and down the steps, landed awkwardly on the river path below. I sat there for a moment, just wanting to cry. I'd grazed my hands and knees and twisted my ankle. But I didn't care. That wasn't important.

I had thought that as soon as Will saw me again, he would want me and just come to me. It had seemed so simple, so obvious. Will and I loved each other. Surely we were meant to be together. So how could he not want me here as he did in our own time?

Yet maybe he did. I remembered the way he looked at me sometimes, the way our eyes met, the way he had held me after the evening at Littlejohn's... Oh yes, Billy was attracted to me...

But he wasn't going to do anything about it, was he? Will might have no one else in his life but me, Will and I might be free to wonder whether we wanted to be together. But Billy and I didn't have that choice. Billy had already chosen, chosen Carol. Now he had a wife and family, and there was no way I could fit into his plans.

I hobbled home, almost glad of the pain in my ankle.

By the time I got back to the house I was in a dreadful state and close to tears. There was blood streaming from my hand and my trousers were ripped. I headed straight up to the bathroom. I needed to bathe my cuts, find some other clothes and just sort myself out. I went upstairs, hanging on to the banister and hauling myself up as my ankle was quite painful now.

I paused, frozen, at the top of the stairs. There was someone in my bedroom.

It sounded as if someone was opening all the dressing-table drawers. I could hear a drawer being opened and someone going through my things. Then another drawer opened...

Burglars. It had to be. Well, there wasn't much for them to steal from my room. But what should I do?

There was a phone downstairs in the hall below me. If I could get down quietly, I might be able to dial 999. But what if the burglar heard me?

I started inching quietly back down the stairs, wincing as I put weight on my rapidly swelling ankle. Then I heard another noise. It was a sort of whimper and a sob. And a familiar voice said, 'Oh where are they?' in a voice reeking of tears and desperation.

'Peggy?' I asked tentatively, hauling myself back up on to the landing. 'Peggy, is that you?'

The noise in my room stopped completely. I knew that on the other side of the door Peggy had frozen at the sound of my voice.

I limped along and pushed the bedroom door open.

There was devastation. All the drawers and the wardrobe were half open with a lot of stuff obviously just taken out and flung to one side. I didn't think I had much, but when I saw it scattered like that, I realised there was quite a lot really. And my handbag had been emptied out on the shiny, slippery green eiderdown.

Peggy was sitting on the bed now. Her face was swollen and blotchy, her eyes red. She looked dreadful.

'Peggy? What on earth are you doing?' I limped towards her.

'Where are they?' she demanded. 'Where do you keep them?' Honestly, she seemed mad.

I answered warily. 'Keep what?' I had absolutely no idea of what she was on about, but she was clearly in such a state I didn't dare upset her anymore.

'The pills. Those tablets you told me you had to stop you having babies.'

'Tablets? Babies?'

I remembered our conversation at the kitchen table, the one that her mother had cut so vehemently short.

'Oh Peggy, I haven't got them with me. Anyway, you have to take them to *prevent* you getting pregnant. Though, of course, there's always the Morning After pill...'

Ah. Suddenly it all became clear. 'Peggy, do you think you might be pregnant?'

And with that she howled. A dreadful, stomach-chilling howl of misery and desperation. 'Don't say it!' she shrieked at me. 'Don't say it!'

'Hey,' I said, as gently as I could. 'It's not that bad. It's not the end of the world.'

'What do you know about it?' she screamed at me. 'It's not you, is it?' She flung herself face down on the bed, sobbing hysterically. 'I don't know what I'll do.'

Gingerly, I put out a hand and stroked her shoulder as she snivelled into my eiderdown. The

209

sobs continued. I handed her one of my little lace-edged handkerchiefs that she had flung out of the drawer and onto the floor.

'I haven't got the pills with me. And even if I had, they're no good to you,' I said as gently as I could. 'How far gone are you?'

'I've missed one of my monthlies,' she said, not looking at me, 'and the other was due yesterday and it hasn't, it hasn't...' She started crying again.

'There's still time for an abortion, just.'

Suddenly I remembered the steamy bathroom, the smell of booze. I've seen *Alfie* and *Vera Drake*. I knew what went on.

'So is that what you were trying that afternoon? Hot bath and gin – you were trying to get rid of the baby, weren't you?'

She nodded. 'I didn't know what else to do. But it didn't work. Nothing happened,' she sobbed. 'I don't know who to ask about ... well, you know. I've heard there's someone who can arrange things. But I don't know who she is. And I'm scared.' She stared at me, panic in her eyes. I certainly believed her about being scared.

Oh God, it was years before abortion would be legal. What a mess.

Peggy was gazing at me in desperation. 'Don't you know anybody? You seem to be ... well ... as though it's the sort of thing you would know.'

'Sorry,' I said. 'Can't help.' And before she could start howling again I asked, 'So, um, what about the father? Does he know? How does he feel about it?'

'He can't do anything!' snapped Peggy. 'Nothing! It's hopeless.'

She looked up at me, her face utterly bereft.

'He's married,' she said simply.

'Oh.'

I remembered the proud smile, the way she smirked at the editor, the country bus to Middleton Parva... 'Oh God, Peggy. It's not Mr Henfield is it?'

She sniffed a bit and then nodded.

'Have you told him?'

She nodded.

'What did he say?'

'He said I was panicking. That it was a false alarm. That I was just late. And I hoped... I thought he might be right. He said women always panicked and I'd soon find out I was panicking over nothing. I thought he knew about these things. After all, he's married. And anyway,' she sniffed, 'I wanted to believe him.' She had screwed the little lace-edged hanky into a knot between her fingers.

'How on earth have you managed to work for him still?'

'He's hardly there. He hasn't been coming in much. And when he has, he just pretends it's all as normal. We always did in the office, in case anyone noticed...'

'Could it be a false alarm?'

'I don't think so. I'm ever so regular normally.'

'Then why...?' I was getting really confused here. 'If you were still trying to talk to Henfield about it, why were you so keen to go out with Lenny?'

She looked at me and turned my little hanky around and around in her hands with such force

211

that I thought it would rip apart.

'Richard's married isn't he?' she hiccuped. 'I knew he couldn't marry me, so I thought...'

'So you thought Lenny might. Is that it?'

She nodded.

'But don't you realise...?'

She clearly didn't realise where Lenny's sexual preferences lay, and I didn't know how to begin to explain.

'I thought ... I thought if Lenny and I, well, you know, if Lenny and I did it, did *it*, then maybe...'

'Then maybe you could get him to marry you?'

She sniffed and nodded.

'Oh God, Peggy, you weren't going to have sex with him and then try and fool him that the baby was his, were you?'

She howled again.

'I guess that's a yes, then. But it didn't work, did it?'

'No. Lenny, well, he, well almost ran away from me. He said there was no point in us seeing each other again. That it was all over.'

And suddenly I felt a bit responsible. Well, very responsible. I'd opened my big mouth and talked to Lenny as if he were Leo, rabbiting on about him and Jake being together. If homosexuality was still illegal then you could see why he wouldn't want that news spread around the office too widely. What better way to quash any rumours than by getting himself a girlfriend? Pretty damn quickly. And there was Peggy, desperately on the hunt for a man, any man...

If I hadn't said anything, Lenny wouldn't have needed a sort of cover by going out with Peggy in the first place. Then she wouldn't have got ideas, and ... oh God what had I started?

Peggy was studying the pattern in the shiny green eiderdown while she tried to explain. 'I tried to, well, you know, coax him ... but he didn't ... he wouldn't ... he just said ... he just said it wasn't going to work and there was no point. And then he went. He couldn't get away fast enough. It was dreadful.'

'Poor girl. Poor, poor girl,' I said. It was all so desperate that the image of Peggy trying to seduce Lenny and get him into bed with her didn't even raise the ghost of a smile. It was a pretty shitty mess.

'Richard won't leave his wife. He says he can't. They have a daughter.'

'Well OK, so might you soon. And what about supporting you? If you have this baby...'

'I can't have it! I can't!'

'Shh now, shh.' I put my arm around her. 'Worst case scenario says you have this baby. And that's not such a bad case is it? A little baby?'

'My mother will kill me!'

She looked really seriously frightened. And I must admit, I wouldn't have relished facing Mrs Brown with that particular bit of good news myself, to be honest.

'OK, I know your mum can be a dragon. But deep down you know she's really kind. Think of how she looks out for Janice and her family. She's got a really good heart.'

Peggy gave me a stunned sort of look.

'And I know it would be a shock to her, when you first tell her. It's bound to be. But I'm sure she'll get used to the idea. I'm sure she'll be great.'

Peggy was crying again. Time to get off that tack, I thought.

'Look, if Henfield's the father then he *has* to support you. It's his baby as much as yours. Even if he stays with his wife, he should give you enough money to live. He can't get away with it, but you've got to tell your parents. You must do that. Apart from anything else, you need to look after yourself, go to clinics, check-ups, that sort of thing.'

I wasn't too clear on the details of ante-natal health but I knew you had to keep getting MOT type things.

'I just want to die.' Peggy flung herself back down on the eiderdown.

'No you don't. What you want is to be well and happy and have your baby. Really, you do. Honestly, lots of women do it where I come from. They have babies all on their own, no man around, and it works. They and their babies are happy and healthy.'

I closed my mind to the *Daily Mail* type statistics here for a moment.

'It can be done. Honestly. No one minds. There's no stigma. Just wait, in a year or two, no one will take any notice.'

And so I went on. We sat there for another hour or more as I extolled the joys of single mother-hood. I don't think she was persuaded but she stopped howling and did seem to be listening. I raked up every example I could think of, friends who had babies on their own, friends who were the babies of single mothers.

Finally she stopped crying, calmed down and we reached some sort of decision. We decided that the next day she would tackle Henfield and persuade him into doing something for the child. And then, armed with that bit of provision, Peggy would come home and tell her parents. Her face still filled with fear at the thought, but I didn't know what else I could do.

'Don't worry,' I said, still trying to be soothing, 'I'll be there for you.'

But this sent Peggy straight back into a panic. 'Where will you be? When will you be there?' she asked, agitated. 'What will you do?'

'I'll help you all I can,' I said. I tried to move and realised my leg had seized up.

'It's no good,' I said. 'I'm going to have to do something about these cuts and this ankle.'

'Oh I'm sorry,' sniffed Peggy. 'You should have done that first instead of listening to me.'

'That's all right,' I said, not wishing to provoke another flood of tears. 'Now why don't you go and have a wash and then get that pie out of the pantry and warmed up. You need to eat, and in any case, your mother will only play hell if she comes home and we haven't eaten it.'

Peggy nodded and dutifully went off to the bathroom. When she'd gone downstairs, I too hobbled off there and tried to clean myself up. I realised as I sat on the edge of the bath, holding my ankle under the icy water from the cold tap, that all the time I'd been talking to Peggy, I hadn't given Will a thought. Only for an hour or two admittedly, but the longest I'd gone without thinking of him since I'd been here.

Chapter Fourteen

'Right.'

'Right.'

Monday morning and Peggy and I were standing outside *The News* office, both of us waiting to pluck up the courage to go in. I knew quite well why Peggy was so frightened. She had no idea why I was dreading the day.

'OK, now remember,' I said, 'you tell Henfield you want to see him and have a proper talk to him. You're entitled to some help and support. After all, he's the one who's married. He knew what he was doing and should take responsibility.'

'Right,' said Peggy again, though she didn't look too sure. 'Rosie you've been a real brick,' she suddenly said, turning to me. 'I'm sorry I haven't been very nice to you, but I thought with you working at *The News* you would realise what was going on and tell my mum. It suddenly seemed a frightful idea, you staying with us, and I wished I'd never thought of it.'

'Well yes, now I *have* realised, but it doesn't matter. In fact that's a good thing. I can help you sort it out. And we will. Promise.'

What was I saying?

But Peggy was smiling – not much of a smile admittedly, but it was something.

'Right,' she said. And in we marched.

216

Billy was sitting with his back to me and the diary open in front of him, talking to Alan and Brian. 'Hiya kid!' he said, turning around and giving me a wonderful smile. 'Good weekend?'

'Yes, yes, fine thanks.'

Should I tell him I'd spent a large chunk of Sunday spying on him and his wife and family? No, I didn't think so either. So I said brightly, 'Shall I make the tea?'

'What a marvellous woman you are, Rosie,' said Billy.

If only he meant it...

I made the tea and brought it in just as Marje arrived in her normal flurry of hat, scarf, cigarette and shopping bag.

'Ooh you've made the tea! What a pet you are!' she said, reaching over and taking the cup I'd meant for myself. I went back and got another as Marje had a good cough and wafted the smoke away. Billy and Alan were busy on the telephone making the morning calls. I had other things and people to think of beside myself. Here was a chance. I'd promised Peggy I would ask. And Marje was the only person I could think of.

'Marje,' I whispered conspiratorially, 'can I ask you something?'

'Ask away, my dear,' said Marje, hunting the ashtray under a drift of yellowing copy paper.

'Well a friend of mine is in a spot of bother...'

At once Marje looked up shrewdly at me.

'Friend?'

'Oh yes, honestly, not me...'

'And what sort of bother would that be then?'

'Well the usual one, I'm afraid.' I whispered

217

across the desk. 'You know, young girl, older man and now…'

'Got caught has she?' asked Marje, inhaling deeply on her cigarette.

'Well yes. And, well, she's desperate. Really desperate. I don't suppose you know anyone…'

I let the idea, the question, hang on the smoky air. I didn't want to have to spell it out, especially not with the men just yards away. Marje had found the ashtray. She put her cigarette in it, blinked the smoke from her eyes and came across to me, put her hands down on the desk and leant over my typewriter until her face was only inches away from mine. I could smell the tobacco on her breath and the powdery smell of her make-up.

'Yes, as a matter of fact, I do know someone,' she said. For a moment I felt a surge of hope on Peggy's behalf. 'I know someone who promises to "help" young girls. Then the poor girl bleeds like a stuck pig and, if she's lucky, she gets over it. They're the lucky ones. The unlucky ones end up in hospital. The really unlucky ones don't get that far. Let me tell you, Miss Rosie Harford, a friend of mine was helped by this woman. A lot of things went on during the war.

'They managed to get her to hospital but she died anyway. Her husband came back from the desert to find his wife dead. Her parents never got over it.'

'Why on earth did the silly kid think her parents would rather have a dead daughter than a live grandchild, whatever the circumstances?'

Marje's eyes glittered.

'Just tell your friend that she's done what she's

done and now she has to live with it. It's her mistake and she has to cope.

'It's not the end of the world. She can put the baby up for adoption and forget all about it. In a few months it will all be over and she can come home, make a fresh clean start and be more sensible in future. She won't be the first and she won't be the last. But please, please, tell her not to go near any woman who offers to "help". Not if she wants to live and maybe have more children one day.'

With that Marje went back to her desk, picked up her cigarette and moved the ashtray from one side of the desk to the other, just for the satisfaction of slamming it down... Billy and Alan looked across at us, sensing the conversation wasn't the normal girly chat.

'OK fellers,' said Marje, with a flourish of her cigarette, 'let's get on with some work, shall we?'

A few minutes later Billy came over with the diary. He stood there, looking at me with that half smile on his face, and as he spoke he waved the pen in the air. Such a Will gesture... I had to swallow hard.

'So there's the village feature, the preview of the spring flower show and the cheque presentation for the Hospital League of Friends. If you and Marje would like to sort those out between you?'

'Sure,' said Marje. 'I could do the village feature – maybe Somerton – if Rosie does the flower show and the League of Friends. Or of course, you could send Rosie to Somerton, and, knowing the way things happen with her, she'll probably find Jack the Ripper and Dr Crippen serving in the sweet shop.'

Billy laughed. 'She certainly has a knack of finding stories. Or of stories finding her. But Marje, I'll put you down for Somerton.'

Clever Marje. She knew the cheque presentation was in the early evening and she didn't like working late.

'Fine with me,' I said. At least the flower show would get me out of the office.

But first I had to go and see Peggy.

She was sitting at her desk, motionless, ashen white.

'Hi,' I said quietly, after a quick check that no one was around, 'I'm sorry. I've spoken to Marje and she doesn't want anything to do with it. Says it's better to go ahead now. Even if you have the baby adopted. Have you arranged anything with Henfield?'

Peggy looked at me glassily. 'He's not coming in today. He rang in. He has to take his wife somewhere. I told him I wanted a proper discussion with him, said I had to see him, we had things that needed to be talked about.' She looked bleak.

'He just put the phone down on me, Rosie. He just put the phone down. I don't know what to do. I don't know.'

'It's going to be all right,' I said as forcefully as I could without yelling. 'Really. Look, we'll talk about it tonight. Now don't panic. You can talk to Henfield tomorrow. He *has* to agree something. I'll see you later. We'll sort it all out this evening.'

A spotty young man from advertising knocked and walked into the office.

'Mr Henfield about?' he asked cheerily.

'No,' said Peggy and fled from the room.

I felt I should go after her, but young George was waiting for me. There was nothing I could do for the moment. I'd speak to Peggy later. I grabbed my notebook and my handbag and left.

The flower show was very straightforward. It was their fiftieth, so I spoke to the organiser and got a bit of history. I spoke to the secretary of one of the gardening clubs, and to a nice old chap who'd been a gardener's boy when the very first show was held. George took lots of pretty pictures of flowers and we were back in the office by lunch time.

Alan and Billy went to the pub.

'Coming, Rosie?' said Billy as he picked up his coat.

'Yes. I'll just finish this. See if you can keep me a cheese sandwich that hasn't yet curled up and died.'

'OK. I shall try and work miracles for you.'

I followed them down a few minutes later. I deliberately wanted to keep it casual, keep it friendly, pretend that everything was normal. In the pub I sat next to Alan, but as I nibbled at my sandwich – no miracles there, even a desperate mouse would have turned up its nose at that cheese – I was aware of Billy's eyes on me. I knew he was watching me, even while he was talking to Alan. And when Alan got up to get some more beers in, it was only easy, only natural, for Billy to slip around and sit next to me... I relished his closeness, but I knew that's as far as it would get. However much I wanted to be in his arms, in his heart, in his bed, it wasn't going to happen. It couldn't happen. This Billy was a family man. He had a wife he cared for. He had children he doted on, children for whom he was determined to do his best. That's why he did the sports shift on a Saturday. It's why he spent so much time on that garden, to keep them fed, well and healthy. It was why he didn't go to the pub that often. He was a solid, reliable, responsible husband and father. He was loyal to his family and he put their happiness first.

The irony was, of course, that it made him such a decent bloke and made me love him even more.

Is this how Will would be? I thought. In a different time, in different circumstances?

Will had never had to take any responsibility for anyone other than himself. That didn't mean that he couldn't or wouldn't. It just meant he'd never had to. He still acted like a kid, because he'd never had to do anything differently. I remembered our row. I thought of what I'd snapped at him when he'd asked me about having a child. I'd said it would be just another toy for him, that he was too much of a kid to be a father.

But here was Billy, a father at seventeen, and a good father.

Did that mean that Will would be too?

My head was spinning...

'You're miles away, Rosie,' said Billy, smiling at me quizzically.

I felt myself blushing. 'Think I'd better go back. Lots to do. Better get on.'

'Time I was going too,' said Billy. And the three of us walked back across the road together. While Alan walked along, whistling blithely, I felt Billy was walking as close to me as he could, almost touching. But maybe that was my optimistic imagination.

In the office, Marje, back from Somerton, had made some tea. She plonked a cup down in front of me. 'Are you all right?' she asked. 'Are you *sure* it was your friend who wanted help?'

'Yes, I...' Oh God! Peggy. I'd better go and see how she was.

I poked my head around her office door. She wasn't there. Her coat was on the peg and her handbag by the desk where it had been the last time I saw it.

'Looking for Peggy?' said a girl from accounts putting some papers on her desk. 'I think she must have gone home. I haven't seen her since early this morning. Nobody else has either. I asked.'

'But her bag and coat are here.'

'Maybe she wasn't well and left in a hurry. She looked very pale when I saw her.'

This was worrying. I went and looked in the Ladies. I ran down to reception. I asked the ladies on the switchboard. They took off their head sets and unravelled the complicated tangle of wires in front of them. 'No, she hasn't been in since mid-morning,' they said crossly. 'And she didn't tell us where she was going. It's been very difficult, with all of Mr Henfield's calls.'

I ran back up to the editorial floor and bumped into George, who was bringing down the pictures of the flower show.

'Do you want to see these?' he asked, handing me the black-and-white prints.

'Very nice,' I said, not looking at them. 'George,

223

are you down to do the League of Friends' cheque presentation tonight?'

'Yes, seven p.m. in the hospital. You know Charlie never goes out after six o'clock – wouldn't miss his tea for anyone. Do you want a lift up there?'

'Yes please. And could we leave a bit early? I just need to pop back home on my way.'

'Right you are. I'll see you in the yard at six-thirty. That do you?'

'Perfect, George. You're a star.' I think he blushed.

I suddenly felt an arm around my shoulder. For a second I hoped... But no.

'Hello, Phil,' I said as cheerily as I could. 'Ships in the night, I'm afraid. I'm just finishing off these few bits then I'm off to the League of Friends cheque presentation. Exciting, eh?'

'You could make anything exciting, Rosie,' said Phil, and it didn't sound smarmy because he was really such a nice bloke. 'Will you be back in time for my break, about nine-ish? I'll buy you a drink if you can.'

'Maybe. Yes. I don't know. I'll see,' I said and blew him a kiss as I picked up my copy to take to the subs' room. I knew Billy had listened avidly to every word. Good.

Still no Peggy in her office. She wasn't at home either.

'Hello, Mrs Brown, just popped in for something I've forgotten. I'll be back later,' I said as breezily as I could.

'Is our Peggy with you?'

'Peggy? No,' I said. 'I haven't seen her. Though' – oh blessed inspiration – 'I think I saw Lenny in the office.'

'Oh well. That explains everything, doesn't it?' said Mrs Brown indulgently. 'But she'll miss her mince and dumplings. She could have shown a bit of consideration and let me know.'

She muttered on as I dashed up to my room, really just so I could look into Peggy's room. She wasn't there. So where was she? I was beginning to get really worried.

It was raining when we left the hospital, cold, wet miserable rain. The van rattled back to the office.

'George, are you going to print those up tonight?'

'Yes, they want them for tomorrow's paper.'

I didn't want to go back into the office. With both Phil and possibly Billy still there it was going to get hopelessly complicated.

'Could you do me a favour, George? Could you look into Peggy's office and see if her coat and bag are still there?'

'Yes of course, but why? Not anything wrong is there? Not with Peggy?' George looked quite anxious. I'd forgotten he'd always had a soft spot for Peggy.

'I don't know. But just do that for me will you?'

He was back in five minutes.

'Coat and handbag still there,' he said. 'Now will you tell me what's going on?'

'How long will you be printing your pics?'

'Half an hour or so.'

'Well I'm going to wait in the van. I've got some thinking to do.'

'Is this something to do with Peggy?'

'Just be as quick as you can, will you, George? Please?'

He turned and ran, his skinny little body flying up the rickety stairs.

He was back in record time. 'Now will you tell me what this is about?' he asked, settling into the scratched leather of the seat as the rain lashed against the windscreen. 'And what's happened to Peggy?'

'I think she may be in trouble.'

George sat up like a shot. 'What sort of trouble?'

'The usual sort,' I said, trying to think. 'Do you know where Mr Henfield lives?'

'Yes, course I do. Big house on the hill, other side of town.'

'Can we go there please?'

George folded his arms. 'Only if you tell me what's happened to Peggy.'

'Not my secret to tell, George. Sorry. But can you go to Henfield's house now please?'

'But...'

'Please.'

Reluctantly he started the engine and we headed to Henfield's house. It was the only place I could think she might have gone. If he wouldn't arrange to talk to her, she might have gone to see him on his home territory. It would be a brave move, but Peggy was getting desperate. We drove slowly through the dark and the rain, George peering at the road as the tiny windscreen-wipers were pretty ineffective, while I kept a look-out for someone who looked like Peggy.

'Oh God,' I remembered, 'her coat's still in the office.'

'If she's out in this, she's going to be soaked through,' said George, pulling up outside the Henfields'. It was a large pleasant 1930s house, with an imposing lawn sloping down to the road.

'There's no one in,' said George, peering through the rain.

He was right. The place was in darkness, the curtains still open as though no one had been in all evening. We sat there for a moment, thinking about what to do. George passed me a packet of sweets.

'Have a Spangle,' he said 'Hopalong Cassidy's favourite sweets.'

'Hopalong Cassidy?' I unwrapped the little square boiled sweet.

'The cowboy on telly.'

'Do cowboys eat sweets?'

'Hopalong does.'

We sat in the van and sucked our Spangles for a while. 'Let's have a look in the garden. She could be there waiting,' I said.

There were no lights, no moon, no streetlight. Finding our way was incredibly difficult. We went up the drive, looked in the porch, went around to the back. In the dark and the rain I walked into the dustbin. There was a huge clatter, but nothing else. No other sound, no other sign of anyone there.

We skulked back down the drive, and into the van. My hair was soaked.

'Now what?' asked George.

'I don't know.'

'Well how about you tell me what this is all about, just why we've been skulking around

Henfield's house in the sort of weather you wouldn't put the cat out in.'

He sounded firm, sensible, adult. And I needed his help. So I told him the story. I had to. I know it was Peggy's story and her secret, but I was desperate for ideas.

'Poor Peggy,' said George, looking shocked. 'Poor bloody Peggy. And that Henfield, he's a bastard – sorry Rosie, 'scuse my language, but he is.'

'I'll not argue with that. But forget about him for the moment. Where can Peggy be?' I asked him. 'I'm not over-reacting, am I? She hasn't been seen since this morning. She hasn't been home. Her bag and her coat are still in the office. She's pregnant and desperate. Where would she go?'

'Well that other girl threw herself in the pond at Friars' Mill, didn't she?' said George.

'Oh God, you don't think...'

He'd already started the van and was turning it around.

I remembered when I'd told them the story of Amy Littlejohn's suicide, how taken Peggy had been by the details. How she'd repeated them. The little van tore through the night. My teeth were rattling in my head and George was leaning forward over the steering-wheel as if he could make the van faster by sheer willpower.

Huge trees loomed big and black around Friars' Mill making it hard to forget the tragedies that had taken place there. George braked hard, nearly sending me through the windscreen, and then drove very slowly along the road above the mill-pool.

'Of course,' he said, trying to sound sensible and cheerful, 'we've no real reason to believe she's here at all. She might really have been out with Lenny and she might be safely at home now, tucked up in front of the fire with a cup of cocoa.'

'You're right,' I said. 'I've probably got everything completely out of proportion and I'm making a fuss out of nothing. Just forget I ever told you anything about it and let's go home.'

'I'll just drive up to the end, just to be sure...'

We couldn't see a thing. Just the trees and the sheet of water shining an even darker black in the darkness. The water looked cold. And deep.

George hunched over the steering wheel, staring into the darkness.

'What's that?'

'What? Where?'

'Over there. Something light.'

I opened the window to see better and was greeted with a swirl of rain blowing into the van. But yes, I could see something. 'Something white, by the edge of the water.'

'Come on!' George was out of the van and already climbing over the wall.

He moved quickly through the dark and I stumbled after him, my feet soaked, rain from the trees dripping down on me and small branches whipping my face as I pushed past. George was now racing along a path towards a small clump of trees at the edge of the mill pond. 'Peggy?' he shouted. 'Peggy!' and he almost fell towards the patch of white.

'It's her! Rosie, we've found her!'

Thank God, I thought, thank God.

George already had his jacket off and was wrapping it around her. Peggy was hardly conscious. The skirt and blouse that had been so neat this morning were torn and covered with mud. She seemed to have no shoes.

'Come on,' said George 'We have to get her back to the van, get her to the warm. Come on now, Peggy, there's a good girl. You can do it. Rosie, you take one arm, and I'll take the other and there you go. Come on, Peggy, not far. You can do it.'

Between us we staggered with her back along the path, slipping and sliding with our burden.

'No,' muttered Peggy, her eyes still closed and her head lolling against George's shoulder, 'leave me ... just leave me.'

'Never,' said George fiercely. 'We're not leaving you anywhere until you're warm and safe.'

George was taking charge. He was brilliant, and we soon had Peggy back by the roadside. 'Right, stay here and I'll run and get the van,' said George.

Peggy was collapsed against me. I put both arms around her in an effort to keep her upright. 'Come on now, Peggy. Don't give up now. Please.'

Somehow, we put Peggy in the back of the van and I climbed in there with her. I took my jacket off and wrapped it around her legs. Then I tried to rub some circulation into her limbs.

'We're going to the hospital,' shouted George. 'Just try and keep her warm.'

I carried on rubbing her hands and arms, talking to her, persuading her to stay awake, to be all right. We drove up to the hospital which seemed tiny by modern standards and all in darkness.

'Are they open?' I asked stupidly.

There was a small door with a light showing above it.

'Night Entrance' it said. I rang the bell, George pounded on the door, then we almost fell in as the door opened and a nurse in a dark blue dress and a fiercely starched white cap stood in the dimly lit hallway.

'Well?' she said.

Then in a blink of an eye she seemed to assess the situation. She reached for a wheelchair from an alcove, pushed it towards Peggy and expertly manoeuvred her into it.

'She's been out in the rain,' I blurted out, 'all day. She's pregnant and the father ... well the father doesn't want to know.'

'Has she taken anything? Tried to do anything to harm herself or the baby?'

'I don't know.'

'Her name?'

'Peggy Brown.'

'Wait here please.'

She disappeared with Peggy along an oak-panelled corridor. I followed. The nurse turned. 'I asked you to wait there,' she said, and vanished with Peggy.

So George and I waited. There was a bench. No coffee machine. It was very quiet. The floor gleamed. It all smelt sharply, cleanly of dis-infectant and polish. Where were the drunks? All the usual chaos of casualty late at night?

George was pacing up and down. 'Is she going to be all right, Rosie?' he asked anxiously.

'I'm sure she will be,' I said, though, like the

nurse, I wondered if she'd taken anything.

'She's always been really nice to me.'

'Yes, I remember you saying. Helped you get the job.'

'Yes and sort of looked out for me when I started. She's a really good sort, you know.'

'Yes George, I know.'

We waited. Eventually the fierce nurse came back. George and I leapt to our feet.

'I'm pleased to tell you your friend is in no danger,' she said crisply. 'Neither is her unborn child. Though whether that will please her I cannot say. She is severely chilled and in a state of shock, but otherwise seems unharmed. We shall probably keep her in for a few days.'

I gave her Peggy's name and address.

'Date of birth?' asked the nurse.

'September twentieth,' said George quickly. 'Same as mine, only she's six years older, so she's twenty-six.'

'Wouldn't it be easier if her parents did all this when they come up? I'm sure they'll be here as soon as we tell them,' I asked.

The nurse snapped the folder shut.

'They can visit tomorrow between two and three p.m.,' she said and must have seen the horrified look on my face because she added, 'Tell them if they telephone between seven-thirty and eight o'clock in the morning I shall still be here and will tell them how she is. But I'm sure' – and she almost smiled – 'that she'll be fine and at home before the end of the week. Goodnight.'

And so we went.

Back in the van I really wanted a cigarette.

'Don't suppose you've got a fag have you, George?'

'No, never smoked. They always told me it would stunt my growth and as I'm so skinny to start off with...'

We almost laughed. But I had to go back and tell the Browns that their daughter was a) pregnant, b) by a married man, c) was in hospital, and d) they couldn't see her until tomorrow afternoon.

By the time George dropped me off it was very late, and then the poor lad had to get the van back to the yard and walk home.

'What if we hadn't found her?' he asked, looking frightened, young again.

'But we did, George and that was because you refused to give up. You probably saved her life.'

He looked pleased and then with a final 'Goodnight,' drove off. I took a deep breath and went into the house.

'Peggy?' said Mrs Brown sharply as soon as she heard the door click.

'No, sorry, it's me,' I said, going into the sitting room.

The fire had died down, but the Browns were still sitting by it. They normally had their last cup of tea and a biscuit at about nine-thirty, but that was hours ago and they'd clearly just had another. The room was chilly but they were waiting up, waiting, worrying, for Peggy.

'Where is she? Where's Peggy?' said Mrs Brown, worry making her angry. 'Has something happened?'

'She's fine. But she's in hospital.'

Mrs Brown leapt to her feet. 'What's happened?

Has there been an accident? Tell me! Why is she there?'

So I told them the whole story. Well, not the bit about Lenny, but everything else. I'd thought about this in the van coming home and I'd decided it would be much easier if they knew before they got to the hospital. If I told them, then at least Peggy wouldn't have to. I thought it would make it easier for everyone. I hoped so.

I probably didn't tell it as well as I could. It was late and I was tired, but I did my best to be gentle. When I told them Peggy was pregnant, Mrs Brown gave a little cry, her hand on her mouth. When I told them the father was Henfield, Mr Brown's right hand clenched into a fist and he pushed it repeatedly into his other hand, as if practising for Henfield's face.

When I told them how we'd found Peggy by the mill pond Mrs Brown went white. 'Silly, silly girl,' she said. 'I should have known, I should have realised...' Her eyes were full of tears, but her mouth set firm like a trap. I told them about the hospital and what the nurse had said.

'She really is going to be all right,' I said.

'And the baby?'

'That's all right too.'

They didn't say anything. Like the nurse at the hospital, I didn't know if that was good news or not.

Mr Brown looked up at me. He looked old suddenly, old and small. 'It seems to me that you've done our Peg a great service today. If you hadn't looked for her and found her, she could still be out there now, and who knows what state she would be in.'

Mrs Brown gave another small strangulated cry, more of a gasp really and quickly choked back.

'...so we are very grateful to you. Thank you, Rosie, thank God you were here.'

Suddenly Mrs Brown started bustling with the tea tray. 'You'll be wet and cold yourself. I shall make you some cocoa, then you must have a nice hot bath even though it's so late. That doesn't matter. Doesn't matter at all.'

She was busying herself in order not to think, I could see that. As she put a cup and saucer down on the tray, she knocked the milk jug flying. I thought she was going to cry.

'Now now, Doreen,' said Mr Brown soothingly as he came back with a cloth. 'No use crying over spilt milk, is there? What's done's done and now we have to think what to do next.'

I made the cocoa myself and went upstairs and peeled off my wet and grubby clothes. As I felt I had a special dispensation, I ran a bath. I used every last drop of hot water and luxuriated in the warmth creeping back into my bones. When I finally got to bed, the light was still on downstairs and I could hear the Browns talking. They would probably be up all night, and it was still a long time until they were allowed to phone the hospital.

Chapter Fifteen

Peggy came home from hospital three days later. She came on the bus. Her dad went to meet her at the bus stop.

While he was gone, Mrs Brown fussed back and forth in the kitchen. She had cleaned the house from top to bottom and had prepared the meal with extra care. There were lamb chops and mint sauce. She had chopped the mint fiercely. She'd made an apple crumble – Peggy's favourite – with the stored apples. Everything was under control but she couldn't settle. It was as if she were expecting a hugely important visitor, not her own daughter whom she had only just seen at visiting hours.

When Peggy walked in I thought there'd be a big welcome. But to my surprise, Mrs Brown just said, 'You're back then,' and went to strain the potatoes.

Conversation was stilted and awkward, with many silences. I could hear Mr Brown's false teeth slipping slightly when he chewed.

'Lovely meal, Mum, thank you,' said Peggy, her eyes pleading for a response, for some relaxation from her mother.

'Well, I never trusted hospital food,' said Mrs Brown, getting up and taking a dish out to the scullery, almost unable to look at her daughter.

Peggy and I did the washing up. 'It's all right,

Peggy, I'll do it if you want to put your feet up.'

'She's not ill now,' snapped Mrs Brown, and Peggy just shrugged. We washed up in silence, suffocated by the atmosphere around us. Then there was a ring at the door.

George shuffled in looking even younger than usual. He was carrying a bunch of primroses. He carried them awkwardly, as if they belonged to somebody else. He was not used to such gestures. 'I brought these for you, Peggy.' He blushed. 'I just wanted to know you were all right.'

'Thank you, George,' said Peggy giving him the first smile I'd seen since she was home. 'That's very kind of you.'

'Yes, George,' said Mr Brown, 'Mrs Brown and I, well, we can't say how much we want to thank you. If you hadn't been there, I don't know what would have happened.'

'Well, it was Rosie really, I just drove the van.'

'We know what you did, and we're very grateful.'

'Well, as long as you're OK now, Peggy.' George was shuffling his feet trying to come up with an exit line. 'So I'll see you at work then shall I?'

'No,' snapped Mrs Brown. 'She won't be going back there. Never.'

'Oh, right. OK then.' George looked awkward. 'Well I only wanted to see that you were better, so I'll be going now. Goodbye.' And he fled.

'Well you might have offered the lad a drink,' said Mrs Brown.

'Drink?' said her husband. 'He doesn't look old enough.'

Later, when Peggy was going up to bed, her

mother suddenly reached out her hand and put it on Peggy's arm, and with eyes full of tears she looked at her and said fiercely, 'Don't you ever do anything that stupid again.'

Whether she meant a suicide bid or an unwanted pregnancy, I didn't know.

'Do you like it?'

Carol was in the reception area at *The News*, taking off her coat to show me her new outfit.

'It's a bit thin for now, but I just wanted to show you.'

It was the material she'd bought on the market, which she'd made into a skirt. Now it was made up I could see that the picture was of a Paris street scene, pavement cafés and people walking poodles. Odd but effective. With the skirt Carol wore a wide black patent leather belt and a fitted white blouse. She looked stunning.

'Did you make that yourself?'

'Yes, of course. It's not as full as I'd like because there wasn't really enough material, but it's all right isn't it?'

'Great,' I said. 'What a clever mummy you have,' I said to Libby who was waiting patiently by the full shopping bag, 'smoking' a sweet cigarette and blowing imaginary smoke rings.

'And what about the blouse?'

'Fine, absolutely fine.'

'It's an old shirt of Billy's that I altered.'

'It's great, perfect.' What wouldn't I give to have an old shirt of Will's around me? 'It makes a brilliant outfit. Time for a coffee?'

Smiling, she shrugged back into her shabby

brown coat, picked up her shopping bag, took Libby's hand, and we went over to Silvino's.

As soon as we got there Libby wanted the loo. So while Carol took her I ordered the coffees and sat doodling in my notebook. 'What's that?' asked Carol as she came back.

'It was my favourite outfit when I was a student,' I said.

I'd sketched a girl – a very long-legged slim girl, not at all like me – in my favourite denim mini, a strappy vest, and my lovely, lovely cowboy boots. I quickly drew in the last tiny detail and showed it to Carol.

'What's that?' she asked, peering at the paper.

'My belly button stud,' I said. 'It was a little fake diamond.'

'In your belly button? You never!' She looked genuinely shocked. 'Didn't it hurt?'

I shook my head, smiling.

'And what did you wear on top?'

'I had a lovely little denim jacket.'

'No, I mean on top of this?' asked Carol astonished. 'You couldn't go out in the streets in this.'

'Yes I did.'

'But... It looks just like your underpinnings!' she said, and it was my turn to laugh.

She looked so worried that I decided to draw her something a bit less revealing.

'Here's the outfit I wore to my cousin's wedding last summer,' I said, and quickly drew the knee-length flippy silk skirt and boxy jacket. 'That's a sort of bright peacock blue and the edging and lining,' I scribbled swiftly, 'are a jade green, and my shoes, ah my shoes...' I tried to

239

draw them, but didn't do a very good job. 'They had really high heels, I could only just walk in them and kept sinking in the grass, and they were the same jadey colour as the edging on my jacket and across the middle...' I jabbed some bits in. 'They had little tiny jewels. Well, bits of coloured glass, really, but the effect was good.'

Carol gawped at my sketch and then looked at me, sheer envy all over her face. 'They are wonderful. Magic,' she said. 'I would love to have shoes like that.'

'You'd be a princess,' said Libby.

'Yes, my love, I would. A real princess.'

She looked hungrily at my rough sketch and I thought of all the shoes that Caz and I had between us, and I just wished that somehow there could have been a way of getting a pair to Carol.

That day Mr Brown went to see Henfield. Gosh I wish I'd been a fly on the wall.

'So what's happening?' I asked Peggy. I'd been in my bedroom putting some ironing away. (By the way, did you know that steam irons hadn't been invented in the 1950s? And everything was cotton, which creased horrendously? So you had to iron everything through a wet tea towel? Brilliant.) Peggy knocked and came in. I think she just wanted to get away from the atmosphere downstairs.

'He denied it. Said there was no proof the baby was his.'

'He can't do that! Anyway, you can get DNA testing and...' No you probably couldn't actually.

240

Not yet. 'What did your father do? What did he say? What happened?'

'There wasn't much he could do. Threaten to tell Henfield's wife, I suppose, but that would just make things worse. I don't know. He said he's going back, but for the moment, nothing. Honestly, I can't believe how stupid I was to get involved with him.'

'Easy to be wise with hindsight. And what will you do? Are you going to keep the baby?'

'I don't know. I really don't know. Don't care really.'

Her blouse was already straining at the buttons. She looked down on the small but noticeable bump and pressed her hands on it. 'I still can't believe it's happening. I keep hoping it's all a nasty dream and I'll wake up and everything will be just as it was. It's hateful!' she suddenly spat out. 'Nothing fits any more and I still keep feeling sick.

'I just want it all to be over so I can start again. But I don't know if I can. Oh Rosie, it was awful when my dad came to see me in hospital, he was so upset. He just kept calling me his little girl and I just felt, oh, I just felt I'd really let him down.

'And as for Mum. She's so ashamed of me I think she'd have preferred it if I'd, if well, if you hadn't found me.'

'Rubbish! Don't you dare think that. If you'd seen them on Monday night, they were beside themselves. They didn't sleep all night for worry and waiting to phone the hospital. And when you came home yesterday she did your favourite food.'

Actually I couldn't understand it. I could see

241

how much they cared, and I thought that they'd be so relieved Peggy was safe that they would be happy about the baby. But it wasn't that simple. It was clear that Mrs Brown especially was having trouble getting used to the idea. It was only a baby after all. As Marje said, she wasn't the first, and she wouldn't be the last.

'Mum's written to my Aunty Emily.'

'Well, she'll want to tell her about the baby.'

'No. Well, yes, she'll tell her about the baby. That's the point. My Aunty Emily lives in London. Mum thinks I should go and stay with her, until ... until the baby's born.'

'But why?'

'Then I can just have the baby and have it adopted. And no one will know. I can come back home and everything will be just the way it was. But it won't be, will it? Nothing will ever be the same again. There'll be a baby. Wherever it is, there'll be a baby.

'Oh I wish I could put the clock back. I would never ever have gone near Richard Henfield. I wish I could go back.' She sank onto my bed looking wretched.

'Peggy!' Mrs Brown was shouting from downstairs. 'Peggy! Are you up there?'

'Yes Mum, just talking to Rosie.'

'Well come down here.'

'What does she want?' I asked.

'Nothing. She just doesn't want me out of her sight, I suppose.' She went downstairs.

This was a grown woman of twenty-six, skulking in her parents' house like a naughty schoolgirl.

Nothing was actually said about the baby. It

was as if by not mentioning it, it didn't exist. But occasionally Mrs Brown would refer to it very obliquely. She would give Peggy an extra helping at meal times and say, 'You've got to keep your strength up.'

There was no question of Peggy going back to work. Instead she gradually took over the house-keeping. She did the washing and ironing and cooked the evening meal. She would then collapse on the sofa while her mother or I did the washing up. Nothing was said, not in my hearing anyway, but the threat of Aunty Emily still hung over the house. Whether Mrs Brown had had a reply yet I didn't know, but we were all walking on eggshells.

The atmosphere in the house had been so heavy that even Janice had kept away, but one day she crept back into the kitchen.

'I really miss the boys,' she said simply, bleakly.

'Oh Janice,' said Peggy immediately giving her a hug. 'It's for the best you know. They're safe at Parkfields. And it must be easier for you at home.'

Janice nodded, unconvinced.

'And there are still plenty of you to keep your mum busy, aren't there?'

Janice nodded again. Then she looked up fiercely. 'Sometimes I really wanted them to be gone. They break things and scream and they ruin everything. Sometimes I *hate* them. But other times ... other times they're just like the little ones. They'll play with Dennis and the baby.'

'Ah yes, but then what happens?' asked Mrs Brown, who had come into the kitchen. 'What happened to Dennis's little truck that your dad

243

made him?'

Janice said nothing.

'They threw it at Dennis, didn't they? Cut his head badly. Could have blinded him. No love, Parkfields is the best place for them. Best for all of you. Now come and have a cup of tea and some cake.' And she led the child towards a chair, her arms protectively around her thin shoulders, as if she could be kind to Janice when she couldn't be kind to her own daughter. And Janice started creeping back into the kitchen with her enormous satchel full of books.

A few days later, Janice was at the table doing her homework – I can't remember whether it was the life cycle of the amoeba or Latin verbs – when she started chewing her pencil and looking at Peggy quizzically.

'Peggy, are you having a baby?'

Peggy went bright red and nearly dropped the kettle.

'What makes you think that?'

'Well, you look as though you are.'

I remembered she had seven brothers, most of them younger than she was.

'Well actually Janice, yes I am, but it's a secret and you're not supposed to tell anyone yet.'

'Well, it won't be a secret for long, will it?' said Janice and calmly went back to the amoeba or Latin, whatever it was.

Mrs Brown must have thought so too. She started producing strange clothes for Peggy to wear, clothes she'd dug out of the attic and altered. Maybe even her own old pregnancy clothes. I'm no expert on 1950s maternity wear but even by the standards of the day they looked pretty bleak. But that evening they inspired Janice to put her pen down for a while.

'Rosie, will you tell me more about the clothes your editor back home wears?' she asked, pushing a lock of lank hair back behind her ears. 'What makes them special?'

'Well,' I said, 'they are always beautifully cut, stylish without being gimmicky and absolutely immaculate.' Janice listened attentively, as if she had to memorise the details for yet another test, as if she were saving up the information for future use.

Peggy watched her for a moment then disappeared upstairs and came down again holding what looked like a tiny leather purse.

'A present for you,' she said to Janice. 'It's a manicure set. Look, there are some nail scissors, some emery boards, and some little sticks to push your cuticles down nice and tidily. See?'

Janice looked, her bright little eyes lighting up her face. 'For me?'

'Yes,' said Peggy. 'Now go and give your hands a really good wash and I'll show you how to use everything. And if you look after your nails properly then next week I'll let you have some of my nail varnish.'

Janice scuttled off to the scullery to wash her hands and then the two of them sat by the range, heads bent down over Janice's hands, absorbed in the manicure. I thought how kind Peggy could be, and how a manicure – however unlikely – seemed the perfect distraction for them both.

Chapter Sixteen

'Job for you,' said Billy, his eyes dancing with laughter as he looked up from the papers on his desk.

I grinned back, relishing the warmth of his smile, the feeling that he and I were about to share a secret joke. 'Just let me get sorted.' I dumped my bag, including my Oxo tin of sandwiches, on my desk. I was glad to be in the office, away from the heavy atmosphere at the Browns', glad to be in the office with Billy, especially glad to be with Billy in this open, laughing mood.

'Sir Howard Castleton,' said 'Billy, 'is a junior government minister.'

'Isn't he the one who talked such rubbish about women drivers?' I interrupted indignantly. 'The one who said women weren't safe driving cars because they would be too busy looking in the mirror to check their lipstick?' My blood boiled at the stupidity and ignorance of the man.

'The very same,' said Billy, his huge smile making him look young and happy, and also making me long to rush forward and kiss him. Kiss him? I could have ravished him there and then on the desk. Instead, I had to content myself with gazing into his big brown eyes. 'And he's coming here today. In fact, he's here to open the new driving test centre.'

'Is he? Well I'd like to tell him just what I think

of him and his crackpot outdated ideas. Everyone knows that women are better drivers than men, much safer, fewer accidents, not so reckless. Just ask the insurance companies. They're no fools. They'll tell you...'

'OK, OK,' laughed Billy, getting up to hand me a piece of paper with the details. 'Somehow I thought you'd feel like that.'

'Honestly, he must be living in the dark ages,' I rattled on, well and truly on my soap box now. 'I mean even in the 1950s. Weren't women driving during the war? They drove cars and buses and lorries then, didn't they? If they're good enough to do it during the war...'

I stopped. Billy was standing close to me holding a finger to his mouth for silence. Then he leant forward and put his finger gently to my lips instead. His eyes held mine for one, two, three seconds. I didn't dare move, didn't want it to stop. We were standing so close, it would have been so easy to kiss him. His eyes looked as if he wanted to kiss me...

But he suddenly turned away, went back to his desk and, without looking up, said, 'He's due at ten o'clock. I've booked a photographer.' He shuffled the papers on his desk for a bit, then glanced up at me. I was still standing where he had left me, clutching the piece of paper in my hand.

'You can drive, of course?' he asked.

'Of course,' I said. 'Since I was seventeen. Passed first time. Bought my own car soon afterwards. No accidents, no speeding tickets, no insurance claims.'

'I thought that's how it would be,' he said, look-

247

ing at me and smiling, almost to himself. 'I thought it would be.'

With that, Alan came in scrunching up a piece of copy paper and muttering about people changing their minds. It looked as though he was going to have to rewrite a story. He booted the ball of paper towards the basket, but Billy suddenly leapt on it and booted it back. As I picked up my bag again and set out for the driving test centre, the two of them were replaying the Cup Final across the newsroom.

I ran down the crowded wooden stairs and out into the spring sunshine, with my hand on my lips, remembering Billy's touch, the expression in his eyes...

At the new driving test centre Sir Howard Castleton was ushered away by his flunkies as soon as he'd made his short and boring speech, so I didn't get a chance to interview him.

But it didn't matter – because Billy had wanted to kiss me. I almost sang it to myself. Billy had wanted to kiss me. He had leant forward, touched my lips, and that look... I dragged myself back to work. Concentrate, girl. Concentrate.

The chief examiner said he was pretty sure that, actually, a greater number of women than men passed their driving test first time. He could give me the figures, if I liked.

'Women drivers are the best,' the story would write itself, though I doubted it would do much to stop the flood of women driver jokes.

Billy had wanted to kiss me. I knew he had wanted to kiss me. I couldn't get the thought or the memory out of my head. Billy...

'Want a lift back?' asked George.

'What? Oh yes please. Thanks.' I got into the van still in a dream. But then we were just getting going when I suddenly spotted the window display in the Home and Colonial. It couldn't be, could it? It was.

'Hang on a minute, George,' I said, 'I've just got to go in here.' In the centre of the window was a wonky-looking pyramid made up of bottles of washing-up liquid. Washing-up liquid! Yup. Squeezy had arrived. I dashed inside and joined the queue.

When I came back and clambered triumphantly into the van with two bottles of washing-up liquid, George asked me how things were going at home.

'Peggy's mum looking forward to being a granny then is she?'

'Not with undiluted joy, no.'

'Is it safe for me to pop around and see Peggy yet?'

'If you take your tin helmet and body armour. But on the basis that you can't make things worse, you might as well. Peggy needs cheering up and I know she likes you.'

'Does she? Does she really?' George seemed quite excited.

'Well I think so. Anyway, you saved her life. She's got to like you.'

I went back up into the office, wondering whether Billy would be there, wondering if he would look at me in the magical way again, wondering if he would say anything...

But the newsroom was empty apart from Marje

at her desk in her little cloud of smoke. She looked up from the notes she was scribbling and, waving the smoke away from her eyes, asked suddenly, 'Did your friend sort out her little problem?'

'Yes, well no, well, she's decided to go ahead and have the baby. Might even be keeping it.'

'Mmm,' more scribbling, then, 'Is Peggy coming back to work soon?'

'No, no I don't think so. I think...'

The official line was that she was on sick leave.

'She was quite close to Henfield, wasn't she?'

'Yes, but–'

'Don't worry. I won't breathe a word. Henfield's secretaries have a habit of leaving suddenly. She should have known. Silly girl.'

'You can't blame her!' I said indignantly. 'Henfield was her boss, older. He shouldn't have led her astray, abused his authority.'

'Henfield is a great editor but a swine of a man. She is old enough to know what she was doing,' said Marje, stubbing out her cigarette and heading down to the subs' room. I shrugged. It wasn't worth arguing about any more.

When I got home from work George was there, sitting at the kitchen table with Peggy, having a cup of tea. He was there to watch my great washing-up liquid demonstration.

'See. One squeeze and it gets everything nice and clean. No rubbing bits of green soap or using washing powder. Simple, isn't it?'

Mrs Brown eyed it all very suspiciously, but later, after she'd done the tea things she came out into the kitchen and said, 'Well it works. I'll grant you that. Very clever, but I bet it costs a lot.'

'No matter, Mrs Brown,' I said, feeling like Lady Bountiful. 'I promise you that as long as I'm staying here, I will buy the washing-up liquid. Anything to make life easier.'

'Oh well, very nice I'm sure,' said Mrs Brown. 'Another cup of tea, George?'

George was very soon quite a regular visitor. He even started helping Janice with her homework. Very knowledgeable about history he was, said it had always been a hobby of his.

But while the atmosphere at home was gradually getting a little easier it still wasn't exactly a laugh a minute. I escaped when I could. I went to a jazz club with Phil. It was very smoky, in a cellar that seemed to smell of damp, and seemed to be full of teachers from the boys' grammar school. I didn't think I liked jazz but I enjoyed the evening there. I drank whisky and ginger and felt quite mellow.

I even went to the theatre on press tickets.

'Anyone want to go to the Hippodrome?' asked Billy one morning, waving a set of tickets in the air. 'Normal reviewer can't do it. It's a thriller. Any takers?'

'I'll have them,' I said – it had to be better than sitting in at the Browns. Phil was doing nights again. 'Do you think Carol would like to come?'

Billy looked surprised for a moment. 'Carol? To the theatre? Yes. I'm sure she would. I'll ask her and let you know tomorrow. I expect her mum will keep an eye on the kids.'

'Tell her to come early.'

I'd been looking out for her shabby brown coat and so I didn't recognise Carol when she arrived

251

at the Hippodrome. She was wearing a boxy jacket and a pencil skirt.

'Gosh, don't you look smart!' I said and then worried that I might seem condescending.

'Are they all right? I made them myself and I'm not sure about the jacket. Billy said reviewers always get the best seats so I thought I'd better look a bit posh,' she said. 'It's ages since I've been to the theatre, proper theatre that is, not just the pantomime.'

'Come on. We've got time for a drink.'

Up in the circle bar hardly anyone had arrived yet so I was served quickly. 'Gin and tonic,' I said to Carol, as I brought them over to the table. 'Is that all right?'

'Smashing,' she said, she lifted the glass and breathed in the fumes of the gin. It was so like Caz I had the most dreadful ache for my own life, my real life. For a moment the yearning was a sharp physical pain – that longing to be in a bar with Caz having a good gossip over a bottle of Chablis at the end of the day. Oh God, how I missed it. I missed it so much. I felt tears coming. I blinked quickly.

'Strong isn't it?' said Carol, happily knocking back the gin.

'I'll just get us another. Before the rush,' I said. 'On expenses,' I added so that she would enjoy it even more and not feel obliged to offer to pay. When I came back with them – doubles again – Carol nudged me and nodded towards a woman just coming in. She was removing a beautifully-cut jacket to show a fitted dress with a boat neckline that showed her shoulders and elegant neck to best advantage.

'What a corker!' whispered Carol. 'Not like her.' She pointed towards a well-upholstered matron, corseted so tightly that she was already having to use her programme to fan her glowing face.

Soon Carol and I were studying all the people coming in. Here there'd be a dress that Carol thought she could copy, there was someone looking frightful in totally the wrong colour. In the circle bar we had the pick of small-town fashion to gaze at, and we made the most of it.

'He's a bit of all right,' said Carol suddenly, gazing at an elegant young man who'd come in with an older woman, probably his mother, 'but no he's got a moustache. That's no good. It would tickle, wouldn't it?' She started to giggle. It was infectious and as the second bell rang and we went in to find our seats, we were shaking with silent laughter.

In the darkness of the theatre while the bodies piled up on stage, Carol sat forward in her seat, totally absorbed in the action, happy and relaxed. Meanwhile, I thought of Billy and felt guilty and miserable. How could I be a friend to Carol when I wanted Billy so much? True, we hadn't done anything. But oh how I wanted to. And I was sure that Billy wanted me as much as I wanted him. The incident of the almost-kiss was part of it.

I'd ordered more gin for the interval and we sat giggling in the corner while the well-upholstered matrons glared at us disapprovingly, which, of course, made us giggle even more.

At the end of the evening, as we made our way with the crowds out into the fresh air, Carol was still bubbling away about the play and the people she'd seen.

'I've had a really nice time,' she said, as we stood at the edge of the town centre where our ways parted. 'Really nice. I think I might be a bit squiffy.' She beamed happily. 'It does me good to get out of the house sometimes and away from the kids – not that I would be without them, of course, but it's good to have a laugh and a chat. Anyway, perhaps we can have a coffee soon. If my slave-driving husband will let you out. My treat next time.'

'Great. Yes. Soon,' I said and managed to smile.

Suddenly I heard footsteps running towards us. I tensed as I turned.

'Hello girls! Have you had a good evening? Was the play good?'

'Billy!' said Caz. 'What are you doing here?'

'Well, as your ma was babysitting, I made the most of it, finished some work and then went for a drink with the subs. Then I thought I'd find you and walk you home.'

'Oooh, romantic,' said Carol. 'Just like when we were courting.' She put her arm through his and pulled him towards her. It couldn't have hurt more if she'd slapped me.

Billy looked at her. 'Have you been drinking, Carol?' he asked, surprised.

'Just a little gin or two with my friend Rosie,' she said.

'Just as well I'm here to see you home then,' he said and although he smiled, somewhere there was an edge, just a little edge of disapproval. He turned to me. 'Will you be all right, Rosie?' he asked, politely, courteously, distantly.

'Yes, of course. Fine. It's only a step away,' I answered, flustered, trying to seem cool. I pulled my jacket around me and set off purposefully. At the corner, I looked back. Billy and Carol were arm in arm strolling down the lamplit street. But as I watched, Billy turned. His arm still in Carol's he looked back at me over his shoulder and kept on looking until the darkness swallowed them up. I ran home.

It was as if Billy was playing a game with me. I often caught him looking at me. He'd be leaning back in his chair trying to think of an intro, and he'd be gazing at me. And I couldn't work out the expression on his face. At other times he would bounce ideas off me – suggestions for stories, how they could be covered.

'I like your American way of thinking,' he would say. 'It's different, fresh. Better than sleepy old England, eh?'

Or he'd hand me a story and go out of his way to be helpful, leaning over my desk and scribbling names and addresses of contacts. It was very much the way Will and I worked together. And although I loved the closeness with Billy, the friendlier he was, the harder it was for me to cope. If I got Billy to love me, then what? What about Carol? The kids? There didn't seem to be any easy solution.

So I did what I always do when things are tricky – I went shopping.

Only there weren't any shops. There was a tiny Marks and Spencer, which was full of cardigans and underpants and dreary dresses. There was no Top Shop, no Zara, Mango, Monsoon, H&M,

Jigsaw, Hobbs, River Island, Next, Principles, Gap, Laura Ashley, no Harvey Nicks, no Primark, no Wallis, Warehouse, French Connection, Karen Millen, Kookai, Oasis, no ... well, you get the picture. Which was very bleak.

There were a number of chichi little shops that sold 'Ladies' Modes' and I actually had to work out what that meant. One had a fur coat in the window. I think not.

There was no Debenhams, John Lewis or Selfridges. The nearest the town had to a department store was Adcocks, which was a series of small shops knocked together, but it actually had a pair of jeans in the window. True, they were in a side window under a handwritten sign saying, 'Teenage fashion!' but it was a start. I went in.

I'd hardly got through the door when a middle-aged woman in a black dress came sweeping down on me. 'Can I help you, madame?'

'Oh yes please. You have some jeans in the window?'

'Jeans? Ah yes, the denim slacks.' She wrinkled her nose as though there was a nasty smell. 'Miss Marshall will help you. Miss Marshall!'

Another woman came gliding over and led me through a warren of rooms, up steps, down steps until we came to a tiny room, where a display model wore a pair of jeans and a peasant-style top. That looked quite fun.

'Could I see what jeans you have please?'

'We have those, madame.'

'Is that the only style you have?'

'Yes, madame. Would you like to try a pair? What size are we?'

I wanted to say 'Well we're a size ten but I don't know about you sunshine,' but I resisted. Instead, 'Size ten,' I said meekly. 'And I'd like to try the top as well, please.'

She looked at me. She sniffed. She showed me into a tiny fitting room with a wonky chair, and then brought me the clothes. I tried the blouse on first. I pushed my arms in. Pushed. And stopped. I was stuck. My arms couldn't actually fit all the way into the sleeves. They had got halfway and no further. What's more, I was trapped.

Let's make this clear. My arms are not Victoria Beckham stringy skinny, but they are not fat. In fact, I can honestly say they are quite decent arms. I can wear skinny fits and never have to cover up!

But now I was trapped in these tight sleeves. My arms stuck out like a scarecrow. I tried to pull the sleeves down. I couldn't. As I tried to reach one sleeve with the other hand, I could feel the cotton material straining around my back, ready to rip. I stopped. Maybe I could sort of shrug it off, backwards... If I pushed both my arms out behind me, then maybe I could just ease one sleeve down a bit and then I'd be able to do it...

So there I was, arms stuck out behind me like a chicken, face bright red, sleeves stuck, when the sales assistant just yanked the fitting-room curtain open and stood there.

It's difficult to feel cool and superior when you're bright pink and stuck in a blouse that's too small. 'What size *is* this?' I asked crossly.

'Size ten, madame, as you asked,' she said frostily, as she eased the sleeves off me. I rubbed my arms. They now had bright red rings halfway

257

up. 'You might find this a better fit.' She handed me another blouse. Size sixteen. Sixteen! I'm never a sixteen.

I tried it on. It fitted. I know when I'm beaten. I didn't even try the size ten jeans, but went straight to the sixteens. Even they were snug and the cut was pretty rubbish, but they were OK. They'd do. Obviously sizes were completely different in the 1950s. I took them out to Frosty Face and followed her back through the warren of rooms to the till.

'It's the milk, I believe, madame,' she said.

The milk?

'I understand Americans drink a lot of milk. It's why you tend to be taller and ... better made ... than us. After all, we went through a war, rationing... We always noticed it when your GIs were here in the war. Such strapping young men...' Her face went suddenly dreamy. I just did so not want to go there. I took my jeans and blouse and fled, feeling suddenly like a giant and even more out of place in this strange world.

When I got home, the first thing I did was cut the labels off. Size sixteen ... never.

Chapter Seventeen

When Phil came around one sunny Saturday morning and asked me if I fancied a day at the seaside, I leapt at the chance. Just the opportunity to wear my new clothes, perfect for the back of a bike. Though Mrs Brown didn't think so. As I came downstairs in my new jeans she looked at me and asked, 'Is that considered decent in America, then?'

Mr Brown laughed. 'Of course it is,' he said. 'Those are cowboy trousers. That's what cowboys wear.'

'Not like that, they don't,' sniffed Mrs Brown.

'These are girl's jeans, Mrs Brown,' I said, and gave a little wiggle. And then I felt guilty because Peggy was standing there in a shapeless old skirt, the only thing that would fit her now, though probably not for much longer.

'Enjoy yourself,' she said. If I could see envy in her eyes, I pretended not to.

It was about thirty miles to the coast. Quite a long way on bumpy roads on the back of a bike, but it was just wonderful to feel so free. Spring was well and truly here. The sun was shining and the wind was blowing my hair, so even the odd bit of grit in my eye couldn't bother me.

There were quite a few cars about, but we drove straight onto the prom and parked up. I felt like a kid. I wanted to rush down on the sand.

'Why not? Race you...' We dashed down. I pulled my shoes off and felt the sand between my toes and the little ripple of waves breaking on my feet.

'Ow! It's cold!'

'Still early in the year,' laughed Phil.

We walked the entire length of the bay and then put our shoes back on to scramble up a path to the top of a cliff. There was a big corrugated tin building in a grim shade of green. On the side in huge white letters was painted TEAS. Phil went in and emerged a few minutes later with a tin tray carrying a tin teapot, a tin milk jug and two thick white cups and saucers, and a couple of solid-looking scones. He carried them over to the top of the cliff where I was sitting on the grass, looking at the huge drifts of pale pink thrift coming into bloom alongside the paths.

'Beautiful, isn't it?' said Phil.

I nodded. And then burst into tears. Oh God, I know it was a stupid thing to do. And I don't even know why it happened at that particular moment. Except maybe because I'd started to relax.

'What's the matter?' asked Phil, looking concerned and frightened.

'I want to go ho-o-ome,' I wailed. Pathetic, or what?

'Right. Fine. I'll just take these things back.'

'No, not home here. Real home. Proper home. Where I belong.'

Phil was hunting through his pockets. He found a nice, big, clean, white hanky and passed it to me. Then after I'd given my nose a good honk, he put his arm around me. 'Well you're bound to get homesick occasionally.'

'I did at first, dreadfully, but then I thought I'd got used to it. I haven't been thinking about home so much,' I said with a sniff.

And I hadn't. I had got drawn into this 1950s life. Sometimes, home – proper home – seemed like a dream. It was getting further and further away from me. And maybe that was the problem. I was scared of forgetting where I came from, where I belonged, who I really was...

Then the floodgates opened and I started.

'Everything's so different here. I want home and my friends and comfy clothes and proper showers and going out at night and big televisions and computers and my phone and texting and fluffy towels and garlic and curry and soft loo roll and cars and the Internet. I want everything to be light and bright and white and clean not scruffy and shabby and smelling of mice. I want creams and shampoos and lotions and potions and mascara you don't have to spit on and my boots and my duvet and my iPod. I want … oh I want so many things and most of all I want people like Caz and my mum and dad. But most of all I want Will.'

I only stopped because I couldn't breathe and cry and talk at the same time. If this was Narnia, of course, there'd be Aslan to guard me. Or a faun or a talking horse. At the very least I'd have a bottle of magic elixir to make things better, or a magic hunting horn to summon help. As it was I just had me. And sort of Phil.

I thought of that hymn again. *Dwellers all in time and space.* Somewhere I'd lost my way in time and space. I was locked out of where I should be. I wanted to go home and I didn't know how. Nothing was sure. Nothing was certain. Everything was out of focus and wrong. Panic was bubbling up into my throat, choking me. There must be some way I could get home. There had to be.

Phil was brilliant. He kept his arm around me and at the same time poured me some tea into the big thick white cup.

'Drink this,' he said. 'It will make you feel better.'

261

Oh God, I'm lost in time somewhere and this man thinks a cup of tea can help. But it did, sort of. Phil really was such a decent man.

'You'll go home again. Of course you will. Don't worry. Home is still there waiting for you.' His voice was gentle, repetitive, hypnotic. I began to calm down. Took deep breaths. Concentrated on Phil's arm around me. Let his voice murmur on, gently, soothingly.

I looked out at the sea and wondered if it was the same sea I'd seen before. Something someone once said about never bathing in the same river twice came into my head. I tried to make sense of it and I couldn't. And suddenly I was too tired to try. For weeks I'd been battling to find out where I was and why I was here. And I just didn't know if I could any more.

At least I'd stopped howling. I sniffed again, wiped my eyes and my nose, and shuddered a bit. 'I'm sorry, Phil. What a scene. You bring me on a nice day out and I just go and cry all over you.'

Phil – bless him – looked relieved that I was talking more or less normally.

'Nothing to apologise for. It's all quite normal, quite natural,' he was saying soothingly. 'We used to see it in the army, time and again. Young lads getting on with things, no bother. Then suddenly, for no reason, out of nowhere, you'd get struck by the most awful homesickness. I remember getting really drunk one night because I suddenly missed my dog of all things, and I was just pig sick of sleeping in a wooden hut with nineteen other smelly snoring blokes and having to queue for everything, queue for a meal, queue for a shower, queue for a sh—Well, you get the idea. It's bound to happen. Only natural. Don't worry about it. Here...'

He passed me a scone. I nibbled it, still sniffing.

'So how long are you going to be over here for?'

'That's the trouble. I don't know. No idea at all, really. It's complicated. I can't really explain. But I didn't think it was going to be very long.'

'Well that's all right then,' said Phil easily. 'If you're not here very long, then all you have to do is make the most of it while you are. Get your head down and get on with it and you might find you enjoy it. Well some of it anyway. That's how most of us got through national service. It's the best way. Honest.'

He smiled at me. He looked so straightforward and cheerful. His pale blue eyes were full of kindly concern and I really wished I could love him.

'Here we are,' he said, 'in glorious sunshine with a marvellous view across the sea. Let's just enjoy this and not worry about what will happen next, shall we?'

It was as good a plan as any. I was already feeling a bit of a fool over my outburst. I managed a small smile for him. So we drank our tea and threw the remains of the scones for the seagulls, and then we walked back along the cliff path to the promenade. The turf was springy under my feet and Phil was holding my hand and whistling. The sun glinted on the waves and we seemed to have the whole world pretty much to ourselves. Wherever and whenever it was – it was a very good moment in time and space. The spring sun was surprisingly warm and I felt as though it was soothing me, taking out the twists and aches.

Back down on the prom we bought an Italian ice cream and had a go at the slot machines in the amusement arcade. Phil almost got a bar of chocolate in one of those crane thingies, but of course it slid out just before it got to the chute.

'Has anyone *ever* won anything from this machine, do you think?'

'Well, I'm sure that chocolate was there when I was a kid before the war,' said Phil.

A kid before the war... Who was this person I was with...?

I shook my head and licked my ice cream. As the man said, enjoy the moment.

Back on the bike, we took a roundabout route home via a tiny fishing village. There was a pub right down by the little quayside, and lots of boats were pulled up on the beach. It was a place of lobster pots and fishing nets and the real smell of the sea. The sort of place so simple and un-spoilt that you don't think it exists any more. And I suppose it probably doesn't. We sat on the wall and ate crab sandwiches, drank a beer or two and watched the sun set. Then climbed back on the bike and came home.

'Phil, thank you. It has been a really lovely day,' I said when we got home. 'And thank you for being so kind. I'm sorry I was an idiot.'

'Shh, not an idiot. Just normal,' he said. He took me in his arms and kissed me gently.

'I don't know who this Will is who you miss so badly. But I think he's a jolly lucky chap.'

Then he went back to his bike and roared off.

Chapter Eighteen

All right I knew I shouldn't have done it. But I had to know how Billy felt. Is that so bad?

It was early evening in the office. Billy had been going through the day's stories with Brian the Night News Editor, ready to hand over to him. Phil, on nights again, had gone straight to a meeting of the Memorial Swimming Baths Committee, and wasn't back yet. I was just typing up a story about a bull in a china shop. Yes really. A young bullock had escaped from the auction mart and had rampaged into the High Street. Seeing its own reflection in a shop window, it had charged at it and broken the glass. The shop actually sold toys and fancy goods, but as it had a display of souvenir mugs and ashtrays in the window, most of which had got smashed to smithereens, I thought it was fair enough to call it a china shop. Call it journalistic licence. The bullock, shocked and shaken, had eventually been recaptured by a couple of farmers and an energetic young policeman. Charlie had a picture of them all leading it away.

'Nearly finished,' I called across to Brian. 'The subs can have this, in two minutes.'

There's always a strange atmosphere in an office at the end of the day. *The News* was a twenty-four-hour operation. Yet after six o'clock, the atmosphere changed. Unlike the twenty-first century, where office and printing centre were separate, in the 1950s they were still in the same building. Evening work was done against a background of the sound of the presses rumbling away in the cavernous press room on the ground floor. Instead of the office and advertising staff in the building, you'd bump into printers in aprons and overalls, covered in ink. Or messengers carrying copy from the subs to the printers. *The News* printed five different editions – the first was for the furthest fringes of its circulation area, the last for the town and its immediate surroundings. By the time the last edition started printing at about three in the morning, the first edition had been printed and bundled up and stacked onto the first of the fleet of vans that rumbled out into the darkness through the big gates.

Although it was still daylight outside, the light had begun to fade, and by the time it had fought its way through the grubby windows of the newsroom and the pile of papers and files tottering on the windowsills, there wasn't much of it left. I had a small light near me, but the atmosphere in the office was closer, more intimate than in day time. I finished typing my story with a very satisfying 'ends', pulled the paper out of the typewriter and separated it into the three copies, making one or two pencil corrections on each copy in turn. I did it almost automatically now. The thought of a computer, with spell check and direct input into the editorial system, seemed a long, long way away. Maybe I'd even dreamt it.

I could feel Billy watching me. I looked up swiftly, briefly, and saw that he was sitting at his desk reading some copy. But I knew he wasn't really reading it. He was waiting for something. Waiting for me. No. He couldn't be.

I checked the corrections and folded the sets of copy paper story facing outwards – making a show of having finished.

'I'll take those along to the subs if you like,' said Billy, picking up the stories with his own copy.

'Thanks.' I deliberately didn't look at him. I wanted this to be casual, accidental.

And yes, I could have picked up my jacket and been down the stairs and out of that building in thirty seconds flat. It was late. I'd finished. I was ready to go home. But I wasn't. And I didn't.

Instead I got my jacket and left it draped across my desk – obvious to anyone that I was still in the building but about to leave – went to the loo and washed my hands. And I waited.

Billy would be a few minutes in with the subs. If I listened hard I could hear their voices, his amongst them, floating faintly down the corridors. Say five minutes, I thought to myself. Five minutes would be about right. And I counted. Sad, isn't it? But I counted down, '300, 299, 298, 297...' standing there by the dingy little wash basin with its grey cloth, hard green soap, and tin of Vim. When I got to 129 – still more than two minutes to go – I wanted to change my mind and go back to the newsroom. But I made myself wait.

And it worked. At a silent triumphant 'One!' I took a deep breath and emerged, back down the corridor and into the newsroom at the same time as Billy. He went to the coat stand and got his jacket. It was only natural that we should walk down the stairs together and out into the Market Place where the air seemed so clean and fresh and quiet after *The News*. Just two colleagues who happened to leave the office at the same time.

We talked about my story, laughed about it. It was the sort of conversation we'd had often enough when we'd been with Alan or Phil. But this time was different. There was a tension in the air – a wonderful toe-tingling tension, a sense of possibilities ... just like the time I first met Will. Only then I wasn't sure if he was the man for me. This time around I knew. I'd never been more certain in my life. All the time we were talking I was so aware that it was just the two of us. And I knew he was too. The conversation became stilted, loaded.

'Well the newsroom has certainly changed since you joined us.'

'For better or worse?'

(Damn! Didn't mean to echo wedding vows...)

'Oh better. We've never had a woman in reporters before.'

'Billy! What about Marje? Isn't she a woman?'

'Yes of course, but well, she's older, isn't she. You're different. You look at things differently. Think differently. It's good. Must be the American way.'

(I had long given up explaining that I wasn't American. After all, it acted as explanation for such a lot of things.)

He was smiling down at me. 'When you talk, well, sometimes I don't know what you're on about – computers, and phones you can put in your pocket, and getting information out of the air. It's like something out of a film, but I like to hear you talk about it.

'And I like your ideas for the paper. You make it sound more interesting. Looking forward, not into the past all the time. It's the future we want to be thinking of. I love to hear you talk about it. In fact ...' and he stopped and turned to face me '...in fact, I just love to hear you talk.'

His words hung on the evening air. The way he was looking at me, you can be sure he wasn't thinking of work. I held my breath and looked at him, waiting to see what he would say next.

'Rosie. Do you have to go straight home? Shall we...? Maybe a drink?'

He looked at me anxiously, seriously, and I knew this was more than a quick after work drink with colleagues.

'Why not?' I said. 'Where?'

And with that there came a shout.

'Dad! Da–ad!'

A small figure on a battered bike was hurtling down a narrow side street and into the Market Place. Oh no, talk about timing...

'Davy. Whoa, careful son!'

The small boy and bike had screeched to a halt with the help of feeble brakes and the toes of his shoes. Around his waist he wore a mock leather cowboy-style belt with holsters, each holding a toy gun. He sat astride his bike, face bright red, hair sticking up on end, and a huge grin on his face.

'Hiya Dad! I thought it was you.' He looked very pleased with himself.

Billy was caught off guard, but quickly laughed. 'Well if it isn't Two-Gun Tex!' he said. 'Howdy pardner!' He looked at his watch and immediately switched to caring dad mode 'Hey, it's time you were home. Mum will be worried.'

'Yes, I know. I've been to Kevin's, but if I'm with you, that's all right then, isn't it?'

Billy tried to look cross, but didn't make a good job of it. 'Right, then we'd better get home as quick as we can. Come on, cowboy.'

He turned to me. 'Nice talking to you, Rosie. See you tomorrow!'

And with that he went, loping along with one hand on Davy's shoulder as the little boy pedalled down the street. I stood there, staring after him, helpless with frustration. What had Billy been planning? He clearly wanted to be alone with me. Where could it have led to? Whatever it was, his son had gone and spoilt it. I leant back hard against a nearby cherry tree, sending a flutter of pink blossom around my shoulders. Like confetti. Well, that was a sick bloody joke, wasn't it?

I longed to be with Billy, but part of me was pleased, maybe relieved, that Davy had come along just when he did. I think...

I walked off home, striding out as quickly as possible in a bid to stop myself from crying. My plan to get Billy to myself had failed miserably – thwarted by a scruffy urchin on a bike. But, of course, he was Billy's scruffy urchin. His son.

Despite that magic, that electricity between us, there was nothing that could disguise the fact: Billy was a husband and father. Apart from in the office, there was no way I could fit into that equation.

And what about Carol? She was meant to be my friend. How could I take her husband away

270

from her? Oh! I wanted to shout in rage and frustration.

Instead, I tried to think of something else, anything else, other than Billy and his family. I wondered what culinary delights lay waiting for me, drying inexorably under an upturned plate in the bottom oven of the range. In fact, I think Mrs Brown had mentioned making rissoles from the final remains of the weekend joint. Rissoles. And probably last night's leftover potatoes and cabbage as a fry-up or bubble and squeak. Not a dish to lift the spirits.

But as I pushed open the back door to the Browns' and went into the kitchen, I knew something was up. Mrs Brown was bustling around with the best cups and saucers, white porcelain with a little blue flower, and the place was fizzing with excitement.

'Oh Rosie! You're just in time! Go on through.'

In time for what? Intrigued, I hung up my jacket on the back of the kitchen door, dumped my bag and walked through to the sitting room.

What a scene. Mr Brown was sitting in his usual armchair, with a bottle of beer and a bemused expression. Meanwhile on the sofa sat George, also with a bottle of beer and looking completely at home, while next to him was Peggy, smiling rather tensely. Mrs Brown came through with the tray laden with tea things, including neatly cut sandwiches, a huge fruit cake, and a Battenberg cake, with its pink and yellow squares. Gosh. That was a real sign of celebration – a shop-bought Battenberg. She placed the tray on the table then went to the dark oak sideboard and opened one of the cupboards. From it she took a bottle of Harvey's Bristol Cream sherry and three small gold-rimmed glasses. She placed the glasses carefully on a cork mat and poured the sherry. She handed a glass to me and one to Peggy.

'It's like Christmas!' giggled Peggy.

'Is this a celebration? What are we celebrating?' I asked, bemused by the sudden lightening of the grim atmosphere that had pressed so heavily on the Browns recently.

'A toast,' said Mrs Brown. 'Shall you do it, Father, or shall I?'

Mr Brown waved a hand in her direction. He looked too stunned to speak.

'A toast? What are we drinking to?'

'To George and Peggy!' said Mrs Brown grandly, raising her glass. 'To their future happiness together!'

The sherry hadn't even got to my lips and I was already choking. 'Together? George and Peggy? You mean...?'

'Yes,' said George, beaming proudly. 'I asked Peggy to marry me and she said yes.' He reached out and held Peggy's hand. He looked young and proud and there were a million questions I wanted to ask him, chiefly, 'Do you know what you're doing?' and, 'Are you sure?', possibly followed by, 'Are you mad?'

But he looked so pleased with himself and so happy that they all died in my throat. Instead I raised my little glass of sherry and said 'Congratulations! I wish you all the happiness in the world!'

And George blushed and looked about fourteen again. Then I recognised the atmosphere in the room for what it was. It wasn't excitement – except perhaps on George's part. It wasn't celebration. It wasn't even happiness. No, it was relief, sheer unadulterated relief. A huge problem had been solved, thanks to young George.

Peggy had found a husband. Peggy had found a father for her baby. Respectability and reputation were saved. No wonder the Browns were so pleased. Just when everything had seemed as black as it could possibly be, George had ridden to the rescue. I was beginning to understand how important it was.

No matter that George was six years younger than his bride-to-be. That they had never gone out together. That Peggy had never considered George as anything other than a young lad in the office seemed of no relevance at all. He had presented himself as husband material and they had been only too eager to snap him up.

Getting pregnant and being abandoned was one thing – a shame too terrible to befall any well brought-up young girl. And her child would be a living reminder. As long as the child was there and the mother was on her own, no one would ever forget that she was a fallen woman, a girl who had sold herself too cheaply. For the rest of her life, and her child's life, she would be labelled as the woman who was loose or foolish. A few might pity her for being too trusting, and condemn the man involved, but more would condemn her for giving herself too easily, for not ensuring a proper father for her unborn child.

And there were the practicalities ... who would support her and the baby? There were benefits, but they were pretty basic I think.

But getting pregnant and getting married, well, that was a different thing. That was just two young people so in love that they couldn't wait. Not ideal perhaps, but understandable, forgivable. Except that it wasn't George's baby...

'Are you sure about this?' I had to ask as the others busied themselves with plates and sandwiches and finding the big sharp knife to cut the cake.

'Never surer. I've loved Peggy ever since I was about fourteen, I thought she was a great girl. And when I was doing my national service, well...' he gave Peggy a quick sideways glance '...I used to dream about her. She was always the one for me and now I'm the one for her too.'

'But ... but you're only twenty.'

'Soon be twenty-one. That's why my mum was so easy to give her permission for us to wed. Said I could do it soon enough without her say-so she might as well give me her blessing.'

'Permission?' I was floundering here.

'Yes, because I'm not twenty-one yet. But that doesn't mean I don't know what I'm doing. We'll be fine, just fine,' he said firmly. Already he had a different air about him. He looked confident, determined. He looked ... well, grown up, I suppose.

It turned into quite a party. The men had another couple of beers each and Mrs Brown poured us another sherry. It was very sweet, but seemed to go straight to my head. Oh God, now I sounded like my gran... Finally, Mrs Brown was clearing the dishes, gathering up the tray.

'Ooh, I must write to our Stephen, tell him he's

gaining a brother. And he's going to be an uncle. Help me with this into the kitchen, would you, Rosie?' she said. 'Then we can leave those two lovebirds together.'

Lovebirds?

In the space of a moment it seems that Mrs Brown had redrafted the entire scene. This wasn't a desperate wedding hastily planned to save her daughter's name and reputation. No, George and Peggy had suddenly been transformed into a pair of devoted lovers, giggling young things who must be left to do their courting in private.

How long, I wondered, before she managed to convince herself that the baby, now growing so obviously, was George's, and Henfield would be wiped out of this cosy domestic picture?

I went to bed early, and I was sitting up reading *Pride and Prejudice* for the umpteenth time, wondering idly how Will would look in breeches and a wet shirt – when Peggy knocked and came in. She hesitated for a moment and then sat on the bed.

I didn't say a thing. I waited.

'I couldn't do it on my own,' she said. 'I know you said you had lots of friends who did. But I can't. I just couldn't.

'And I couldn't give it away either. I know that. I thought I could.' She put her hands over the little bump, already protecting her unborn child. 'But I knew life won't be like it was before, whatever I do. So this is the best way.'

I still didn't say anything.

'I know George is a lot younger, but well, he's always had a bit of a crush on me. He's a nice lad, a good lad. I'm fond of him.'

It was no good. I couldn't keep my lip zipped any longer.

'Look, if George had asked you out six months ago, six weeks ago even, you wouldn't have considered it. You would have laughed at him for his cheek. And now you're thinking of marrying him. Marrying's for ever, Peggy. You and George. If' – I remembered something Carol had said – 'if Gregory Peck came by tomorrow, you'd have to say "Sorry. I'm marrying George."

'And what about George? Are you being fair to him? He barely earns enough to keep himself and you're saddling him with someone else's baby. What if there's a girl waiting for him somewhere? A nice young girl, who he can have a bit of fun with for a few years before they even start thinking of babies? Have you thought about that?'

'Of course I've thought of it!' snapped Peggy. 'I've thought of so much that my head's bursting with thinking! All I know is that this is the best way for me. It's best for my parents too. And it's best for the baby. And as for George...

'You know I remember what it was like when I was ... when I was down by the mill, when you and George found me. I know what I felt like then. Everything was black, it was the end, I couldn't see any way out, any single little way that life would be worth living again. Even when I was in hospital I couldn't say, I really couldn't say that I was glad to be alive. I couldn't. I wasn't. Part of me still wished that you and George hadn't bothered, that you'd just left me there to die in peace.

'No listen, please. I'm not ungrateful, I'm really

not. Because the one thing that kept coming into my head as I was lying in hospital was George's voice saying, "Come on Peg, you can do it. It'll be all right." And his arm around me as you carried me back to the car. You and George saved me and my baby when we didn't want to be saved. And now I'm so pleased and grateful that you did.

'No, I'm not madly in love with George, but somehow, he brought me back to this life. I know he cares about me. He always has. And I'm beginning to care about him. Really. And if he looks after me and this baby, I will look after George. He's a good man – and he is a man, although he's only twenty – and I'm going to do my very best to make him happy. I promise that. It's what he deserves. And I won't forget that.'

She looked up at me. 'It's the best solution, Rosie, the best there can be.'

I clambered out of bed and reached out and hugged her. What else could I do?

Chapter Nineteen

Billy was ignoring me. Not nastily or obviously, but he was definitely ignoring me.

I knew it was because he'd nearly made a pass at me. Oh God, I would love to know what would have happened next if Davy hadn't come along. Would we have gone to the pub? For a walk? Would he have told me what he thought of me? He had already been saying nice things.

But the moment – if moment it had been – had definitely passed. And Billy was clearly regretting the little bit he had said. He hardly spoke to me. And when he did, it was brisk and businesslike. Perfectly polite, but he was definitely avoiding eye contact. Yet sometimes, I knew he was looking at me across the office. I could feel his eyes on me. If I turned around, I'd see a tiny movement just out of eye range, but Billy would be bent over his typewriter, or the diary, or his notebook. It was wonderful that he cared, that he felt the same as I did. But he wasn't going to do anything about it. I knew he wanted to, but he wouldn't, because he was a married man, a family man.

I admired him for that. Loved him even more. I loved his loyalty to his children. I loved the way he spent time with them, teaching them things. He didn't try and pretend he was a kid too, fooling around with them. He was their father and he took that seriously.

Most of all, though, I loved him for his loyalty to Carol. I knew he was falling for me, but he was trying hard not to, because of his loyalty to his wife. I genuinely admired him for that – even if it made me feel utterly miserable.

I was sitting in the newsroom, typing up a very dull story about Bob-a-Job week (sending small boys to knock on doors offering their services. Paedo fantasy or what?) and trying not to put my head down on the typewriter and weep, when young George came bouncing in.

'All ready for Thursday then, Rosie?' he asked happily, to a chorus of comments from the men in the room.

Word had got around about the wedding and had stunned everybody, hardly surprising since George and Peggy had never even been out together. Marje had guessed the story but I knew I could trust her to say nothing, so everyone presumed Peggy's baby was George's, which meant he got all the sympathy – and the rude comments.

'Hey George, hear you been paddling without your boots on!' yelled one of the young messengers walking past the door.

George took it all, responded merely by grinning. He really did seem so pleased to be marrying Peggy. I hoped she'd make him happy.

It was a special licence job. Bit of a rushed do.

'Well,' said Mrs Brown with her mouth full of pins that evening, 'it's not as though we're inviting anybody. We haven't got much to organise.' She was busy trying to alter a dress for Peggy to wear, letting-out seams, moving buttons.

'It's not the way I thought my only daughter would be getting married. Not the way at all.'

'My friend Kate had a lovely dress when she got married, even though she was six months pregnant,' I said chattily as I brought them a tray of tea. 'You can get nice posh maternity dresses, even wedding dresses.'

Mrs Brown nearly choked. 'I never heard of such a thing! Maternity wedding dresses! Well really!'

I could have pointed out that Peggy was far from the only girl in need of such a thing, but guessed I'd be wasting my breath.

The wedding was going to be extremely quiet,

in the register office. Just the Browns and George's mum, and George's friend Derek as best man. It all seemed very hole in the corner to me, not exactly a celebration.

'There!' Mrs Brown handed the dress to Peggy, who slipped it on. To be fair, her mother had done a good job. The dress, a pale silk, looked dressy and flattering.

'What are you going to wear on top?'

'I don't know. My coat I suppose.'

Oh dear. Her coat was fine, but it was very fitted. It was some time since she'd been able to do it up.

'There's no point in buying anything new just for the day,' snapped Mrs Brown. 'You've got plenty of other things you'll need to spend your money on.'

Which gave me an idea...

In the window of Adcocks, I had spotted a very nice jacket. I had fancied it for myself but dismissed it as I had nothing really to wear it with. It was a mid colour blue, short, loose and fastened with one huge button. It was young and fun. It would, I thought, go perfectly with Peggy's let-out dress, be fashionable but yet would fit nicely over the burgeoning bump, and I wanted to buy it for her.

I would have liked her to have come with me to choose it and try it on, but until the wedding, Peggy was practically in purdah, hardly allowed out until she had that wedding ring on her finger and was respectable again. So I went back to Adcocks and faced Frosty Face and tried the jacket on. It was – as Frosty Face pointed out – a bit tight across the shoulders for me, but Peggy was narrower there than I was, so that would be fine. And it was plenty big enough in the middle to flow over the bump. So I forked out a week's wages for it, and took it home. Janice was sitting at the kitchen table with her homework (railways of Canada; functions of the lungs). The room smelt of the onions in the corned beef hash bubbling on the top of the range for supper. Peggy was sitting in her dad's chair, sewing, surrounded by huge swathes of old sheets, much patched and darned. She looked tense and tired, not a bit like a bride only days before her wedding.

'What are you doing?'

'Making cot sheets. These are all Mother's old sheets that she was keeping for tea towels, but I think I can manage to cut a few cot sheets out of them.'

'Gosh,' I said, 'are cot sheets that expensive to buy?'

Peggy laughed. 'You don't *buy* cot sheets. What a waste of money that would be. Mind you, I think I'll be hemming sheets in my sleep. What have you got there?'

I pushed the old sheets out of the way and placed the big box ceremoniously on the table.

'For you.'

'For me?'

'Yes. Open it.' I grinned and Peggy giggled and looked years younger. She stuck her needle carefully into the small cot sheet, put it down on the table, stood up wiping the stray bits of cotton off her, and picked up the box.

'It's from Adcocks!'

281

'Yes.' Peggy unfastened the string and opened the box to reveal a cloud of tissue paper. She removed it carefully, putting it on the table to be folded and used again.

'Oh! It's a jacket!'

'Yes, it's a jacket. What's more, it's a jacket for you to wear on your wedding day. I just hope the colour's right.'

Peggy carefully took the jacket out of the tissue paper and looked at it. Oh God, I thought, she doesn't like it... Quite the opposite. 'It's beautiful!' she said.

'Try it on.'

Even over the old jumper and shapeless skirt she was wearing, the jacket looked good. We took it upstairs and tried it against the dress.

'It goes perfectly,' said Janice, who had followed us up. Janice stroked the jacket and looked in admiration at the big button, the silky lining. 'It's wonderful, isn't it?' she said, almost in awe. 'Very special.'

'Here Janice, you try it on for a second,' said Peggy, and popped it over Janice's scraggy gymslip and threadbare cardigan, where it hung like a clown's coat. Janice looked at herself in the mirror and her eyes widened. Her hands, I noticed, were spotlessly clean and her nails looked pink and cared for. She'd soon have her nail varnish from Peggy.

'It would be lovely to have clothes like this all the time. It would be like a fairy tale, wouldn't it?' said Janice. After another long look, she solemnly handed the jacket back to Peggy, who was nearly in tears.

'Oh Rosie, I've never had anything as posh as this. It must have cost a fortune. Thank you.'

'It's your wedding day. You deserve to have something new. It's a special day.'

'Yes it is, isn't it?' she said, looking determined. 'It's the start of my new life. With George. It will be a good life, Rosie. I promise I'll do my best. It will be worth celebrating.'

Mr Brown obviously thought so too. He came home later and said he'd booked a table at The Fleece for us all after the ceremony.

'But I was just going to do something for us here,' said Mrs Brown.

'It's our only daughter's wedding. We'll do it properly, or at least as properly as we can,' he said firmly.

We could have walked to the register office, but Mr Brown insisted on a car to take us. When Peggy came downstairs in the altered dress and the new jacket, he walked towards her and wrapped her in his arms. 'My little girl,' he said, 'you look lovely.'

She did too. Very smart. Though I say it myself, the jacket was a triumph. I was so pleased. Best of all – from Mrs Brown's point of view – was that you couldn't really see that Peggy was pregnant, especially when she held her bouquet in front of her.

'Something old, something new – that's the dress and jacket,' said Mrs Brown. 'Something borrowed. Something borrowed! Quick, Peg, borrow something.'

'Here,' I said, quickly, 'borrow my hanky!' It

283

was one of the little lace ones I'd found in the trunk the day I arrived.

'Thanks, Rosie. Now I've got everything I need to bring me luck.' She tucked it into her pocket.

'And the something blue is my dress and jacket again. And,' she whispered, almost giggling, 'my new slip.'

With that the car arrived and we all bundled into it quickly, while the neighbours peered out of their windows or stood on the doorsteps waving, 'Good luck, girl!'

The register office wasn't really a register office, it was just part of a solicitor's office, with a big old-fashioned desk and chairs and rows of leather-bound books. But they'd done their best with it. It smelt of polish and there were vases of flowers on the windowsills. George had a new suit, one which fitted, unlike the one he wore to work. He looked nervous, but when Peggy walked in his face lit up.

And so began the ceremony to unite Margaret Elizabeth Brown and George Arthur Turnbull. I realised I hadn't known what George's surname was. Turnbull. George Turnbull. 'So officially, Peggy would now be Margaret Turnbull. Margaret Turnbull ... Margaret Turnbull... The name niggled away in my brain. It meant something. There was something about that name that I should recognise.

The ceremony was brief. With a bit of hand-shaking and congratulations, it was all over and we were out in the street again.

'Come on then, Mr and Mrs Turnbull,' said Derek, the best man, a pleasant-faced young man

284

with slicked-back hair and a cheerful grin. 'Time for the first drink of your married life!' and he led the way the fifty yards or so to The Fleece. It was as we were walking into the lounge that I remembered.

Margaret Turnbull.

She was the woman I'd been on my way to interview when I'd fainted and had landed in the Browns' house. That had been the start of these weird weeks, the start of my trip back in time. I looked at Peggy, smiling now, looking happy, young and glowing. I remembered that brief impression I had of an old lady getting up from her chair to come and answer the front door.

'I say! Are you all right?'

Derek was looking at me anxiously.

'Sit down!' Mrs Brown commanded. I sank into one of the armchairs by the fire. 'You've gone as white as a sheet. Frank! Get Rosie a brandy!'

The brandy hit my system and I could feel its warmth spreading through me. Margaret Turnbull. Peggy. It was too much of a coincidence. My head filled with fog and cotton wool as I tried to work it out. Whatever it was, this wasn't the time and place to think about it.

The brandy and the fire did the trick. Well, they didn't really, but enough to bring some colour back to my cheeks and enable me to join in with what was going on. The last thing I wanted to do was ruin George and Peggy's wedding day.

'That's better!' said Mrs Brown approvingly.

Peggy was laughing. 'You all right, Rosie? Not going to have to plan another wedding are we...'

Everyone laughed with her. And somehow the

day turned into a party. We were in an alcove off the big dining room so had a certain amount of privacy from the business men and old ladies enjoying their lunch. Just as well. George's mum got quite tiddly on a couple of glasses of sherry. She was a nice old dear. Confided in me that she was very worried about George marrying so suddenly, but she could see that Peggy came from a decent family.

There was a small heap of cards and telegrams and after the pudding, Derek stood up and read these out. The lads from work had sent a card saying, 'We never knew you had it in you!' and Stephen from Cyprus had telegrammed, 'May all your troubles be little ones!' Both of which caused huge hilarity.

I remembered Peggy slumped in the wet grass down by Friars' Mill, remembered the deadly atmosphere in the house afterwards and couldn't really see the joke. But the others did, so that was all right.

There was a collection of cards from friends of George and Peggy's, including a very nice one that said 'Wishing you both every happiness, with best wishes, Lenny', which made everyone go 'Aah' and Mrs Brown to say, 'You know I thought he was going to be the one.' Mr Brown and George just exchanged glances and Mr Brown made a funny face, which meant that he exactly got the measure of Lenny.

There were cards from the girls at work, from Peggy's friends and from Janice's mother.

'Oh that's nice,' said Peggy, 'very thoughtful.'

The last card looked big and fat and expensive.

'This looks a posh one,' said Derek cheerfully, tugging it open.

A shower of notes cascaded onto the linen tablecloth, drifting onto the uncleared plates and bowls, piling up against the glasses. Mrs Brown gathered them up.

'There's a hundred pounds here! A hundred pounds! I've never seen so much money.' Her eyes were wide with shock.

'Who's it from?' asked George's mum, though the rest of us knew.

'With all good wishes, Richard Henfield.'

There was a small silence.

'I don't want his money,' said Peggy quietly.

'Oh yes you do, my girl,' said her mother. 'You can buy a lot of baby things with a hundred pounds.'

'Or it can go towards the university fees,' I said merrily.

'University fees?' George's mum was gawping at me.

'Why not?' asked George cheerfully, putting his arm around Peggy. 'Our baby will go to university if he wants. Or she... A student with a briefcase and a gown and one of those long stripy scarves.'

Everyone laughed and the party mood was restored.

'That Mr Henfield must have thought a lot of Peggy,' whispered George's mum to me.

'Oh yes,' I whispered back. 'She was such a good secretary. He's going to be lost without her.'

If still suspicious, George's mum at least looked mollified.

'Twenty-six,' she said, looking at Peggy. 'That's how old I was when I was widowed.' She was in danger of getting maudlin.

'Well don't say that too loudly!'

'No love, I won't. But it will be nice to have a baby in the house. I'm looking forward to that. I'm glad they decided to come and live with me. I wouldn't like to be on my own. Be better when we move, mind.'

I remembered that George's house was in the line of the new bypass. They too had been offered a house at The Meadows. Sometimes it seems as if the whole town was moving up there. I was also doing my sums. If George's dad died at Dunkirk when his mum was twenty-six, then she'd be, gosh only about forty-two. And I'd thought she was about sixty...

The head waiter was bustling towards us with a stand, which he placed alongside the table. Next, he came with a bucket full of ice and a bottle.

'Your wine, Sir,' he said to Mr Brown.

'Champagne!'

'Well near enough,' said Mr Brown. 'It's fizzy anyway.'

'Oh, I never thought I'd drink champagne,' said Peggy, already giggly. 'Aren't we grand!'

George's mum just kept saying 'Champagne, well I never.'

I caught sight of the label. Not champagne, Asti spumante. Oh well. The waiter brought those saucer-shaped champagne glasses and opened the bottle with a huge pop! We stood and drank a toast to the long health and happiness of Mr and Mrs Turnbull.

'It's bubbly!' laughed Peggy. 'They go up your nose! Oh isn't this special!'

As we sipped the fizz – one bottle between seven of us – I reached across the table and picked up the cards and the telegrams and idly looked through them. Many of them featured intertwined hearts, pink and pretty and satiny, as if love were simple and straightforward, clean and uncomplicated.

I thought of Peggy and Henfield, the scene at Friars' Mill, Amy who had killed herself, and Peggy who'd wanted to. I thought of Will, whom I loved, and of Billy who loved his children, and sort of loved Carol but who also wanted me.

Love hearts weren't neat and pretty like a sugared sweet. No, they were like those hearts I'd seen soaking in the bowl at Carol's – messy and bloody, staining the waters all around them.

Soon it was time for the newlyweds to rush and get their train. They were off to stay with Aunty Emily in London and do the sights. A bit different from the trip there that had been planned for Peggy just a few weeks ago.

Peggy and I were in the Ladies, washing our hands side by side. I looked at her reflection in the mirror. She looked pretty and pink. I wondered how much was due to happiness and how much to sherry and sparkling wine. She dried her hands on a slightly damp roller towel behind the door. With her back to me and avoiding the small mirror so she couldn't even see my reflection, she said, 'Thank you Rosie. Thank you for all you've done. For, well you know. And for the jacket. And everything really.'

I was standing there, hands in the air, waiting to dry them. 'It's been a nice day,' I said. 'Have you enjoyed it?'

'Yes, I have. I really have. To think I'm in The Fleece drinking champagne with my husband! And to think... Well, to think it might have been different. Anyway, I just...'

'Peggy!' Mrs Brown was pushing her way through the outer door. 'Get a move on, girl, or you'll miss that blessed train!'

Peggy gave me a quick smile and leapt to do her mother's bidding.

We saw them off at the station. George already had the confidence of a married man, dealing with tickets and luggage. Derek had tied a 'Just Married' sign to George's suitcase and try as he might, George couldn't undo all the many knots that Derek had tied so devilishly.

'Give you something to do at bedtime!' yelled Derek as the guard blew his whistle and the train started to pull out.

George and Peggy leant out of the window of their compartment and we all waved until they vanished in a cloud of steam.

'Well,' said Mrs Brown with the air of a job well done. 'Let's go home and have a proper cup of tea then, shall we?'

Chapter Twenty

I was standing in Boots looking glumly at the shelves waiting for super strength conditioning extra volume mousse to be invented ... and lemon cuticle cream ... and high definition lip liner ... and summer glow body moisturiser ... and lustrous length waterproof mascara ... and smoky grey eye-shadow ... and skin serum ... and whitening tooth-paste ... and long-lasting luxury lipstick, and gloss, and concealer, and ... oh ... everything really.

'Hi Rosie!'

I turned around to see Carol standing there clutching a package. 'Home perm,' she said. 'Going round to do my mum's for her.'

'Oh right.'

'How are you then, Rosie? Still enjoying *The News?*'

What do I say? Do I say, 'Hello Carol I'm in love with your husband and I think he might fancy me'? or, 'I'd really love it there, Carol, if I could just work with your husband all day, gaze into his eyes and get a bit too close to him as he explains something in the diary to me?'

No you're right, I didn't.

'Fine, fine.'

'I heard Peggy got married to George.'

'Yes, just a few days ago.'

'Well, she's a dark horse, isn't she? They kept that quiet. Did you go to the wedding?'

'Yes. It was low-key, you know, but very nice.'

I was torn. I longed to have a coffee with Carol, sit and gossip, tell her all the details, the way I would with Caz. And I wanted her take on it all too. Not that I would tell her the Henfield involvement. I couldn't believe everyone would have been as po-faced about it as the Browns. Carol was good company, kind and funny... I wanted her as a friend.

And I wanted her husband. And if I felt that so strongly, how could I be friendly with Carol? She was standing smiling at me. She might have mousy hair and crooked teeth, but that was still Caz's cheeky grin, and I missed her.

'Got time for a coffee? Look – no kids!'

Well, why not?

I abandoned any hope of buying anything I wanted and followed Carol out of Boots. We slid into a booth at Silvino's.

'Come on then,' said Carol, 'tell me about the wedding. I didn't even know Peggy was going out with George. She must be six or seven years older than him.'

'Six.'

'Well,' she grinned, 'he obviously knows what it's all about then. Never had Peggy down as a cradle snatcher, still he'll have plenty of energy for her. So tell me all about it. Did they have a do?'

'Yes, at The Fleece.'

'Oh very grand.'

So I told her about Peggy's dress and jacket, and about the meal and the 'champagne'.

'Ooh,' said Carol, hungrily. 'There's posh. When Billy and I got wed we just had sandwiches and cake at my mum's, while Billy's gran sat and looked as if there was a bad smell under her nose.'

'Didn't she approve?'

'No, thought it was all my fault. But, as my dad said, it takes two to tango... Still it's worked out OK and even Billy's gran thinks I'm all right now, and she worships Libby, really spoils her.'

She spooned some of the froth from her coffee in its shallow Pyrex cup. 'Have they gone on a honeymoon then?'

'Yes, a few days in London. Peggy has an aunt who lives there, so they'll see the sights, but they're back tomorrow. George is in work on Monday.'

'Where are they going to live?'

'With George's mum. I'm not sure where she lives now, but I know it's in the line of the bypass, so they'll all be moving up to The Meadows. It looks as if everyone will be up there.'

'That's good. I like Peggy. It'll be nice having her near. Anyway ... tada! I've finished the dress!'

The dress. The dress she was making to go to the mayor's ball with Billy.

'Oh great. Does it look good?'

'Yes I'm pleased with it. In the end I had to take it up to my mum's to finish it, I just couldn't get the light in our house.'

The little dark house with no electricity and a smell of earth and damp.

'Does Billy like it?'

'He hasn't seen it yet. I've decided he's not going to see it until we go out. I've got it all worked out. My mum's coming down to ours to babysit, but we're going to go up there at teatime, so we can have baths and I can wash my hair and dry it properly, not like in our house with the tin tub in front of the fire. I'll take Billy's suit up there so he can come in from football and have a bath too and we can go out from my mum's. See, all organised. I'm really looking forward to it.'

'It should be a good evening.'

'It's a shame you can't come, Rosie. They've got a proper dance orchestra and everything.'

'Haven't been invited. Don't know the right people.'

'And at the end apparently they have a great net of balloons that come down from the ceiling. It's going to be lovely.' Her eyes were shining. I thought of Caz. Caz would hate going to a mayor's ball. Wild horses wouldn't drag her there. But for Carol it was the height of sophistication, the social event of the year. I wanted her to enjoy it. I tried to forget that she was going with Billy and just hoped she would have a good time.

'Oooh, it will be lovely when we're up at The Meadows and can have our own bathroom. I shall have a bath every night, with lots of bubbles like a film star.'

I laughed.

'What's funny?' asked Carol.

'My friend Caz – the one who's so like you. She loves relaxing in the bath, and the funny thing is, she switches the lights off and just lights scented candles around the edge of the bath.'

'What's the point of that if she's got electric light?'

'It's more romantic.'

Carol snorted. 'She should try it in the tub in

front of the fire with a draught howling under the back door and mice scurrying past. That would be romance for her. Anyway, this won't get the baby bathed, time I wasn't here.'

She picked up her shopping bag.

'Maybe Phil could get you an invite to the ball and you could both come with me and Billy? That would be good, wouldn't it?'

'Yes, maybe,' I said, but dismissed the thought instantly. In any case, I wanted to keep Phil at arm's length, as a friend. I think he was beginning to get ideas.

'Are you seeing Phil this weekend?'

'No. Well, we haven't arranged anything.'

He'd asked me out for Saturday night and I'd turned him down vaguely. I regretted it now. Without Peggy, the house was already feeling empty.

'Blooming heck! It's raining and I haven't got a brolly!'

Standing in the doorway of the café, Carol tugged a scarf from her coat pocket and tied it over her hair. Then, with her head down, she dashed out into the crowds.

'Tara Rosie. Maybe see you in the week!'

I pulled my coat around me and splashed through the puddles, headed for home.

There was no smell of cooking, not even the lingering smell of something drying up in the oven. Instead Mrs Brown was looking busy and harassed.

'You can have bacon and eggs and a bit of mash for your supper. I'm making a start on Peggy's room.'

'Making a start on what?'

'Well we're going to be moving soon. That first phase is just about finished up at The Meadows. Frank heard from his mate Les that the decorators are starting on Monday and that's the last thing to be done. They'll be allocating them soon. I don't suppose we'll get first phase, but we'll probably get second if they want us out of the way to start on their precious new road. And there's a lot to be done.'

I realised she had been struggling with an old suitcase, on which the zip had broken as it was tied together with a dressing-gown cord.

'All these are clothes ready for the jumble sale. I'll leave it in the scullery and if anyone comes around – I think the Guides are due one day soon – just give them that will you, love. Now where's Frank? He's late this evening. Just as well as I'm not ready for him.' And she struggled with the case through the kitchen and into the scullery.

With that, Mr Brown came in, stamping the rain off his shoes.

'You're late, Frank,' said his wife.

'Yes and for a very good reason.'

There was a silence.

'Well aren't you going to ask me what that reason is?'

'Oh go on then,' said Mrs Brown, not looking at him, but tipping potatoes into the sink and turning the tap on.

'Why are you late?'

'I've bought a car.'

There was a very satisfying clatter as the potato knife dropped into the stone sink too. 'You've done what?'

'I've bought a little car, a Morris Minor.' Mr Brown looked very pleased with himself.

'A car! Us?'

'Why not? I've been thinking about it ever since it took us all day to get to that christening and all night to get back from it. If we had a little car, we could have done it in an hour.'

'Can we afford it?'

'I had a bit of money put by for our Peg's wedding and well, in the end it didn't cost as much as I thought, so let's spend it on something we can enjoy.'

'What do you know about cars? Do you know how to drive one?'

'Course I do. Learnt in the army, didn't I?'

She bombarded him with questions over kind, colour, cost.

'And have you got it here now?' Mrs Brown darted out to the front, to see if it was in the street.

'No, no. It will take a few days to get the paper-work arranged and everything done.'

'Well, well,' said Mrs Brown, finally absorbing the idea. 'Fancy that. A new house, a new baby, and a new car, all at the same time. We *are* going up in the world, aren't we?'

'If you want to put it like that,' said Mr Brown, looking pleased with himself. 'Right then, where's my supper?'

Mrs Brown scuttled back into the scullery and started speedily peeling potatoes.

As we sat down to bacon and egg, with the egg yolk mopped up by the mash to fill any gaps, Mrs Brown was still dreaming of the difference a car would make.

'We'll be able to go to the seaside. And for drives out in the country. Oh, Frank, we could go on a holiday, a touring holiday. You see it in the papers, don't you, in the wedding reports. "The couple will spend their honeymoon on a touring holiday of the West Country." We could do that – a touring holiday along the open road.'

She cleared our plates and brought out some fruit cake for pudding. 'Cornwall, now I've always wanted to go to Cornwall, they say it's very quaint. Can we go to Cornwall, Frank?'

'Why not?' Mr Brown was beaming like an indulgent uncle.

Janice came in later to finish the fruit cake and her English homework ('Describe Shakespeare's use of the imagery of blood in *Macbeth*'), and was very impressed to hear about the new car.

'After all, Mr Brown,' she said solemnly, 'we are the New Elizabethans, and we have to explore our world.'

Mr Brown laughed, 'Well pet, I think I explored more than enough of it in the desert with Monty, but yes, we'll explore a bit more now.'

Chapter Twenty-One

It had rained all day and all night. From the moment Carol and I had come out of Silvino's on Saturday afternoon, and all through Sunday, it hadn't stopped. It had blown George and Peggy in through the door on Sunday evening, their cheeks glowing, their eyes dancing with excitement. Was it the weather or the honeymoon? I wondered.

'Can't stop long, Mum,' said Peggy, 'George's mum will be waiting for us. But I'll come over tomorrow afternoon, when you're back from work and tell you all about it. But we've had a lovely time. We've seen Buckingham Palace and the changing of the guard, and we saw the Houses of Parliament – it's just like on the sauce bottle!'

Over a quick cup of tea and a slice of the sponge cake Mrs Brown had baked that morning, Peggy handed over a little plate with a picture of Buckingham Palace. 'Present back, Mum.'

Mrs Brown smiled and put it on the dresser, slap bang in the middle of the shelf. 'I'll put it there so people can't miss it,' she said proudly, 'and I can say my daughter and son-in-law brought it back from their honeymoon in London.'

I could see again how the story of the wedding was still being re-written.

After a quick hug for Peggy from her parents, she and George had dodged back into the rain. George with one hand carrying their small case and the other protectively holding Peggy's arm.

'I don't know, it doesn't seem right her not being here,' said Mrs Brown, peering out of the sitting-room window trying to watch them going down the street.

'She's a married woman, now. Her place is with her husband,' said Mr Brown.

Mrs Brown fussed around clearing away the cups and plates and taking them out to the kitchen. I could have offered to help but thought that really she would prefer to be on her own.

All night it rained. The wind whipped along the streets and blew the blossom off the trees. The blossom bobbed on the ripples whipped up on the puddles. As I sat eating my breakfast por-ridge, glad of its stodgy comfort, the rain slashed angrily against the kitchen window, making the old frame rattle and turning the outside world into a cold wet blur.

'More like blooming winter than nearly sum-mer. I hope Peggy wraps up well when she comes around,' said Mrs Brown, tugging on a pair of rubber boots and tying a scarf firmly around her head. 'No point in taking a brolly today. It'll be blown inside out before I'm across the doorstep.'

'When you get your new car you'll be able to have a lift to work, or drive yourself,' I said.

Mrs Brown stopped, her hands in midair where she'd been tugging at her scarf. 'Ooh, I couldn't do that. We couldn't use the car for that. Though Frank might. No, I'll be back to Shanks's bloom-ing pony. Anyway, I'm off now. Make sure the door's shut really tight when you go out, won't you? Otherwise we'll come back and find the wind's whipped it right off.'

I finished my breakfast, washed the dishes and did my make-up in the kitchen mirror – powder, lipstick and a quick spit on the mascara. Then, wrapped up nearly as securely as Mrs Brown, I tugged open the front door and launched myself into the storm.

Ouch! The rain slapped me in the face, blew my skirts up and tugged through my hair. It was a battle to get over the doorstep, never mind down the street. How I missed my car, my nice, warm, safe, *dry* little car... I would have caught a bus, but there was no direct route between the house and *The News*. I would have caught a cab if I could have found such a thing. Come to that, if I'd spotted the milkman and his horse I'd have hitched a lift on that. As it was, I had to walk, hands in pockets, head bent against the wind and the rain that was stinging my face.

By the time I got to work I was soaked. My feet squelched in my sensible shoes, I had mud splashes all up the back of my legs and the rain had even started to come through the shoulders of my sensible mac.

'Lovely weather for ducks,' said the receptionist cheerfully as I squelched into *The News*, water dripping off the end of my scarf.

The office smelt of wet clothes and wet shoes, horribly reminiscent of wet dog. It mingled with the smell of musty newspapers and all the cigarette smoke. It made me long to get out again, but one look at the smeary, rain-spattered windows, the panes rattling in their frames, made me equally desperate to stay inside, smell of wet dog or not.

Despite the damp and the smell, I went up the stairs with that small sense of excitement, that fluttering in your insides that comes from fancying someone you work with. Only this was much more than simply fancying. I squelched up the stairs with a spring in my soggy step.

'Bit damp are you there, kid?' asked Billy as I dripped past him, my face bright red with the rain and the wind. I grinned – if he'd called me

301

'kid' back at home in our own real time, I would probably have hated it, but here it was great, a sign of comradeliness, affection almost... I shook my head so the drops flew off and spattered all over the newsdesk diary, and then ran quickly as he shook his fist in mock horror.

'Just for that,' he said sternly, 'I think I will send you on a nice little door-stepping exercise...'

My face must have fallen because he laughed.

'No, you're OK, I wouldn't send a dog out today, though,' with a grin over his shoulder, 'I'm going to send Alan. No, Marje is off today, so could you do the women's page please, Rosie? Oh yes, and we need Kiddies' Corner too.'

I groaned. But at least it kept me out of the rain, which got no better as the morning went on. At lunch time I was still bashing away at my typewriter when Alan came back in. Rain was dripping off the rim of his hat and he looked soaked to the skin.

'The river's very high,' he said, peeling off his sodden raincoat and draping it over the back of a chair. 'Sergeant Foster was down there, looking worried. Apparently the Civil Defence are on standby. They're filling sandbags. It looks as though they'll be needed. It's getting serious out there.'

He looked at Billy. 'I don't know if you want to go and check on your house...'

But Billy was already pulling on his raincoat.

'Alan, can you run the desk for a while? I must check on Carol and the kids. If the river's running high, it could be well up towards the house.'

'Glad to,' said Alan. But Billy was already gone. I could hear him dashing down the stairs two at a time to get to Carol. So much for that small show of affection for me. So much for my anticipation, the fluttering insides, my eagerness to get into the office to see him. He was well and truly spoken for, and by someone who could get him leaping downstairs two at a time, a wife and family he had to look after and protect.

'Are you making the tea then, Rosie?' asked Alan as he shook his hair dry and looked at the work left on Billy's desk. I turned, deflated, to get the kettle. I knew my place.

The rain didn't let up. I ate my sandwiches at my desk and was finishing the women's page ('Meals in a hurry for busy mothers'), and Kiddies' Corner (this week's competition is how many words can you make from 'Thunder and Lightning'?) when the electricity went off. It was so dark that we'd had the lights on even though it was early afternoon.

Alan cursed, lit a cigarette and then went groping around in the back of a cupboard from which he produced a paraffin lamp. He cleared a space for it in the middle of all the clutter and lit it. After a few failed and smoky efforts it finally got going and cast a cosy glow over the office, though God knew what would happen if anyone knocked it over in all those heaps of paper...

By now phones were ringing from reporters in other offices and members of the public wanting to know what was happening. Alan was already talking on two phones at once when the third rang and I answered it. It was Billy.

'Is your house OK?' I asked.

'Probably not for much longer. But we've moved all we can upstairs and Carol and Libby have gone to her mother's. There's nothing more we can do.'

That little house already smelt of damp. How much more so now?

'Look Rosie, can you get Alan? We need to be out and about. The river's burst its banks and people are going to have to be rescued. There are great stories. I've seen George and Charlie, but we need another reporter out.'

'I'll come!' I said.

There was a crackly silence on the other end and hope in my heart. 'Alan has only just dried out, and he can run the desk better than I can,' I said. I let the thought hang in the air.

At the end of the phone line I could hear the wind and rain – and almost hear Billy thinking. It took a second for him to make the decision.

'OK. I'm down by the old quay, so get yourself to Watergate and see what's happening there. But for goodness' sake be careful! Now put me on to Alan.'

I interrupted Alan's two phone calls, handed him the receiver and fled.

Floods! A real story! Worth getting wet for! And Billy had told me to be careful. Maybe he did care about me after all. Adrenalin and happiness were surging around my system.

Now I know journalists are always said to like bad news, but the truth is that they are the dramatic stories. It's when you feel part of the action. You spend so much time doing routine stuff –

those worthwhile things about concerts and councils – that you long for something different. It's exciting, an adventure, and also you feel useful and part of the community at the same time. So it wins on all fronts – and you know that lots of people will buy the paper the next day.

As long as *The News*' generator worked of course...

The receptionist on the front desk looked horrified as I clattered down the stairs. 'You're not going out in this are you?' she said, and when she saw that obviously I was, she said, 'Well at least get yourself something sensible for your feet. Haven't you got any wellies?'

'No. Where's the nearest place to get some?'

'Woolies, of course.'

It was only across the road. I dashed in and found some wellies, the last pair in my size said the assistant, and some woolly socks. I went back to *The News* to change and left my soggy shoes in reception. Certainly, as I strode down to Watergate my feet felt warm and dry, about the only bit that did. I slipped my bag across me, like old ladies do, and marched out into the storm.

Down at Watergate it was chaos. The river was already over its banks and the road was disappearing. A stream ran down into the river under a low old bridge. The water was already up to the arch of the bridge and was roaring through in a torrent, bringing branches and debris down with it. It looked as though it would start backing up soon.

I splashed along on what had been a pavement but was now about a foot deep in water. It was already lapping near the top of my wellies and rising fast. I moved away, up higher towards the Market Place and the water seemed to follow me.

A policeman in fisherman's waders was standing in the middle of the road, directing traffic, up to his knees in water. A tractor and trailer were ploughing through the water sending up huge waves, but people were wading across to get into the trailer, bringing babies and possessions. A little short fat man came waddling out nearly bent double under the weight of a huge cardboard box full of papers. I was sure the rain would make the box collapse and the wind whip all the papers away before he got to the trailer, but he made it. Just. Then he dumped the box and went waddling back to his office for more.

You could see the water rising as you looked. A lorry load of volunteers arrived with sandbags and a fireman sent them elsewhere. He was shouting into the wind and rain, but his voice was whipped away.

Normally on occasions like this I dart in and out talking to people, grabbing a chance and a quote where I can. But it's tricky to dart when you're wading in water in wellies. It was hard going. Police and firemen were too busy to talk, but generous enough to throw remarks out into the wind and rain. I guess they were pretty excited by it all too. Someone was waving out of a bedroom window. A fire engine arrived and the firemen put a ladder up to the window. It looked very puny in such weather.

But a fireman – in a huge and heavy uniform, made even heavier by the weight of the rain – climbed up and took a bundle from the woman at the window. The bundle shrieked. It was a baby. The fireman in his yellow helmet took the baby down the ladder and it was handed from arm to arm to the safety of a lorry parked in the shallower water. Then there was a slightly larger bundle, a little girl of about two.

At that point, hooray! George arrived. He got some good pictures and I paddled through the water to the trailer and got the names of the mother and children.

I tried to write them down in my notebook but it was hopeless. I struggled into a covered alley-way that led around the back of some derelict-looking houses. Quickly I scribbled down the names of the people I'd talked to, ripped the already wet pages out of my notebook and stuck them deep down in the pocket of my bag where there was a chance they might not get any wetter.

The alleyway was damp, but at least the rain wasn't as heavy there. It was quiet too. I hadn't realised how noisy it was outside. I leant against the wall and took a breather. There was a strange whispery noise…

A rat. It sleeked past my toes and down the alley. I yelped and went back into the rain.

The little fat man with the cardboard boxes was shouting at the policeman, who didn't want him to put any more on the trailer as it was fully loaded and starting to go. 'But my businesses! My papers!' the fat man was shouting.

He would have gone on like this for some hours, I'm sure, only his cardboard box really did start to collapse and he ran, cradling it like a baby to scrape into one of the lorries.

By now I'd had to retreat. What had been the road was just part of the river which was growing wider every second. A group of lads, about fourteen or fifteen years old, appeared. They had their shoes tied around their necks and their trousers rolled up.

'Right you lot!' bellowed the policeman in waders. 'Make yourselves useful and get along to those houses at the end. See if anyone needs help getting their stuff shifted upstairs. If they want to leave their houses then wave something out of the window so we know. And be bloody careful!'

The boys splashed off up the waterway, full of excitement and adventure and ready to help.

My sense of adventure was definitely beginning to pall. I was soaked and getting cold. It had been a long day, and I had been walking back and forth in the deep water for a long time. My leg muscles were killing me. My feet were wet now and I was probably getting blisters. Time, I thought, to get back to the office. The policeman was shouting at me to get out of the way, when suddenly I saw a rowing boat coming up what had been the street, but was now under about four foot of water.

It was a bright red little boat with the number forty-two painted cheerily on its side. Despite the wind and rain and current, the man rowing it was doing so competently and confidently, regular easy strokes as he guided the little craft around the lamppost and past a telephone box.

'Want a lift?' he yelled across at me. It was Billy.

He brought the boat as close as he could to me and I waded across and climbed in. The boat rocked terrifyingly, but Billy got it steady as he helped me in. 'Do you like it?' he asked, grinning. 'I requisitioned it from the boating lake.'

'Brilliant!'

'Yes, the bloke wanted five bob – five bob! – for the hire charge, but I told him it was a national emergency and as a member of Her Majesty's Press I demanded the use of it and he couldn't countermand my air of authority. Mind you, I did promise to look after it carefully and bring it back when the floods have gone down.'

I clung to his arm for maybe a fraction longer than necessary and then settled down opposite him. It was a very small boat and our knees were touching.

'Where are we going?'

'Have you got some decent stuff from here?'

'Oh yes, babies being rescued, businessmen complaining, boys helping, old ladies hugging policemen. Everything.'

'Great stuff. So have I. But I thought we'd have another look around, see what's going on.' He grinned at me and suddenly I didn't feel cold any more

It was really weird rowing around the streets. The water had spread all through the town. I thought that the Browns' house would be all right because it was quite high above the river, but I imagined the cellars were well and truly flooded.

The water was running fast, and every now and then a particularly fierce current would catch us and the boat would swoop and dip before Billy could steady it. We were on the main road between the Market Place and Watergate when a sudden torrent came. Billy tried to keep the boat on course but in the end it was easier to let the current send us down a narrow pathway, one of many that led through Watergate down to the river.

The buildings were grim. Suddenly I could see why Mr Brown thought the whole lot would be better off demolished. They were narrow, dark and virtually derelict – certainly the flood would finish most of them off. There were no lights anywhere and although it was still only late afternoon, it was dark.

'All right?' asked Billy as I clung to the sides.

'Never been better!' I yelled back up at him.

And as I did, I spotted a face at a window above him.

The window was broken and part of it was stuffed with old material, but there was a woman looking out, clearly terrified. 'Help me! Please help!' she shouted.

Billy managed to pull the boat around and tie the rope around the spear-shaped top of a railing – all that showed above the water.

'We need the fire brigade!' I said to Billy. 'We can't get her out of there.'

'And I can't see how the fire brigade would get down here – even if we could get to them in time,' said Billy.

By now he was out of the boat – rocking it hard in the process – and had pulled himself up onto the railings, one hand holding on to an old light bracket that can't have held a working light for decades.

'Pass me an oar up, Rosie,' he shouted.

I did and, telling the woman to step back, he smashed the window. Not that it took much doing. The frame was rotten. He took the bit of blanket that had been stuffing one of the missing panes and laid it across the windowsill to protect her from the splinters of glass.

'Now what I want you to do,' he said to the old woman, 'is to sit on the windowsill with your legs outside.'

'I can't! I can't!' yelled the woman who seemed to be wearing a heap of raggedy clothes, her hair escaping from a greasy, untidy bun.

'Yes you can, of course you can,' said Billy soothingly. Even though he had to shout over the noise of the wind and rain and roaring water, his voice was kind and gentle. And, still perfectly balanced, he caught hold of the woman in her ragged clothes and battered shoes and guided her down.

'Pull as hard as you can on that rope, Rosie! Right,' he said to the woman, 'can you just jump into the boat? It's not far. Just a step really.'

'No I can't! I can't!' yelled the woman, clinging harder to Billy. Quick as a flash Billy bundled her into the boat. They landed with a thud and a scream and the boat rocked wildly. I was sure it was going to capsize and flung myself to one side to try to balance the weight. It sort of worked. The boat rocked a bit more, and the woman lay in the middle of it whimpering, but at least she had the sense to stay fairly still.

'Are you all right there, love?' asked Billy.

'Been a bloody sight better,' muttered the woman, so we knew she was all right really.

311

The little red boat was not designed for an adult lying across its middle seat. It meant Billy and I were forced to either end. The boat wasn't very deep and was filling quickly with water.

'Come on!' yelled Billy, passing me an oar and untying the rope. 'Let's paddle.'

Once loose, the boat swirled out into the water and, with Billy kneeling at the front and me perched on the little seat at the back, we paddled through the streets, our oars working together in perfect rhythm as we raced for dry land. Under the heavy clouds, it was already getting dark, and it was wet, cold and a bit frightening, but it was also exhilarating. There I was with Billy, working together as a real team. I paddled faster, Billy adjusted his rhythm to match mine, and our heavily laden little pleasure craft seemed to sing over the water.

The raggedy woman stopped whimpering and looked up warily at us.

'Blimey,' she said, 'I've been rescued by a pair of blooming Red Indians.'

Billy and I laughed out loud in shared pleasure. Soon we came to higher ground and the boat started bumping along the pavement. There was a lorry with a couple of civil defence volunteers in it.

'Where are you taking people to?' Billy yelled across to them.

'Church hall,' one of them shouted back. 'They're doing soup and sandwiches for them.'

'Ooh,' said our raggedy woman sitting up, and looking quite bright, 'I could just do with a drop of soup.'

'Hop aboard then!' shouted the civil defence man. The woman bundled up her raggedy clothes around her knees and waded out towards him.

'Thanks for the lift,' she said to us and then turned conspiratorially to me.

'You hang on to him, love. He's a bit of all right. Wouldn't mind jumping into his arms again.'

And off she went while Billy and I laughed, with only a little embarrassment. Then we splashed along the road, pulling the little red boat behind us.

'Well kid,' said Billy, 'we certainly have some adventures, you and me, don't we?'

My heart did somersaults. 'We certainly do. And it's a lot more interesting than writing Meal Ideas for Busy Housewives. Thinking of which, we'd better get back to the office. I've got a lot of stuff to write up.'

'What time is it?'

I pushed my soggy sleeve back up to see my watch.

'Five to six.'

'In that case, I've got a better idea. I'll just make a phone call first.'

He disappeared into a phone box while I stood outside hanging on to the rope of the little red boat. I couldn't hear what Billy was saying but he was obviously telling someone how to do something, his hands and arms talked for him. Just like Will. Caz always said that if Will broke his arms he'd be speechless.

'Right,' he said, emerging from the phone box and taking the boat rope from my hand. 'Follow me.'

We splashed along for a little way until we came to the steep steps that led up to the old town wall. There was a tapas bar up there in my day, I remembered. Will and I had been there once or twice. But right now on this stormy rainy night, it was a pub. Billy tied the boat to a lamppost.

'Don't let me forget it. I did promise to take it back. Come on, up the steps.'

The steps were narrow and crumbling. There was no light anywhere, just a dim glow from the window of the pub. With the town wall stretching out in the gloom, it was almost medieval.

'Jolly good, Bert has got the fire lit,' said Billy.

The tiny bar was lit by candles and the glow of a coal fire. I went straight towards it and within seconds there was steam coming up from my soggy coat.

'Oh, it's you,' said a voice from somewhere in the gloom behind the bar. 'I might have known it would have to be some daft beggar out in weather like this. Even the dog's got more sense.'

As if to prove it, a small terrier uncurled itself from a chair and came to sniff at my wellies.

'And a good evening to you too, Bert,' said Billy. 'A pint and a half of bitter please. And can we take a couple of these candles over to the table? We've got work to do.'

'Help yourself,' said Bert. 'Give us a shout when you want another drink or if any more daft beggars come in. I'll be out the back.'

'Right,' said Billy. 'They're managing fine at the office. Phil's in with Alan and the others are back. So I thought we might as well write our stuff up here and then we can phone it through. Much nicer, wouldn't you say?'

'I would. I most definitely would.'

So we sat on either side of the table, working by the fire in the glow of the flames and the candlelight. Just us in this strange little world at the end of a strange little day. It twisted my heart to watch Billy working because, of course it was Will's way. He flipped through his notebook, marking something here, underlining something there. I just wanted to watch him, that little frown of concentration as he thought, the way his eyes lit up when he spotted something worth using, the quick, confident notes.

'Right, that's me done,' he said.

'But you haven't written anything!'

'Yes I have. Well, I've got the intro and a few bits. The rest I'll just do on the phone.'

'Oh.'

I really admired the way some people could just write a story off the top of their heads, especially dictating it to someone else. I was carefully – but quickly – writing out my whole story. I wanted to be sure I'd got what I wanted, where I wanted it. When Billy disappeared outside to the phone, I concentrated harder. There were so many differ-ent stories, all good. In the end I wrote them up as separate pieces, ready to slot anywhere on the page. I scribbled quickly.

'OK, your turn with the phone. The copytaker's waiting for you,' said Billy, clearly not even con-sidering the possibility that I couldn't be ready. Which was a sort of compliment I suppose.

'Don't forget this.'

I looked. It was a torch, well a bike lamp really.

'You've got to be able to read what you've written.'

Now that's what I call being prepared...

I wriggled back into my sodden mac and out into the rain and to the phone box at the bottom of the steps, and started the long process of dictating the stories to the girl at the end of the line.

'Gosh,' she said. 'It's all really exciting, isn't it?' When I walked back into the pub, Billy was getting us some drinks.

'I don't suppose there's any food, is there?' I asked. 'I'm starving.'

'Can do you crisps,' said Bert.

'Oh right, um, anything else?'

'Pickled eggs.'

'Pickled eggs? Well thank you, but I think I'll pass on that.'

'Go on,' said Billy, 'local delicacy you can't miss out on. Two bags of crisps and two eggs please, Bert. My treat.'

'Thank you. I think,' I said.

Bert took two packets of crisps and opened them. Then he unscrewed an evil-looking jar on the counter. Using his fingers – his fingers! – he reached in and pulled out an egg and placed it on top of the crisps in the open bag.

'There you are, kid,' said Billy, handing the crisps and egg to me. *'Bon appetit*, as they say in France. Or, get stuck in, as we say here.'

I have to say that a pickled egg is not my idea of a delicacy. In fact it was pretty gross, *and* it made the crisps soggy. I wasn't a great fan of beer either, but it seemed the right thing to drink somehow. I ate and drank and steamed gently by the fire and just counted my blessings for being here alone with Billy.

I remembered in those first days how I'd been desperate to be alone with him, convinced this was all a reality game that we had to win. But now I knew that this was no TV show. Today's rain, for instance, couldn't have been a studio stunt. Not even Cecil B. DeMille could have organised that lot.

When you eliminate everything else, what's left must be the truth... Dwellers all in time and space...

Somehow I wasn't so bothered about it any more. Well, maybe at three o'clock in the morning I was, but the rest of the time I was getting used to the 1950s. Take each day as it comes and enjoy the moment, Phil had said. He was right. And I was certainly enjoying being alone in this snug little room with Will...

'You've done a good job today,' he said, 'as good as many of the men could have done.'

He meant it as a compliment. I tried not to feel patronised. Or want to hit him. He was laughing now. 'That old dear was right. You were paddling like a Red Indian. A very wet Red Indian.'

'Was that old woman living there?'

'Yes, there's all sorts of people living in there. It's a warren, and probably not safe really. But it's a roof, so I suppose it's better than nothing.'

We leant back on the bench, cherished the warmth of the fire and talked about the day's work – and the hope our hard-won words would get a decent show in the next day's paper. And I watched the way the firelight showed up his

317

cheekbones and the hollows and shadows of his face.

He told me what he knew about the floods elsewhere in the region – bad everywhere, but we had had by far the worst. And I looked at his hands curling around his beer glass. Working hands, callused hands, but with neat and tidy nails. Billy might not have the same shelf full of beauty products that Will had, but he had the same pride in keeping himself well groomed.

We talked of the rain and whether it would last, of the tidying-up operation, of the people in the church hall. And I watched the way his hair went into small curls at the nape of his neck as it dried.

We had another beer. And possibly another.

We talked of Gordon and when he might be back, of Alan and what a decent bloke he was. And even in the candlelight I could still see his long eyelashes and his deep brown eyes.

We talked of the plans for tomorrow, the way the story would develop. And I gazed at the outline of his broad shoulders reflected in shadows on the opposite wall. And I wanted to bury myself in his arms, and I wondered what would happen if I did. Just the two of us in this strange small room with the warm smell of beer and the glow of the fire and the candlelight. Just me and Will, his eyes never leaving mine, his body getting closer...

'Right you two! Ain't you got no homes to go to?' Bert was doing things to the fire, closing down at the end of the night sort of things. He took our empty glasses and one of the candles back to the bar.

'OK Bert, we can take a hint,' said Billy. 'I've left a boat tied up at the bottom of your steps. I'll be back for it later.'

'Boats on my steps. What next?' muttered Bert, wiping down the bar.

We went out by the light of the bike lamp. I went to go back down the steps, but Billy stopped me. 'Let's walk along the walls for a way. It's probably quicker, and certainly a drier way home for you.'

The rain had stopped and the wind had died down. It was actually a mild spring night.

'But doesn't everything look weird?'

Being up on the town walls was a bit like being in the middle of a lake. Vast stretches of water now reflected back the moonlight. There was a fire engine at the edge of the water, and far below us a few uniformed men gathered in a little group, but there was no real activity. Everywhere was very still but for the sound of water lapping halfway up shop doorways, across roads and over windowsills.

'This is the highest flood since 1888,' said Billy. 'I don't suppose we'll ever see it like this again. If you could forget about the damage it caused, it's beautiful in its way. Careful...' He grabbed my arm as a pothole suddenly appeared in the path along the walls. In my day it was all smoothed and tarmacked, with a safety rail, but now it was uneven and rubbly with weeds growing in sudden holes and a sheer drop to the water below.

He didn't let go of my arm. Instead he pulled me around to face him.

'You were a lovely little Red Indian today,' he said. 'I'll never forget you. You were so wet, rain was streaming down your hair but you were paddling away. You looked so determined. So...' he hesitated, '...so beautiful.'

I knew what was coming next and I did nothing to stop it. He took me in his arms, brought his head down to mine and kissed me, a long lingering kiss that tasted slightly of beer and crisps and rain, and was utterly wonderful.

Oh the joy of it! To be wrapped in Will's arms again, to feel his arms around me, to put my head on his chest and be cocooned in that little world.

We kissed again. And again. Each kiss fiercer than the last. It was strange, the clothes were unfamiliar, the scent of his skin was not what I knew, but yet it was still Will, still the man I loved, the man I'd missed so dreadfully. And now here I was wrapped up in him again. I was in Will's arms. I was home. I wanted to burrow inside his soggy mac and jacket, feel his skin against mine...

We disentangled ourselves and I looked up at him. He was smiling down at me and his eyes were Will's eyes, laughing and loving. He started to say something and stopped.

'I–' I started, but he put his finger gently on my lips to silence me and I fitted myself back under the curve of his shoulder with his arm around me, holding me tightly against him. We ambled along the top of the town wall, with just an old bike lamp against the dark and the only sound was the lapping of the flood water and the flump flump flump of our wellies.

That Frank Sinatra song drifted back into my mind. *They can't take that away from me.* I knew I would have this memory for ever.

We came down from the town wall about fifty yards from the Browns' house. In the darkness of the steps once again we wrapped ourselves around each other and kissed long and hard, not saying a word, just trying to get so much of each other...

Billy finally pulled away and said, 'It's all different since you arrived. I don't know what it is, but you make life exciting. You're different, you think differently.'

He buried his face in my hair, then kissed my neck, my throat... 'Oh God, you don't belong here. It's as if you come from another world, not another country. All I know is,' and he took my face and held it gently in his hands so I was looking up at him, 'all I know is that I think a tremendous lot about you, Rosie. I didn't mean to, and I don't want to, but I have. You really are very special. I could love you, I really could. In fact...' he stopped and looked at me helplessly, hopelessly, 'I already do.'

It was what I had longed to hear all the weeks I'd been there. I closed my eyes and reached hungrily to kiss him again.

But something had happened.

I could feel his hands holding mine. He was taking my hands and removing them from around his neck. I could feel the strength in his wrists as he pushed my hands away. I tried to push against him, but it was no good. He was holding my arms down by my sides and holding me away from him. 'It's no good, Rosie,' he said, and his face looked desperately sad. 'I am married. I have a wife and three children. I can't hurt them. They have done nothing wrong. Don't you see? They are my responsibility. I can't let them down, not even … not even for you.'

I stared at him, not believing what I was hearing. Had I won him only to lose him just a few heartbeats later? One look at the pain on his face told me the answer.

'Carol is a good wife and a brilliant mother. She works hard and we're happy. We were happy, until you came along. And we will be again. I think you're wonderful, magical, different from any girl I've ever known. I would love to leave everything and be with you, but I can't. It can't happen. I must stay here with my family and you must go back to where you came from. I'm sorry, I shouldn't have kissed you. I shouldn't have said what I said.'

'But you did!'

I was so angry. So hurt. This was what I had wanted ever since I had first set eyes on him in the newsroom. And now he was saying it was over before it had begun?

'No! You can't say that! That can't be the end. We're meant to be together, you and I. You're the only one. There's no one else.'

Billy put his hands on my shoulders and looked at me gently, sadly. 'I can't let Carol down. I can't. It's not fair, not right.'

And it wasn't. He was right. Oh I knew that really, deep down. 'Then why did you tell me you love me? Just so you can snatch it away! That's not fair, Billy! That's not fair!'

'I'm sorry, Rosie,' said Billy, brushing some of my tears gently away, 'I'm sorry. I just wanted to hold you in my arms. I wanted to know what it would be like. I thought I could just ... but I can't. I shouldn't have done it. I'm sorry. This has been a magical night and I wish, I really do wish... But it can't happen. Pretend it hasn't happened. Wrong time, wrong place.'

Wrong time. Wrong place. And how.

But he was right. How could I blow in and wreck his marriage, his children's lives? Wrong time. Wrong place.

If Billy and I were meant to be together, it wasn't in the 1950s. I made myself stop crying. I tried to act casual. It took a few goes to get my breathing under control before I could speak, but I did it. Made a decent fist of it. 'Well, it was only a kiss. What's a kiss between friends?' I said, though my tough-girl attitude didn't quite work between sniffs. 'It's been a funny old day, funny old night. We'll blame it on the weather, shall we? Here's another friendly kiss.'

And I reached up and kissed him gently on the cheek.

He bent down and kissed me in return, the same gentle way. I could feel his eyelashes brush my face. I swallowed hard.

'OK, I'm nearly home now. Goodnight, Billy. See you tomorrow.'

He was still holding my hand. As he let go, he rubbed his thumb over mine the way Will always did. That nearly finished me off. I broke free of him and ran the few yards to the house.

'Rosie!' I heard Billy shout. And it echoed strangely over the lake of moonlit water. 'Rosie!' as if it were coming from a very long way away. Another time. Another place.

Chapter Twenty-Two

I didn't sleep.

When I got home the Browns had long since gone to bed. Walking into the kitchen I tripped over sacks of potatoes, tins of paint, a clothes horse, an old wash boiler – all things that had presumably been rescued from the cellar when the flood waters had soaked in. They brought the smell of mud and damp into the normally cosy kitchen and reminded me of Billy and Carol's house.

There was a pan of warm milk sitting on the side of the stove waiting for me. I heated it up, made some cocoa and crept into the sitting room to the cupboard where the Browns kept a bottle of sweet sherry and another of brandy, for medicinal purposes. Sambo followed me, wrapped himself around my legs, unsettled by all the upset. I definitely needed medicine. It would be months before they got the bottle out. They wouldn't notice. But it didn't calm me.

I paced back and forth in the kitchen wondering what on earth I was to do next. Wondering why I was here. I was as confused – more confused even – than when I had first arrived. There was no future here for me and Billy.

OK, maybe I could have tempted him further, persuaded him into an affair, maybe even to leave Carol.

But it wouldn't have worked. He was good and

324

loyal. And – oh bitter bitter irony – that made me love him even more. He had made promises that he would keep even if his heart wanted to be elsewhere. Even if it left me in despair, you had to admire a man like that, you had to respect him. And his, well, decency I suppose. Now there's an old-fashioned word.

But Billy was just Will in another age, other circumstances. And, I realised, quite suddenly, that I could trust Will too. In every way, with my life, my future. Why couldn't I have seen that before? I had built up spiky little barriers all around me, afraid of letting him in, in case he let me down. But there was no need. He wouldn't. I knew that now. Once Will committed himself to me, it would be for life. No question. As I would to him. If only I could get back to him to tell him so...

I finally went up to bed as dawn was breaking, but I still couldn't sleep. When my alarm went off I dragged myself downstairs to get a cup of tea. But even wrapped in my huge blanket of a dressing gown, I was still shivering.

Mr Brown was out looking at the garden. It was a chaos of mud and branches where the river had flooded. Already the water level had dropped right down, but the devastation was clear.

'I'll never get that garden back the way it was now,' said Mr Brown. 'The bulldozers will be through here soon enough. Still, I might rescue a few of the early spuds.' He went optimistically down the path to investigate.

I leant over the range, trying to get some warmth into my bones. 'And you're not going anywhere today, young lady,' said Mrs Brown.

'You're not well. You got yourself chilled with all that trailing about in flood water. Get yourself back up those stairs into bed and I'll bring you up a hot-water bottle.'

She did too. And some more tea. And some toast cut into soldiers, which I couldn't really face, but which was a nice thought. I heard the front door slam a little while later when she went out to work. Then I slithered gently down the pillows and gave up.

I thought about Billy, remembered the way we just fitted together as though we were meant for each other. I thought about Carol and the dark little house and what it must be like now after the river had raged through it. I thought of his kids, especially Peter, so like him, and little Libby. I couldn't make sense of anything. Where did I go from here?

I tossed and turned, half slept, half woke, dreamt weird dreams, imagined worse. And sometimes when I closed my eyes I could hear Billy's voice, calling to me from far away.

'Rosie! Rosie! Are you there? Can you hear me?'

Eventually I got up, re-made my bed and went and had a bath, which warmed me a little. I had got dressed because I couldn't stand getting back into my night clothes, when I heard a 'Yoohoo!' from downstairs. Nothing ghostly about this call. Peggy had arrived.

'I saw Mum and she said you weren't well so I came around to see you. Did you write all the flood stuff?'

She was looking at *The News*. There was our story all across the front page, with George's pictures. 'By our News Staff', it said. I glanced at it. They seemed to have used plenty of it, but it hurt my eyes to read it.

'I think George took most of those pictures,' she said proudly. Then she looked up at me. 'You look awful.'

'Married life suits you then,' I said, with only a little bit of cynicism.

'Yes,' she said matter-of-factly. 'It does.'

She poured me some tea and cut a slice of the cake her mum had baked for her homecoming. I couldn't face it and let it sit untouched on the plate, though I managed some of the tea.

Already Peggy looked different. Partly it was because she was so obviously pregnant now and no longer trying to hide it. She'd gone past the early morning sickness stage and had that glow of pregnancy that seemed to light up the kitchen.

But more than that, she had the confidence of a married woman. As she fussed with the teapot and pushed the cake bossily towards me, there was an air about her... She knew she had a place in society, a standing. However it had been done, she had been chosen and someone had made a commitment to her. She was a respectable married woman, and I knew that even though I knew what I knew, she still somehow felt one better than me.

I couldn't hack it.

But she was looking concerned.

'Is it just the chill that's making you feel bad?'

'I don't know.' I was damned if I was going to tell her about Billy. She might have had a long affair with Richard Henfield but right now she was a paid-up member of the married women's club, and I knew her loyalties had swapped right over without so much as a blush or a backward glance, so I didn't even go there.

'I suppose I'm wondering why I'm here really. What's been the point of it.'

And that's when I realised I'd got Peggy wrong, because she put down the teapot and gazed at me earnestly.

'I don't know where I would have been without you,' she said. 'Me and my baby and George, we're a family now. And that's thanks to you. If you hadn't turned up ... if you hadn't got George to come looking for me... I don't know what would have happened. We're all here for a reason, Rosie, and I think that was your reason. You saved me and my baby.'

Was that the reason? Could that really be why I was there?

When Lucy went through the wardrobe to Narnia, she and her brothers and sister had a mission to save Narnia, the whole world, not just one person. Everyone who ever travelled in time had some great and noble mission. I didn't know why I was there, but I knew all that it had really achieved was to make me realise how much I loved Will. And, too, what he was really like if he had the chance to show it.

If I ever got the chance to tell him, I would never let him go again.

I was still wondering how to reply to Peggy when we both heard a strange noise out in the street. We looked up, looked at each other, tried to work out what it was, when we heard it again.

'It's a car horn,' said Peggy, and then, with a

squeal of excited realisation, 'Dad's got the car!'

She rushed to the front door. Mr Brown was sitting at the wheel of a little black Morris Minor. 'What do you think?' he asked. 'Isn't it grand?'

Peggy had rushed out to look at it. I had sunk onto the wooden bench of the hallstand, my legs seemingly made of cotton wool.

'Oh there's Mum! Cooeee! Mum!' yelled Peggy down the street. Soon Mrs Brown arrived home from work with a bulging basket.

'Well, will you look at that!' Mrs Brown walked all around the car. Mr Brown showed her the boot, the little finger-shaped indicators. He switched the lights on and off.

'Can we go for a ride, Dad, please?' asked Peggy, as excited as a two-year-old.

'Ooh wait, let me get ready!' said Mrs Brown. She ran into the house, dumped the shopping on the kitchen table and then started brushing her hair. Back in the hall, she took off her everyday beret that she wore to work and instead put on a slightly posher felt hat.

'You don't need a hat to go in the car!' said Peggy.

'It's my first outing in our car. I have to look my best,' replied Mrs Brown firmly.

'Come on, Rosie,' urged Peggy as she climbed into the car, 'you've got to come too!'

I really didn't feel like it. I wanted to crawl back to bed, but they were so excited that it seemed churlish to refuse. Mrs Brown had to get out again, to push the front seat forward for me to get into the back.

'Right, where shall we go?' asked Mr Brown.

'We can't go down near the quayside because there's still a lot of water around.'

'I know, Dad! Let's go up to The Meadows and see where we're going to live.'

'Right you are then.'

Mr Brown turned the engine on. 'Self starter motor,' he said proudly. The car hiccuped a bit before we chugged off down the road.

In the weeks I'd been working on *The News* I had never yet been up to The Meadows. The estate was slightly above the town, the new road curving around from the end of the old High Street. Squashed in the back of the car next to Peggy, I couldn't see much out of the small windows, though I could feel the car struggling up the hill with the four of us inside it. Ahead of us I could just make out a higher bit of hill full of lorries and cement mixers, but Mr Brown turned off onto the bottom road, the first of the new estate. There were just a couple of vans parked there as workmen were doing the last of the decorating or tidying up.

Peggy and I scrabbled out of the back of the car and I had a shock.

The view from The Meadows was tremendous. You could see down over the town, and the fine old parish church. Although the flood level had dropped you could see the river still overflowed its banks. The bottom half of the Market Place was a small lake, and there were fire engines down by Watergate. 'Still pumping out the flood water,' said Mr Brown.

The road we were standing in was like a scar on the hillside. The gardens were churned-up mud,

330

but workmen were fitting in fences and the houses looked fresh and new. They hadn't yet acquired that bleakness so typical of The Meadows as I knew it. 'Isn't this grand?' said Mrs Brown, walking along. 'They're lovely houses, so new and clean. And look at the size of those windows! They'll be lovely and light. No mouldy old cellars here.

'Proper front gardens, and look, the gardens at the back are a tidy size. Plenty of room for your vegetables there, Frank. And not far to walk into town, Peg. Be a nice walk out when you're pushing the pram! Oh and look, we're almost in the countryside.'

True, at the end of the road was a field with horses, and beyond that some woods. 'What a grand place to grow up. Oh it will be lovely for the baby here. And the air's so clean. No smuts on your washing up here, Peg!

'I just hope we get some good neighbours. These houses will be wasted on some of those people from Watergate. Bathroom! They wouldn't know what to do with one. Keep pigeons in it I expect.'

Peggy laughed, 'Well there's you and my dad. Then there'll be me and George and his mum. And Billy West and Carol and their three kiddies will be moving up here. So that's a good start.'

I thought of Billy living up here with his family, making a new garden, playing football with his boys, riding his bike down the hill to work, his coat flapping behind him. The thought hurt so much, I bent double.

Peggy and her mum walked up the path of one

331

of the houses and peered in through the windows. They enthused over the size of the kitchen, tiles around the fireplace, the boiler, the concrete shed by the back door. Everything met with their approval and delight.

Mr Brown was poking his toe into the soil in the garden. 'I'll get some potatoes in, get that clear, then I think it will do very nicely,' he said. 'We could have a bench out here, sit here of an evening and look out over the town.'

'Come and look, Rosie!' yelled Peggy. 'If you look in through this window, you can see into the kitchen and through into the front room!'

Anxious to please and not wanting to dampen their enthusiasm, I started to walk up the path, but my head was hurting and my legs were like lead. Everything was out of focus. I was ill, I realised, really ill.

'Can we go home please?' I said quickly in as strong a voice as I could muster, though I knew it came out as a squeak. 'Can we go home please? I don't feel very well.' Somehow I knew I was going to be ill, and I didn't want it to be here. I didn't want to spoil their delight and excitement in their new home.

Suddenly they were all fussing around me, squashing me back into the car. Peggy was holding my hand, rubbing it to get warm. I knew I was icy cold. I couldn't stop shivering and I couldn't keep my head up. It felt so heavy. As we bumped along in the car, I felt so sick, I didn't know where to put myself to get comfortable, but I couldn't move.

The car had stopped, I think. Hands were pulling me, helping me, trying to support me. Voices swirled above my head. They were telling me I'd be all right soon. That I could lie down. Get to bed. Get warm. Sleep. Suddenly I seemed to fall through all those helping hands. Everything was dark, and I was falling, falling, falling ... and somewhere in the darkness, Billy was calling to me.

Chapter Twenty-Three

Lemons. I could smell lemons. Definitely lemons. But mixed with something else, something woody. And soap. There was soap in there somewhere too. It was a very clean smell, a zesty smell, a familiar smell.

I knew I had smelt it before, long ago, somewhere. But also that it had been near me a lot recently. I realised it had been there, on the edge of my consciousness for a long time. It had become comfortable, familiar. But I knew it belonged to an earlier time too. Not just now.

I struggled to place it. I knew I knew it and that it would make me happy. But I didn't know why it made me happy. And it seemed such a long way away. Maybe I could try and go towards it. But it was such a long way away, I didn't think I could reach it. Everything was such an effort, such a struggle...

The smell was closer now. I was breathing it in. It was filling my nostrils, my head. Maybe I could reach it if I tried very hard. If I just tried a bit harder...

'Rosie! Rosie! Are you there? Can you hear me?'

If I concentrated very hard, I could open my eyes. I flickered them open. There was someone bending over me. Someone familiar. Billy?

'Rosie! It's me, Will. Can you hear me?'

Will? Of course. Lemons. Will always smelt zingy and zesty of delicious woody citrus. Billy smelt of sweat and beer and newsprint. This was Will. Will!

I opened my eyes and smiled at him and he was crying.

'You're back! Oh Rosie, you're back!'

And then I was sick. Horrible vile-smelling dribble. Will whipped a bowl over and caught most of it. I closed my eyes again to get away from the smell of it, the awful all over pain and, yes, the embarrassment.

Then there were all sorts of things going on. People talking, testing, beeps of equipment. There were nurses and a woman in a white coat. And my mum was there and Dad. All those people. I opened my eyes and tried to smile at them all. It was nice to see them. But my head still hurt and I felt as though I had the most tremendous hang-over so I closed my eyes again. Just for a little while...

But I could still smell lemons and I knew wherever I'd been, I was back.

I was in hospital. I worked that out. A nice twenty-first century hospital. It had to be. Mum and Dad were there. And even in this one room, I could tell this hospital wasn't like the one we took Peggy to. But it was Will I had to be sure about. As nurses prodded and poked and measured and tested and asked me how many fingers they were holding up, Mum and Dad were either side of my bed. Mum was holding my hands and I could feel her trying not to cry. Dad was stroking my shoulder, about the only bit of me that was easily accessible.

My head hurt and I felt wretched, but a nurse cleaned me up swiftly and efficiently, and my mother was murmuring soothing things that made me feel safe. They adjusted one of the many drips that seemed to be plugged into me and gradually I calmed down and felt more relaxed.

Will, meanwhile, was standing at the back of the room, leaning against the windowsill, watching me intently. I knew he must have found my parents and then stepped back to let them be close to me in my newly-awakened state. It was hard to keep my eyes open. The light hurt my eyes. My head felt very peculiar – like one of those diagrams for headache tablets where you see a cross section of a scalp in wildly pulsating colours.

But it was Will, not Billy.

The clothes – well-fitting jeans and polo shirt, the decent haircut, a face less lined, less raw-looking, all gave the game away. But even in my dopey state I realised the big difference.

Will was looking at me with an expression of pure love. And concern. No guilt. No worry. No thoughts about a wife and children. Here life was simple. Despite the pain and the doziness, I felt suddenly light-hearted. I slipped away from the pain and back into sleep. But I knew I was smiling.

It was meningitis. What I thought was a cold and sore throat meeting a huge Monday-morning hangover and the stress of a row with Will had actually been a very serious illness. I was lucky to be alive. Apparently, I'd walked up the path to Mrs Turnbull's and had collapsed at her feet. Literally at death's door.

'Mrs Turnbull's house?' I asked, a day or so later when I was well enough to talk and was trying to get things straight in my head. 'Mrs Brown's house in Cheapside where I'd been staying?'

'Cheapside? No,' said Will, exchanging a glance with my mum. 'No. Mrs Turnbull's house at The Meadows.'

'Ah, the new house, George and Peggy's new house...'

'Not that new,' said Will. 'It's been there fifty years, one of the oldest on the estate.'

I think I might have had to go back to sleep again before I could work this one out and ask any more questions. My head was seriously confused. Mum and Dad had gone to get something to eat and I was lying in bed watching the sun set while Will held my hand, rubbing his thumb on mine, the way he did.

'So I haven't been in the 1950s house then?'

'No, you've been here, in hospital. You went a week ago on Monday afternoon to interview Mrs Margaret Turnbull at The Meadows. You were meant to be doing a feature on fifty years of The Meadows. Do you remember that?'

'Yes. I got a taxi because my car was at the pub.'

'That's right.' Will looked relieved. 'And you'd just rung the bell at Mrs Turnbull's house, when

336

you collapsed. She opened the front door and found you lying groaning on the doorstep.'

'No, it was Mrs Brown's house and she gave me tea and cake and I began to feel better. And I stayed there and I thought it was the 1950s house, and I was looking for the cameras.'

'No, my love,' said Will, gently. 'You dreamt that. The doctors said that your memory would be shot to pieces for a while. But you never went into the house. You never got over the doorstep.'

It was too confusing to argue. So I didn't bother. I just listened to Will's version of events.

Mrs Turnbull might have been getting on a bit but she was no slouch. Apparently she took one look at me, realised immediately that not only was I very ill, but that it was meningitis. She didn't mess about, but got straight on the phone and told them precisely what was wrong. The ambulance was there in minutes and had whisked me here. If it hadn't been for Mrs Turnbull's quick actions, I would not have lived to tell the tale. Which takes some getting your head around, believe me.

As it was it had been touch and go.

I had been in hospital for over a week, they told me, and Will and my mum and dad – and my brother Dan too – had been at my bedside pretty much all the time.

'So I haven't been living in the 1950s?' I asked Will.

'No, just nearly dying here in the twenty-first century.'

'And the farmer didn't shoot himself?'

'Not any farmer I know.'

337

'And there haven't been floods and you didn't borrow a boat from the boating lake?'

'Not guilty. No floods. No boat. No boating lake.'

'And ... and ... you're not married to Carol? Caz? And you haven't got three children?'

Will laughed gently. 'No, last time I looked I definitely wasn't married to Caz and I have no children at all.'

'You're not married to anyone?'

'No, no one at all.'

'And it's all right to love you?'

'It's very all right to love me,' he said, kissing my hand and smiling.

'That's good,' I said and fell back onto the pillows, trying to avoid the sore bits on my head.

The next day my mum was helping me wash, oh so gently sponging me down. I couldn't wash my hair yet, or get in the shower, but already some of the wires had gone and at least I could put on a proper nightie, and not the hospital issue open-backed thing.

'Oh, Rosie, I thought we'd lost you,' she said as she eased the cotton nightie over my head. It was one of my old ones she'd brought from home, I realised, and it smelt of soap and sunshine and warmth.

'I felt lost. In my head I've been away for six weeks or more. I thought I was living in the 1950s. I was working on *The News* but it was all different. It was very real.'

'Of course it would be, you were very ill. Your brain was swollen and you were full of goodness knows what drugs. Being somewhere else sounds very sensible to me. Though I think I would have chosen somewhere more exotic than the 1950s. A nice warm bit of foreign coast might have been nicer.'

'It was ... interesting. Do you remember the 1950s, Mum?'

'Not much. I was born just after the Coronation. I remember wearing hand-knitted cardigans and Clark's sandals and watching *Muffin the Mule* and *Roy Rogers and Trigger*. And your gran wearing a pinny all the time. Except for going to the shops when she would take the pinny off and put a hat and coat on.'

'Did you eat hearts?'

'Hearts? Yes, I think we did. I think Gran used to stuff them. Goodness, if you've been dreaming about hearts, then you *have* been having strange dreams. But you rest now. Will will be here soon.'

And so the days drifted by. I spent a lot of time sleeping, dozing, trying to make sense of what had happened to me. Life in the 1950s had been so vivid, the memories were not fading away. It seemed more real than what was going on around me. I knew I was physically back in the twenty-first century, but I think my head was taking a bit longer to catch up.

Mum, Dad and Will took turns to be with me, though no one stayed the night any more. My dad just sat by my bedside and did the crossword. He would read the clues out loud as if I could join in. I was never any good at crosswords at the best of times, and certainly not when I was having great difficulty getting my head to work, but it was very soothing and companionable.

'It's nice to have you here,' I murmured to him one day, half asleep.

'It's what dads are for, princess, to look after their little girls, however old they are. And to look after their mums as well. I look after Mum, so she can look after you. It's quite a good system really.'

'Mum can look after herself.'

'Of course she can. And so can I. And so can you. But it's nicer when we all look after each other, isn't it?'

I drifted back to sleep and thought about it.

We got into a routine. Morning was hospital stuff, tests and doctors and physio and things, and visits from the consultant, Mr Uzmaston, and the registrar Dr Simpson. Mum and Dad came in at lunch time to be with me all afternoon. Will came in the evening. He'd been off work all the time I'd been unconscious, but was back now. Mum and Dad were doing their jobs long distance for the moment. Dad, who has his own business, was apparently spending the mornings on the phone and computer. Mum – who teaches sixth form – spent the evenings marking her students' essays and tutoring them via email. Hooray for the internet.

I hadn't realised they were staying at the flat.

'Will insisted,' said Mum. 'After all, he says it's your flat. And it's much nicer than staying in a hotel. Will insists on sleeping on the sofa. It means Dad and I can do some work, and I can get a meal ready for Will when he comes back from the hospital.'

Strange to think of this cosy domestic life going on without me.

The doctors were right about my memory being shot to pieces. I could remember every detail of my time in the 1950s, but was struggling to recall much of what had happened before.

One evening Will was taking me for a walk. This was a big adventure. We were going all the way along the corridor to the small lounge area that not many people seemed to know about. It had wonderful views over the town and tonight we had it to ourselves. The first time we'd walked there – all of a hundred yards, Will had had to bring me back in a wheelchair as I felt so faint and dizzy. But I was getting good at it now.

'You'll be running along here soon,' he said, as I made my way extremely slowly to one of the armchairs and collapsed into it.

'I wish!'

I was not a pretty sight. Unlike heroines in films who fade away with perfect skin, beautiful hair and full make-up, I looked a mess. My skin was clammy, my hair filthy, with a small shaved patch where something had been done. My body was covered with blotches and I had bruises where so many drips and needles had been in me. Although the nurses and my mother had bathed me, I knew I smelt stale and sour. Yet here was Will with his arm around me, holding me close.

'Do I smell?'

'We-ll, I've known you smell sweeter.'

'Oh Will, you're so kind and patient.'

'You've been very ill. You need looking after. Don't think you're quite up to killing dragons at the moment.'

That rang a bell. Jamie talking about redundant

341

dragon slayers. Something about being able to kill my own dragons...

'Will, did we have a row just before I was ill?'

'Shhh. It doesn't matter now.' He gently stroked my lank hair.

'We did, didn't we? I can remember! You wanted to go to Dubai. You wanted a big television. You're not going to Dubai, are you? Are you?' I could feel my voice rising in panic.

'No sweetheart, I'm not going to Dubai. But don't worry about things now.'

Suddenly scraps of the row came back to me. Will telling me I was selfish. Me telling him he was a big kid with no sense of responsibility...

Was that true?

I thought of Billy. Billy had taken on the responsibility of marriage and fatherhood when he was seventeen, and had made a brilliant job of them. Was Billy just Will in different circumstances? If Billy hadn't had to get married and had had plenty of money, would he have just wanted fast cars and big televisions?

I called the gadgets Will had a passion for his toys. But why not? He had no need to grow up, so why should he? If he was like Billy, then he would grow up when he needed to.

'You asked me what I wanted for the future. If I wanted children.'

Will put his finger gently on my lips.

'There are lots of things to talk about. But not now, not yet. First thing is to get you better. Then we will have all our lives to sort things out. Just a few days ago, the chances of that looked slim. Take it gently, Rosie. We have all the time in the world. And I'm not going anywhere.' Then he grinned and laughed at me. 'And you're not exactly running marathons yet, are you!'

He helped me up and I started the slow hundred-yard totter back to my bed.

But slowly, I got better. I know I owe a huge debt to the medical team who saved my life, but my immediate undying gratitude went to the two student nurses who helped me have a shower and wash my hair. Bliss! You just feel so much more human, don't you?

And I was allowed more visitors. I'd had scores of cards and flowers and get-well messages, and now the doctors thought I was up to a few more visitors. First to come was Caz, who bounced into my room, with an aura of fresh spring air around her.

Her blonde highlights gleamed, and when she smiled she showed perfect even white teeth. I thought of Carol and her crooked smile.

'Caz, did you ever wear braces on your teeth?'

'Oh God yes! From twelve to fifteen, *just* the age when you're most self-conscious,' she said, helping herself to some of my grapes. 'Dentists have a lot to answer for. Ruined my social life.'

'Not really?'

'Well no. But I do remember that I had the braces off when we went into Year Eleven, and I could finally flash my winning smile at Will.'

'And it worked.'

'Oh yes. However, not for long, which only goes to show that dentists can give you perfect teeth but cannot also be responsible for finding you a life partner.'

'But what if you had?'

'How do you mean?'

'Well,' I was struggling here, 'but what if you'd got pregnant and you and Will had got married, could it have worked?'

'Well, we wouldn't would we? I mean I didn't get pregnant. If I had, I would have got rid of it. And the thought of marrying Will aged seventeen. Um no. Let's not go there, Rosie. I know you've been ill, but that is just bizarre.'

I wasn't giving up. 'Seriously, think about it. Could it have worked?'

'Oh Lordy, I don't know. Basically I would say no, because Will and I – though I love him dearly as a friend of course – would drive each other mad. But, if you really want to be serious for a moment, I suppose, yes, in a parallel universe sort of way, it might have worked.

'I mean, arranged marriages work, don't they? Will is a decent bloke, not given to wife beating or eating babies for breakfast. Give or take the odd all-night poker game and a passion for football, he has no seriously bad habits that I know of. So yes. I suppose, in your bizarre hypothetical situation, if Will and I had been forced to marry, we might – if we'd both tried hard enough – have made a reasonable fist of it. But honestly, I'm so glad we didn't.

'If nothing else, if I'd married Will, that would have left you and Jamie. And I've bagged Jamie, thank you, so let's leave things the way we are!' She put the grape stalks in the bin and took one of my tissues to wipe her hands.

'One more thing...' I had to ask. 'I know it's

none of my business, but are you sure you don't want children?'

'Not that again!' Caz laughed. 'As sure as sure as sure,' she said. 'Honestly Rosie, Jamie and I have talked about it a lot, so it's not a whim. We are both adamant. Jamie has enough of kids in school, and me, well, I don't think I have a maternal bone in my body. Much too selfish! We've got too many things we want to do, places to go. Children don't fit into that. We've both got nephews and nieces and if the day ever comes, I shall happily be an indulgent godmother to your sprogs. If you want me to be, of course. But any of my own? Perlease... No thanks.'

I thought of Carol and the way she looked after her children, the way they were pretty much her whole life, the way her eyes beamed with pride and delight when she was with them.

Caz settled down to tell me all the juicy gossip I had missed while I had been ill.

But as I smiled and listened, all I could think of was Libby, the little girl with the shy smile and the bright inquisitive eyes who was the image of her mother. Who in this age would never be born.

Chapter Twenty-Four

'Right then, where's my darling girl?' The voice drifted down the garden where I sat on the bench, relishing the early summer sunshine.

'Grandad! Granny!'

I hadn't heard them arrive, but now here they were, coming down the garden path, their arms wide open for hugs and kisses. They looked terrific. Life in Spain suited them. They were trim, tanned and toned, their tans set off by their bright clothes and white hair. My brother Dan had just collected them from the airport and was in the house, no doubt grazing around the kitchen picking at bits of food.

'We had to be sure you were all right,' Granny looked worried and, for a moment, old.

'I am, I really am. A bit wobbly still, but getting better all the time.'

'And where's this wonderful young man of yours?' asked Granny, looking around as if expecting to see Will pop up from behind a bush.

'He'll be down later, Gran. He's got to work.'

'We've been hearing all sorts of good things about him.'

'Yup,' said Dan, coming out into the garden, a chunk of cheese in one hand and an apple in the other, 'the man's a hero, a regular Florence Nightingale. Actually, sis, he must think something of you because let's face it, when you were ill, you looked really crap. I thought sick people were meant to look all frail and beautiful. You looked really minging. Bit better now, though,' he added hastily, as I tried to throw my book at him. 'Almost human,' and he dodged back up the path.

Everyone was laughing, but Gran was holding my hand. 'People die from meningitis, pet,' she said.

'I know, Gran, but I didn't. Thanks to the woman I went to interview. What a quick thinker.

I shall go and see her as soon as I'm back to normal,' I said. 'She saved my life, the least I can do is say thank you.'

And then, of course, I had to go through the whole history of the illness with them, all the gory details. What is it with old people and illness? Why are they so fascinated by it?

Anyway, then Mum was calling that lunch was ready. Grandad had to rummage through all the bags to find some wine they'd brought over from Spain, and he insisted that I sit next to him. It was wonderful to be back with my family, safe and loved, listening to their chat.

'We have plenty to celebrate,' said Granny, glass in hand. 'And it's our fifty-fifth wedding anniversary this year, so we thought we'd celebrate that too. Live for today is our motto these days. So would you all like to come out to Spain? We'll rent another villa near ours and you can all come out for a week, longer if you can. All of us together. It would be a real family gathering. What do you think?'

'Brilliant!' said my mum. 'Absolutely brilliant!'

'Yes, and if we're still fit, we can do it all again for our sixtieth,' said Gran laughing.

Dad poured Grandad whisky, 'for the jetlag,' he said, and Grandad winked at him, and I thought how good he looked for someone well into his seventies. The sunshine and life in Spain suited him. Apart from his white hair, he could pass for someone ten years younger. Gran too, in yellow trousers and matching gilet, a heavy silver bracelet showing off her tan.

Grandad cradled his whisky glass and smiled.

'Who would have thought it, eh?' he said. 'Here we are still together after fifty-five years, and planning a party in Spain as easy as if it was at the end of the street.' He looked at Gran fondly.

'"Castles in Spain",' he went on. 'That's what we used to say when we wanted to describe a dream, something we never thought we'd have. "Castles in Spain", and now that's just what we've got. Well, a villa anyway.'

Gran was beaming too, leaning back in her chair. 'Every morning in Spain when I get up and go for a swim in the pool, I just think how wonderful it is. Time was I'd have been happy to have warm water in the tap, never mind a whole pool full of it. Ooh it's grand, really grand.'

Gran poured herself another glass of wine. She was getting quite tiddly now, and she hadn't finished...

'Times change, but I don't care what anyone says. If you've found yourself a good young man, you stick with him.' She wagged her finger at me, and then knocked back her wine. 'You listen to your old granny.'

'I will, Granny, I will.'

And with that, right on cue, Will arrived, clutching a bunch of flowers for my mum and a scruffy carrier bag for me. He shook hands with Grandad, had a kiss from Mum, a beer from Dad, a cheerful shout from Dan, and a huge hug from Granny, who made him come and sit next to her while she alternately cross-examined him and flirted with him outrageously. He knew when he was beaten. He grinned back at her and answered all her questions like a lamb.

348

Within two minutes she'd got all the information she needed from him – where he was from,
where he'd been to university, what his parents
did, what his hobbies were, whether he was a
vegetarian, preferred football or rugby, and did
he want to be an editor. And she kept her arm
through his all the time, so he couldn't get away.
She could teach Jeremy Paxman a few tricks,
could Gran.

But they were both laughing when she turned
to me and said, 'I think he'll do for now, Rosie.
He's passed the first interview.' Then she said in
a fake whisper, 'He's lovely, isn't he? If you don't
want him, I'll have him myself, but don't tell your
grandad.'

Finally she only let him go when Mum insisted
on feeding him and brought him through a plate
of meat and salad.

Soon it was time for Mum and Dad to take
Granny and Grandad back to the small flat that
was their base in England. Granny stood on
tiptoes to kiss Will goodbye. 'And mind you look
after Rosie,' she said in mock severity, 'she's very
precious to us all.'

'And to me too, don't worry,' he said, walking
down the drive arm in arm with her.

They finally drove off, with much waving and
blowing of kisses. Dan went off to see his girlfriend, and at last Will and I were alone together.
Which is when I remembered the carrier bag. I
found it behind my chair, opened it up carefully
and peered in. Inside was an ice-cream tub full of
soil, in which was a small plant with a couple of
tiny green things growing on it.

'Um, lovely. What is it?'

'Chillies!' said Will proudly. 'I grew them from seed. Bloke I interviewed gave them to me. He makes all sorts of chilli sauces. Really hot stuff. And I planted them – went down with a serving spoon and got some soil out from the base of one of the cherry trees outside the flat. Then I watered them and put them on the kitchen windowsill and they've flourished. See. I'm a gardener, a horny-handed son of the soil. There's a couple more back in the flat, a regular production line. I just brought this one down to show you.'

'Well I'm impressed. Eat your heart out Alan Titchmarsh.'

'Definitely. On the other hand, it's a sort of magic, isn't it? You put a little seed in some soil and then eventually it turns into something you can eat. Pretty cool when you think about it. I might do some more.'

'More chillies?'

'Well, more anything, well, anything you can grow on the kitchen windowsill. I will also have you know that I had to eat an awful lot of ice cream for my chilli crop. Honestly, the sacrifices we gardeners make.'

I remembered a garden stretching up a hillside, a garden planted and tended so carefully. Neat rows, little paths, tall wigwam frames for runner beans. And a man like Will leaning on his spade, watching his sons helping...

'Rosie, you've got that faraway look again. Still in your dream?'

I shook my head to shake the memory away and smiled. 'Yes a bit. It still seems so real. Much more than a dream really.'

I had tried to explain it all to Will, but you know what it's like when you try and tell people your dreams? They never make sense, and you feel an idiot, and you can see their eyes glazing over as they lose the will to live.

'Why don't you write it all out, everything that happened? If nothing else it would make a great piece for the Health page – "Me and My Meningitis". It would be a neat way of getting back into the way of work.'

'Well, that was something else I was going to tell you. I'm ready to go back to work.'

'Rosie, you mustn't rush it.'

'I'm not, but the doctor's said it's up to me now. I've just spoken to the Vixen and I'm going to go back a week Monday. She says I can do as much or as little as I like until I'm back in the swing of things. It's been lovely being at home. Mum and Dad have been absolutely fantastic, but I want my own space, our own space back again.'

'If you're sure…' Will was looking worried. 'But it would be wonderful to have you back, to be back to normal.' He lay down on the sofa beside me, pushing his great long legs under mine and wrapping an arm around me.

'I've missed you horribly, you know,' he said. 'I don't like it on my own. I hate going back to the flat. I miss having you there, miss talking to you, miss your opinions, miss just having you around. Good God, I even miss your singing – that's how bad it is! I know, Rosie, all this has made me realise that, well, basically, I just don't want to live life without you.'

I lay there in his arms, not looking at him, but gazing out of the windows where I could see the high branches of the apple trees in the garden. I could feel the bones of his chest, the warmth of his skin through his shirt. I could smell his citrussy aftershave, I could hear his heart beating. He was so alive and so close to me that I felt almost part of him. I remembered watching Billy go home to another woman and her children. It might have been a dream, but the pain was real and hadn't faded. I knew I didn't want to live without this closeness to Will for ever.

'The day before I was ill, and we had a row...'

'Well, yes.' I could feel Will's muscles tensing slightly at the memory of it.

'You said you wanted to go away to Dubai or Barbados or somewhere.'

'I was angry.'

'I know, but why? Please, Will, I really want to understand.'

'Do you really want to talk about this now? Are you ready for it?'

'Yes, I want things to be clear.' I settled myself into the curve of his shoulder.

He took a deep breath. 'Well, it's partly because I don't know what you want. I'm not sure sometimes how I fit in. It's like you think of me – of men in general really – as an optional extra.'

'No! That's not ri–'

'Shh, shh, let me try and say what I want to say. It's as if you have your life planned out and if I can fit in around the edges, then, well, that's fine. But if you've got more important things to do and I don't fit into your plans, then well, forget it.

'I mean, I don't want a wife who's a little woman, waiting at home for me all the time. God forbid. But I don't want someone who's just going to skip off and do what she wants, just as if I'm not around. That's why I thought then I might as well do my thing too. Travel a bit, the sort of things I'd planned to do before I met you. I was getting too used to being with you. Working with you, going to the pub with you, cooking, even just goofing out in front of the TV. And of course, bed...'

He picked up a strand of my hair and wrapped it gently around his fingers, then stroked my cheek. I could feel my insides tingling.

'It all mattered to me more and more,' he had twisted himself around now, so that he was looking at me, 'and I found myself hoping that we would always be together. The problem was I wasn't sure about you. Every now and then you'd just announce that there was something you wanted to do, just as though it was absolutely nothing to do with me. And I was like, I'm not saying anything to her, because let's see how it pans out.

'Then when I saw you in that hospital bed, when I knew there was a very real chance that you could die, I felt as though my whole world was knocked sideways. Without you, there just didn't seem any point in anything. Without you, I'm lost. Sad isn't it? But there you go,' he shrugged.

'So there, that's me, Rosie. I love you and I'm pretty sure I want to spend the rest of my life with you. Those are my cards on the table. If that's not what you want, then just say so.'

I curled around even closer to him. And took a deep breath. 'I didn't think you wanted any commitment. I thought if I let on how much I wanted to be with you, that it would scare you, that you would run a mile.

'I wanted my own life, because I thought I would need it when you left me. I thought you didn't want to grow up. No commitment, no responsibility, no putting down roots. I didn't want to let you hurt me, so it was easier to pretend that it didn't matter.'

Suddenly an image of Billy in the garden showing Peter how to build the cold frame flashed into my head. The grown-upness, the gentleness of it.

'Then we had that row and I thought I'd lost you. I realised that more than anything else I wanted to be with you. And I also realised that you could be all those things if you needed to, if you had to. It's just that so far you hadn't needed to. I mean, I'd never needed to scrape burnt porridge off a pan with no washing-up liquid, or face a gunman, or walk miles, but I know I could if I had to. Like Caz could live without electricity or hot water and Mr J's wizard concealer.'

I could feel Will looking puzzled.

'Rosie, what are you talking about?'

'Tricky to explain.' And how. 'But I guess it's just that I've realised we don't know what we can do until we have to. Sometimes we've just got to trust people and take the leap.'

And I knew I could trust Will. He was absolutely rock solid.

He was also baffled. 'But what's that got to do

with porridge pots and gunmen?' he asked.

'Nothing. Everything. I can't explain. All I know is that, well, I just know I don't want to live without you. I knew it before really. Being ill just made me certain.'

Will was still playing with my hair. I could feel his breath, warm and gentle, on the side of my face. All the time he'd been coming down to my parents' house since I'd left hospital he'd been sleeping in the spare room. Not because of any prudery on my parents' part, just that I'd still felt so ropy and could hardly bear to be touched. As Will started kissing me, as our legs wrapped around each other on the sofa, as I took him in my arms and pressed his head close to mine, I knew that had changed.

'So, Rosie, is it you and me against the world? A couple? Are we going to stick together and see how it works out?'

I nodded. 'Somebody told me that you and I were a great team, that things happened when we were together. I think that's right. Together we can conquer the world!'

Will's laugh came from somewhere around his fourth shirt button. As I lay with my head on his chest I could feel the laugh bubbling up before I heard it. I felt part of the bones of him, which was just what I wanted. I untangled myself quickly, took hold of his hand and led him upstairs to my bedroom.

'Are you sure?' he asked.

'I'm sure. I'm sure about everything.'

Chapter Twenty-Five

'Oh you lovely, lovely computer!' And can you believe I patted its sleek black casing, as if it were a favourite pet.

There was a snort of familiar laughter behind me. I turned around and the Vixen was standing there smiling. 'Welcome back, Rosie. It's very good to have you back and looking well. But I didn't think you'd have missed your computer that much!'

'I was just thinking...' How could I explain? '...just thinking of what it was like in the old days when they used typewriters and you had to put in paper and carbon paper...'

The Vixen smiled. '...and two blacks each time, and correcting mistakes was a bugger. We must have spent so much time on it. Yes, that's what it was like when I was starting out. Then you'd send your copy to the subs, and then it would go to the typesetters and then the printers. Seems positively medieval now. Well, the basic printing press was pretty much the same as in the middle ages I suppose.'

'Were the subs all men when you started out?'

The Vixen perched elegantly on the edge of my desk. 'Always until around the 1970s I think. They'd sit around their table in a fug of smoke – they all smoked pipes – and I used to hate going in there.'

'Oh so did I! I mean, well, aren't we lucky things have changed.'

'Yes, we are,' said the Vixen, looking at me oddly. 'Oh yes, by the way, that 1950s house thing isn't going to be in The Meadows any more. Apparently they're filming it in Birmingham instead. Shame, it would have been fun to have it on our doorstep. And you heard about Margaret Turnbull?'

Yes I had. The old lady I'd been about to interview, who had been so quick to get help for me, was now in hospital herself. She'd had a stroke.

'Yes, I rang up because I wanted to visit her, thank her. If it hadn't been for her... But her daughter, the headmistress, was at the house and answered the phone. Said she was there fetching things that her mother needed in hospital. She said she'd let me know when she was up for visitors.'

The Vixen picked up her sheaf of papers that looked like a set of sales figures – good again, I bet – and turned to go to her office. 'Anyway, I'm very pleased to see you back, but for heaven's sake, take things gently. Don't push yourself. Well, not for the first week or two at least. We don't want you going off ill again.'

Off she went, her immaculate red bob catching a streak of sunlight streaming in through the windows.

That was the other thing I couldn't get used to – the office was so big and light. There were plants on the windowsills, not piles of yellowing newspapers. True, most people's desks were chaotic, but there were sleek black computers everywhere and every desk had a phone. That seemed such luxury. The whole place was clean and spacious and tidy with carpet – carpet! – on the floor, an iced water machine, and a proper pot of coffee smelling delicious in the little alcove.

As I was taking it all in, some people arrived, two men and a girl wearing striped shirts, with a little tree logo. They carried watering cans and a little tool box of cleaning equipment. The girl took out a spray and a duster and polished the leaves of the big cheese plant near the news desk, while the two men nipped dead leaves from the plants in the huge tubs by the water cooler and watered the other plants scattered around the office. And oh, how I just wished Gordon could have seen that. I could just imagine what his out-raged and spluttering reaction would have been.

Honestly, I never thought I would be so deliriously happy to be back in *The News* office – and that wasn't even counting all the hugs, kisses and welcome back messages from friends and colleagues. There was a balloon tied to my key-board and a bunch of roses by my phone. I took a deep breath of their scent and sat down at my desk again, switched on my computer, and checked my email. My Inbox was full, going back to the day I was ill. So I just deleted the lot. Fresh start. I went on Google for the simple pleasure of having instant access to all sorts of information. Then I emailed Will just to say Hi. It was so good to be back...

It was good to be back in the twenty-first cen-tury too. I'd gone back up to the flat at the end of the previous week. I'd driven my little car. I'd downloaded a whole new load of tunes onto my iPod. I'd upgraded my mobile. And yes, Will and I had bought a new TV... Well, I know we didn't have room, but we soon would have.

Because that was the plan. We were house-hunting. We didn't quite know where we were going in our careers – we both had dreams and ambitions, but we would see what happened. We were a team. We could work things out.

And that was another thing. Apart from that initial splurge and the extravagance of the TV – which was really my present to Will for all the hours he'd spent by my bed or charging back and forth to be with me – we were having a bit of an economy drive, to get a deposit together for the house. And do you know what? I hardly minded.

Whether the 1950s was a dream or reality, it left a lingering influence. I went shopping for some new outfits and I looked at the racks and racks of clothes. I thought of Carol wearing the same coat, the same skirt, the same jumper, the same shoes, day in, day out and not minding. Don't get me wrong – I didn't stop shopping overnight, but I certainly thought a bit more about what I bought. And I certainly cut back on my bag habit. I mean, how many bags does one girl need – and certainly at a few hundred pounds a pop?

It was wonderful to have proper extra long length luxury waterproof mascara again, all on a double-ended twirly applicator – not some disgusting little scrap of something that you spat on and then scrubbed at. And back home, on my first day out in town with Mum, I'd had a little mini raid on the Bobbi Brown counter. But

359

really, when I looked at all the stuff I had on my dressing table, I thought maybe I could manage for a while.

The first time I went into Waitrose after I'd been ill, I cannot tell you how wonderful it was. All that food! What's more, all that instant food, all that really interesting delicious food that you just bung in the microwave or assemble on the plate. I was in foodie heaven. Bliss. Even though it was summer, I bought some microwavable porridge for the sheer extravagant delight of heating it up in a minute and a half and throwing the plastic pot away afterwards. I will never forget that big grey pan, the green soap and the manky bit of steel wool.

I was making supper one night. Well, let's be honest, I was putting a goat's cheese tart on a plate with a bag of mixed baby leaves (washed in spring water, of course), with some baby plum tomatoes, all followed by a delicious sharp lemon tart, and washed down with a nice glass of chilled Chablis (barely a glass in my case, I was drinking very little) and I remembered the hearts soaking in the mixing bowl, all those potatoes I'd peeled, the rhubarb, and the hours it took to cook it all...

But there again, there was something about all those stacked shelves that made me feel a bit queasy. One of the first features I was asked to do when I got back to work was about all the ways we could save energy, save the planet, and save money at the same time. Yawn.

'That is incredibly worthy,' I said to Stan, the Features Editor, my heart not exactly sparkling at the prospect of writing it.

I sat at the computer, looked up all sorts of facts and figures when it suddenly dawned on me – if we lived the way we had in the 1950s, it would solve the problem pretty well instantly. The intro snapped into my head. 'How green was your granny?' I typed and recalled all the things I remembered from the 1950s house.

Stan grinned when he read it. 'I knew you'd make a decent fist of it,' he said.

The piece hit a nerve. I had all sorts of letters and emails from people remembering how they – or their mothers or their grannies – used to do things.

'Do you think there's a column there?' the Vixen was asking. 'We're all meant to be recycling more, and using less, and reducing our carbon footprint, etc, etc. Not too worthy though. We might as well try and make it fun. Give it a bit of glitz and glamour. Glitzy green. Just your style.'

'Well, great, yes, why not?'

'If you ever run out of ideas, come and ask me. I was a child of the 1950s.'

So in a way, I couldn't let the 1950s go. Or they wouldn't let go of me. My dream still troubled me. It hadn't really faded. One day I even went up into the bound file room and pulled out the huge dusty volumes from the 1950s shelf. I got very excited when I read the report of the great flood. No byline, of course, just 'By our own staff'.

That was it! I thought, carefully turning the pages. That was the bit that I had written. And there was Billy's story. And George's pictures. That was the story we had written up by candle-light in that little pub in the walls, where we ate crisps and pickled eggs. It *had* happened.

For a moment I could smell the old newsroom, the piles of papers, the damp coats, the cigarette smoke, and the masculine smell of beer and sweat. But then I opened my eyes and I was in the bound file room in a very modern building in the middle of a very modern industrial estate. And I realised, of course, that I'd probably been reading that story just when I was getting ill. That's why it stuck in my mind. That's why I dreamt of it. And put myself in it. There was no magic. No time travel. Just a nasty illness and vivid dreams.

Other stories were there too, for the same reason. The bull in the china shop, Princess Margaret's visit, the murder in Friars' Mill.

I put the huge file back in its place on the shelf, brushed the dust off the front of my T-shirt (stretchy, Lycra, no ironing – bliss) and felt somehow disappointed.

It had felt so real. I still felt I had lived it, not dreamt it – the little boat, rescuing the old lady, wading through the flood water dragging the boat on a bit of string, sitting in the pub with Billy and then walking along the walls in the moonlight...

For a dream, it had been pretty powerful.

I asked Kate, the Vixen's secretary, if there was a way we could check back former members of staff. I wanted to know if Billy had been real, or if I'd dreamt him too. But there was no way of checking, no way of finding out. Even the accounts department had no record.

'Most of the old paper files got ditched when we moved out of the old offices,' said the Assistant

Accountant, 'we transferred the relevant ones to computer, kept a few from the early years for historical interest, but I don't remember a Billy West. Can't remember seeing that name, sorry.'

But Richard Henfield was real, of course, his picture on the Vixen's office wall, the nice eyes, the weak chin – and I remembered the wandering hands...

One day when I was home before Will, I spent hours trawling through the internet looking at articles on time travel. I'd hoped there might be a simple explanation, but I soon got lost somewhere between the arrow of time and the collapse of wave function, neither of which meant much to me.

When you've eliminated everything else, then what's left must be the truth.

One day I had an email from Margaret Turnbull's daughter, the headmistress Rosemary Picton.

'Mother's by no means totally recovered and is still quite confused,' she wrote, 'but she is much better and we are going to try a spell in her own home, with plenty of care and support, to see how she gets on. We hope that being surrounded by familiar things might help a bit more.'

A few days later I went to visit her. Will came with me. We took a huge bunch of flowers, an enormous box of chocs and a bottle of brandy. It felt really odd going up to The Meadows. I could remember the day I came up before, feeling so ill and also that time – in my dream – when the houses were still bare and the gardens unmade and bleak.

'Oh, the view's gone,' I said to Will as we got out of the car.

'What do you mean?'

'You used to be able to see right down to the town and the church and along the river. But now it's gone.'

'It's a long time since anyone could see the river from here,' he said. 'There are all those office blocks in the way. Some of those must have gone up in the 1960s. And the leisure centre and the multi-storey car park. I remember that going up when I was at school, must be about twenty years ago. Long before your time.'

We were walking up the path to Margaret Turnbull's house. I took a deep breath and rang the doorbell. I expected everything to go black again, the ground to come up and hit me, or to find myself back in Doreen Brown's kitchen, with the range and Sambo.

But no. The door opened and Rosemary Picton – scary head teacher of The Meadows School – was ushering us in. She had blonde hair, going grey, and a pleasant open face. She reminded me of someone.

'How lovely to see you. I'm so glad you've re-covered. Mother will be so pleased. Come on in.'

We manoeuvred our way through the tiny entrance hall into a spacious sitting room that seemed full of light and sunshine. As well as the big window facing onto the front garden, there was another window in the side wall, and the sun streamed in. The views were still far-reaching and must have been stunning when the house was first built. Mrs Turnbull, in black trousers and bright pink sweatshirt, was sitting in a chair by the window. We went towards her with all our offerings and, as she smiled in welcome I could see that the right side of her face drooped slightly, but her eyes still held a hint of sparkle. She had been a formidable woman. It was thanks to her that the south side of The Meadows was still a decent place to live – not like the no-go area to the north.

'Rosie!' she said, quite clearly, lifting her left hand out towards me.

I passed the flowers to Mrs Picton and turned back to her mother, took her hand in both of mine and gripped it hard. She was trying to thank me for the flowers and chocolates and, I think, especially for the brandy. But I was the one who had thank yous to say. 'Mrs Turnbull, I hardly know what to say. Thanks for saving my life! Because you did. If it hadn't been for you...'

There was a low stool next to her chair and I sat on that, still holding her hand.

'You ... better ... now?' she asked me. The words came out slowly and slightly slurred.

'I'm fine. Fine. In fact' – with a quick glance at Will – 'I'm better and happier than I was before, than I've ever been. I am very, very lucky. And that's largely down to you. But how about you?'

'Getting ... there. Getting ... there.'

'I'm sorry I never did the piece about the fiftieth anniversary of The Meadows.'

A freelance had done it while I was ill. It had been a competent enough piece but, of course, she hadn't been able to interview Mrs Turnbull.

'Very different ... when moved in. See for miles.

Woods at end of road... Tried to keep nice.'

'Yes, you did wonders for this area, community initiative and everything. This part of The Meadows is still a good place to live. And now your daughter's doing wonders with the school.'

'Good girl ... good girl.'

'She is, a remarkable woman.'

At that moment Rosemary Picton was coming sideways into the sitting room carrying a large tray with tea things which she put down carefully on a low table.

'Best china!' she grinned. 'Mum insisted.'

I looked at the cups and saucers, white porcelain with a little blue flower. There was something familiar about them.

Will, meanwhile, having got up to hold the door open for Mrs Picton, was looking at some of the photographs. The room was full of photos. Wonderful local scenes on the walls, and a great rack of family photos – weddings, babies, graduations – in front of the books on the shelves.

'Of course,' said Will, 'your husband was a photographer with *The News*, wasn't he?'

I looked up, surprised. I hadn't known that. I was sure I hadn't known that. How could I have done?

'Yes,' replied Rosemary for her mother. 'He started there at fourteen and was still working there when he died in 1994. Tragic, he died much too young. He was a lovely man. Both my brothers have followed in his footsteps. Tony works for the Press Association and David's a cameraman with the BBC. I'm afraid the photographer gene missed me totally. I was the person digital cameras were invented for,' she laughed.

'Was he called George?'

'Yes, that's right. There he is. There's my parents' wedding photograph.'

I looked at the photo she was holding towards me. A boyish young man was beaming proudly beside a slightly older young woman, who was holding a bouquet of flowers very carefully in front of her as if to hide something. She was wearing a dress and jacket, the jacket was loose and stylish and fastened with a single large button...

Mrs Turnbull was struggling to say something.

'You ... bought ... jacket ... wedding ... beautiful ... jacket...'

'What, Mum?' said Rosemary Picton gently. 'No, this Rosie didn't buy your jacket for you. It was another Rosie. You were married long before this Rosie was born. I'm sorry,' she said to me, 'but she still does get a bit muddled.'

All my nerve ends tingled. I wasn't going to faint, I told myself, I was *not* going to faint. But there were so many questions. So much I wanted to know, and Margaret Turnbull was in no position to answer them. I looked quickly across at Mrs Turnbull. For a second there was a flash of knowledge, recognition. 'Yes,' it seemed to say, 'you're right. It is me.'

Rosemary poured just half a cup of tea and placed it carefully, without its saucer, into her mother's hand. I remembered where I'd seen those cups before. It was the night of the engagement. Peggy and George's engagement. Mrs Brown had got them out because it was a special occasion.

367

I felt frightened, excited. Was this old lady, drinking her tea so carefully, really Peggy? It couldn't be. Could it?

Mrs Turnbull was lifting the cup shakily to her mouth. She took barely a sip and then set the cup on its long journey back to the saucer again.

'Mrs Turnbull,' said Will, 'what really impressed me was the way you didn't mess about, didn't hesitate. You knew instantly what was wrong with Rosie. If you hadn't, if you'd dithered, she wouldn't be here now. Rosie means a lot, every-thing to me. So really I owe you everything too.' He turned the full power of his smile onto her.

Mrs Turnbull smiled with half her mouth.

'It's quite sad really,' explained Rosemary. 'When Mum was young, just about the time my parents were married, she had a friend, an American girl who was lodging with them, who died of meningitis. Very suddenly. That's why my mother recognised the symptoms. She'd seen them before and always felt guilty that she couldn't save her friend. Always thought that if they'd called the doctor sooner, they might have saved her. She had a bit of a thing about it. Long before there was all the publicity about menin-gitis, my mother was always telling us the signs and symptoms to look out for. She knew speed was so important. Funnily enough, the American was called Rosie too.'

'Rosie ... saved ... my ... life,' said Mrs Turnbull, 'Rosie ... and ... George.'

'She's never told me the full story,' said Rose-mary, 'but she always said that if it hadn't been for this American girl, she wouldn't be here today. And neither would I – that's why she named me after her.'

Rosemary.

Suddenly there was a woman of fifty named after me. I poured myself another cup of tea and wished I could have poured a generous slug of the brandy into it.

Will was admiring some of George's photos of Watergate before it was pulled down to make way for the ring road. While he and Rosemary talked about them, I took Mrs Turnbull's hand again. 'Peggy? Is it you? It's me, Rosie. Rosie, the one you thought was American, Rosie who lodged with you. Rosie who came with George looking for you.'

Oh God, if I found it hard to accept that this was Peggy, how on earth would this muddled old lady realise I was Rosie? She couldn't, of course, but I had to try.

'Peggy,' I whispered, urgently, 'Peggy. Is it you? Is Rosemary the baby you were expecting when I knew you? Were you happy with George? What happened to Billy and Carol? Did they move up here? Are they...' oh God, this was seriously weird, 'Are they still here?'

I was desperate to know. If Peggy was an old woman, now, surely Billy would be an old man somewhere. Did Carol ever get her bright house, her TV and her washing machine? Did she ever get a better job? Did she and Billy stay happy together? There was so much I wanted to know.

It was no good. Of course I shouldn't bombard Mrs Turnbull with questions. She was confused enough. I would only make it worse. It was my dream. What was I doing trying to use her to explain it?

Mrs Turnbull was gearing herself up to say something.

'Want to say ... happy life ... wonderful husband ... best daughter ... good sons ... all thanks ... Rosie... Lovely ... see her ... again...'

She reached for my hand again. I hugged her.

'It's all worked out, Peggy,' I found myself saying. 'Everything worked out. Everything worked out fine.'

She looked tired, but was still trying to smile her lopsided smile.

'I think it's probably time we went, Rosie,' said Will, putting his hand on my shoulder. 'We've exhausted Mrs Turnbull.'

We exchanged pleasantries, made our farewells and went to the door. I looked across the room and for a second I could see Peggy again, the young Peggy who was laughing when she came back from her honeymoon, her expression flitting quickly over the half-frozen, lined and wrinkled face of Mrs Turnbull.

'G'bye Rosie,' she said, and then 'G'bye Billy.'

'It's Will, not Billy, Mum.'

'It's all right. I answer to anything,' said Will as I tried desperately to see Peggy again in Mrs Turnbull, but her eyes had clouded over, the side of her face seemed to droop even more. She had switched off, didn't even seem to know any more that we were there.

'Thank you for coming,' said Rosemary. 'That's the most lively we've seen Mum since she was ill. I'm sorry if she was a bit confused. She's tired now. But you've done her good. You must come again.'

'Thank you,' I said.

But I knew we wouldn't. Peggy, Mrs Turnbull, was already struggling with words and life. Using her to sort out my dreams or the mysteries of time was not only pointless but downright cruel. We had said our thank-yous to each other. I had saved her life and her daughter's. She had saved my life. Peggy would like that. It balanced everything up. The debt was paid. The past was over. I didn't belong there. I had my own life to lead, here and now.

Chapter Twenty-Six

It was a perfect day. The sun shone and the garden of the Shire Hall was rich with the scent of roses. Leo and Jake, looking incredibly smart in matching morning suits, were posing happily at the top of the steps, while the rest of us waved and cheered and cameras flashed.

It had been a simple and moving ceremony of civil partnership, in which Leo and Jake had promised to love and support and care for each other, and each to help the other flourish and achieve his dreams.

'Nice vows,' said Will. 'Very egalitarian. None of that obeying nonsense.'

'That's not in the ordinary wedding service any more,' I said, bopping him lightly with the order of service. 'Not if you don't want it.'

At the end of the service, Leo and Jake had hugged and now here they were on the steps, their arms still around each other's shoulders looking incredibly proud and happy. 'Now to the important part!' shouted Jake. 'Champagne!'

A little brigade of waiters and waitresses carrying trays of champagne were strategically placed around the garden. We all took it in turns to congratulate Leo and Jake before we moved down the steps into the garden to collect a glass and then gather in little clusters. Somewhere in the background a jazz band played. The air was full of saxophone and laughter, glasses and the pop of more champagne corks.

Both sets of parents were there, the two fathers looking only occasionally bemused. Leo's dad was deep in conversation with Jamie about the latest education proposals, happy to have something solid to discuss. A couple of Jake's more excitable gay friends were gushing congratulations. Leo's dad started talking earnestly about alternatives to A levels.

The two mums were talking politely to each other, each making an effort to be nice to the other for the sake of their sons. Caz was talking to an incredibly camp young man in a pink suit, who was enthusing about her dress.

'It's vintage,' she was saying. 'It's actually a 1970s copy of a 1930s design, and I've just tarted it up a bit.'

'Well, you look just like the Duchess of Windsor, only much much more delicious,' he said.

Two little girls, Jake's nieces, were sitting on the

grass making daisy chains. We stepped around them, careful not to spill champagne on their heads.

'Good do,' said Will, helping himself to another glass from a tray offered by a passing waitress.

'It's a lovely day. A perfect day. About as far away from hospitals as you can get, thank God. I know it sounds corny, but I can't think of any other way of putting it – I'm so glad to be alive.'

'Not nearly as glad as I am that you are,' said Will, kissing my nose.

There was a big contingent from *The News*, including the Vixen, in designer shades, who was holding court on a stone bench in the shade of a tree. She was explaining something to someone, then she got a pen out of her bag and scribbled on the order of service. She looked up, pushed her sun specs back up her nose, and looked from under her fringe straight at me.

Suddenly I was back at the Browns' kitchen table. I *knew* I'd recognised her.

'Will ... what's the Vixen's first name?'

'Jan, of course.'

'Yes, I know, what I mean is, what's Jan short for?'

'I don't know. Is it short for anything? Janet I suppose. No, hang on, I remember seeing something somewhere. Janice, that's it. I remember thinking she wasn't a Janice sort of person, but she is. Or was.'

I looked at Jan Fox in her sharp designer outfit, her gleaming hair and immaculate make-up, her style and confidence. I remembered the small and smelly girl with the broken specs and the ravenous appetite for food, for learning, for life. I couldn't ask. I just couldn't.

I shivered, and Will put his arm around me. 'All right?'

'Yes, yes. It's nothing.'

A maître d' was summoning us in to eat. There was delicious food, more wine, crackers with jokes and streamers. Leo and Jake both made speeches and referred to 'My partner and I'. Their fathers started to relax. Their mothers looked proud. The magic of a wedding – or a civil partnership – was beginning to work.

'Mind you, I could murder a decent pint of beer,' said Jamie.

'Don't even think about it,' hissed Caz.

Back out in the garden in the early evening the jazz players had been replaced by a small band playing hits from the 80s and 90s. There were jugglers near the rose bushes and a magician doing tricks.

'Have you a note there, sir?' the magician asked Will.

Laughing he took out his wallet and handed the guy a twenty pound note.

'Could you just write something on it?' asked the magician. 'Your initials perhaps.'

Will duly scrawled his initials and handed the twenty pound note back to the magician, who promptly ripped it up and seemed to throw the pieces in the air. Will's face was a picture. The magician opened his hands wide. No note. Shook his sleeves. No note. Turned out his pockets. No note.

Will was still smiling, but not so confidently...

Then, apparently equally puzzled, the magician scratched his ear and, lo and behold, there was the twenty pound note, complete with scribble.

This time Will's laugh was genuine.

'How did you *do* that?' I asked. 'I was watching your hands all the time, and I never saw anything.'

The magician smiled a mysterious smile.

'There are more things in Heaven and Earth... Sometimes you cannot believe your own eyes,' he said, and moved on to the next group.

'But I was watching...!'

'Clever stuff,' said Will, examining his twenty pound note carefully, before putting it back in his wallet. 'Just shows that things aren't always what they seem.'

'Now that's something I *have* learnt.'

The party was now in a blissful mood of post-meal, lots of wine relaxation. One of the beautiful young men was dancing with one of Jake's nieces. They both wore daisy chains like crowns on their heads. Jamie was having a bit of a bop with someone's elderly aunt and Caz was flirting outrageously with Leo's dad. The two mothers were sitting on a bench, their smart hats and their shoes in a heap beside them.

'They seem really happy together,' one was saying.

'They are. They will be,' said the other firmly. 'They are good for each other. Anyone can see that they were made for each other.'

'All I wanted was for my son to be happy.'

'That's all I wanted too. And look at them. You couldn't have a happier couple.'

With that Leo and Jake, arm in arm, came

laughing up to their mothers, took their hands and danced them gently across the lawn, all four joined together, the mothers laughing at their sons' happiness, and relief at the cool grass on their hot stockinged feet.

And suddenly they were going. Waiters came around with ice-cream cake, coffee and trays of liqueurs, and there were Leo and Jake at the top of the stairs, thanking us all for coming, blowing us all kisses and getting huge cheers.

'I've got no bouquet to throw,' said Jake, 'but instead I shall throw you my ... button hole.'

And he freed the flower from his jacket and tossed it with a flourish down into the group standing at the bottom of the steps. The lad in the pink suit reached for it, as did a few others. But, to my surprise, it was Will who leapt high into the air and grabbed it from above the heads of them all.

'I always was great in the line-out,' he said, amid cheers and cat calls and foot stamping.

There were even more yells when he tucked the flower into the very low neckline of my dress.

'Your turn next!' shouted Jake. 'And so far I can recommend it most strongly.'

Off they went to catch their flight which would eventually take them up to the edge of the Arctic Circle where they wanted the twenty-four hours of daylight. After cheering them on their way, the guests split into little groups, some making leaving noises, others ordering more drinks, a few energetic souls planning to go clubbing, the parents and aunties by now the best of friends and beaming with happiness that the day had gone well.

'What would you like to do?' asked Will as I shrugged into my tiny jacket.

'Well, I don't want anything more to eat or drink – not for a week at least.'

'I think we're ready for home. Shall I call a cab?'

'No, let's walk.'

The Shire Hall was in the old part of town, and I knew which way I wanted to go. We slipped through the gardens and along the path through a small secluded square and along the crescent of lovely Georgian houses that are now the offices of solicitors and PR firms, until we found ourselves by the steps leading up to the old town walls. The tapas bar was bouncing, and people were overflowing up the steps and onto the walls, but after twenty or thirty yards their noise faded into the distance and we were alone.

In the soft evening light we could see along the river and across to the banks on the other side. The click click of my kitten heels echoed against the old stones.

'The last time we walked along here I was going flump flump flump in wellies.'

'I don't remember that.'

'Well no, it wasn't you, not now.'

'Your dream again? My alter ego?'

'That's it.'

There was a bench now just where there had been a bench before. New bench, old walls. We sat down and I looked across the river. All the streets of little old houses had gone. Instead there was a block of very expensive apartments, a green open space, a car park, and a neat and tidy cycle path.

'There was a little house over there, where your alter ego lived with Caz and the children. The house was horrible, very picturesque, but dark and damp and smelly, no electricity and the only tap was a cold one in the kitchen. But you had a huge garden that stretched all the way up the hill and you had lots of very neat rows of vegetables. And a rickety old shed that you wanted to replace, and cold frames that your son helped you build.'

I remembered the togetherness of the little family and the pain of being excluded from Will's life. I couldn't believe that he was here beside me now. I leant against him, pleased that I had the right to snuggle up to him, to claim him as my own.

'That reminds me!' Will sat up suddenly.

'What? That you have a wife and children and a passion for gardening?' I could almost, almost, joke about my dream now.

'No, there was something in the post this morning from the estate agent. The postman arrived just as I was going out to bring the car around and I stuffed the letter in my pocket and forgot all about it.'

He pulled out an envelope from his inside pocket and ripped it open.

'Don't suppose it'll be any more interesting than the rest of the overpriced dolls' houses he's sent us.' He looked. 'On the other hand...'

I snatched the details from him and peered in the dying light. I could see a picture of a house, a square-ish no-nonsense sort of a house, solid and surrounded by gardens. I liked the look of it. It immediately appealed to me.

378

'Three bedrooms ... two reception ... original fireplaces ... needs some work ... plenty of room to extend.' Will read the details out loud as I peered over, still looking at that picture. '...large well-maintained garden including lawn, orchard and vegetable plot.

'I think I could take to gardening,' said Will. 'I mean, I've grown those chillies haven't I? I can learn. I quite fancy going out and picking nice fresh veg. Could get used to that.' Already he could see himself as the new Monty Don.

'Anyway, we'll ring them tomorrow to take a look, shall we?' he said. 'If it needs doing up that's why the price is almost affordable. But we can do that. We've got the rest of our lives, haven't we? When I'm not growing prize marrows or what-ever.'

I was laughing. 'Tell you what,' I said, 'I'll even buy you a shed.'

'A shed! It's a deal!'

Will pulled me to my feet and put his arm around me. The bench and the wall and the river, and the memory of that dark damp little house faded into the darkness as Will and I walked into our future together.

Epilogue

Newspaper cuttings

Joy for journalists

Two journalists on The News *were married yesterday at St Bartholomew's church. Will West (30) was recently appointed Deputy Editor of* The News, *and Rosie Harford (29) writes the popular Glitzy Green column. The wedding comes a year after Ms Harford nearly died from meningitis.*

**Best Sellers
Non Fiction**
A Load of Balls, Footballing Lives
by Clayton Silver
Nigella's Sumptuous Suppers
Think Yourself Thin by Summer by Anna Hardy
Eat Less, Exercise More, the Ultimate Diet Book
Glitzy Green, a stylish way to save the planet by Rosie Harford
Misery, my Wretched Childhood by Belinda
O'Connor

West. On 4 September to Will and Rosie (Harford) twin sons, Adam and Owen. Mother and babies doing well, Father still in state of shock.

(Pic caption) Former *News* journalist Caz Carter stars in her own story this week when she opens Spangles, featuring vintage and retro clothing reworked into new fashion. Caz (left) models an original 1950s full cotton skirt in a design of a Paris street scene. Her partner in the enterprise is former colleague, the columnist and author Rosie Harford who has helped make green living glamorous.

Honour for local Head Teacher

Rosemary Picton, head of The Meadows Comprehensive School, has been awarded the OBE for services to education. Mrs Picton (57) has been head of the 1600 pupil school for eight years, and is credited with its transformation. From being on the verge of special measures, it is now the highest achieving school in the area, with a waiting list for admissions.

'I'm proud to accept this award on behalf of the children at The Meadows, whom it is a privilege to teach,' said Mrs Picton. 'Also on behalf of the staff who work so hard and so willingly. My only sadness is that my mother did not live to see it, for she was my inspiration. She was the one who always insisted that every child deserved a chance.'

Editor to retire

The Editor of *The News*, Jan Fox, is to retire at the end of the year. Since she returned to *The News*, the paper on which she trained in the 1960s, Ms Fox has won many accolades and awards for *The News*. 'We have always tried to make the most of modern technology while retaining our traditional values,' said Ms Fox, who had her own television shows in the 1980s and early 1990s.

She will be taking over as Honorary Director of the Parkfields Trust, a local charity for mentally disturbed children. 'It has long been a cause close to my heart and I am grateful for the chance to be more actively involved,' said Ms Fox.

Windfall for local school

Children at Prendergast Primary School will be a lot more adventurous thanks to a legacy from a former pupil. Australian newspaper proprietor Philip Tasker, who died recently aged 80, was a pupil at Prendergast before the war. He has left the school £100,000 on condition that it is used for trips to broaden the children's horizons.

Mr Tasker started his career on *The News* before moving to Fleet Street and then to Australia where he owned a number of newspapers.

His son David said, 'My father had many happy memories of his childhood in England and wanted to give something back to the school, which had given him such a good start in life.'

The publishers hope that this book has given you enjoyable reading. Large Print Books are especially designed to be as easy to see and hold as possible. If you wish a complete list of our books please ask at your local library or write directly to:

Magna Large Print Books
Magna House, Long Preston,
Skipton, North Yorkshire.
BD23 4ND

This Large Print Book for the partially sighted, who cannot read normal print, is published under the auspices of

THE ULVERSCROFT FOUNDATION